Praise for Sarah Harrison

'A consummate storyteller'   *Woman & Home*

'Harrison shows herself to be more than equal to the complexities of her plot . . . impeccable timing'
The Times

'Written with Sarah Harrison's usual verve, this story offers new insights into the dangers of a mother's overdependence, and the absolute necessity of letting go'
Good Housekeeping

'Harrison is a writer with a gift for mixing candour, compassion and comedy'   *YOU Magazine*

'Written with Sarah Harrison's usual perception and telling eye for detail . . . warm, moving and believable'
Home and Life

'A lovely, uplifting, gentle read that is both captivating and charming'   *Booklist*

'Full of unforgettable people, places and passions'
Woman's World

'Smashing . . . a story which hurried you along from page to page at breakneck pace'   *Daily Mirror*

'A nice dry, wry style . . . you who have tears to shed, prepare to shed them now'   *Northern Echo*

'Harrison's cinematic story has it all: history, war, passion, love, and heartbreaking loss'   *Library Journal*

Sarah Harrison is the well-loved author of more than thirty books. As a broadcaster she was a long-term panellist on *Stop the Week with Robert Robinson* and on the book panel of Radio Five Live's *Simon Mayo Programme*, and has appeared on *Question Time* and *Any Questions*. Her novels *The Flowers of the Field* and *A Flower That's Free* were bestsellers around the world. Visit Sarah's website at www.sarah-harrison.net

By Sarah Harrison

The Wildflower Path
The Flowers of the Field
A Flower That's Free
An Imperfect Lady
Hot Breath
Cold Feet
Foreign Parts
Both Your Houses
Life after Lunch
Flowers won't Fax
Heaven's on Hold
That Was Then
A Dangerous Thing
The Divided Heart
The Grass Memorial
The Dreaming Stones
The Next Room
The Red Dress
Swan Music
The Nightingale's Nest
A Spell of Swallows
Rose Petal Soup
Matters Arising
Returning the Favour
Secrets of Our Hearts

The Wildflower Path

SARAH HARRISON

An Orion paperback

First published in Great Britain in 2013
by Orion Books
This paperback edition published in 2014
by Orion Books,
an imprint of The Orion Publishing Group Ltd,
Carmelite House, 50 Victoria Embankment,
London EC4Y ODZ

An Hachette UK company

5 7 9 10 8 6 4

A CIP catalogue record for this book
is available from the British Library.

ISBN 978-1-4091-2889-2

Typeset by Input Data Services Ltd, Bridgwater, Somerset

Printed in Great Britain by Clays Ltd, St Ives plc

The Orion Publishing Group's policy is to use papers that
are natural, renewable and recyclable products and
made from wood grown in sustainable forests. The logging
and manufacturing processes are expected to conform to
the environmental regulations of the country of origin.

www.orionbooks.co.uk

For Patrick

Welcome to *The Wildflower Path*.

When as a busy young mother in the late 1970s I was writing *The Flowers of the Field*, it was as a single, life-changing, all-consuming project. I certainly had no idea there would be a sequel.

But a good story has a way of growing, and three years later I embarked on *A Flower That's Free*, another saga big in scale and heart. This time I considered I was definitely finishing the story. But readers thought otherwise and here I am in 2013, having written, with enormous pleasure, the third and final book about the Tennants, Kingsleys and Drakes, and a whole new generation besides.

Each of these books was written to be complete in itself, with its own unique narrative. But just in case you'd like some context, there follows a summary of the main characters, and a little about each of them. I do hope it adds to your enjoyment.

Sarah Harrison, 2013

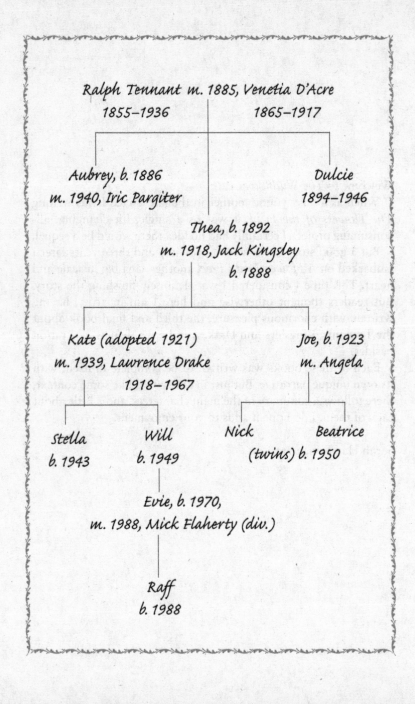

Ralph Tennant m. 1885, Venetia D'Acre
1855–1936   1865–1917

Aubrey, b. 1886   Dulcie
m. 1940, Iric Pargiter   1894–1946

Thea, b. 1892
m. 1918, Jack Kingsley
b. 1888

Kate (adopted 1921)   Joe, b. 1923
m. 1939, Lawrence Drake   m. Angela
1918–1967

Stella   Will   Nick   Beatrice
b. 1943   b. 1949   (twins) b. 1950

Evie, b. 1970,
m. 1988, Mick Flaherty (div.)

Raff
b. 1988

Character List

Ralph Tennant
Paterfamilias, formerly buccaneering, self-made industrialist, now widowed and retired.

Venetia
His aristocratic wife, died towards the end of WW1.

Aubrey
Their son, a solid citizen, married his former housekeeper, looks after his father.

Thea
Aubrey's younger sister, Ralph's favourite; an ambulance driver in WW1, now married to Jack and living a tough life in Kenya.

Dulcie
Youngest of the Tennant offspring – a beautiful flighty opportunist.

Jack Kingsley
Saw distinguished army service in WW1, emigrated to Kenya as soldier-settler with his wife, Thea.

Kate
Widow in her eighties. Adopted by the Kingsleys at five years old. Wayward and adventurous as a young woman, mellowed by a long and loving marriage.

Lawrence Drake
Kate's husband, career army officer. Distinguished service in WW2. Retired at time of his death.

Stella
Their unmarried, independent daughter, tough-minded but tender-hearted.

Will
Stella's younger brother, romantically impulsive and brave, but unreliable.

Evie
Will's daughter, a spirited young divorcee and working mother.

Raff
Evie's young son, a boy chorister.

Mick Flynn
Evie's ex, Raff's mercurial father.

Jacqueline Praed
Will's grand passion, Evie's mother.

Bill Maguire
Journalist, war correspondent in WW2.

Andrea Avery
Former school friend of Thea's. Died in HMS City of Benares disaster.

Ernest Mallory (Marx)
Wealthy restaurateur, started out as a waiter, finessed his way up the ladder.

AUTHOR'S NOTE

Any resemblance between the broadcast carol service in *The Wildflower Path* and that of King's College Cambridge is not coincidental. My college choir school is fictional but I could not resist using elements of the Nine Lessons and Carols.

Christmas Eve 1999

There were now over a thousand people in the chapel. The combined body heat of the congregation poured upwards to be lost among the fan vaulting. Evie and Kate, sitting halfway down the nave on the north side, had priority tickets but they'd still had to be here early and the cold of the stone floors was beginning to bite.

Evie felt for her grandmother's hand, gauging its temperature. Outside the midwinter was nothing if not bleak, the afternoon rapidly darkening towards a clear, freezing night. In here, though, it was softly bright, and the crowded pews gave off a murmurous rustle of anticipation, like waves on shingle. Stone fountains leapt. The candlelit choir stalls glowed. This was an atmosphere beyond price, and everyone knew it. Evie closed her eyes for a moment and thought, intensely, of those who weren't here; and of Raff, waiting with the others for the choir's entrance. This piercing, yearning feeling – was this, she wondered, what it was to pray?

Kate felt and appreciated that little squeeze of the hand. Her granddaughter wasn't an especially demonstrative girl and had quite enough to think about without shepherding an old lady to church on this always hectic day. It was sweet of her, and so much appreciated. Kate's part of the bargain was to enjoy it to the full. Heaven knows how those who'd queued must be feeling. But, oh—! No matter how often she came here, she never tired of the beauty of the building's soaring splendour. She tipped back her head, gazing upwards in wonder. Just to be here, away from the retail frenzy, the processed pop music and the blitzkrieg of advertising, was balm to her soul. Peace – that was what she hoped for, for all of them. Peace, and strength, on this most potent day of the year, freighted with memory, sadness and hope, especially for her.

She closed her eyes for a second, and when she opened them, Evie was looking at her.

'All right, Gran?'

'Never better.'

'Are you missing Stella?'

'Yes,' said Kate. 'I am. But I'm sure she's not missing us. And I don't wish her back.'

The first small figures of the choir appeared in the south doorway. The congregation stood, with a sound like a giant sigh. A soft blanket of silence fell over them. Snow on snow ... This time it was Kate who felt for Evie's hand, and held it tight.

Evie closed her eyes as the pure lone voice curled up into the still air like a thread of smoke. After a few seconds, unable to contain herself, she looked over her shoulder. Across something like twenty rows of people behind her, through a chink in the thickly clad figures she could see, clearly magnified as if through a pinhole, the ramrod-straight back of the choirmaster.

Incandescent with pride and emotion, she glanced across the aisle at the pews opposite: all the rapt faces, caught in this moment; all those memories that would hold it, all those voices that would describe it, over the years to come.

As she scanned the faces, her eyes were drawn as if magnetised to one that she recognised. Even as she told herself it couldn't be – could it? – she knew that it was him. His expression in profile, listening, was weary and quizzical, with the hint of a wistful smile; the habit of charm so strong it could not be broken, even here. Oh God, it *was* him. Changed, but not out of all recognition, still as fond and familiar, as infuriating, as her own reflection.

With the second verse, the organ and the massed voices of the choir released their powerful wave of sound, and Evie's tense heart unfurled.

Chapter One
1944-1946

Stella's earliest memories were a mixed bag – disordered, but separate, vivid and distinct, like the collection of old buttons her paternal grandmother kept in a satin handkerchief sachet.

The very earliest (she was almost certain she had not been told) was of the V-2s. She and her mother had certainly been in south London for a while at the end of the war, at Great-Uncle Aubrey's (to her) grand and gloomy house, before they went to join her father in Berlin. She definitely had a clear recollection of toiling up the stairs to the bedroom she and her mother shared on the third floor. There were different kinds of stair carpet on the different levels, beginning with a thick, woolly one covered in red and purple flowers with a black and red border. That gave way to a paisley leaf pattern in faded mauve, and finally to a plain dark red with threadbare patches of hairy beige string. It was the same with the stairs themselves, the edges of which were a shiny varnished brown between the ground and second floors, then becoming a dull, scarred black. (There was a cellar full of old trunks, flowerpots and bric-a-brac, but the stairs down to that were of icy grey concrete.) They would joke about how the two of them were in 'the servants' quarters', as if they'd been banished there, but in fact Kate had chosen the room because, though low-ceilinged, it was large, and had a view, of sorts.

'In Africa, where I grew up,' she used to say in a wondering, wistful voice, 'I could ride my pony in one direction for two hours and still be on our land. In London, you're lucky if you can see the next street.'

They weren't lucky; they couldn't see the next street, but they could see the backs of the houses that lined it, and the gardens in between. The houses were tall, like this one but seen from behind;

without the steps and porticos and porches and mouldings that they presented to the outside world, they looked rather scruffy. One afternoon, when she was in the garden, Stella had checked, and theirs was no different from the back. And the garden itself, which at ground level appeared imposingly long and set with giant trees, was just a strip among many similar strips when viewed from the top-floor window. Still, they liked being up high.

Other memories of that house: mealtimes, which she liked because of the sense of security they gave her – the way the grown-ups talked across and around her and complimented her on her appetite. It was easy to be good when eating; she liked food, and wasn't fussy. A 'good doer', her Great-Uncle Aubrey said, an expression more usually applied to horses, but a compliment nonetheless, and a characteristic that was to stand her in good stead at boarding school.

No, she did remember the V-2s – the drone that became a whine, then a high-pitched howl, a hunting-wolf shriek of approaching danger ... Then the awful split second of silence when your heart stopped beating and your skin prickled and shrank ... And finally the thunderous boom and crash of someone else's house, and life, being blown to smithereens. They hadn't had an Anderson shelter; she hadn't even known such things existed until later – they used to go down to the cellar when the air-raid warning sounded. She remembered the solid chill of the steps, and the smell of the paraffin heater, and the wonderful thrill occasionally of seeing Great-Uncle Aubrey in his whiskery dressing gown and slippers, all of them sitting round on boxes and drinking plastic-smelling tea poured from a Thermos. And then coming up, stiff and bug-eyed, in the morning to find that everything here was all right, but that not far away there were piles of smoking rubble where houses had been, and the acrid smudge of burning brick dust on the morning air. Sometimes she and Kate went out to shop or do errands the day after a raid, and they'd have to take a roundabout route because of bomb damage, and there would be ARP wardens, firemen and ambulance crews going about their business, taking no notice of anything else, moving doggedly between the pedestrians and the groups of exhausted displaced people, bereft of everything but what they stood up in – women with babies and frightened, peaky-faced children wrapped in rough brown blankets, whatever the weather. 'Because of shock,' Kate explained. 'It makes you cold and shivery.'

Mainly, these experiences had given the young Stella a sense of her own good fortune, because once again the Bad Thing had happened to someone else. She hung on to her small store of pity, as yet unformed by experience, to apply to herself when – if – the time came.

What did sometimes make her cry was the absence of her father. She felt a homesickness for the texture of him, the scratch of his battledress, the smooth prickle of his evening face when he read to her, his hands, which, though stronger than her mother's, were more tentative from lack of practice, his infectious carefree laugh, which made his scalp move back slightly so his whole face smoothed out and looked young. She knew Kate missed him too, because she became snappy if Stella complained about it once too often.

'Oh, he'll be in touch when he's ready. The war'll be over soon,' she'd say, or something similar, briskly and determinedly putting the feelings back in their box.

Great-Uncle Aubrey had been a comfort. Kate had once called him 'a funny old stick', but whatever that meant, Stella thought, it couldn't have been that bad. He was nice: big, and solid and unchanging – she almost believed that a V-2 wouldn't dare hit the house in Mapleton Road while he was there – and though he didn't say very much, she found him always approachable. She would go into his dressing room (a masculine preserve, quite separate from the large, two-bedded room he shared with Aunt I) in the morning, and sit on the narrow camp bed, the grey blanket tickly beneath her bare legs, watching him perform the unvarying rituals of his masculine toilette: hair-brushing with two brushes, shoe-cleaning, snapping on of sock-suspenders, insertion of cufflinks, vigorous application of the clothes brush – he allowed her to stand on the camp bed and brush the back of his jacket – and finally the replacing of everything in its rightful place on top of the tallboy. When standing on the bed, she could see that the tallboy was like a sort of altar, everything arranged symmetrically before the mirror, with its twisted columns: the tortoiseshell cufflink box, the dappled ivory shoehorn and the silver-backed hairbrushes with their thick yellow bristles. There was a drawer – the top

5

right-hand drawer – which was more mysterious. Aubrey would take a clean handkerchief from this drawer and thrust it, folded, into his trouser pocket, or less frequently into the breast pocket of his jacket, but then quite often he would peer into the drawer and move the contents about, stirring them slightly and thoughtfully as if they were potpourri from which he was trying to coax scent. She'd been too small to see into this drawer, so a mystery it remained.

On the wall over the bed was a framed photograph of a school rugger team, with Great-Uncle Aubrey – he had pointed himself out – third from the left in the front row, sitting very upright with his arms folded. All the boys wore striped shirts and skull caps with dangly tassels.

The two of them rarely conversed. Her great-uncle was a man of few words and an inherent reserve. He did what he had to do, and she watched him do it. She liked the austere, business-like air of the dressing room, with its smell of starchy cotton and shoe polish. As well as the jacket-brushing, Aubrey encouraged her to tie his shoelaces; that was where she had learned to tie bows. Stella knew her mother thought him grumpy, but she herself found him patient and was comfortable with him. But then she'd been a small child. As an adult, she often looked back and wondered how it had been for Kate – an attractive, impatient, energetic young woman – to be stuck in that house without her husband and with only fuddy-duddy Aubrey and homely Aunt I for company. Had there been tensions? What did they talk about in the evenings, when Stella had gone to bed? How in God's name had her mother borne it?

Immediately after the war, they'd gone to join her father in Berlin. Once there, she had been protected by her parents' happiness in being together once more. Her child's world was a small one, its parameters extended only so far. She peered out at the biting cold of that first post-war winter, the desolate city of ruined buildings and thin, sad-faced people, from a cocoon of security and contentment such as a person feels at their fireside during a storm.

There had been three German people working at the house in Charlottenburg: the live-in maid, Gisela, a minxy girl in her twenties; an easy-going mother's help, Hildegarde, who came in daily on the tram from Spandau; and Heinz, the scrawny teenage odd-job boy, son of a previous cook who had left under a (to Stella) unspecified cloud. Stella sensed that there was not just expediency but kindness in the arrangement. Outside the tall brick house on Meikelstrasse – a house not unlike Aubrey's in Mapleton Road – Berliners faced a harsh world. 'The Russians' were referred to in hushed tones. There were matters in the recent past not spoken of, things she did not and was not supposed to understand. Gisela, Hildegarde and Heinz worked for the Drakes not simply for a wage, but for protection.

One morning, Gisela was not in the kitchen. The table had been laid the night before, but no further preparations had been made. Hildegarde arrived and took over the making of breakfast. She positively bristled with annoyance and disapproval. Heinz kept his head down as he brought in the coal. When Kate asked, tentatively, where Gisela might be, Hildegarde mumbled without meeting her eye.

'She is still out, madam. She is not in her room.'

'But it's' – Kate consulted her watch – 'eight thirty.'

Stella felt the tremor of anxiety in the air. Hildegarde's cowed silence was broken by the arrival of Lawrence, trotting down the stairs, buttoning his battledress jacket.

'Am I keeping everyone waiting?'

'No,' said Kate. 'We haven't started. Gisela's not here.'

'Is she not?' He picked up Stella and gave her a kiss. 'Does she need waking?'

'Hildegarde says she's not in her room.'

'Don't let's panic. Morning, Hildegarde. Heinz, *guten Tag*.'

'Good morning, sir.' Hildegarde mouthed a prompt at Heinz, who managed a stifled syllable.

'No news is probably good news.' Lawrence plopped Stella down again and went into the dining room. 'Let's have breakfast and see what the situation is by the time I leave.'

Stella caught the sharp look her mother gave him. She thought her father should have been more angry, or worried, or – *something*. They sat down at the table in the dining room, a room so chilly their breath smoked. Lawrence touched Kate's hand and she pulled a rueful smile. Stella felt a little flop of relief in her stomach. Her father decapitated her egg neatly for her and cut

7

toast into soldiers. She was munching the third soldier when they heard the back door open and close, and tense, lowered voices in the kitchen. Kate made a move, hardly more than a twitch, but Lawrence shook his head. A minute or two later Gisela came in, her face as pale as her apron, bluish-white except for the dark scoops under her eyes and a blurry colour around her mouth where she – or perhaps Hildegarde – had scrubbed the lipstick off.

'Gisela,' said Lawrence in his pleasant way. 'We're glad to see you back.'

'I'm sorry to be late, sir.' She looked close to tears. Stella hoped she wouldn't cry; she hated grown-ups crying. 'I have missed the train.'

'We were worried about you,' said Kate, more pointedly.

'I know, I'm sorry, madam. It won't happen more.'

'As long as you're all right,' said Lawrence. 'Could we have a couple more slices of toast?'

'Yes, sir.' Glad of the excuse, Gisela snatched up the toast rack like a talisman and fled.

'Oh dear,' said Kate. 'She looks ghastly. Do you think I should give her the day off?'

'Why not just let nature take its course? She can sleep it off this afternoon.'

'Poor girl. I feel awful.'

'Never mind.' Lawrence winked at Stella as if they were in on something. 'She's back, and no harm done.'

'No ...' Kate looked as if she were about to demur, but restrained herself. Because of her, Stella inferred.

When Gisela came back in with the toast, she had regained something of her old swagger, and nothing more was mentioned. Much, much later, Stella learned, from other sources as well as her mother, about the *Zigarettenkultur* of the Ku'damm, and the money to be made from it. A girl like Gisela was going to snatch her opportunities wherever she could. Now she slid Lawrence an oblique glance from beneath puffy lids as she left the room.

It was obvious to Stella that while Gisela and Hildegarde liked Kate well enough, they adored the Major. Not only did he embody the basic decency and fair-mindedness of the upright English officer, he was so tall, fair and handsome. As a child, Stella took her parents' good looks for granted, but as a grown woman not herself endowed with beauty, she could, with hindsight, fully appreciate theirs. Hildegarde's admiration showed itself in a quasi-motherly doting, though she couldn't have been more than thirty-five herself. Gisela's was more straightforwardly flirtatious. There was nothing calculating in this; she was the kind of girl for whom flirtatiousness was a reflexive reaction to any attractive man. She had dark red hair and luminous porcelain skin. There was a smudge of amber down on her upper lip, too, and a pungent slick of it under either arm which showed when in warmer weather she wore one of her sleeveless blouses. Stella thought Gisela beautiful, but recognised there was something else about her too, something more grownup and dangerous.

Weaker marriages might have been vulnerable to the sultry Gisela of the bedroom eyes and nocturnal habits sashaying about their house, but Stella was sure she had never posed a threat to her parents. Gisela's little ways were a sort of shared joke between them. Besides, one of Lawrence's outstanding qualities was his capacity for happiness. It was a gift. Even in those dark and difficult times he'd been a glass-half-full man, able to take pleasure in his family and the everyday happenings of their lives. The notion of Stella's father, or her mother, straying would have been literally unimaginable; the stability of family life was a given. Her parents had something rare that made them almost unassailable: a true love match.

Christmas came, and was even more thrilling than usual because of the thick snow. They had a big Christmas tree in the drawing room, brought in by Heinz and Gisela's brothers, two lads of about twelve and sixteen. Once the giant tree with its black-wet smell had been wedged in a coal bucket near the window, they'd stayed for tea and cake, perching self-consciously on the edge of the sofa, melted snow making dark patches on the rug around their cheap split shoes. Kate made conversation in her spirited pidgin-German and Gisela translated, elaborating where necessary. Heinz and the older lad did the talking, while the younger one gazed mutely at the ground and Stella stared, fascinated, at his hands; they were thin and dirty, the stubby nails torn and the knuckles scaly and red. Those hands were a message from outside, and she was glad when the brothers had gone, carrying the bag of clothes Kate had given them 'in case you know anyone who'd find them useful'.

Something strange happened that Christmas Eve. Stella didn't know what, to this day. It had taken place elsewhere; she had only been conscious of an atmosphere – strained and tense, hanging in the air like a single long-drawn-out note on a violin, or as if that horrible V-2 howling sound were going on for hours and hours. The explosion had not come, but the foundations of family life had been momentarily shaken, and shifted in some invisible way.

There was a children's party in the gym of the army infants' school. Stella hadn't really wanted to go – she was shy and would know none of the other children – but there was firm, gentle pressure to attend; it was expected of her, and Kate would remain there with the other younger children's mothers for the two hours of the party's duration. To sweeten the pill, Kate had found her some pretty party shoes at the army thrift shop, but even they did nothing to dispel the feeling of dread. Even the proximity of Christmas itself was no comfort.

She tried not to think about the party. The night before, she was allowed to stay up quite late in her dressing gown, colouring by the fire in the drawing room. When the phone rang, her mother answered it in her usual cheerful, businesslike way, but the next time she spoke it was in a quite different tone, low and urgent, the words inaudible. Stella scrubbed away with her red crayon at Santa's coat.

The phone went down and her mother came into the room and sat on the sofa just behind her with her hands laced on her knees. She wore a knobbly green jumper with an orange scarf knotted round her neck, and loose tan trousers. Out of the corner of her eye Stella could see her socks, and thick-soled shoes with tasselled laces. She lifted her crayon from the page and Kate leaned forward to admire.

'Good colouring, darling. He looks very festive.'

'What colour is his sack?'

'Whatever you like …' Her mother took a cigarette from the box on the side table and lit it. 'Brown usually, I suppose.'

Dutifully, because she wanted to soothe her mother, who seemed agitated, Stella took a brown crayon and began to apply it, round and round inside the outline of the sack. Kate got up and went to the window. The tree was decorated now, but the lights wouldn't be lit till four o'clock, when it would be dark. The dreaded party tomorrow was at half past three, so they would be on when she got back; she'd be able to see them from the road, welcoming her. Not that it was proper daylight even now – they already had a lamp on, and the road outside was grey and bleak. Her mother stood with her shoulders slightly hunched, the elbow of her right arm cupped in the hand of her left, cigarette poised. Someone went slowly, stooping, past the window, collar up and hat down, pushing a loaded wheelbarrow. Kate turned back into the room and Stella coloured busily as her mother returned to the sofa and stroked the back of her hair.

'Darling … Stop a moment?' Stella stopped. 'Look at me?' She looked. Her mother's face was very bright, and nervous. Stella realised that she, Stella, was in a position of power, though she didn't know why or how, and she didn't want to be. Kate stubbed out the half-smoked cigarette.

'Would you mind if Hildegarde took you to the party tomorrow?'

She turned back to the safety of the colouring book. 'Why?'

'I have to go out. I'm really sorry, sweetheart, but it wouldn't make any difference, would it?'

'Will you be able to come?'

'Oh, of course I will. We both will, a bit later.'

'What are you doing?'

'Just seeing a friend, someone I haven't seen for ages. Good girl.' Another quick stroke of the hair. 'I bet I will be along.'

Stella noticed the slightly different form of words. Her mother dropped a kiss on her head – another slightly absent-minded caress – and went upstairs.

The next day was even more bitterly cold, dark and short. That morning, before her father left for work, her mother followed him into the hall and there was some sort of very quiet conversation, clearly not intended for Stella, still finishing her toast at the table, to hear. She knew there were secrets at Christmas – nice ones – but for some reason she didn't think it was one of those.

The day slunk by. Her mother was preoccupied. Gisela was snappy. Heinz trudged about, keeping his head down. Hildegarde took Stella out to the nearby park, crunching and slipping through the frozen streets. They took stale bread for the starving ducks, Hildegarde kept it stuffed deep in her big coat pockets because there were plenty of people who would have taken it.

As the time for the party bore down on her, Stella sat and turned the pages of *Babar the Elephant*. She could hear her mother walking quickly about upstairs, short intervals of silence, then more walking around. She sounded brisk and purposeful. Perhaps everyone would forget about the party.

But Hildegarde was looking forward to it, and it wasn't long before she put her head round the drawing room door.

'*Alles alein?* Where is *Mutti?*'

'Upstairs.'

'The time!' Hildegarde pointed at the clock on the mantelpiece. 'We are going to the party?'

Against every instinct Stella said, grudgingly: 'Yes.'

'You should get ready.'

'Okay.'

'"Okay"!' Hildegarde pulled a face. 'Come come, *liebchen*, let's go!'

Reluctantly, Stella stood up, then, in response to Hildegarde's stern look, put the crayons back in their tin. Hildegarde laid a hand on her shoulder and steered her gently towards the stairs.

While Hildegarde got her things out, Stella looked in on her mother. Kate was sitting in front of the dressing table in the bedroom. She wasn't actually doing anything; just sitting there with her hairbrush in her hands, gazing at her reflection in a preoccupied way.

'Mummy?'

'What?' Kate jumped slightly. 'Oh, hello, poppet.'

'Hildegarde told me to get ready.'

'Ready? Yes!' She glanced at her watch and got up with almost comical enthusiasm. 'Come on, I'll come and help – and you've got those lovely shoes!'

Stella's party dress was dark red velvet with smocking, long sleeves and a narrow trimming of white lace round the collar and cuffs. Granny Drake had made it for her and everyone thought it was beautiful and so clever, but she was less than enthusiastic. Neither the skirt nor the sleeves puffed out, and there was only a small floppy bow at the back, not a full butterfly sash. But once Kate had hitched her hair up in a green and white ribbon, and the shoes were on, set off by gleaming new socks, she felt a little better.

Hildegarde stood back in fond admiration. Kate bent to give Stella a kiss; she had put her evening scent on and its fragrance washed over Stella.

'You look so pretty. You'll be the belle of the ball.'

This wasn't the sort of thing her mother usually said, and anyway, Stella took leave to doubt it. She was *not* pretty. Though she quite looked forward to going with Hildegarde in the staff car, there was no doubt she was being fobbed off. She felt again the curious sense of her own power in this situation, and tested it with a whine:

'Do I *have* to go?'

'Yes!' Her mother's voice was impatient, then she changed it: 'You're all ready. Anyway, there'll be super food, and games – it'll be fun!'

The mention of games was no comfort at all. Games featured heavily in Stella's worst nightmares – the cheating, the covert bullying, the screeching, her own uselessness, the not-being-picked. And the food would be wasted on her; she'd be too nervous to eat. There would probably be a Father Christmas, and she would be asked what she wanted – what was she supposed to say, in front of all those people? But now her best coat had been removed from its hanger and was being held out. The inexorable process had begun.

Naturally, the party wasn't nearly as bad as she'd feared. Her father came early. Tea was as scrumptious as an army of wives and Red Cross helpers could make it, and the games were well regulated; she won musical bumps. She still, however, drew the line at Father Christmas, even though her father explained he was really Drum Major Watts, whom she liked. The German children got their presents first, and then sang carols. They sang beautifully. Hildegarde beamed and dabbed her eyes. Stella's father clapped his hands and said 'Bravo!' – but quietly. The two dreaded hours had passed, and it was going-home time.

'Where's Mummy?' she asked.

There was a tiny pause before he answered. 'She'll come soon, I expect.'

But by the time Stella lined up with the others to say goodbye and thank you to all the ladies who had given the party, and to the Drum Major, now out of his Father Christmas costume, she had still not come. Watts handed her father a small package, then he bent down from his immense height and addressed her jovially.

'Now then, young lady. Promise me you'll have a happy Christmas!'

'I promise,' Stella muttered.

The sergeant major seemed to find this funny and laughed like anything.

'With plenty of presents.'

'I promise,' she said again, this having gone down well the first time.

Hildegarde rode with them just as far as her bus stop. Stella's father jumped out and held the door for her, pressed something into her hand. Once he was back in the car, his good humour seemed to desert him. He sat deep in his corner of the seat, with one hand covering his mouth. When he caught Stella peering at him, he dropped his hand and smiled for a moment as if to re-assure her, but she was sure the smile didn't last once his mouth was hidden again. When she asked again about her mother and why she hadn't come, he said he didn't know. It was obvious he didn't want to talk about it, perhaps because of the driver, Corporal Baker. Feeling slightly car sick Stella opened the Father Christmas present and found a paper doll with three sets of cut-out clothes. This cheered her up; she looked forward to getting home and undoing the packet and carefully separating the clothes along their perforated outlines.

The house felt lonely and empty without her mother. When Stella's father had hung his cap on the hook in the hall, he paused for a moment as if listening, but there was only a solid, resentful silence. They went into the drawing room, where the tree lights had at least been turned on by someone, and the fire was banked up so that it looked like a wall of black, veined with sulky red, behind the tall hinged fireguard. Lawrence turned on the lamps but left the curtains open.

'That'll be welcoming for Mummy when she comes back,' he

said. He rubbed his hands and sat down on the sofa, patting the cushion next to him. 'Now, what shall we do?'

What Stella wanted to do was play with the new paper doll, but her father seemed to want her attention. They talked 'best bits' and 'worst bits' of the party.

'Drum Major Watts thought *you* were the best bit,' said Lawrence. She wasn't quite sure how she should reply. 'He said you favoured your mother.' This time she didn't know what he meant, and anyway he seemed to be talking to himself. 'Hmm.' He took her face in his hands and scrutinised her with a comically stern scowl. 'Do you look like Mummy? Hard to say. You're like her in other ways, though.'

'What ways?' asked Stella, with interest.

'What ways, right. You're independent, and you know your own mind, you can be quite bolshie when crossed. But you're also' – he kissed the top of her head – 'my sweet girl. Stay here and keep warm, I'm going to get a spot of Scottish cough medicine.'

Stella hadn't understood most of this, but she recognised a slight improvement in her father's mood. While he was out of the room, she opened the packet and took out the doll and the clothes. When he came back, he said: 'That your present? Looks like a good one,' and sat down with his glass and the BFO newspaper. A moment later he got up and turned on the wireless, twiddling through a variety of digestive sounds until he found some dance music.

'This do us?' he asked, and she nodded. All these questions that didn't seem to require an answer – her father was restless. She kept her head bowed over her task, but soon became aware that he was looking at her round the paper.

'Isn't she smart?'

She held up the doll for his inspection. 'Do you like her shoes?'

'I do.' He leaned forward and tapped one of Stella's feet. 'Not as much as yours, though.'

'They're new.'

'I thought they must be. Did Mummy get them?'

'Yes.'

No one else *could* have bought them, thought Stella; he just wanted to mention her. He picked up the paper again and she started on the next sheet of doll's clothes, a beach ensemble of shorts, shirt and straw hat. A few quiet, but not peaceful, minutes elapsed.

'You know,' he said, and she looked up politely. 'You know, we ought to get changed. Kate would have our guts for garters if she could see you on the floor in your party dress and me lolling about in uniform.'

'Mummy' had become 'Kate', Stella noticed.

Suddenly there was a patter down the stairs, and clack-clack across the hall and Gisela appeared, slightly flustered, with bright eyes and a shiny red mouth, feet like Minnie Mouse in high heels. She'd laid the table and put supper out, had the Major noticed?

Lawrence hadn't. They thanked her and did their best with the cold meat and potato salad, but after the party tea they weren't hungry. Stella's father found Gisela's Christmas present (stockings – Stella had helped to wrap them) and sent her on her way on a tide of thank yous.

Now the house was even emptier.

'When's Mummy coming back?' she asked.

'Any minute, I should think. How about a bath – that be nice?'

So her father didn't know and didn't want to tell her. Stella didn't ask again because he was in such a funny mood and the atmosphere between them was so awkward and wobbly. But as they went upstairs – he carried her most of the way – she felt a cold lump of anxiety bobbing in her chest. It made her feel a little sick.

He took off his battledress jacket and tie and his clumpy shoes and put on a khaki jumper and leather slippers. Then he ran her a bath. The bathroom was freezing and the hot water steamed like a volcanic spring. He helped her get out of the party dress carefully, and then said, 'Hop in,' and took her clothes to the bedroom. When he came back, he soaped her back and sat on the stool by the bath, trailing one hand in the water. He rubbed the soap in his hand and tried to blow bubbles through the 'O' of his finger and thumb, but it didn't work.

'Your mother's the expert,' he said ruefully.

He'd often bathed her before, but this time was different because there was no Mummy in another part of the house, wondering how they were getting on, looking in on them so it felt like a game. This time Daddy was in sole charge, and they didn't know where Mummy was or when she would be back. They didn't play any more, and after a very few minutes she stood up and he pulled out the plug and lifted her out wrapped in a towel as the water gurgled and growled down the plughole.

When she was in her nightie, a yawn rose up from deep inside Stella, fought its way round the anxiety lump and forced her mouth open, until her whole face was stretched wide as a cat's.

'Bedtime?' She nodded. 'I think so. I'll read to you.' He stood and lifted her up. 'Now that I *am* good at.'

She leaned against his neck. He carried her across the landing and into her room. She had a white wooden shelf full of books – Beatrix Potter, Alison Uttley, Enid Blyton, *A Child's Garden of Verses*, Hans Andersen and the brothers Grimm (the pictures in that one almost too frightening) – but on the bedside table there lay just *The Wind in the Willows*, which her parents were taking turns to read aloud to her at night. It was quite a grown-up book with few pictures, but she loved the sound of it when they read it to her. She took off her dressing gown and Lawrence hung it on the bedpost. When she was sitting comfortably, with her pillow against the headboard and the covers tucked snugly under her armpits, he began to read. The last part had been rather sad, with poor Mole missing his home, and knowing it was nearby but not able to find it, and then when he did, feeling sad because it was neglected and empty – rather as this house felt tonight, though she tried not to think of that.

But it was Christmas time in the story, too, and Ratty bustled round and found some food, and said, 'Capital, capital!' and cheered the Mole up, and then there were carol singers at the door, little field mice with lanterns who sang in piping voices. Ratty invited them in – her father was particularly good at doing Ratty – so it was quite a party, and Mole was cheerful once more, tired and happy.

They didn't hear the front door. Stella saw her first when she appeared in the doorway with her big coat undone, her scarf trailing and her red wool gloves in her hand. There were snowflakes still twinkling in her hair and on her shoulders. Her face was shiny bright with the cold, and with that other something that Stella had noticed earlier, before she went out, only now the light seemed directed at the two of them.

'Here's Mummy,' Stella said. She gave her father a little push. 'Make room for her.'

They looked at her, and she at them. She smiled. She was beautiful, a wintry angel.

Stella felt her father smile too, as he moved both of them to one side so she could join them.

Chapter Two

1918

Ralph Tennant stood at the drawing room window, whisky in hand, scowling. The bleakness outside accorded with his mood. Bare trees, with peeling trunks and knob-jointed branches like arthritic fingers, lined the road. In the gutter on the far side an elderly street-sweeper stooped to pick up sodden leaves and rubbish between two planks, transferring them with wavering slowness to an already overflowing cart. On the pavement below Ralph, a nanny pushed a pram containing a dull-faced baby up the hill at a funereal pace, killing time. A couple of refugee seagulls perched on the chimneypots of the house opposite, though why they would choose this God-awful suburb over the majestic Thames was a mystery. A woman drew the curtains in an upstairs room, and they flew away.

He glanced at his half-hunter. Only two thirty p.m. on December the twenty-fourth and the drab, drizzly afternoon was already beginning to shut down. He wouldn't mourn its passing, except that then there was tomorrow – Christmas, the prospect of which appalled him. He could no longer produce seasonal bonhomie to order. It had been easier when his wife was – was there, when everyone rallied round, and engaged in the various rituals, which had never formed part of his own upbringing but in the performance of which he was happy to indulge her and the children. Allotted the role of clan chieftain, he'd played it, he fancied, pretty well. But he needed the prompting of someone to whom these things came naturally. Like Venetia, whom he still missed painfully. And now Thea, his darling daughter, the natural inheritor of his affections (he knew one shouldn't have favourites, but there it was), was gone too. He was deserted.

Somewhere in the lower reaches of this large, serviceable but dingy house, Dulcie, God help them, was at this very moment attempting to organise some kind of frippery Christmas. Aubrey, even in the old days not noted for festive merriment, had trudged off to the high street in search of a tree. Ralph's shoulders twitched at the thought of their solicitous fuss and bother. The whole thing was bound to go off at half-cock. How the devil was he going to get through it? He took a swift, angry swig. He was bloody sorry for himself; someone had to be.

Dulcie's scent, a little sweeter and heavier than was appropriate at this time of day, reached him just before her voice.

'Papa?' She gave the two syllables equal weight in the French manner. 'What are you doing?'

Without turning round, he moved his head slightly to acknowledge her. 'As little as possible.'

The scent wafted over and around him as his younger daughter came to stand beside him at the window.

She sighed theatrically. 'What a perfectly vile day it's been.'

'It has,' he agreed, adding with gloomy relish, 'And it's not over yet.'

She turned and sat down on the windowsill, tilting her head to look at him. Her exquisite make-up, her golden cap of perfectly coiffed hair with its rippling finger waves, the very sheen of her top-to-toe Parisian chic jarred on Ralph's nerves.

'Are you all right?' she asked.

'Of course, why shouldn't I be?'

'I can think of lots of reasons.'

Ralph made no comment, and she looked away from him, up the road. 'Would you mind terribly if I had a cigarette?'

'I shan't like it, but I don't imagine I can stop you.'

He was being a little unfair, applying a double standard. With Dulcie, he affected to find smoking flashy and fast, though in other women he secretly found it rather dashing.

'It doesn't matter.' Head still averted, she tapped her nails on the edge of the sill and added, 'I know you're miserable, Papa, but do you have to be so ungracious?'

Ralph put down his glass and folded his arms to contain his fury. By what right was she, of all people, censorious? He just managed to contain himself. This wasn't the moment to bite back. She would be gone soon.

There was a crash and a clatter from somewhere below, followed by raised voices, one strident, the other querulous.

'Oh lor',' said Dulcie listlessly. 'What's she done now?'

'Let them deal with it.'

'I'm glad I'm not in that poor girl's shoes. She means well but she is utterly useless.'

Ralph retrieved his glass. The small offstage disaster, by uniting them in their dislike of all things domestic, helped bridge the gap. He took another medicinal gulp.

'No such shenanigans for those spending Christmas on an ocean liner,' he said, knowing Dulcie wouldn't want to discuss her sister. 'Unless it gets rough, of course.'

'In which case no one will want to eat anyway. I swear I'd rather die than be seasick.'

Ralph could tell by the way she closed her mouth that she wished she'd bitten her tongue, but she had not offended him. Too much tact in this house of death and departure and one might never speak at all!

'Oh, look—' She pointed, the other hand placed affectedly on her breast as if stilling her heart. 'Here's Aubrey, with the tree!'

She flew from the room – any excuse – and there was the short sigh of the door being pulled to behind her. Her footsteps pattered across the hall.

Aubrey, stumping up the steps to the front door, glanced at the window. He gave the tree a triumphant shake and Ralph lifted his glass stiffly. Where, in the name of all that was holy, were they going to put that?

The front door was opened. Dulcie exclaimed, and Aubrey said, 'What do you think?' in a hearty voice, to which she replied more quietly. There followed a short exchange that Ralph could not and did not wish to hear. Talking about him, no doubt.

They were doing their best, but it wasn't enough. Nothing they did could make them what they were not. Or who. Ralph was frozen with loneliness. Deep inside his chest he seemed to hear his atrophied heart groaning like pack ice as it slowly imploded under the strain, and began to break.

Aubrey left the tree in the porch and went down to the kitchen to find a container and to fetch Sidney the garden boy to give him a hand. Ralph did not emerge. Dulcie, her small supply of filial patience exhausted, went upstairs. Family life had never suited her, but the atmosphere in this tall, glum brick villa, just one of the phalanx that marched up both sides of Mapleton Road, stifled her. At least in the country there had been plenty of space, both indoors and failing all else outside, in which to get lost. You could never get lost here. The three of them crept about, trying not to get in each other's way, but there was never a moment when each of them didn't know where the others were.

She went into the room she had been allocated, and flung herself full-length on top of the counterpane. On the other side of the wall behind her head was the room – the very bed – where Maurice had died. *Affreux!* She was only just getting over the funeral, grim beyond belief. But this was her bolthole for the time being; she had hung scarves on the frame of the dressing table mirror, and necklaces on the wardrobe handles, draped her fur coat over the chair and sprayed her scent everywhere like an animal marking its territory. The discussion with Cook about tomorrow's lunch had left her shaking with agitation; it was probably the reason she had been sharp with her father. Not that she felt any remorse. Ralph's vile ill humour was casting a blight over an already difficult time. At least the rest of them were *trying*. Even Aubrey, she conceded (she had not enjoyed cordial relations with her brother over the years), after all he'd been through, had put his shoulder to the wheel. But they did miss Thea's gusto. Dulcie still couldn't quite believe that with every dreary minute that passed, her sister was drawing further and further away. Seasickness apart, she herself had always been attracted by the notion of shipboard life. Her own experience had been confined to crossing the Channel, and an ocean liner would be as different from that as the Savoy from a seaside guesthouse. She pictured cocktails, dancing, lounging or playing quoits on deck in a variety of stylishly casual ensembles. The captain's table, perhaps ... She would know how to make the most of it. She just hoped Thea and Jack were enjoying the voyage and not pining – that would be simply too ironic. She flung her arms over her face.

A few minutes later she heard her brother directing operations in the hall, and a little after that, the staccato rumble of Ralph's voice. So he had decided to stop sulking; about time too. She would leave them to get on with the heavy work and go down when it was time to hang the decorations.

Not long, she told herself, and her duty would be done. Then it would be back to Paris, and peace.

Chapter Three

1918

HMS *Morgana*'s passengers had had an easy ride so far, but that was over. Now that they were past Finisterre and broadside on to the Atlantic swell, there were noticeably fewer in the first-class dining room. The ship's doctor was in constant demand. Stewards hurried along the companionways with the dance-like steps evolved to counteract the pitching and rolling of the ship, carrying precariously aloft trays of tea and tureens of thin broth to the cabins of the afflicted. Even numbers in the bridge saloon were down from eight tables to three, the clientele of both bars reduced to a handful of diehards, and the decks empty except for the walking-sick and the incorrigibly energetic, both, for their different reasons, in need of fresh air. Wisely, the captain always delayed his full cocktail party until Gibraltar, when experience showed his charges would have rallied enough to enjoy themselves.

The Kingsleys had so far remained unscathed, and it was Christmas Eve. Changing for dinner, they looked forward with varying degrees of enthusiasm to an array of seasonal festivities. A printed note from the liaison officer had been slipped under the door of their cabin that morning.

You are invited to join the choir of the ship's company in singing a selection of traditional carols in the forward saloon at 9 p.m.

Divine service tomorrow, Christmas Day, will be Matins, at 11 a.m. in the forward saloon, conducted by the padre. The preacher will be Dr R. J. Manning, who is travelling with us to Cape Town.

Captain Compton, his officers and crew take this opportunity to wish you all a very happy Christmas and a peaceful and prosperous new year.

Jack studied the last words for a few seconds before dropping the sheet of paper on the table next to him. He hooked a finger inside his stiff collar, easing it slightly away from his neck. Incredible to think that for the first time in four years, peace and prosperity were not out of the question.

'Remind me what it says?' Thea, doing her hair in the bathroom, legs braced to steady herself against the swell, looked past her own reflection in the mirror to her husband's. 'Are we asked to something?'

'Everyone is. Carols after dinner.'

She appeared in the doorway, thrusting in one pin, removing another from the corner of her mouth. 'That's right. How lovely.'

He shook his head slightly. 'You'd like to go, I take it?'

'Naturally.'

Naturally. He watched his wife as she went back to the mirror, as always baffled but moved by her guileless enthusiasm, the open heart that he, astonishingly, had captured and was now towing thousands of miles across the ocean, away from everything – at least everything but him – that she knew and loved.

The ship heaved and the sheet of paper slithered to the floor. Jack bent to retrieve it. 'Then we shall go,' he said.

At dinner, the bursar's table included new people, the pleasant but stuffy Collinses and the frankly dreadful Mr Steen, the dining room having been reorganised to disguise the yawning gaps left by the cabin-bound, of whom Mrs Steen was one.

The bursar, smiling expansively, expressed the hope that they were all in good voice.

'I'm not sure we'll be singing carols,' said Mr Collins. 'Berths and books for us.' He glanced at his wife for corroboration. 'How are you feeling now, Vi? You look a bit peaky.'

'I feel it, to be truthful.'

'You poor thing,' said Thea, with a sympathetic look. 'Surely you don't want to be here.'

'Well, no ... I don't know ...' Violet gazed wanly at her plate of egg mayonnaise as it slid gently this way and that. 'I should probably try and eat something ...'

Steen raised an eyebrow for the benefit of the others. 'What makes you think that?'

'As a matter of fact, it can help,' said Jack. 'A little food can settle the stomach.'

'If you say so.' Steen turned to Thea. 'No queasiness for you, I see.'

'I've been lucky so far.'

'And a seasoned traveller, I bet.'

'Not particularly. This is the furthest I've ever been.'

'Well, Mrs Kingsley, you're going to God's own country.'

'Oops!' This was Collins, as his wife clapped her hand over her mouth and scuttled from the table. 'Excuse us, everybody!'

The bursar speared a last anchovy with relish. 'Let's hope everyone has their sea legs by the time we reach the Cape!'

Thea looked anxiously after them and Jack laid a hand on her wrist. 'Leave them to it. Don't worry, they'll be fine.'

Steen, vindicated, smirked. 'And then there were three.'

They took their coffee at the table, as chairs were being set out in the saloon. Steen excused himself – 'not a carol man' – and headed unsteadily for the bar.

Jack muttered, 'What a oncer. I swear he was actually pleased that poor woman was sick, because it proved him right.'

'I feel sorry for his wife.'

He leaned towards her. 'My own wife is the most beautiful woman in the room.'

'That is such dear rubbish.'

'But true.'

Embarrassed, she looked away. Her half-averted cheek was pink. 'Thank you.'

Jack remained at the table to take port with the bursar, and Thea excused herself, sidestepping those ladies who were already congregating near the entrance to the saloon. She ran down the staircases, zigzagging to and fro and ricocheting off the balustrades as she went, fetched her coat from the cabin, tied a scarf round her head and headed back up to the boat deck.

She emerged on the leeward side, but even here an icy fist of wind struck her full in the face. She staggered and gasped, and the door, torn from her hand, crashed back against the bulkhead. With difficulty she dragged it shut behind her. Beneath her feet the tilting deck streamed with water. The tarpaulins covering the lifeboats snapped and smacked beneath shuddering ropes. Hissing spouts of spray leapt high above the rails, and beyond them the huge waves, pitted with hard rain, reared up, forming a landscape of racing cliffs and black, sucking valleys. Thea stood with her back against the bulkhead, on the other side of which was the snug, civilised shipboard world of bridge, and drinks, and polite conversation. The wind tore at her scarf, and she pulled it off and fought her way to the rail, shouting with wild laughter that she couldn't hear.

Even Jack, a slightly unwilling participant, had to concede that the carols were splendid. The atmosphere was more music hall than church, with the massed ranks of the ship's company flushed and beaming after an evening of good wines. The choir, consisting as it did of professional sailors unaffected by the weather, was in excellent voice and did justice to old favourites like 'God Rest Ye Merry, Gentlemen', 'The Holly and the Ivy' and 'O Come, All Ye faithful' (omitting the last verse as it was not yet midnight). Because of the difficulty of keeping music stands steady in these conditions, accompaniment was confined to the white grand piano, imported from the ballroom for the occasion. The hundred and fifty or so passengers attending – not a bad turnout all things considered – had found hymn sheets on their gilt and velvet chairs, and joined in spiritedly as they grew in confidence. Thea rushed in at the last minute – just before nine, Jack had moved from the centre to the end of a row to prevent a disturbance – with wild hair and damp skirt and shoes, her face flushed and exhilarated. He whisked her carol sheet from the seat and handed it to her under cover of 'While Shepherds Watched'.

'Thank you!' she whispered. 'I've been out on deck!'

'I'd never have guessed.'

'Oh lor', sorry.' She scraped at her hair. 'But it was wonderful. Now ...' Her eye ran down the sheet and she began to sing. 'Glad tidings of great joy I bring, to you and all mankind!'

Jack entertained the mildly blasphemous thought that those words suited Thea to a T – she brought great joy to him and to most people. In the warmth of the saloon the sea spray on her skin and clothes began to evaporate and give off a sharp, briny scent. Drying salt made white streaks on her face. As always, he felt more at ease now that his wife was beside him, her cheerful mezzo soaring above his diffident baritone. The Atlantic might still be fretful, but in here, at least, balance and harmony were restored.

At the end of the carol they sat down to listen to a solo of 'Silent Night' from the liaison officer, who had once been a boy chorister. His adult voice was a lyric tenor in the Richard Tauber mould.

Stille nacht, heilige nacht
Alles schlaf, einsam wacht …

The cultured beauty of his singing delayed his audience's moment of realisation. Goodness – German! What to make of it? A murmur of uncertainty ran round the saloon, a rustle as heads were turned and programmes lifted. Jack glanced at Thea, but she showed only rapt attention, sitting slightly forward on her seat with her hands on her knees, her programme lying forgotten at her feet.

The moment passed, the uncertainty stilled. The liaison officer was a popular fellow; everyone was now listening intently. When he finished singing, there was another murmur, this time of appreciation, a ripple of clapping and even a lone 'Bravo!'

Jack bent to retrieve Thea's programme and handed it to her as they all stood, unsteadily, to sing again. Her eyes were shining.

'Wasn't that quite wonderful?'

'He has a good voice.'

'Yes, but not just that. The words, in German!'

'A bold move,' agreed Jack. 'But he carried it off.'

The ship gave a particularly violent lurch. There was a flurry of consternation and a shriek. The captain in his role as master of ceremonies advised that they each hold the back of the chair in front, to steady themselves and to keep the chair in its place. But the rows had begun to waver and several people, alarmed by the surging deck and the banshees howling beyond the portholes, were overcome by a sudden pressing need to be horizontal on their bunks. Those remaining embarked determinedly on the next carol:

> It came upon the midnight clear,
> That glorious song of old,
> From angels bending near the earth
> To touch their harps of gold ...

Now it was Jack who sang lustily. Thea's throat seemed to close; singing had become impossible. She covered her mouth with her tightly held programme, and closed her eyes, swamped by a memory more powerful than the Atlantic storm.

She was back in Merville, northern France, driving the ambulance from the station to General 16 late on Christmas night; the last hospital train of the day. That afternoon there had been a concert party for the convalescents at Quatre Pins; she'd taken part and still had a silly false moustache in her pocket. The passengers, three of them, had been in high spirits in spite of their wounds, because they were safe, and it was Christmas, and they would be going home. One, a stocky little Welshman, had lost an arm but was positively chipper.

Infected by their spirit, she'd put the stupid moustache back on and made them laugh. Behind the wheel, she'd begun to sing. This same carol, these very words.

> Still through the cloven skies they come
> With peaceful wings unfurled ...

They'd been bowling quite merrily up the hill, with her singing away, when all of a sudden it was too much – the exhaustion, the men's terrible injuries, their optimism, her own homesickness – and the lump in her throat threatened to choke her. She'd driven on in silence, through a dazzle of unshed tears.

Then out of the darkness at the back of the ambulance, one of the men, the amputee, had raised his own voice and picked up the verse where she'd broken off.

> ... And man, at war with man, hears not
> The love song that they bring ...

Hesitantly, the other two joined in, recognising the tune but not the words, droning softly beneath his confident rendition.

... Oh hush the noise, ye men of strife
And hear the angels sing!

Thea was there now, in that rattling, groaning ambulance with
the rain pattering on the windscreen, the air rank with the stink
of petrol, sweat, Lysol, blood and dirt, rotting skin and bandages.
The first man, knowing all the words, sang on, and his compan-
ions accompanied him in their lowly, generous way. She heard
their singing for what it was – a present to her.

... When with the ever-circling years
Comes round the age of gold;
When peace shall over all the earth
Its ancient splendours fling,
And the whole world give back the song
That now the angels sing!

There had followed a pause which she'd been unable to fill. Then
one of the men had suggested 'Ding-Dong Merrily' and they were
off, swooping up and down the switchback of glissandos with
comical brio.

After she and the orderlies had unloaded the stretchers,
she'd been sufficiently composed to thank the Welshman for his
singing. He told her he'd been in his chapel choir, back in Mountain Ash. As he was carried away, he shouted something and she
put her hand to her face. On her upper lip, damp and askew, was
the handlebar moustache. A couple of days later, the Welshman
had died.

'Thea?'

Jack grasped her hand and gave it a little shake. 'Darling? Are
you all right?'

'What? Yes.' In response to his gentle pressure, she sat down,
with everyone else. The pianist began to play a rippling sonata.

'It's nearly over,' Jack whispered. 'Do you want to leave?'

'No, I'm fine. Really.'

He dug out his handkerchief and passed it to her. 'If you say so.'

'I was remembering, that's all.'

'Ah. Yes.'

He gazed around, leaving her in peace as she pressed the hankie to her eyes and cheeks. The sonata glided on. Jack's own memories threatened to crowd in and he once more possessed himself of his wife's hand, feeling it turn and open in his. They remained like this, quietly, until the music ended.

Chapter Four
1998 (1967)

Will Drake liked everything about the Tudor Hotel, Cairo, especially the bar. It was on the first floor, accessible either via a staircase, flanked by ranks of murky framed photographs, its treads coated in treacle-coloured varnish and a threadbare patterned runner, or an antique lift. Will often took the lift for purposes of time travel – to experience the clank of the iron concertina doors and the ghostly rattle of heavy chains.

Once in the bar, nothing could have been more agreeable than to settle into one of its massive scarred chairs, with a fat tumbler of whisky in your fist, soothed by the brown Windsor decor: more ancient photographs and the odd dim watercolour spotted with humidity and tiny dead insects, day-old English newspapers drooping from wooden rods like faded flags of empire, and rangy, dust-furred plants clinging to life against all odds.

This evening there towered, near the entrance, an artificial Christmas tree of jarringly vulgar magnificence, tricked out in scarlet, pink and gold and attended by a clutch of sparkly creatures – reindeer, penguins and elves – due to stand there till well into January in deference to the Coptic calendar.

The Tudor's clientele did not, by and large, accord with its image. Since falling on hard times it had been obliged to drop its rates, and a characterful, reasonably priced hotel in the city centre, however lacking in modern facilities, was going to attract the young and strapped. There was a serious danger of its becoming cool. The moment some bright spark labelled its gloomy grandeur and down-at-heel gentility 'shabby chic', that would be it as far as Will was concerned, and he had strictly avoided doing so in his column. For now, there was a certain charm in being surrounded by backpackers eking out bottled beer while they consulted their

Rough Guides, and lone women travellers reading prize-winning novels. There was even the occasional laptop and cell phone, not actually banned, though the atmosphere discouraged it. And then – Will blanched – there was the man with the cough: an elderly Egyptian with lustrous iron-grey hair, skin yellow as buttermilk and a chest that heaved and bubbled with contaminated phlegm. At frequent regular intervals this glutinous burden needed shifting, and the man would launch into a storm of explosive hawking and hacking, aided by much robust hankie-work. Egypt was one of the last outposts of unashamed free-rein smoking, so you were going to get these historic nicotine coughs, but there was still something shocking about the way the man threw himself into the process, a lighted filter-free cigarette held delicately all the while between the fingers of his well-manicured right hand. It occurred to Will, not altogether fancifully, that the crepuscular colours of the bar might actually be the product of a century's worth of vigorous expectoration. It wasn't a pretty thought, and he took a large gulp of Chivas to banish it.

Still, it was good to see a local here other than Yusef, the barman. Will liked this country and its people, always had, and not only because this was where he'd met Jacqueline.

Not in this very spot – it had been at a different hotel, smarter than this even thirty-odd years ago when the Tudor had been not quite so dilapidated; a Victorian palace down on the corniche, with a glass-roofed veranda overlooking the Nile and a man playing a white piano in the bar. Oddly, that hotel had long since been bulldozed to make way for a thirty-storey American excrescence, while the Tudor mouldered on undisturbed. Too prime a location to leave alone, he supposed.

It was before the army, or any other job, was even a gleam in his eye. He'd been twenty-one, in his final year at Sussex, travelling with a friend in the Easter vac. They were staying in a backpackers' hostel in a seamy part of town but had got scrubbed up to have a drink at the Bellingham. They'd walked less than halfway through the chaotic streets when Mart had been taken short (it had been only a matter of time before certain unwise food choices caught up with him) and was forced to dip out. Will's debate with himself was short-lived: the carefully husbanded stash of Egyptian pounds was burning a hole in his pocket; he was gasping for a beer; and he'd had, to use one of his father's army expressions, 'a shit, a shirt and a shave'. He was ready to sample the good life.

In the spacious bar of the Bellingham there were a couple of waiters in burgundy jackets sashaying about, so he found himself a window seat in the corner of the veranda where he could see the comings and goings along the river. Five minutes later, he'd taken delivery of the frosted pint of his dreams. He took a first, measured sip ... The soft kiss of the froth, the icy, invigorating nip of the beer and the attendant swoosh of alcohol hitting his bloodstream brought on a high that was better than hash, better than sex (at least any Will had had to date). Plus there was the buzz of being in this fantastic place (sorry, Mart) on his own. Nobody here knew him for the potless fraud he was. He could be anyone, do – within reason – anything! Was it possible to be happier?

Being strapped for cash, the two of them had been pretty abstemious till now, dossing around in pavement cafés where the thick coffee and syrupy *shai*, the Turkish ciggies and on-tap *nagileh* had kept them pepped up. But now he wondered how he'd managed for so long without a beer. Sitting here with the chilly condensation trickling down his hand, he felt just like that bloke in the film *Ice Cold in Alex* that his parents liked so much.

Fifteen minutes later, he was still euphoric and contemplating a second beer, when the woman swept in. There was nothing tentative about *her* arrival; it punched a space in the air of the room which only she could fill. Will couldn't have said what age she was, except that she was older than him, very tall in high heels and a severely elegant suit, with big glasses, and thick brown hair slicked back and caught in a velvet ribbon on the nape of her neck. Ignoring the tables, she hitched herself confidently on to a high stool at the bar, crossing her legs with a neat swish before ordering a drink.

Clearly unfussed about the no-ice rule, she poured tonic into a clinking glass, took the little green cartwheel of lime off the side and dropped it in. Then she lifted the glass, turned her head and looked right at Will, as if she knew she'd find him staring. Fortunately at that moment the waiter arrived, blocking their view of each other.

'May I get you another drink, sir?'

'Um, hang on ...'

The waiter stood by politely while Will's hand instinctively went to his pocket and then away again as he did some mental arithmetic.

'Er – yes thanks, I'll have a half. Please.'

'Of course, sir.'

Will made sure that he was gazing out at the Nile as the waiter moved away, so as not to be caught staring. With his peripheral vision he saw the waiter return, put his glass down on the table and hold out the tray towards him.

'Sir ...'

Bloody hell, surely not the bill already! And what about a tip? He was in a posh hotel in the biggest *baksheesh* culture in the world; it would be too humiliating to be found short. His hand twitched nervously towards his pocket again.

'The lady at the bar sent you this, sir.'

'Really?'

He picked up the small piece of card, noting with a surreptitious glance that she was now sitting with her back to the room, a cigarette in one hand. The waiter, who had taken a couple of steps backwards, stood patiently, gazing over his head, holding the tray in both hands over his genitals.

It was a business card with the name 'Jacqueline Praed MLitt' – engraved, which he recognised as classy – and underneath that, 'Professor of English, Fairfield College, University of London', with a phone number and email address. On the reverse was written, in black ink: *Care to join me?*

He studied this message for several seconds to be sure he'd understood it correctly, and then there was nothing for it but to look back at the bar. She was the only woman there, but she wasn't helping: her back was still turned.

'Umm ...' He flicked the card back and forth against the fingers of his other hand. What, he wondered, was the done thing in these circumstances? The waiter was still there, perhaps expecting some sort of reply, but surely that was a bit elaborate, unless, of course, he was going to say no. He glanced up.

'Thanks – that's all right – I'll, er – thanks.'

'Thank you, sir.'

The waiter bowed slightly and withdrew. Will picked up his glass, took a fortifying swig and walked over to the bar.

'Good!' she said, her expression amused. 'You made it. I thought I might have embarrassed you.'

'You did, a bit. I wasn't sure what the form was.'

'Form?' She laughed out loud. '*Form?*'

'What's so funny?'

'I'm sorry, it's just your suggestion that there's some kind of protocol involved.'

'There might have been.' He felt, and to his chagrin sounded, somewhat nettled.

'Well – there is none that I know of.'

'In that case, can I buy you a drink?'

To his intense relief she replied smartly, 'No you may not. Insofar as there *is* a protocol, I invited you, so this will be my round.'

'Thank you.'

She held out her hand, ringless but with a heavy gold bracelet. 'Jacqueline Praed.'

'I know.' The hand was cool and dry. 'Your card.'

'Yes,' she said, keeping hold of his hand, 'but you see, I'm hoping you'll return the compliment.'

'Sorry. Will Drake.'

'No need to apologise, Will.' She took a plain silver cigarette case from her bag and offered him one. 'Turkish – it's all I've got, I'm afraid. Are you man enough?'

'I've been practising.' He took one. 'Cheers.'

The barman lit their cigarettes, and she took a long drag and puffed the smoke over her shoulder before asking: 'Are you staying here, Will?'

'No.'

'I didn't think I'd seen you before. So where are you?'

'You don't want to know.'

'Yes I do.'

'Trust me. A flophouse.' In response to her look of not quite serious sympathy, he added, 'Actually, it's not that bad, we've known grottier. But we decided to live the high life for one evening.'

'We?' She glanced over his shoulder. 'Did I miss something?'

'No, no. Mart was taken ill on the way over.'

'Oh dear. Poor Mart.'

'Don't waste your sympathy, he deserved it.'

'And his loss is my gain.'

She stared at him with a gleaming, quizzical smile, lips tight closed and eyes narrowed. She smelt fantastic – something sweet, and powerful. He wondered, with a shock of pure excitement, if he was being picked up. Jesus H! He could already taste the story he would tell Mart at some later date.

He felt suddenly confident. What the hell? She didn't know him from Adam. This whole thing was surreal, like a scene in a film, and he knew how the dialogue in such scenes went.

'What are you doing in Cairo?' he asked. 'Is it work or pleasure?'

'Let's see ...' she murmured, gazing down as she tapped her cigarette slowly on the lip of the ashtray. Then looked up again.

'It's been work, Will. Up until now.'

Next morning, Mart, largely recovered, but weakened by the gastric maelstrom, had been gratifyingly gobsmacked.

'You jammy bastard! I don't believe it! And me with my arse on the bog and my head in a bucket in this hole!'

Will, beaming, shrugged. 'Sorry.'

'Don't be such a sodding hypocrite!'

'No, I meant it, it's a real bugger about the shits –'

'And the rest!'

'– but what can I say? She was determined to have her wicked way with me.'

Mart's face turned ferrety. 'Go on then.'

'What?'

'Don't give me "what", you know what. How did it go?'

'Okay.'

'That's no answer.'

Will gave a bland grin. 'Only one you're getting, I'm afraid. Now if you're all done evacuating, can we find a coffee?'

Had he but known it, this uncharacteristic and unprecedented reticence was the sign – the indication that something had started that was more than just the one-nighter to end all one-nighters; that along with a more or less permanent stiffie, he harboured a hopelessly enslaved heart.

While Mart paid a further precautionary visit to the bogs, Will headed for their preferred café, ordered an extra sweet one and sank into a reverie. Oh, what a night! If he'd had the remotest idea where she was right now, he'd have gone there just to see her, perhaps to grab a moment of her attention, the briefest, slightest contact with her slim, strong body that had become so soft in his arms ... That had been a revelation – the way she'd given herself up to him as if he, not she, had been the seducer. It was the greatest, sexiest, most exhilarating compliment he'd ever been paid, the most lavish and enchanting gift. Even the embarrassing swiftness of the first round hadn't been a problem – it had turned out to be a sort of overture, a prelude to the succession of varied movements that followed. The moment he was done, he was ready again, and she, as it were, had never gone away. From there on in it had been not just about gratification, but – he took a scorching sip of strong, sugary coffee – *communication*. That was it, a sort of conversation of the flesh, quite different from the spoken one they'd had at the bar; much more subtle, complicated and mutually respectful, as if that had been only play and this was the real, grown-up thing. She'd examined him carefully; deduced, correctly, that the white scar on his neck was from childhood chickenpox, and the insect bites on his ankles the result of riding a flea-bitten camel at Giza.

'What on earth possessed you?' she mocked. 'That is *such* a shameless con.'

'We thought one of us should.'

'So Mart persuaded you.'

'I volunteered.'

She shook her head. 'Foolish, foolish ... Don't scratch those, they'll turn nasty. And you're so lovely.'

No one had ever called him lovely, and if it had ever been suggested to him that they would, he'd have found it toe-curlingly embarrassing. But in her mouth the word became the most erotic of endearments and he had almost spilled into her searching hand.

Sometime in the small hours she'd ordered a taxi for him. They'd scarcely spoken as he left; this, he was certain, had not been from any awkwardness on his part or coolness on hers – their farewell kiss had been both tender and tumultuous – but because neither of them had wished to break the spell. Only trouble was, there was no plan in place, no promise of another meeting, nothing. He had her card, but the details on it related to her job in England.

He could scarcely go round to the Bellingham and sit in the bar waiting for her to come in again. That would be pathetic, and obvious; and anyway, as someone, probably his mother, had said, you couldn't step in the same river twice. She had laughed at him for worrying about protocol, but in the changed circumstances he was pretty sure there was one at this stage, of which – again – he was entirely ignorant. Now that something tremendous and significant had happened, had he been granted some sort of status? Permission to take the initiative? Or did that still rest with her? Could he perhaps ring the Bellingham this evening and ask to speak to her (she had said she was there for two more nights), or would that be an appalling solecism, displaying a presumption on his part from which his reputation, such as it was, would never recover?

'Oi!' Mart snapped his fingers in front of Will's face. 'Wakey wakey, love god.'

'Piss off.'

'Steady on.' Mart indicated the coffee cup and did a dumb show to order another two. 'Don't take it out on me; it's not my fault you're knackered.'

Will rubbed his face with both hands. 'What do I do now?'

'Take a cold shower.'

'I want to see her again.'

'I bet you do.'

'Should I ring the hotel?'

'Up to you, mate. Remember, I don't know the lady, so it's hard for me to advise.'

Will interpreted this as his cue to spill the beans.

'True.'

Mart's face fell.

What was left of the morning idled by. They walked through the market and found a desiccated triangle of garden with a patch of shade where they lay down and dozed. When Will woke up, Mart was gone. There were women sitting on a bench, and kids playing in a sandpit, which struck him as kind of weird in this desert country. In fact it was all weird, and he felt groggy. The women looked at him suspiciously as he raised his head and sat up. Brushing at himself, he found a piece of paper stuck in the pocket of his shirt.

Thought I'd leave you to it, Sleeping Beauty. See you at Abdul's, sixish?

He struggled to his feet and thrust the scrunched-up note into the pocket of his jeans. He supposed it was fair enough. After last night, Mart was entitled to a show of independence. He left the garden, conscious of the mothers' heads inclined to one another in relief, and zigzagged between the careering black taxis and donkey carts to a stall selling flatbread and olives, which he washed down with a can of 7 Up. It was one fifteen; he pictured Jacqueline sitting in some cool, shady courtyard restaurant or swish hotel dining room, talking to her interesting, cultivated colleagues, sipping white wine. Did she, he wondered, fix everyone with that look? Was she thinking about him at all? He was a miserable exile from her life. It was intolerable.

He had to do something, so in the end he bought a pad and pencil in a corner shop and wrote her a note. It took him several goes to come up with the simple and, he hoped, effective *Can I see you again? W.*

He then trudged across town in the punishing afternoon heat and suffered the lofty disfavour of the Bellingham's reception staff for his sweat-stained shirt and dusty jeans.

'I'd like to leave this for Miss Praed, please.'

'She is not here at the moment, sir,' purred a huge man with the superb manner and pomaded hair and moustache of the Egyptian alpha male.

'I know. Please would you give it to her when she comes back.'

'Very well.' The man took Will's note fastidiously between finger and thumb and put it in one of the cubbyholes at the back: Room 223.

A coolly courteous smile played on him from the man's great height. 'May I do anything else for you, sir?'

Will could take a hint. 'No, thank you.'

Turning his back on the inviting portals of the bar just a few yards to his left, he went back out into the street. Now that he no longer had a purpose, the heat and noise were overpowering; he felt drained and slightly nauseous. He missed Mart, the swine. There was no point in going back to the hostel, which didn't open again until five. He headed for the museum.

He'd been twice already, once with Mart and the second time

alone. There was more there than one person could absorb in a month, and it was relatively cool. Failing all else, he told himself, he could sit on the steps outside the main entrance and watch the people come and go and take photographs of each other. Will owned a camera, one his parents had given him last Christmas with his travels in mind, but he couldn't be bothered to have it with him, to be one of those people with cameras round their necks like harnesses, driven by the need to record everything. It had been duly stolen from his rucksack in Naples; he hadn't told the parents. Though he didn't miss the camera himself, he felt a bit shamefaced at having lost their present through sheer lack of interest. His plan was to tell them he'd put it down for a moment at some enthralling site, not that it had been pinched from the youth hostel.

When he reached the museum, he had to queue to get through the turnstile, and the forecourt garden, where he'd pictured himself restfully observing his fellow tourists, was heaving: school parties and at least three coach tours had converged on the way in – or out, it was impossible to tell. Harassed teachers and tour guides were trying to impose order on the melee.

Will shouldered his way through the throng to the entrance, and went straight up the stairs to the Tutankhamun gallery. This was the business; you could spend all day every day here and never get bored. He'd been hooked the first time he saw the picture of the tomb as Howard Carter had discovered it. Just like any old box room or garage with stuff piled up haphazardly – except that it wasn't any old box room or garage, and there was more, and more fantastic, stuff than any nineteen-year-old, even if he was a pharaoh, had any right to own. Will had to keep reminding himself that Tut, in pharaonic terms, was not much more than a comma, a footnote, an obscure boy king of no great wealth or distinction. Christ knows what the others must have been buried with before it was all nicked.

There were plenty of people up here too, but the exhibits in their glass cases were like bubbles of stillness in the hubbub. And the people were somehow nicer, bonded by their common fascination; he was happy to be one of them. When he saw someone put their face really close to the glass and stare and stare, turning their head slightly this way and that, he knew just how they felt – they were trying to absorb the thousands of years in between, to come to terms with the detailed reality of the thing before them, still as perfect as when it was made, all present and correct and infinitely fascinating. But unlike most, he didn't head straight for the golden treasure; amazing though that was, it wasn't his favourite. The small, peripheral stuff was what he liked most – the models and games and miniature boyhood furniture, the weapons and chariots and spoons and jewellery, some of it quite crude. Not a single thing had been left out. He was looking at a whole life, from top to bottom.

He joined the line processing, awestruck, round the giant Russian-doll sarcophagi. After that, the golden treasure beckoned, but he'd seen that before and didn't have the cash for the special ticket. He wandered back via another room, one he hadn't visited before, not King Tut but a gallery of fresco portraits, even older according to the information plaque. The millennia involved in Egyptian history were enough to give you brain-ache.

He saw her first. She was standing looking up at one of the portraits, arms folded, leaning slightly forward, wearing exactly that expression that he remembered – the pressed-together lips with a hint of a smile, the narrowed, quizzical gaze, as though urging the regal lady in the portrait to respond. She appeared admirably cool; her cream suit looked freshly laundered, her hair, in a chignon this time, was perfectly groomed. Will instinctively lifted an arm to assess his own sweat level.

'Don't worry about it, Will,' she said. 'No one else does around here.'

He was mortified. 'Oops.'

She straightened up and smiled at him. 'That was mean of me.'

'How did you know I was there?'

'I didn't smell you, if that's what you're worried about. You were reflected in the glass.'

'Damn.'

'I was hoping this would happen,' she said. 'But I was afraid it probably wouldn't.'

'Me too.'

They were standing a couple of yards apart. There were half a dozen other people in the gallery. Will thrust his hands into his hip pockets.

'I left a note at the hotel for you.'

'Oh, did you?' She sounded touched and amused, as if that were the sweetest thing in the world. 'What did it say?'

'That I wanted to see you again. I left the address and number of the hostel.'

'I'd have tracked you down,' she said. 'Don't you worry.'

'Really?'

'Why so surprised?'

'I don't know. I thought ...' He shrugged. 'I don't know what I thought.'

She pulled an oh-yeah grimace. 'You thought I casually seduced young men all the time, only to cast them aside heartlessly when I tired of them.'

'No!' he objected.

'Good, because I don't. Or at least I do sometimes, but this was qualitatively different.' She took a couple of steps towards him. 'Wouldn't you agree?'

Overwhelmed and on fire, he could only shrug. She laughed.

'What does that mean?'

'I agree.'

'But not all that much, perhaps.'

'No ...'

'I have a suggestion to make,' she said. 'Why don't we take a cab back to the Bellingham? I can help you decide.'

In the bar of the Tudor, Will's hand, jostled by the memory, shook slightly as he picked up his glass. He was sweating. He wondered if his face, as he daydreamed, had shown something, or if he had made some embarrassing small sound. But the readers were reading, the planners planning, the historic cougher embarking on another spasm. He took his folded handkerchief from his pocket and dabbed his brow and the slippery outside of the glass. Calm down, everything was okay.

Other people, his contemporaries, often remarked that they felt the same under the skin as they had at twenty-one; that it was only the outer cortex that changed. They reflected ruefully and at length that this was a damn shame. Will didn't feel the same; not at all. Remembering his youthful self was like watching a character in a film – Will Drake as played by some attractive, callow actor. Jacqueline had been only eight years older than him – in her early sixties now; there was a thought – but light years ahead in terms of maturity and experience. Her interest in him had been pretty incredible at the time, and from where he was sitting now scarcely credible at all. It was eerie to reflect that there must have been something about him, some quality of voice or manner or appearance, some 'vibe', as today's young might have said, of which he himself was completely unaware but which had attracted her to him. Equally amazing had been his own naivety; he'd never even had a steady girlfriend. A savvier chap would have played it cool and been less open-hearted. So perhaps – Will nodded to himself – his innocence had been his trump card.

The barman, thinking the nod had been for him, took a fresh glass from beneath the bar.

It was bizarre returning to the foyer of the Bellingham just two hours after he'd last been there and if anything even more scruffy, and to watch as Jacqueline was handed the key to Room 223 and the note he'd left for her. Fortunately there were different staff behind the reception desk, and if they were interested in their guest's visitor they didn't show it.

In the pristine surroundings of the hotel room he felt pretty disgusting, but she wouldn't let him shower.

'Before and after,' she said, taking off her glasses and removing the pins from her hair like a secretary in a film. 'Plenty of time.'

They had sex at once, still half dressed, with him sitting in an armchair and her sitting on his lap, pumping and squeezing him between her thighs, her breasts against his face, her arms cradling his head. He was frantic and far too quick, but she stroked back his sticky hair and covered his forehead in kisses.

Then they showered together. She washed him firmly and thoroughly and he came again, leaning back against the Ottoman tiles, his knees buckling under the onslaught. Then it was his turn and she let him do whatever he wanted, a half-drowned woman, her wet body heavy, her eyes slits and her hair streaked across her face.

On the glacial expanse of the double bed they lay quietly, deciding that it would be nice to sleep for a while, but it was hopeless;

their hands strayed and their mouths came together and in no time at all they were wrapped in each other, arms, legs, body and soul.

She had to attend a dinner that night, and his clothes were too grubby for the hotel bar, so at six thirty she took him for a drink on the corniche.

'I go back to the UK tomorrow,' she said. 'So this will have to be au revoir.'

He was desolate. 'We're not due back for weeks! I must see you again. How can I contact you?'

'Don't worry, I'll get in touch.' She took a small black diary from her handbag, 'University of London' stamped on the cover. She removed the pencil and opened the diary at a back page. 'Here. Your particulars, please.'

He hesitated. 'I'm kind of – between things at the moment.'

She was insouciant. 'It's up to you.'

'I'll put my parents' address.'

'Good idea.'

He wrote *Hallowfield, Meeting House Lane, Upper Bradstone, Nr Westerton, Cambs*, and the number. The words of home, as well-worn and familiar to him as a handful of old marbles, nearly unmanned him. He had undergone this massive seismic change, but back there everything would be the same, quietly and trustingly waiting for him.

When he got back, Mart was sitting on one of the plastic chairs in the hostel's narrow hallway, a half-smoked fag between his fingers. When he saw Will, he got to his feet and dropped the fag in the tin ashtray on the counter. The bloke behind the counter, an Australian, was watching them. Mart had a funny look on his face.

'Hi there. No need to ask where you've been.'

'Nice of you to wait. Fancy supper? I'm starving.'

'Will – you've got a message, mate.'

'Have I?' Will saw that the Australian was holding a piece of paper. It seemed to be the Day of the Note.

'It's not her,' said Mart. 'It's from home.'

'Oh, okay.' Will took it. 'Cheers.'

*

Will remembered thinking that it was an odd coincidence how not half an hour before he'd been writing down his parents' address, and now here they were getting in touch, as if by doing that he'd summoned them up.

Please call home reverse charge. Mum. Urgent.

'Okay,' he'd said again. The Aussie had pushed the phone across the counter towards him.

'Want me to place the call? Save time?'

'Can you? Thanks.'

He and Mart stood there while the Aussie got through. Mart lit another cigarette. That 'Urgent' was a cloud no bigger than a man's hand on the horizon. They didn't look at one another.

'You don't have to hang about,' said Will. 'Just tell me where you're going and I'll see you there.'

'It's fine, I'll wait.'

'There you go.' The Aussie handed Will the receiver. Mart went and sat down on the step just outside the door.

'Hello?'

'Will?'

'Oh, hi, Mum.'

The Aussie retreated to the small office at the back.

'Will ... Oh God.'

'Mum? What's up?'

Remembering this, Will was glad of the second large gin that stood waiting on the table. He'd had his share of life-threatening moments in the army, but none of them had had the ice-water effect of the call to his mother on that sweltering long-ago evening in Cairo.

Lawrence Drake had died at almost the very moment his son and a virtual stranger were rogering each other rigid in a Cairo hotel room. Will's first thought, once he'd absorbed the shock, was:

Now God knows when I'll see her again.

Chapter Five
1998

Stella had been minding eighteen-month-old Toyah all afternoon. Though the time had passed pleasantly enough, she was glad to hear Shannon's key in the lock.

'There's Mummy,' she said, rising awkwardly from the floor with the aid of the nearest armchair. 'Hey, you – your mum's back.'

Toyah took no notice and continued to play with My First Laptop, even when Shannon swept into the room, dumped a clutch of supermarket bags on the sofa and descended on her daughter with outstretched arms in an attitude that mirrored – probably unconsciously – the famous clip of Princess Diana greeting the little princes on *Britannia*.

'Hello, darlin'!' She gazed winsomely at Stella over the toddler's head. 'How's she been?'

'She's missed you, of course,' said Stella. 'But she's been as good as gold.'

'Ah, bless.' Shannon planted a kiss on her struggling daughter's cheek before putting her down. 'Thanks ever so much, I really appreciate it.'

'Pleasure, it's what I'm here for. Did you manage to get everything done?'

'Yeah, not bad. I couldn't find that bathroom storage thing I was telling you about, but I got the rest and I made the doctor's appointment.'

Stella was struck as always by the perfection of Shannon's turn-out, all her own work. Her already flawless skin was enhanced by immaculate make-up, her manicured nails twinkled, her hair was streaky and silken. How on earth did she manage it, a single mother on benefits? It was a gift, Stella decided, one she herself did not possess. She smiled benignly as she took her tea mug out to the kitchen. Now that her scheduled stint was almost over, she felt able to go the extra mile. Returning, she asked:

'Is there stuff that needs putting away?'

'Yeah, but it can wait. I'll do it when she's in bed.'

'Are you sure? It won't take a moment.'

'No, no, for goodness' sake, you've done enough. I don't know what we'd do without you. Eh, Toy? What would we do without Auntie Stel?'

'She's a sweetie,' said Stella. For all that she wore her out, she was genuinely fond of Toyah. 'All right, well, if there's nothing else I can do, I'll run along and see you the same time next week.'

'Sure, that'd be great.' Still carrying Toyah, Shannon accompanied her into the hall and watched as she put on her coat. 'How are you, anyway, you all right? Done all your shopping? Not long now – what you doing for Christmas?'

Stella went for the last question only. 'I'll be with the family as usual.'

'That's nice. Best place.'

'I think so.' Stella turned her collar up and took her woolly gloves from her pocket. 'Right, that's me. Bye-bye, Toyah.' She patted the baby's cheek. 'Be good for Mum. Bye, Shannon, look after yourself.'

'I'll be fine,' said Shannon, opening the door.

'You know where I am if you need me.'

'We do! Bye-bye, Auntie Stel!' Shannon waggled Toyah's plump hand, then waved her own. 'See you!'

Opening the front door of her Victorian tradesman's terraced cottage, the opposite side of town from the Cherrydown Estate, Stella reflected that as with Shannon's person, so with her environment. Her housekeeping put Stella's to shame. Stella told herself she had no aptitude for housework, was not the domesticated type, and that the state of her home was not something an intelligent woman should lose sleep over. But with the image of Shannon's shining surfaces, burnished sink and radiators draped with spotless, fragrant washing still imprinted on her retina, the comparison with her own surroundings was dismayingly unfavourable. She plonked her coat and bag down on the already overloaded hall chair and spent ten minutes wandering between kitchen and living room, a distance of some three metres, trying to decide where to begin, before giving up and pouring herself a Scotch.

She derived a real sense of satisfaction from her afternoon's work. Of course it was no more than Shannon did every day of her life, but not having had children of her own, Stella found the peculiar mixture of inertia and responsibility exhausting. When she'd taken early retirement from her job as senior administrator at the local FE college, she had completed training as an adult literacy teacher, but the work that generated, though interesting, was only part-time. With no dependants, she'd accumulated decent savings and had a good pension, with more to come in a couple of years' time when she was sixty. She planned to engage in some adventurous travel, to see more of old friends (many of them from her boarding school days; she was good at keeping up) and to resume the piano lessons she'd abandoned at eleven. Since then, she'd been on a gorilla safari in Uganda, and a guided walking holiday in Tuscany, had advanced to page 20 ('Once I Had a Secret Love') in *Playing for Pleasure* before abandoning the project for a second time, and discovered that former head girl Penny Backwell had turned into a braying crypto-fascist. In other words, it was becoming increasingly clear that she needed something else to occupy her and she had cast around for ways to make herself useful. A mild political involvement – envelope-stuffing, making rice salads for fund-raisers – was one, and Child Friendly was now the other. It had struck her as a thoroughly sensible, practical sort of charity, local and hands-on, without the huge running costs of more high-profile good causes. Volunteers were allocated to particular hard-pressed young families to whom they became surrogate aunts, available on predetermined days (and at other times at their own discretion) to help with child-minding, shopping, lifts and the occasional treat. She herself had been familiar with Universal Aunts when she made the regular journey back to school in England, so she appreciated the value of the role, the peace of mind it had given her mother and the comfort to her small self, soggy with homesickness. With no child-rearing experience, Stella wasn't sure if they'd want her, and took it as a compliment that they'd practically bitten her hand off. Perhaps it was as a concession to her childlessness that she'd been allotted Shannon and Toyah, who surely constituted a cushy number.

She stretched across to the coffee table (used for and laden with everything but coffee cups) and switched on Radio 3, a clarinet concerto. Then she moved last Sunday's papers, thus dislodging others on the far side, and leaned back, putting her feet up on the resulting space.

It wasn't quite true that Stella had no dependants. She might not have borne any, but the other reason that she needed one or two solid commitments was to prevent her from being subsumed in the roles of dutiful daughter and maiden aunt (she was no maiden; the title was generic). Since her mother had chosen, as an intelligent pre-emptive measure following a fall, to move out of Hallowfield into sheltered accommodation nearby, and Will's daughter Evie had been elevated to giddy executive heights at the bank, the calls on her time had multiplied exponentially. She collected her great-nephew Raphael from school twice a week, and on Tuesdays he stayed for supper so that Evie could go to Pilates straight from work. But those were just the regular dates; life was dotted with steppings into the breach which she felt obliged to undertake unless there was a cast-iron reason not to.

With her mother, she was more reliant on conscience, but Stella's conscience was a stern mistress. Kate was far from being a difficult old lady – rather the opposite – and the warden carried non-interference to extremes, so unless Stella went over to Rectory Court, she wouldn't necessarily know that her mother had cut herself on a tin lid, or the kettle had packed up. She was not in the loop because there was no loop; she simply visited on a frequent but random basis to keep herself informed.

She might well go tomorrow – no Raff, and she should also shop (there was next to nothing in the fridge), so a round trip would kill several birds with one stone. Tonight, she decided to take advantage of the lack of supplies and have a takeaway curry. She glanced at the grandfather clock and subtracted the obligatory ten minutes. Half an hour and she could place her order with Mohan at the Pride of Bombay, an exercise which only meant giving her name; she was a good customer and always had the same thing.

She put her glass where her feet had been and went into the hall to fetch the handset and the few letters that she'd scuffed to one side on her way in. The bills she dropped on top of her handbag, the three letters she took back into the living room. Two of them were Christmas cards, one from the chairman of Child Friendly, the other from a married couple, fellow envelope-stuffers, whom she occasionally supped with. The third was a postcard bearing a picture of the Sphinx. Just like her brother to ignore all easier forms of communication, and keep his distance.

Staying on here pro tem so not back for Xmas festivities. Sent Evie a cheque to spend on herself and the songster. I'll try and call the mother, give her my love. Hope you're well, love Will xx

She tore the postcard in half and tossed it in the hearth. What did he mean, 'staying on'? Doing what? And with whom? What was there more important than his own family, to keep him hanging about in bloody Cairo over Christmas? And what was all this about 'trying' to call Kate? How hard could it be?

There were times when, if Will had walked into the room, Stella would (she fantasised) have picked up the poker and walloped him over the skull with it. By what right did he operate in a different moral universe to the rest of them? He was one of those people – of whom there were a surprisingly large number – who had spent a lifetime developing the role of licensed character, so that the rest of the world would put up with their self-indulgent fannying around. As far as Stella was concerned, it wasn't clever and it wasn't funny. It was bloody unfair. Will had been indulged as a small boy, and as a youth, and he had taken advantage. But as a man in late middle age, he should know better. Time to get backside in gear. No wonder dear Evie was so anal, such a slave to order in all its forms – she had been exposed from her earliest days to a terrible object lesson, from both parents in their different way, in irresponsibility and fecklessness.

She tossed aside the pieces of postcard, and got to her feet. A bit of tidying would be therapeutic, and the lamb passanda would be her reward.

Kate thought about ringing Stella. Her hand hovered over the phone more than once, but she managed to resist. After all, she was perfectly all right, just a bit blue, and it wasn't fair to call people in order simply to moan. It was, notoriously, a difficult time of year, when those who lived alone were more aware of their solitary state. And she mustn't forget that Stella was on her own too.

When the phone rang, she nearly jumped out of her skin, and gave her old Hallowfield number by mistake.

'Now then – I recognise that voice, and that number. Kate?'

'Joe, sorry, you made me jump!'

Her brother chuckled. 'Not too high, I hope.'

'Chance would be a fine thing.'

'I was just saying to Angie that I wondered how my estimable sis was, and she suggested quite forcefully that I pull finger and find out.'

'It's lovely to hear from you,' said Kate. 'I was sitting here in a complete daydream.'

There was a murmur in the background. 'Ah, yes,' said Joe. 'Angie's also reminding me to ask if you've heard from Will.'

'No.'

'We haven't, I hasten to add. Any idea how he is? Or, indeed, where?'

'I believe he's in Cairo at the moment. Evie spoke to him a couple of weeks ago.'

'Will he be in your midst for Christmas, d'you think?'

'I've no idea.' Kate bristled slightly. She had her views about Will, but she kept them to herself, and she didn't like being pushed on the subject or, as her younger brother quite often did, being treated as complicit in a prodigal-son scenario. Joe and his wife Angela lived in north Norfolk, and their twin offspring were models of their kind: Nick was something well paid in the City and had married a former Miss Finland, with whom he had one son currently on a sports scholarship at Millfield; Beatrice, 'Bee', lived with her vicar husband and a brood of tow-headed teenagers near Norwich. Beside these two, her own unmarried daughter and absentee son, though she adored them both, appeared in an un-flattering light.

'... Bee's doing Boxing Day, and she did mention that if you and yours could be bothered, she'd love to see you. We all would.'

Kate told herself he didn't mean to rub it in. 'That's kind, how sweet of her, I'll spread the word.'

'Donald will be enjoying a well-earned rest by then, so it's a case of the more the merrier, you know how she is.'

'I'll definitely ask.'

'Want to speak to Angie? She's flapping at me.'

'Yes, please.'

'Kate!' Angela Kingsley had one of those voices that seemed always to be on the end of a laugh. 'How are you *really*?' It was another of her quirks that she believed no woman would ever tell a man the whole truth.

'Hello, Angela. I'm very well. Really.'

'It would be *so* lovely if you could make Boxing Day. A real gathering of the clans.'

'Let's see if we can.'

There followed a short pause, before Angela said:

'And if the wanderer wanders back, bring him along.'

'Of course,' said Kate, adding, 'If I can. That will be up to him.'

To keep her end up, she told them about going to see *The Browning Version* with Stella, and a boozy Sunday lunch with her former neighbours in Upper Bradstone, and for good measure threw in her two-mile walk along the river (though she didn't mention that she'd done it alone, for fear of unleashing a flurry of fussy warnings). The conversation ended with a repeat of the Boxing Day invitation. She was able to sign off by saying honestly, 'It's so nice to hear your voices. Bless you for calling.'

'I'm glad you prodded me, darling,' said Joe to his wife. 'That definitely cheered her up.'

Angela, rising to see to supper, shook her head admiringly. 'She's a great lady, your sister. Will they come, do you think?'

'Lap of the gods – depends on whether one of the others is up for the drive.'

'You'd better sow the seeds amongst them then, smartish.'

'I shall. I don't want her brooding over that toerag Will. He's clearly got no intention of honouring any of us with his presence.'

'Poor Kate,' sighed Angela. 'I do feel for her.'

*

Kate was going to dine in the main house this evening. Twice a week and at lunchtime on Sunday, the independent residents of Rectory Court could book to eat in the dining room there at very little extra cost, and it was surprisingly nicely done: good, light food, well-chosen wine, Sheffield plate, linen napkins, flowers and, at this time of year, candles. Ian Macky was going to call for her at six thirty so they could go over together for a drink in the drawing room beforehand. She changed into a satin shirt with a velvet jacket, and added Lawrence's regimental brooch, the white horse picked out in diamond chips, before slipping into shoes with a low heel. When she heard Ian's knock, she brushed Lawrence's photo with her finger before going to the door.

'Kate, good evening. You look especially elegant, if I may say so.'

'Thank you.' They touched cheeks and he helped her on with her coat. She picked up her handbag and patted her pockets. 'Now, have I got everything?'

'It scarcely matters here.'

'Don't say that, for heaven's sake.' She closed the door behind her. 'Once I stop taking responsibility for my keys and specs, I'll go gaga in no time.'

'Good point. But please, take my arm. I need something to hold on to even if you don't.'

She laughed and linked her arm through his. It was a dank and overcast night, but the paths of Rectory Court were well lit. She knew she was fortunate to be squired to dinner; women outnumbered men here by a factor of six to one. That didn't mean she was available. In the more than thirty years of Kate's widowhood there had been several suitors, all of them ardent and some persistent, but she had turned them all down with the utmost grace and finality. It wasn't that she closed her mind to the possibility; she liked male company and respected the often-voiced view that swift remarriage was often a compliment to the departed, but that presupposed you'd met someone you wished to marry. The simple truth was that she wasn't going to settle for second best.

As a young married woman all those years ago in Berlin, she had been almost lost, on the brink of a catastrophic decision. Sometimes she had only to close her eyes to see that other figure disappearing into the swarming curtain of snow at the end of the tunnel, to hear the tumbling clangour of the bells proclaiming *Heiligabend* and to feel the tears turning to crystal on her cheeks. But she had made her choice and stuck to it. She too had walked out of that tunnel and never looked back. And if at any time since she had been tempted to consider another life, she had only to relive the moment of her return; to recall the two of them, her husband and child, side by side in the lamplight, and their faces as he looked up from the book they were reading together and saw her there ... Then she would be certain, as she had been then and every day since, that she had come back on that long ago Christmas Eve to her heart's home.

She and Ian entered the rectory through the handsome front door, and he took her coat and hung it on the hook in the hall. He had perfect manners; she took pleasure in his attentiveness.

'So,' he said. 'An aperitif by the fire?'

'I think so,' she said. 'How nice this is.'

In the drawing room, the warden and his wife presided over a loaded drinks trolley. The log fire leapt up the chimney. Dolly, a former actress, was playing 'People Will Say We're in Love' from *Oklahoma!*.

Kate smiled, but did not look at Ian, in case she saw something in his face it would be simpler not to see.

Chapter Six

1967

Lawrence Drake had collapsed and died while mowing the lawn, after a vigorous three sets of tennis with friends. A good clean death, caused by a massive heart attack quite undeserved in a fit man in his fifties who drank in moderation and hadn't smoked for years. He'd taken the golden bowler a couple of years before and was working happily with SSAFA, assessing pension claims and fund-raising for war veterans' causes. He and Kate were universally liked in the village and beyond, an obviously happy couple who, everyone agreed, were always a pleasure to be with.

It was his father's untimely death that had sowed the seeds of an army career in Will. Or perhaps 'career' was too solid and sensible a word – the urge to join up, to go for a soldier, something stirring and romantic of that kind. He'd certainly had nothing else in mind, but those were the days when there existed a notion of choice, so he'd simply put off the decision on the assumption that when he'd done travelling and pissing about, he'd be able to go into something interesting, undemanding, and well paid enough to fund his leisure.

But the powerful emotional effects of going home to his widowed mother, to his stressed, responsible older sister and the time-polished sonority of the Anglican funeral with its strong military presence had affected him deeply. He'd returned from Egypt full of dread and the wildly improbable fear that in his absence Mart might assume the mantle of Jacqueline's chevalier.

The dread had mostly been associated with his mother. Recent adventures notwithstanding, Will was still at heart enough of a child that the thought of his mother broken with grief, not in control, perhaps weeping on his shoulder, appalled him. The first

56

tentative question he asked Stella when she met him at the station in her VW camper, was:

'How's the mother doing?'

'Brave and calm. Amazingly so. I imagine if there's going to be a reaction it will come after Friday, but there's no sign of it at the moment.' She glanced quickly at him. 'Relieved?'

'Yes.'

'I was too. Unnatural, I know, but I couldn't imagine myself comforting her. It would have felt all wrong, embarrassing somehow.'

'Exactly. God, sis ...'

Stella's understanding was a second cause of relief. With the restraint of tension gone and the Upper Bradstone road, familiar as his own face, spooling out before them over the soft Cambridgeshire fields, he could feel the tears threatening to break their banks. He turned to look out of the window and felt Stella's hand briefly squeezing his forearm.

'Poor Dad,' he muttered.

'Actually no, not poor Dad. He dropped out *in media res*, textbook stuff. It's poor the rest of us. Especially Ma.'

'Yes, you're right, I know you're right, it's just ...' He broke off on a croak and felt Stella glance at him again.

'Don't be afraid to have a good cry, Will. We all are, all the time. Ma does it in private, but she does it all right. I mean, for heaven's sake, if we can't cry now, when can we?'

'Fair point.'

But he still kept the lid on it for the rest of the drive. This was partly due to some vague, outdated idea of his now being 'the man of the family', and also because he could not help remembering where he had been and what he had been doing when it happened. And with whom. At this precise moment, his mourning was as much for himself and for Jacqueline as for his father.

That started to change when they turned into Meeting House Lane and then after a couple of hundred yards through the open gate of Hallowfield. The house looked tranquil and welcoming on this early summer afternoon, the garden lovely in its green, abundant Englishness. Past the side of the house Will could see the back lawn still showing the pattern of the mower his father had been pushing thirty-six hours ago. He jumped quickly out of the van and took a moment retrieving his rucksack and rummaging for something – anything! – in the outer pocket. Footsteps scrunched on the gravel.

'It's you!' His mother's voice.

'It's us,' said Stella. 'I brought him back.'

He hauled out the rucksack and dropped it on the ground before facing her. Stella had already gone in; the door stood open.

'Hello, darling.'

His mother at first held out her arms, but intuitively translated the gesture into one of welcome, and didn't embrace him but simply placed her hands on his shoulders and kissed him with a little appreciative sound, as though he tasted good.

'Mm ...' As she drew back, she touched one hand to his cheek and let it rest there for a second.

'Come on in.' She turned towards the house. 'You must be whacked.'

'I'm so ...' He hoisted the rucksack on to his shoulder. 'Mum, I'm so sorry ...'

'I know,' she said. She met his eyes briefly. 'I know, Will.'

'I mean ...' His face contorted with the struggle of what to say. 'How are you?'

She paused before replying in a matter-of-fact way, 'Pretty bloody, to be honest. No point in pretending, and anyway, I don't quite believe it yet. Well, no, I believe it, of course I do, but it's awfully hard to imagine the rest of life without ...' Her voice cracked a little and she cleared her throat. 'Without him.'

'No,' he said, 'nor me. I couldn't help noticing the lawn ...'

'Yes, oh dear. Awful. Wait till you see the rest. It's only half done.'

'Jesus, Mum!'

Now she did give him a hug, rucksack and all, and he sobbed loudly and uncaringly for a couple of minutes, coughing, honking and spluttering like a big kid.

'Sorry ... Shit ... Sorry ...'

'What for?' She stepped back, tweaked a hankie from her shirt cuff and dabbed her own eyes before handing it to him. 'Refreshment, that's what we need.'

Stella appeared at the back of the hall. 'Tea, coffee? Or a sharpener?'

'What will it be, Will?'

'I could murder a beer.'

'And I'll have my usual, darling. Thank you so much.'

'Coming up!'

Will blew his nose, and in response to his mother's gesture thrust the handkerchief into his own pocket. She tapped the side of his rucksack.

'Put that thing down. Let's go out in the garden, it's easier out of doors. Even with the wretched lawn.'

He knew what she meant, but as they walked, arms linked, across the grass to the bleached wood and canvas chairs by the strawberry tree, he saw where the wavering tramlines left by the mower came to a sudden halt, and began weeping again. She squeezed his arm before releasing it, and sitting down. Below the hem of her pale green cotton skirt, her long legs, elegantly crossed, gleamed pale and slim.

'You know, Will,' she said lightly, 'that's something you could do – finish the job. Stella's been meaning to, but she simply hasn't had the time.' She looked at him imploringly, but he knew it was more an order than a request, for his own and the general good. 'Could you face it?'

'Of course I can. That's fine, I will. Good idea. Might even do it this evening.'

'Whenever you're ready. Although I suppose it needs to be before Friday; we don't want that wretched reminder staring everyone in the face over the wine and bakemeats.'

Stella came out with a tray bearing a glass and two cans for him, a whisky on the rocks for Kate, and tea in a Swinging London mug.

'I'm not being virtuous,' she explained. 'We've been hitting the bottle together, haven't we, Ma? But it does give me the blues rather. Or should I say it makes the blues harder to deal with.'

They agreed that this was sometimes the case but that they would all deal with it in their separate ways. Then they began to discuss funeral arrangements, the readings that they would do, and the regimental involvement.

'Sam Payne's been so kind,' said Kate, 'but I sense that unless I retain a firm hand, the whole thing will be hijacked by the military. It's perfectly understandable and the army was a huge part of Lawrence's life, but just – you know – not all of it.'

'This is primarily *your* day,' agreed Stella. 'You're in charge.'

'Well, mine and Dad's.'

'Oh Ma, naturally! But you're the best judge of what he would have wanted, so you mustn't let yourself be railroaded. And we're here to help. Aren't we, Will?'

He nodded vigorously. He had never felt less adequate to a task. The discussion continued, with Stella in the role of *ex officio* chairman, all through their supper of cold chicken and potato salad. He seemed to have almost nothing to contribute. He knew what his sister was doing, keeping the tone practical, steering it away from the emotional abyss. She was trying to help by avoiding the messy, dangerous, emotional heart of things. In one way he was grateful to her for keeping the party polite. In another he wished they could dive in and – what? Get it over with? It would never be over with, not in that way. This was it: this fatherless household, this widowed mother, this having to imagine what Dad would have wanted because he was no longer here to ask. All the opportunities missed, the things unsaid or not understood, the memories that were no longer part of an experience, a continuum, but had to stand alone, like framed pictures to be preserved and cherished. They had to keep the focus short, maintain this febrile level of activity at least for a few days, because beyond it was the drab reality of Dad's absence, in which he could foresee the end of freedom, just as freedom had never looked sweeter. He and Stella were going to have to step up to the mark, become responsible, help look after their mother now that she was on her own. And oh, bloody hell, how he didn't want to!

They'd just finished eating when the phone rang. Stella answered it, and came back into the kitchen wearing an enquiring expression.

'Mum, it's Uncle Joe. Are you up to talking?'

'Yes, I am, I'm coming right away.'

Their mother went into the hall, and Stella pushed the kitchen door discreetly to behind her. She lowered her voice as they transferred the supper things to the sink.

'The phone's been ringing endlessly. I suppose it's good, and it's certainly well meant, but it must be wearing for her endlessly fielding all that sympathy.'

'But Uncle Joe's different, surely. Family's different.'

'I suppose. Yes, you're right. Although it's more sort of potent. It was ghastly for her having to tell Gran. That sense of things being in the wrong order. Two widows ...' Stella broke off and ran water noisily. 'I'll wash.'

'Okay.' Will took a 'country flowers' tea towel off the Aga rail. 'I don't suppose Gran's coming over, is she?'

Stella shook her head. 'No point. Even if her legs were okay, the flight would knock the stuffing out of her. But you know what she is, incredibly – earthy. Emotionally sensible, because she's been through a lot. When she said she'd be with us in spirit, she meant it, and Ma knows she will be. But it was a pretty wretched conversation, as you can imagine.'

Will had only met his Kenyan grandparents a few times, most recently on the last occasion they came over before his grandfather's death. He could certainly relate to that a bit now, although Grandpa had already been in the early stages of his long and painful terminal illness. Always a slightly forbidding figure, aloof and reserved, Jack Kingsley had been understandably even more withdrawn on that visit, and Will had avoided being alone with him. His grandmother Thea, on the other hand, was her usual exuberant self, game and good fun and openly affectionate, an old lady in whom the young one was still very much present. He remembered playing croquet – him, Dad, Ma and Gran – and there being a lot of laughs and some pretty evil cheating.

'... don't know about you.' Stella was saying something.

'Sorry?'

'I was saying we've been going to bed pretty early. Ma's got something to help her sleep. But you don't have to, obviously.'

'I don't know. My body clock's a bit out.'

'Just so long as you won't feel abandoned if we slope off.'

'Don't worry.'

They'd finished the washing-up and were putting away when Kate came back in.

'All right?' asked Stella.

'Fine. Just asking how I was and so on. They're coming on Thursday night. I must run the rule over the spare room and whatnot.'

'Don't worry,' said Stella. 'I'll do that.'

'Actually, darling, I'd like to. Activity, you know.'

'Okay.'

Will said: 'Sorry, I haven't cut that grass. I'll do it first thing tomorrow.'

'That would be wonderful.'

There was a slightly awkward hiatus, which Kate ended by saying, 'Well, I'm afraid it's bed for me.'

'Me too,' said Stella. 'I warned Will we'd be retiring early.'

Kate came over to Will and kissed him. 'Night-night, darling. It's lovely to have you here. See you in the morning.' She went to Stella. 'Night-night, and thank you for everything. We'll probably pass each other on the landing ...'

'Night, Ma. Hope you get some sleep.'

'I shall. Courtesy of Dr Coleman's little helpers.'

She smiled, and they smiled back rather wanly. When she'd gone, Will said, 'God, do you think she's going to cry herself to sleep?'

'Possibly.' Stella pinched the bridge of her nose; she looked worn out. 'Probably. I've not heard anything, ever. But what can we do?'

'Nothing, you're right.'

She fixed him with a worried frown. 'Are you going to stay up? Will you be okay?'

'Sure. I'll just watch TV or something.'

'I feel we're deserting you.'

'You're not. I'm fine.'

'Fine?' Stella snorted.

'I'm tired, but if I went up now, I couldn't sleep.'

'Night, then.' They touched cheeks, and she rubbed his arm briefly. 'See you in the morning.'

'Yup.' As she made to go, a thought occurred to him. 'This may sound odd, but I might take a walk up the lane.'

'Good idea. Don't talk to any strange women.'

'Chance'd be a fine thing,' he replied.

Stella's remark was one of those that people made automatically, without thinking about it, and his reply had been purely reflexive, but it was enough to bring thoughts of Jacqueline rushing back. When Stella glanced down at him on her way up the stairs, he thought it must be because she could hear the thump of his heart, but it was only to waggle her fingers and whisper again, 'Good night.'

It was not yet nine thirty. He went out into the soft dusk and across the gravel, noticing that his mother's bedroom curtains were only half drawn; she'd always liked to sleep and wake with the light. She and his father had occupied twin beds pushed together; Will supposed that the other bed would still be tidily made up with smooth sheets, the same ones his father had been sleeping in before he went. Presumably the bedside table would be the same, too – his book, his radio, his battered snakeskin-covered travelling clock that had been all over the world, and the cut-glass tumbler of water. Empty now, of course.

He walked a few hundred yards in the direction of the village, as far as Green Gates farm, where an alert Border collie began to bark at his approach and he turned back, conscious of causing a disturbance. His parents had been going to get another dog, their old black Lab Alma having gone to a better place six months ago, and he hoped his mother would do that now. It would be good for her, he thought. Not immediately obviously, and perhaps not a puppy; that was a hell of a lot of work. But some nice rescue dog, or one in need of rehoming whose owners were going to live abroad ... He grimaced. He'd caught himself doing it, thinking solicitous, fussy thoughts about his mother, who was only in her fifties and currently coping a lot better than the rest of them.

A barn owl flapped over the lane in front of him and he experienced, briefly, that exhilaration and sense of privilege that accompanied a rare sighting. Following this, he was aware of an equal and opposite sinking of the spirits as he closed the gate behind him for the night and went back into the house.

He snaffled a shot of Jameson's from the drinks cupboard and was fiddling with the telly when the phone rang. The loud, peremptory blast in this sleeping house made him nearly jump out of his skin, and he dashed into the hall to catch it before it woke anyone.

'Hello?' For a moment he couldn't remember the number, and said again in a fierce stage whisper, 'Hello?'

'Now then. Is that Will?'

'Jacqueline!' He lowered his voice and sat down on the carpet next to the hall table. 'God, you gave me the fright of my life!'

'It's only the telephone.'

'Yes, but my mother and sister are already in bed. I went for a walk; you were lucky, I just got in.'

'I hope I haven't woken them.'

'I don't think so. God, it's good to hear your voice!'

'Will, I saw your friend.'

'What, Mart?'

'He told me about your father. I rang to say how terribly sorry I am.'

'Thank you.' Will tried – not altogether successfully – to tune down from elation to respectful melancholy. 'It is pretty bloody.'

'What an awful shock.'

'Yes.'

'He can't have been any age at all.'

'Coming up to sixty?' Will squinted with the embarrassment of not being exactly sure. 'I think he was about that.'

'That really is so sad. I'm truly sorry.'

'Thanks,' he said, and then: 'I wish you were here.'

'No you don't,' she said in her less solicitous, more recognisable voice. 'Think of trying to explain me to your family, especially under the circumstances.'

'You know what I mean.'

'Oh, yes. Yes, I do. And I feel the same.'

'Do you?'

She ignored this. 'But it's the utterest no-no, Will. Out of the question. You have to concentrate on the job in hand. Which is mourning your father, supporting your mother and taking care of yourself, in that order.'

'I will!' He couldn't keep the resentment out of his voice. 'I am. I've only been here five minutes.'

'Yes, and look, I'm ringing already. I must miss you.'

'Do you?' he asked again, and this time she answered.

'Yes.' Her voice softened. 'Strangely, I do.'

'Can I see you again?' he asked urgently. 'After the – when all this part is over.'

'That would be good. I tell you what, call the main switchboard number and leave a message for me, and I'll call you back. But Will …'

'What?'

'After a decent interval. Please.'

'What do you take me for?'

He heard a little sigh. 'For now, you take care of yourself and your family. And think about your father.'

'I will. Jacqueline—'

'Bye for now, Will.'

The line went dead, and he replaced the receiver to silence its dull buzz. He hoped that neither his mother nor Stella was still awake, and so had heard anything. He tried to rerun what he'd said: perhaps nothing more than he'd have said to any concerned friend ...

'Will?'

Stella was on the stairs behind him. 'Sorry if I made you jump. What are you doing down there?'

'Taking a call, about Dad ...' He scrambled to his feet. 'Hope I didn't disturb you.'

'I heard something, but I was only dozing. Who was it?'

'Oh. Mart. The friend I was travelling with.'

'That was nice of him,' said Stella, coming down and heading towards the kitchen. 'I'm going to make cocoa; do you want one?'

'Might as well.'

She gave him a wry look as she opened the fridge. 'Don't force yourself.'

'No. That'd be nice, cheers.'

He leaned against the worktop as she poured milk into a saucepan and stirred cocoa powder and sugar.

'Mum asleep?' he asked.

She nodded. 'I looked in. I might as well warn you, though, she'll be up at the crack of dawn.'

'She was always a lark.'

'They both were, but at least they used to have a cuppa and listen to the wireless for a bit. The last couple of mornings she's leapt out the moment she opens her eyes. I think she can't bear to stay in bed and be prey to her thoughts.'

'I can't say I'm looking forward to it myself.'

She poured out the hot milk and handed him a mug. They sat down at the table.

'Have we ever done this before?' she asked.

'I suppose not.'

'It's funny ...' She cupped her hands round her mug and gazed down at the gently rotating bubbles on the surface. 'Everything we do now is going to be different, isn't it?'

'I don't know,' he said warily. 'Is it?'

'Will, come on! It's bound to be.'

'I suppose.'

'Gosh, I loved him!' Stella pushed the mug away and covered her eyes. 'I loved Daddy so much. He looked after us all ... I miss him, Will, I can't stand it!'

He was shocked, though he knew he shouldn't have been. It was only what he himself had done as he stepped over the threshold with his mother, and would do again, probably, many times. It was his sister's use of the childish word 'Daddy' that startled him; that reminded him that she had been his parents' firstborn, his father's darling daughter, for years before he had come along. Years when there had probably been a particular closeness between them. Awkwardly, overcoming a twist of jealousy, he reached across the table and laid his hand on her arm.

'Stel?'

'It's okay ...' She got up and tore a piece of kitchen towel from the roll by the sink, mopping her eyes and blowing her nose. 'I'm okay, honestly. We all will be, in the end.'

He thought about that when he was in bed, about half an hour later: 'in the end' implied that there would come a time when his father would be safely stashed away, consigned to the curio cabinet of memory and not, as now, still at their shoulders, round the corner, a fresh and vital absence.

The next morning he dragged on a dusty pair of shorts and a clean T-shirt from the drawer and went straight out to the garden shed to confront the mower. Just do it, he thought. It was eight o'clock, and his mother and sister were in the kitchen. Stella pushed the window wide and called to him.

'Hey – breakfast?'

'I'll make a start and then come in!'

'Okay.'

A thought struck him – one he would never have had before, and he realised that the reason he was having it now was, as it were, on his father's behalf.

'Will it matter – making the noise?'

His mother waved her arms and shook her head. 'Weekday morning!'

Conscious that they might be watching him, he prayed that the mower would start first time, or even at all. On the second tug, it sputtered into life. He headed straight for the point where the pattern ended – where his father had died – and started there. As soon as he'd done so, he realised that the two days' worth of summer growth behind him meant that he would have to do the whole thing again anyway.

The days between then and the funeral were characterised by periods of intense, welcome activity, during which there was a sense almost of excitement, and others of stunned tiredness when everyone's emotional water table was high. Of the three of them, their mother was the most stoical. He could only suppose that this stoicism was the fruit of her decades as an army wife. Perhaps, he thought, she was able to see this as just one more absence, like the others but with these two crucial differences: she knew where her husband was, and she was sure he wasn't coming back.

At the funeral, there was one particularly memorable moment in a day full of such moments. The sixteenth-century village church was packed, and the whole service was perfect of its kind, but played with what his father would have called a straight bat. Regimental colours were presented and stood at the altar rail. Flowers arranged by Kate's local friends spilled and tumbled in every corner as if growing out of the stone. The words were traditional, the hymns stirring; the singing shook the rafters of the nave. He and Stella had read from the King James version of the Bible – the passage 'In my father's house are many mansions', and the first chapter of Revelations respectively. The eulogy was delivered by Lawrence's brother officer Sam Payne, who resisted the temptation to focus entirely on his friend's military career and spoke movingly and humorously about the man and his family, naming names and using anecdotes that Kate and Stella had supplied. The vicar, a relatively new incumbent enjoying the fullest house of his tenure, had enjoyed saying, with a smile in his resonant, boyish voice: 'Lawrence – rest in peace, and rise in glory!'

His wish had been to be interred, not cremated. 'Not that it was a topic we bandied about much over the dinner table,' Kate said, 'but I do remember him mentioning it after David Hanwell's funeral.' The two pall-bearers from the undertakers were joined by four young cadets from the local barracks. Just before they lifted the coffin, the vicar motioned them to wait. Kate and Will were already in position, his arm ready to take hers. She stepped forward and laid a hand very lightly on the coffin, the fingers of her other hand brushing the regimental brooch, her soldier husband's favour, that she wore on her lapel, as if by doing so she were creating a current that flowed down her arm between the two. It was the tiniest gesture, a butterfly-wing touch that might almost have been missed by someone not standing so close. But Will felt her tremble as she took his arm, and he placed his own hand firmly over hers as the coffin was lifted on to the pall-bearers' shoulders and borne away down the aisle between the solemn ranks of those who had held his father in high esteem, and dear.

Six weeks later, he applied for officer training at Sandhurst.

Chapter Seven
1998

Stella cleared the dining table for the evening's lesson, plonking things on the floor because there were no other free surfaces.

She did not file either this, the literacy teaching, or her involvement with Child Friendly under the heading 'good works'. Both had been embarked upon out of self-interest rather than altruism: they were interesting, amusing even, and their usefulness to others was a valuable by-product. The last thing Stella wanted was to be thought of as a good woman, when she was no such thing. Many people would have been surprised to know that she was actually quite bad – in both the old and the modern sense; plain single women weren't supposed to be bad. Not to overstate the case – she was not *that* plain, not painfully so, but when she caught sight of herself in a shop window, or was obliged for some reason to study herself in a mirror, she was enough of a realist to acknowledge that in an age when presentation mattered, her own was substandard. Oddly, this was a comfort, proving as it did that the perceived plainness was within her control; that given the will and the application a different Stella was not out of the question. But then it was like the old joke: how many psychiatrists does it take to change a light bulb? One, but the light bulb must really want to change. Stella didn't really want to; or not enough to make the effort.

She'd had a good many men in her life, and a varied lot they'd been. There was a corny song she liked, 'To All the Girls I've Loved Before'. They played it on Radio 2 from time to time, and she'd often hum it to herself while she was making supper. Of all the men she'd slept with, those she remembered with special affection included financial consultant Veejay, with his chocolate and buttermilk eyes, his velvet-soft, patchouli-smelling skin, and the

69

scattering of pockmarks decorating his cheeks. He was a hedonist, proud of flitting from flower to flower. She was sure that if she had fallen pregnant by Veejay, he would have been entranced, though uncommitted, and given gold to their baby.

Then there was Dan, the computer doctor, whose appeal had largely consisted in his ability to fix things – to banish the bugs on the screen, to restore connections and solve the myriad intractable problems of technology. That had been quite sexy for a while; she liked the sense that the hands stroking, kneading and exploring her were the same ones that could bring order to cyberspace and sanity to her desk. But after a while, it wasn't enough. She began to notice his inward-pointing teeth, his too-tight shirt, and the way the black hair that covered his chest thrust out of his cuffs and crawled over the backs of his hands right down to the first knuckle of his fingers. She went right off those hands, and sent Dan back to his wife on a wave of mutual relief.

The one she remembered with the most regret was Mike, a rugged care-home worker who on the face of it ticked all the boxes. Mike was not only good in bed but fully available; he even suggested marriage. But as Groucho Marx to clubs, so Stella to men: she could not have contemplated marriage to any man fool enough to ask her. Mike's proposal diminished him in her eyes. What, was he mad? It wasn't in her to be a wife. How could he have known her all this time and not seen that? Her current lover Paul had a long way to go before he made the running for the Most Memorable list, and she knew she wouldn't have the patience to wait.

Here was another interesting thing. People – those who knew no better – assumed she'd remained single because she'd failed to attract anyone. She knew she was one of those women of whom others still used the near-obsolete term 'spinster'. Whereas on the contrary, Stella's private life was exactly to her taste and of her choosing. She had lovers but she didn't do dating; sex was both important and desirable but it didn't require courtship, just mutual consent. Plus she looked so much better with her clothes off. That was the one advantage of poor presentation: there was a far greater likelihood of providing a pleasant surprise. She loved that disclosure moment, and the power it gave her – the man's jaw dropping as his penis gave its involuntary salute.

This afternoon's pupil was new, a man who'd seen the poster on the notice board at the Jobs Café, picked up a flyer and contacted her through the central number. He'd have needed help to do so, of course, and would probably have resorted to all manner of elaborate deceptions to get it; she was well aware of the struggle most people had been through before they even called her. His name was Edward Guise, a Huguenot or old Norman surname she'd supposed, but when during their first phone conversation she'd pronounced it 'Geez' in the French manner, he'd been quick to correct her.

'No, that's Guise.'

'Ah – like blokes.'

'Correct.'

'Sorry about that.'

'No worries.'

From the moment she answered the doorbell on his first visit, the issue of his surname and its pronunciation became irrelevant. She believed in informality.

'Edward?'

'Yeah. Hi.'

'Stella.' She held out her hand. 'Hello.'

'Ted's fine, by the way.'

'Come in, Ted.'

She had an established routine with new people; not rigidly prescriptive, there was room for manoeuvre, but having it in place avoided the awkwardness of uncertainty with men and women who were often already crippled by shyness and low self-esteem.

She would begin with a general chat over tea or coffee, the purpose of which was to find out what, if anything, they could read or write, and what their aims were. The *Sun*, for instance, only required a reading age of eight, Sebastian Faulks rather more. Forms, the understanding and filling-in of same, were one of the biggest stumbling blocks, and they often required whole sessions to themselves.

She had three other students: Lucy, a mother of school-age children; Richard, a nice young man with slight brain damage; and Arthur, a pensioner who had been functionally illiterate for his whole working life but who now regretted having the leisure to read without the ability. She was paid a small salary by the city council, but would have been prepared to do the work for free; the measurable good effect that her lessons had and the pleasure she herself derived from them were their own reward. But since she needed to live, she was prepared to take the Tory council's tainted shilling for doing something she enjoyed.

Ted Guise was harder work than most. Men, especially those in their prime, were often prickly and taciturn. They'd swallowed their pride to get this far, and now it rose up again and nearly choked them. But Ted was unforthcoming even by the standards of his peers. He was a jobbing gardener (eliciting this information had been like pulling teeth), a big, heavy man who looked a little overweight, but still fit; attractive, actually. She put his age at mid-forties, and he lived in Thurlmere, one of the city's satellite villages. There had been no mention of a partner or family.

At the end of forty minutes, Stella still wasn't quite sure why he was there. Perhaps, contrary to what he'd told her, he'd been under pressure to come because he'd been rumbled and someone, maybe one of his employers, had delivered an ultimatum. She certainly sensed if not a reluctance at least an inbuilt resistance to addressing the problem.

'You're the customer, Ted,' she said. 'Tell me what I can do.'

There followed a silence you could have cut with a knife, during which Ted gazed out of the window, twiddling his shiny new pencil between his fingers. Nice big hands, she noticed. To distract herself, she went on:

'For instance, what about travel – signs, and so on?'

'I'm not so bad with that,' he said. 'I can usually make those out.'

'Good. Or shopping? That can be an awful nuisance.'

'You get to recognise things.'

She wanted to shout at him: 'Yes, but think how much better it could be! Imagine being able to choose things that you didn't recognise! Wouldn't that be great?' But she'd learned a lot over recent months: don't argue, use positive reinforcement; this isn't school.

'Look, I'll leave it with you, Ted. Bring a newspaper or something, anything you'd normally take a look at, and we'll make a start with that. And if you think of anything else specific we could work on, let me know.'

'Okay, will do. Cheers.' The session over, he brightened visibly. 'Thanks for the tea.'

'My pleasure. See you next week.'

She saw him out, and poured herself a drink. This was going to be heavy going. But when Paul rang and suggested he 'drop by', she told him she was tied up, and he accepted the brush-off with surprising equanimity.

The following afternoon was one of those when she collected Raff from school. Putting her simmering resentment towards her brother to one side, she delighted in these great-auntly duties. She was extremely fond of Raff himself, who, in her admittedly limited experience, was about as nice, amusing and personable a boy as you could wish. She knew, because she had it from the horse's mouth, that he could be 'a complete nightmare' at home with his mother and that he gave Evie's boyfriend Owen short shrift (referring to him as 'the thicko'). But none of that was Stella's concern. Hers only to provide food, shelter and company when required. She allowed him to sound off about things, and was the soul of discretion concerning what she heard. She always thought she'd have made a good grandparent, so Will's loss was her gain.

Strictly speaking, she didn't need to meet him at the gate. At nearly eleven, he was quite old enough to make his own way home, but her house was appreciably further away than his own, and they had developed a ritual which involved popping into M&S in the market square to pick up a treat for their six o'clock tea. Evie had remonstrated with Stella about this.

'That's frightfully extravagant!'

'But it's the only time I do it. And it's fun.'

'You really don't have to. He'd be perfectly happy with toast.'

Funny, thought Stella, how in this context 'perfectly' meant, literally, 'imperfectly'.

'But it's my treat too,' she explained.

'Just so long as it doesn't give him ideas.' Evie gave her a sidelong glance. 'He won't be getting lobster thermidor at home.'

Lobster was a slight exaggeration, but they were both keen on the fisherman's pie with herb mash, preferably accompanied by a heaping helping of petits pois, and garlic bread (naff but nice).

Sometimes they went the pudding route – beans on toast the mere prelude to tiramisu, blueberry cheesecake, lemon meringue or banoffee pie, accompanied by Cornish ice cream.

She was usually first at the gate. She never tired of the solemn, mellow beauty of the choir school building, in winter lit from within like a great stone lantern, in summer festooned with wisteria and the bronze scales of Virginia creeper. Another reason to arrive early was so she could stand and listen to the closing minutes of choir practice, the pure, pan-pipe voices climbing and cascading over one another, and the pauses – silences to those outside but actually so that the choirmaster could give direction – before the singing began again, like magic, to his unseen signal. Through Raff she'd learned to love the stately polished phrases of the ancient church music, the thrilling drama of Britten and the measured harmonies of Taverner and Tippett. Though wary of faith, Stella was not against organised religion, and was an occasional churchgoer. She hadn't spoken the creed since her schooldays, and even then had only moved her lips, but she believed in the healing power of church buildings, and of the shared communal activity of services.

So she was happy to stand and listen, or simply to think, as one by one the handful of other collectors arrived and also listened, or talked in a respectful, muted way, as if they were actually in a concert, or a church.

Raff's best friend Alfie (a sign of the times; whoever thought that was a good idea?) was a boarder whose parents lived in Brussels, so Stella hadn't met them. Raff usually emerged in a loose scrum of other day boys, and this afternoon (no choir practice) she spotted a couple of mothers she recognised and a lone father. One of the mothers was a striking beauty in the Joanna Lumley mould, tall and queenly in her big black coat, fur hat and slouchy boots. They exchanged a mouthed 'Hi!' and a smile. The other was a thin, intense woman, an older parent not far off Stella's own age, her long hair tied up in a scarf. The man was handsome and prosperous-looking in a Barbour jacket over a suit. His clothes, his luxuriant groomed hair, particularly his stance (mobile phone in palm, otherwise engaged) stated unequivocally: *I am no house-husband*. When he did look up, his glance swooshed over Stella and the other women (perhaps a nanosecond's double-take on the Lumley-mummy) before settling with languid impatience on the school door.

When the door opened and the boys began to come out, Stella was struck as always by how cool they were, these chosen few, with their floppy hair and disarranged uniforms, their mobiles and music cases – so much confidence so young, she was in awe of them. At their age she had been a shy, stolid bundle of self-conscious awkwardness whose voice (in those days seldom heard) sounded strange even to her. The experience of nearly six decades had brought confidence, but it had been hard won, whereas these boys seemed to have it from nature, a gift from God along with their seraphic voices.

She watched as the other parents were reunited with their off-spring. The Lumley woman's son was a Milky Bar kid, blond and bespectacled; the skinny artistic mother left with two, a slim black boy and a Just William bruiser. Not-a-house-husband began to turn away as his son approached, leaving the tall, gangling lad to fall in beside him with no greeting that Stella could see or hear.

'Hiya.' Raff stood before her, but looking in the other direction, waving to friends.

'Hello there. How was the day?'

'Okay.' The word had a sanguine upward inflection. 'I did all right in the test.'

'Super.' They started to walk. 'What test was that?'

'Problem-solving?'

By now Stella was used to the interrogative answer and didn't lose a beat.

'Maths?'

'Citizenship.'

That stumped her. 'What about rehearsals? No singing today.'

'No, we had theory. Bor-ing.'

'I suppose it has to be done, like grammar.'

'But it's pants,' Raff pointed out.

'I don't like that expression,' she said mildly.

'Everyone says it.'

'QED.'

Because Raff didn't know what this meant, it effectively put a stop to the exchange, in which there had anyway been no rancour.

75

They walked on companionably, past clothes shops, jewellers, two coffee houses, Boots the chemist, till they reached the trainer emporium – here, they drew to a halt.

'Okay,' said Stella, 'which are this week's must-haves?'

He scanned the window with narrowed eyes, then pointed. 'Those. Zone PXs. Darius has got them.'

'Gosh,' said Stella. 'How much do they cost?' She asked not because she was interested in the price but because, as a desirability indicator, Raff was.

'A hundred quid? Bit more?'

'Crikey, lucky Darius. Which one is he?'

'He's the same age as me but really, really tall? His dad works for Virgin records.'

'Ah,' said Stella, 'I think I know the one. Was his dad there today, picking him up?'

'Yeah. He gets cool concert tickets.'

'I bet.'

There followed a respectful pause during which they gazed at the Zone trainers and thought about Darius in their respective ways. As they moved off, Raff said: 'He can really sing, too.'

'Good for him.'

That was why she loved her great-nephew so much. He had all the trappings of the modern pre-teen – the obsessions, the acquisitive longings, the argot and the attitude – but buried underneath these were the right instincts, the fertile soil in which maturity would grow and flourish in spite of the cold competitiveness and commercialism of the modern world.

In the food hall they wandered round, salivating over the options, revelling in their power to select or reject, capricious as Hollywood matrons on Rodeo Drive. They never decided beforehand; they were creatures of impulse. After discussion, Stella invariably let Raff choose anyway, so that later on she could congratulate him on his choice. Simple pleasures! This afternoon they were in a savoury mood and plumped for duck breast in black cherry sauce, with which Stella would serve her special small, crunchy cubed roast potatoes and the petits pois.

'Gressingham duck with green peas,' she declared as they joined the queue at the checkout. 'A classic combination.'

Back at the house, the deal was that Raff did one module of

homework while she got supper ready. She was pleased that on this occasion he chose piano practice. Some time ago she'd bought an elderly upright out of the *Evening News* classifieds for her own stumbling efforts, and Raff's playing was an unlooked-for bonus. It provided the accompaniment to her potato-peeling. She did not look in on him or make any comment; that would have been to break the unwritten contract. Stella was no expert, but she thought he played well. Though this was a new piece, and he halted and had to break off occasionally, those parts he'd mastered he played fluently and expressively. It fascinated her, this gift for music, which, her aborted lessons testified, she so signally lacked. He was Grade 5 now, and the assigned piece was something she recognised; she wondered if it was Chopin and was childishly pleased to be told afterwards she was right.

With homework over, it was their habit to watch whatever was the current teatime quiz programme on telly before they ate. There was a great deal of innocent fun to be had from bitching about the ignorance of the contestants, and their appearance. They'd long ago stopped interjecting the caveat that they themselves would hate to be exposing themselves to the mocking scrutiny of the viewing public – these people had been daft enough to sign up for it, and were therefore fair game.

They had teamwork going on. After the TV interlude they laid the table – cloth, napkins, tea lights in saucers, the whole nine yards – and Stella slung the hash. Then she poured herself a glass of Chilean red and Raff a Coke, and they sat down opposite one another and clinked glasses.

'How's Alfie?' she asked when the first few mouthfuls had gone down.

'Okay. I might be going to stay with him at Easter.'

'In Brussels?'

He nodded. 'We've got a tour to France in April at the end of term and I can go back there with him afterwards.'

'Fantastic. Where in France?'

'Battlefields of the First World War.' She could hear him quoting the syllabus. 'We're doing six concerts.'

Stella never failed to be impressed by her great-nephew, the seasoned performer. She let him shovel down a bit more duck before asking, 'How much do you know about the Great War?'

'A bit. We've started on it. Life in the trenches, and the Battle of the Somme.'

'They thought it was the war to end all wars, you know.'

'All over by Christmas.' Raff speared a potato and wagged his fork, ticking boxes. '"Keep the Home Fires Burning".'

'Lions led by donkeys.'

'"Silent Night".'

'You won't be singing that at Easter, surely.'

'No, we're doing mostly Britten, Mariner and Handel. But "Silent Night" was the football.'

'It was,' said Stella. And then heard herself utter one of those remarks that seemed to have sprung fully fledged from the subconscious: 'I wish I could come.'

'You can if you like.'

'Really?'

He shrugged. 'I don't know ...'

'I do.' She pulled a face. 'Excess baggage.'

He either ignored or didn't hear this. 'Is there any more?'

Evie arrived at seven, straight from Pilates, long and lean and stressed in grey sweatpants and a puffa jacket. She aimed an abstracted kiss at Raff, who was on the computer in the living room, and accepted a glass of the Chilean red – 'Only a small one or I'll undo all the benefit.'

'Hardly.' Stella topped up her own and they sat down at the table together. 'Look at you!'

Evie took no notice of this; she was, as she said, rubbish with compliments. 'Something smells nice.'

'You bet. Duck with cherries.'

'Duck with ...? You jammy things!' She leaned sideways, peering into the other room. 'Raff – Raff? You had duck for supper?'

'It was wicked.'

'You know us,' said Stella. 'We don't hold back.'

'Hmm ...' Evie raised an eyebrow. 'Just so long as he doesn't get any ideas. Still, I suppose it's cheaper than eating out.'

'And a lot better than my cooking.'

'There's nothing the matter with your cooking, Stella. You have a small but dependable repertoire.'

'Too kind.'

'God, this is nice, I'm so glad you twisted my arm.' Evie closed her eyes, which smoothed the sculptural planes of her long face, making it almost beautiful. At this moment, Stella thought, there was a distinct look of her father about her. She sighed, and rubbed her eyes before opening them. 'I'd better move soon, or I never will.'

'Nonsense,' said Stella. 'What's the rush?' They both sipped. 'Raff tells me he's going to France in the spring.'

'That's right,' said Evie. 'It should be a super tour. And good for them. There's a plan for him to go and stay with his mate in Brussels afterwards. I'm sorry' – she rummaged in her handbag and produced cigarettes – 'do you mind?'

'Yes, she does,' said Raff from the other room.

'I wasn't asking you.'

'None of my business,' said Stella.

'I am trying to give up.'

'Not so's you'd notice!' This was Raff.

'Don't be chippy, I'm doing my best!' Evie lit up and lowered her voice. 'He's so on my case. No, this trip – they want a couple of parents to go along as deckhands, nose-wipers, crowd control ...'

'Mum!'

'Anyway, my number's come up, and strictly speaking I should; it's aeons since I contributed.'

'You did that toy tombola last year,' said Stella, ignoring Raff's snort of derision.

'I did, but that only involved standing behind a table for a couple of hours with tea on tap in a nice warm hall. It didn't exactly change the course of history.'

'But they can't expect – I mean, you work full time.'

'So does everyone else.'

'And you're on your own.'

'Thanks, Auntie,' said Evie drily. 'In theory I could take a few days off, but this particular trip clashes with the annual staff weekend, and anyway ... No, it can't be helped, it's just lousy timing.'

Stella inferred an additional, possibly Owen-related reason for Evie's reluctance to go. Here, surely, was her opening.

'Tell me,' she said, 'what's the cost of this trip?'

'Modest.' Evie tapped her cigarette into the tea-light saucer. 'Incredible value, actually, but then they are singing for their suppers.'

'And what about for the helpers?'

'Can't remember precisely.' Evie shrugged. 'Not out of the way.'

A quarter of an hour later, when she was seeing the two of them off, Stella said: 'Heard anything from Will?'

'You are joking.' Evie snorted. 'My wonderful, caring and supportive father – what do you think?'

'Yes,' said Stella, thinking of the postcard. 'I am sorry.'

Though Evie's attitude accorded pretty well with her own, Stella didn't like to hear her talk like that. Whatever his shortcomings, she had always loved her brother, and she wanted others, especially his only daughter, to love him too. If he would only shape up, find his better self and come back to them, he would see how readily he would be accepted and forgiven, welcomed back with open arms. Prodigals, lost (and black) sheep – how come they always emerged smelling of roses?

That night in bed, in spite of all this familiar fretting, her mind kept returning to the other, more cheerful topic of Raff's trip to France. Here, she told herself, was something she'd always meant to do, a pilgrimage she'd long promised herself she would make into her family's history; one of those trips, small in distance and duration but huge in significance, she could in theory have made at any time over the past forty years but had never got round to. And here she was at this late stage being handed a golden opportunity!

The next morning she rang Evie at seven, before she left for work. Her niece was brisk and slightly harassed.

'Stella, hi – did I forget something?'

'No, sorry about the hour, but I wanted to catch you.'

'What can I do for you? I'm on the run.'

'I know, I'll be quick. If you want to keep your end up with the school, you can put my name forward to help with the trip.'

'What? France? Really?'

'Yes. I'd like to, and I've got the time.'

'Great! Star by name and star by nature, thanks so much! Look, I have to dash but can I give your number to Mr Hutchins so he can ring you?'

'Of course.'

'Fantastic, speak really soon. Thanks so much, Stella. Bye!'

As she put the phone down, Stella thought how simple it was completely to change someone's mood, to lift their burden and make them happy, and she wondered why her lazy sod of a brother couldn't pull finger and do the same.

Chapter Eight
1998

She was standing outside her mother's door when a woman wearing a dusty Persian lamb coat, velvet hat and gloves came out of
the door next but one, very slowly, because she was using a walking frame.

'Are you looking for Mrs Drake?' the woman asked in a voice
of wavering gentility.

'Yes, hello, Mrs Armitage.'

'Have we met?'

'I'm her daughter, Stella.'

'I think you'll find she's gone out to lunch with Mr Macky.'

'Has she?' said Stella. 'I'm delighted to hear it. When was that,
do you happen to know?'

'Um, let's see ...' The woman tweaked at her coat sleeve in a
vain effort to consult her watch. 'What time is it now?'

'About two.'

'A little while ago, then.'

'Thanks. In that case I'll wait in the car for a bit.'

'Are you sure? Do you want to come in and wait?'

'That's such a kind offer, but you're on your way out' – Stella
felt she should remind her – 'and I shall be fine.'

'The Saracen's Head is where they usually go.'

'Thank you, Mrs Armitage.'

Stella got back in the car. 'Usually' now, was it? She turned
on the radio to find Linda Snell in a snit about the Christmas
production.

Ambridge had given way to a seasonal play about ghostly
goings-on on the Fens when a blue Polo came round the corner
and pulled up between her own car and her mother's front
door. Covertly, Stella studied Ian Macky in the light of that

'usually': a handsome man for his age in a lanky, Gary Cooperish way. He climbed out slowly from behind the wheel and went around the front of the car to open the door for Kate, who waited for him with ladylike patience. Stella decided it would be polite to let them get their farewells out of the way uninterrupted, and anyway she was curious to see what form the farewells would take. If Ian Macky went in, she'd simply have to intrude – discretion in this case being much the smaller part of filial duty.

He saw Kate to the door and they stood there for a moment, Kate smiling as she said her thank yous and Macky presumably declaring that the pleasure had been all his. Stella watched as their hands met in a chaste handshake, before he leaned across and kissed her mother lightly on the cheek. Kate waved to him as he returned to his car and then went in and closed the door behind her. Macky got back in the driver's seat, flipped the mirror down and ran his hand over his hair. This little glimpse of personal vanity endeared him to Stella, but when he glanced her way she became instantly bound up in tuning the radio to save his embarrassment.

Her mother answered the door still in her unbuttoned coat and silk Jaeger scarf.

'Stella! Darling, what a nice surprise. Were you sitting out there? I didn't recognise … Come in, come in.'

'A bit too much of a surprise, I expect,' said Stella as they exchanged a kiss and removed their coats. 'I know you only just got back – I spoke to your neighbour.'

'Evelyn? Was she compos? She's a dear, but a bit wandery these days.'

'She said you'd gone to the Saracen's Head.'

'Quite right, we do usually, but they were chocka today so we took our custom such as it is to the King William.'

Stella followed her mother into the tiny living room with its white poinsettia on the hearth and bronze Christmassy twigs in an African vase.

'And how did it compare?'

'Food not as good, but sweet people, they made us so welcome. What would you like? I'm not going to because we've just had coffee.'

'I shan't either, thanks.'

'Aah!' Kate sat down in her armchair and heeled off her court shoes. 'Very heaven!'

Stella envied her mother the tall, athletic figure that Will, not she, had so unfairly inherited. Kate was no classic beauty, but she had the sort of looks, based on good bones and a sound constitution, that stood the test of time and defied many of its ravages. It was scarcely decent, Stella considered, to have such great legs and such straight, narrow feet at her age.

'So,' she said, 'tell me about your week ...'

The room they sat in was small; it had been a nightmare selecting what to bring from Hallowfield, a process not unlike *Desert Island Discs*, where each item had to be chosen not just for practicality but for its special value and significance to Kate, its embodiment of a particular strand in a long and full life: the wing-backed chair, the African pot (one half of a pair), the regimental drum, the piecrust side table covered in ghostly drink rings ... Too much, really. There were several framed photographs: one of Kate and Lawrence on holiday in Cornwall; a nice triptych of Stella and Will, a studio portrait of the two of them together as children, flanked by individual pictures of their young adult selves; a couple of now rather poignant ones of Evie's wedding; Raff as a baby, on his own and with his parents, and others showing him at various stages of his boyhood – on a Cornish beach with his father, at playgroup, in the mini-rugby team and, of course, the choir.

In the bedroom next door, on the bedside table, there stood a photograph of Stella's father as a young man in his army uniform, and on the chest of drawers was a whole gallery of sepia and black-and-white photographs, many of them laid out beneath the glass on top of the chest, others upright in their original slightly battered metal or leather frames. Whenever she had cause to go in there, Stella was drawn to these, picking them up one at a time and studying them minutely. This was the cast of her personal history, both its mystery and its mundane detail. She felt that she bore a responsibility – well, somebody had to, and it wouldn't be Will – to know who these people were, so that their names and stories shouldn't be lost. And it was important that in time Raff should know them too, and understand that, though first and foremost himself, he bore the legacy of this array of disparate individuals that spread behind him like a comet's tail.

The undisputed beauty had been her great-grandmother Venetia, a luminously lovely debutante, the catch of the season, whose world had been rocked (and shocked) by the rough self-made industrialist Ralph Tennant. She had died before Kate had returned to England, so there was no one left who remembered her, but the studio portrait of her with her husband proved the received view correct. It showed a tall young woman, slender but statuesque in the Edwardian manner, with pale hair piled high and a perfect oval face with an expression both sweet and cool, the expression of a woman born to privilege and admiration. She was seated, and Ralph stood next to her with his hand on the back of her chair, his broad, dark bulk slightly forbidding; a tough, handsome alpha male, hard-wired to know what he wanted, and to get it.

Most of the photos were of the next generation. There was Stella's paternal grandmother Loelia Drake; Thea and Jack Kingsley, 'the East Africa Company' as Lawrence had called them, Kate's adoptive parents; Thea's ravishingly pretty sister Dulcie, their stolid, serious-faced brother Aubrey and their shy cousin Maurice. Considered dispassionately, Stella reckoned that the one she most resembled was Thea – dark and striking, her clothes unremarkable, her hair left to go its own way. Dulcie was her sister's polar opposite, but Stella knew that though she looked like a good-time girl, it was Dulcie who had been Kate's benefactress and had acted as an *ex officio* godmother when Kate arrived in London as a girl. The photos showed a slender, vivacious sprite, dressed and coiffed in the height of fashion. Whereas Thea and Jack stood four-square and arm in arm on the veranda of their Kenyan bungalow, Dulcie sat in the passenger seat of a gleaming sports car next to a sleek cat of a young man in dark glasses, whose right hand rested on the wheel and the other on the seat behind her shoulders, one finger lifted so that it touched her neck. In another photo she was larking about, posing with a cigarette in a long holder, blowing smoke – or a kiss – at whoever was behind the camera. Stella sensed an underlying difference in mood between the two: the woman in the car was a stylish but restrained Dulcie; the one with the cigarette was playful and abandoned, childlike in spite of the vampish pose. It made you wonder who the photographer had been, but Kate, when asked, hadn't been able to tell her.

There was a picture Stella especially liked of all the Tennant children – the young girls vivacious and wide-eyed in shapeless white dresses with bows trailing from their long hair; their brother Aubrey a little stern and superior, dissociating himself from the feminine silliness; cousin Maurice, the shortest of the four, looking as if he'd rather be roasted over a slow fire than forced to be part of this family group.

As well as the photographs on the dressing table, there were a dozen or more albums and boxes of loose photos in the ottoman at the foot of the bed – a chest meant for linen, but the pictures had been put in there along with a stack of board games the day Kate moved in and remained there ever since. 'When the great day comes,' Kate was wont to say, 'I shall go through all of that lot and get them properly organised.'

But for now she was saying, 'This is so nice, darling. It always makes my day when you turn up out of the blue, and don't think I don't appreciate it.'

Stella made a brushing-aside gesture. 'It's an oasis of calm for me too, you know, Ma. Anyway, it sounds as if you've been keeping busy; you look wonderfully well.'

'Um, let's see.' Kate did a little dumb-show of feeling her neck, her hip, her knee. 'All in order. Some days the aches and pains are a nuisance, but when I look around me, I realise I should be damn grateful. And a drop of the hard stuff works its magic every time.' She raised her glass and then caught Stella's expression. 'Don't worry, I'm not a secret drinker.'

'Have you heard from anyone?'

'I had a call from Joe, very chatty. I expect Angela put him up to it.'

'Probably.'

'You'll hear no complaints from me, I enjoyed talking to him.' Where family was concerned, Kate, like Stella, was a pragmatist. 'She's a jolly good sister-in-law.'

'She is. I only wish I had one like that. Or one at all.'

Kate smiled ruefully, but was not to be drawn. She seldom spoke ill of Jacqueline. Which in Stella's book was interesting psychology, because there was at least a case for saying that the whole mess – Will's absenteeism and the associated flak – was directly attributable to her.

Kate said, 'And I had a sweet conversation with Raff. Evie rang to see how I was, and she put him on. He told me that he was growing his hair for what he called a skater look, whatever that may be.'

'You might think of it as surfer.'

'Ah, got it. I can't imagine it will be allowed.'

Stella shook her head. 'So far and no further.'

'How long is it at the moment?'

'Let's just say it's got several inches to go before the desired look is achieved, and long before then it will either have been scotched by the authorities or some other trend will have taken over.'

Kate laughed. 'Poor Evie! I *do* like her. She rolls her sleeves up. And with everything that's gone on, she's raised a delightful boy.'

Stella agreed and they smiled benignly together at the thought of Raff. Then there was no avoiding the question that had to be asked, the one that lurked on the sidelines of every conversation. She introduced it as casually as she could, aware that the casualness would fool no one, least of all her mother.

'Heard anything from Will?'

Kate gave a short laugh. 'Joe asked that.'

'I'm sorry.'

'Anyway, the answer's no. But then I don't expect to.'

'Perhaps not, but you must admit it's pretty lame. Worse than lame; downright neglectful.'

'I don't feel neglected.' She brushed at her skirt. 'That's Will.'

'You say that, but it doesn't have to be.' Stella felt the familiar rising tide of exasperation. 'He's perfectly capable of behaving respectably. He's an educated middle-aged man with a medal for bravery, for heaven's sake!'

The minute she'd said that, she regretted it. Her mother turned on her a look so coolly challenging that her own eyes dropped.

'When,' said Kate, 'did age have anything to do with virtue? And as for courage, darling, it comes in all sorts of different forms.'

Chapter Nine

1998

Stella didn't work to terms. Except for August (a sullen, overripe month which held no charms for her but which seemed to have a near-mythical significance for others, whether or not they were the parents of school-age children), and the Christmas period (susceptible to mission creep and getting ever longer), she was more than happy to continue with lessons as per, if that was what her clients wanted. In the main, it was – having signed up for a life-changing exercise, they were keen to press on.

Ted Guise was an exception. His first lesson had been in late November. At the end of his third, he asked: 'So when do you start in the new year?'

'I don't stop,' she said. 'You can come the week before Christmas and then again the first session after Boxing Day.'

She saw his face fall, but he caught it and rallied. 'I'm going to be a bit tied up between now and Christmas.'

'That's fine.'

'I can start again mid Jan.'

'Listen, Ted,' she lifted an open hand, 'you're the customer.'

'Yeah, well ...' His expression managed to be both sheepish and irritable. 'That's what I'll do, then.'

'I'll put it in the diary.'

He rose from the table, gathered up his notebook, paper and biro and stuffed them unceremoniously into his North Face rucksack. Stella accompanied him into the hall and stood with arms folded as he shrugged on his jacket.

'Ted – tell me something.'

'What's that?' He was noticeably more relaxed now that he was on his way.

'Are you happy with how it's going?'

'Yeah. I am, very happy.'

She tilted her head, challenging him. 'Really?'

'Yes!' He half laughed.

'Only you must say if there's anything in particular you'd like to do. Or conversely, if we're doing anything you consider a waste of time.'

'I will,' he said. He pulled on his beanie. 'But it's going great.'

'In that case,' she opened the door, 'happy Christmas. Have a good one and I'll see you in a few weeks.'

'Cheers, thanks. Happy Christmas to you too.'

She watched him walk away. He had a long stride, a loping gait, big shoulders hunched round his ears. A man's man, eager to escape.

Sweetly, Shannon had invited her to tea, 'to say thank you' following a late babysit Stella had undertaken while Shannon attended her boyfriend's office party (a black-tie do at the Moathouse: Lee was an estate agent). The evening was no trouble; Stella had passed a happy few hours watching TV and reading *OK!*, which Shannon had bought specially. Toyah had cried only once, a mere fretful chirping, and by the time Stella had gone upstairs, she was lying quietly again; nothing but a dream, or a touch of indigestion. She stood by the cot for a minute or two, gazing down at the baby, who lay on her back with her arms flung above her head. Her beauty – the beauty of unmarked infant perfection – fascinated Stella: the downy hair, the exquisitely pure skin, the lashes like feathers, the rosebud mouth, the hands curled like ferns, clutching the future.

Stella remembered Raff's birth, or at least going to visit him and Evie soon afterwards. He hadn't had time to fill out and get beautiful; in fact she had found something eerie about seeing her niece cradling this seven-pound alien who less than twenty-four hours earlier had been inside her belly. You mean *that* was in *there*? Stella was not abnormally squeamish, but the simple, brutal fact of birth made her eyes water. How was it that ordinary women, of all sorts, shapes and sizes, managed it? Young girls, even? Shannon, for heaven's sake, she of the lip gloss and highlights, had come through thirty-six hours of labour (at least thirty of which had been graphically described to Stella) with flying colours and no stitches and been back in Diesel jeans within three weeks! Leaving Toyah's bedroom that night and going back down the stairs to Shannon's comfy sofa, Stella had concluded that the level and type of involvement that she had with Raff was exactly right for her. If she'd had one of her own, she would have been, to use Raff's expression, pants.

She was touched by the tea party. Shannon had brought the folding table out of the kitchen and covered it with a disposable cloth – red, with gold holly leaves – and had set out gold card-board plates with little sandwiches, cocktail sausages, crisps and a mini Christmas cake which she confessed to not having made herself.

'Thought you'd probably rather have a proper one anyway.'

'It all looks smashing,' said Stella. 'Mind if I dive in?'

They did justice to everything. Shannon and Stella washed down the carbs with first tea, then a small glass of rosé. When they raised their glasses in a toast, Toyah lifted her spouty cup, prompting an 'Ah, bless!' from her mother. When Toyah was back on the floor playing with her talking dog in front of the telly, Shannon said, 'Honestly, Stell, I don't know what we'd do without you.'

'You'd manage perfectly well, is what.'

'We're going to miss you.'

'Why? I'm not going anywhere.'

'But you'll go sometime. You'll have to move, or just want to pack it in. You might reckon you've had enough of us.'

'Well,' said Stella, 'I might, but I don't think it's very likely. I suppose the powers-that-be might think I'm having too easy a time of it and move me for training purposes.' She caught the look of genuine consternation on Shannon's face, and added hastily, 'Joke. I'm afraid you're stuck with me until her ladyship starts school.'

'I hope so, Stel,' said Shannon. 'I really do.'

The evening of the tea party, Stella had what she supposed most women would have called a date. But even if she had been disposed to call it that herself – even if she did 'dates' – she knew the moment she saw Paul in the Saddlers Arms that it was going to be anything but. Having come straight from Shannon's, she was a tad early and had been sitting there quite happily with a mettlesome crossword for half an hour by the time he arrived. The second she looked up from the paper, she knew it was all up: his shifty, glum expression, his restless body language, the timbre of his voice as he said 'Sorry to have kept you waiting' like some brain-dead dental receptionist.

Stella didn't much mind either way – easy come, easy go was her motto – but she wasn't going to give this particular morose man the satisfaction of being the dumper. He'd probably spent the past hour psyching himself up. She only needed a few seconds.

'It was – you know ...' He twiddled his hand vaguely to imply, what? Traffic? Work? Mother? Terrorist attack? 'Shit happens.'

She pushed the folded paper and her biro into her bag. 'No problem, I've been happy as Larry.'

'Good, glad about that. Get you the other half?'

'No thanks.' She gave him a brilliantly cheerful smile. 'I'm a bird of passage this evening.'

'I went to call on a mate,' he said, as if she hadn't spoken. 'He was getting a load of grief from his partner. Male partner. Hell hath no fury, et cetera.'

She didn't bother to correct him. 'That's okay. You weren't late, I was early. And anyway, as I say, I've got to get going.'

'Why's that?' She hadn't given him a chance to get a drink, and he was glancing anxiously over his shoulder at the bar as though it might run away.

'Oh, I don't know ...' When it came to this sort of thing, Stella recognised in herself all the conscious, manipulative power of the courtesan. A courtesan in comfort-fit trousers. She got up and picked up her bag and duffel coat. 'I just have.'

He looked her up and down, baffled. 'Where are you off to?'

'I'm not sure. Fresh fields? Something like that.' She slid out between the table and the banquette. "Scuse I.'

'Sorry.' He stepped aside. 'I see.'

'Something tells me, Paul, that you won't be broken-hearted.'

'No. Well, you know ...' He cracked a half-arsed smile. 'What can I say?'

'Here's to the good times?' she suggested. She put a fiver in his hand. 'Have one on me.'

He glanced down at the note. 'Hey, Stella – we've had some of those, haven't we? Good times?'

'Speaking for myself, yes, we have.'

'Me too.' She could see the misplaced regret in his face now. Relieved of the initiative by an expert, he was starting to consider what he'd be missing, and (more to the point) who would be getting it in his place.

'So.' She looked with tender amusement into his eyes. 'You take care.'

'Hang on.' He frowned, still not sure if this was really happening. 'Stella …'

'Bye, Paulie.'

A brisk kiss, and she was gone.

Out in the street, she marched the couple of hundred yards to her car still carrying her things clutched to her chest like a person moving house. Was there, she asked herself, any better feeling than that of shaking the dust from your feet? Stella knew that by many people's standards she lived a small life, but in her mind, heart and imagination there were great spaces waiting to be explored.

And, in the spring, the vasty fields of France!

Chapter Ten

1969

The Sovereign's Parade of Will's term was a vintage one, a classic of its kind. The sun shone, the flags beat and fluttered in a stiff breeze as if their chests were as puffed up with pride as the friends and relatives below them in the stands. There was scarcely a hint of the memento mori that had lent the parade an elegiac note in their fathers' and grandfathers' day, and would do so again in the future. It was a source of some regret to this batch of newly com-missioned officers that they did not seriously expect to fight a war in the foreseeable future. They told each other they had not joined up to hang around on exercise on Salisbury Plain or in Snow-donia, or mark time on some dull BAOR posting, all married quarters and cross-country running with NCOs and men made mutinous and mean by boredom. They wanted action! Adventure! Parents who remembered the last bout of action and adventure were content for it not to be repeated, and wished only for an extended period of peaceful tedium.

Kate was elegant and warm in a long grey trench coat trimmed with black and a black velvet beret. Stella, who at that time fan-cied herself a pacifist, was there on sufferance; having only a lim-ited sartorial repertoire and no hats, she had managed the warmth without the elegance. Her coat was serviceable; it had a hood, but she hadn't liked to put it up amongst so much chic headgear, and her hair flew about and kept getting in her eyes and mouth. At least her hands were snug in woollen gloves and her feet cosy in moon boots, so she didn't look starved with cold. Walking from coffee and biscuits in the mess to the parade ground, she felt like the ugly duckling in a procession of swans. The miniskirt had reached new heights, and there was an array of trim little suits and cutaway dresses, revealing coltish legs and chunky T-strap shoes. Even some of the mothers were displaying their kneecaps, not altogether advantageously. Handbags were square boxes, or else tiny round purses on long chains. The girls' faces reminded her of cartoon Jersey cows, with feathery lashes, dark eyes and pale, pouty lips. Hair was either shoulder length with an eyebrow-grazing fringe, or bobbed – shingled at the back and with glossy bangs or two sleek wings framing the jawline. Her own hair was unstyled. She had such lovely hair, people told her, but she had no idea what to do with it except have it cut to a serviceable mid length every six months.

'Oh God, Ma,' she muttered. 'Am I letting the side down?'

'No, you aren't. This isn't a fashion parade.'

'But these girls are dressed up to the nines ...'

'Well, there are a lot of smart young men about.'

This would never have occurred to Stella. Was watching a march-past and lunching in the officers' mess some kind of man-hunt, then?

'Anyway,' said Kate, 'I shouldn't worry. They're all going to freeze and you'll have the last laugh.'

War or no war, they were both moved by the occasion. The programme gave a diagram of the different sections' positions on the square, so they were able to find a seat with some chance of seeing Will in action in 21 Platoon, Khartoum Regiment. When they all came marching on to 'Soldiers of the Queen', Stella could suddenly, for a moment, understand why all these sisters and cousins and girlfriends had made themselves beautiful for the day. They were like the ladies of the court on their dais, and these dashing young men were potentially the heroes who might carry their favour into battle. The sexiness of the situation was not lost on her, but she herself was still glad to be warm.

Kate had brought binoculars and they located Will in the second row of his platoon, clearly visible because of his height. Stella was struck by the transformation.

'Can that really be my scruffy brother? He looks so smart.'

'Wonderful, isn't it, what a really ferocious drill sergeant can achieve?'

Stella lowered the binoculars, and at once Will disappeared and all she could see were the rows of stiffly regimented uniforms. As they watched the march-pasts, slow and quick, the inspection by the sovereign's representative, the presentation of the colours and awarding of prizes, she wondered what possible necessity there could be for all this ceremonial discipline and drill. There might be some point in reducing the rank and file to automata (distasteful though that was), but these men were destined to be leaders – the ones who gave the orders.

Her mother's expression was one of calm, thoughtful interest, as if gazing at a view. An army wife and now an army mother. Those phrases, especially the first, were used as if they referred to clearly defined roles, something a woman took on and must learn to perform. Had Kate been subjected to a process of ironing out and bringing to heel in order to accompany her husband's regiment around the world? Did that experience make it any easier to see Will being put through the soldier-making machine? There was a lot, Stella thought, that she didn't know and needed to ask; though not perhaps today.

At the end of the parade, the new recruits marched up the steps of the main building, disappearing two by two through the wide porticoed entrance, the adjutant on his white horse bringing up the rear. It was a scene familiar both anecdotally and from photographs but peculiarly, annoyingly powerful in the flesh. The poignancy of the symbolism – the young men being swallowed up by the darkness, the great gentle horse seeming to shepherd them in – brought a lump to Stella's throat and made her furious. She did not want her emotional buttons pushed by this propaganda exercise! She wished Will all the best in his chosen career, but that was all it was: a job, not some mysterious dynastic vocation, freighted with notions of glory, brotherhood and sacrifice.

Dulce et decorum est? Bollocks, thought Stella, rummaging for a tissue.

'There he is,' said Kate. 'Not so very different after all.'

He was with a couple of other young men, who were duly introduced. Stella entertained a fleeting regret about her lack of a miniskirt, for Will's rather than her own sake, but when he said 'And this is my sister', they beamed and shook her hand and addressed her by name as if she were the loveliest young thing in the world. She had grudgingly to concede that if all the army taught was chivalry, it had achieved something that added to the sum of human happiness.

'Did you enjoy it?' he asked eagerly. 'We thought it went pretty well.'

'It was absolutely wonderful,' said Kate. 'We were bursting with pride.'

Stella allowed this. 'We scarcely recognised you.'

'That's the idea, really.'

'And nobody keeled over. I was quite disappointed.'

'That doesn't happen very often. One chap did in rehearsal, but he had the mother of all hangovers and richly deserved it. Shall we head off to lunch? It's in this direction.'

Gradually, the spell of the parade and its associations dissipated. Over drinks there were encounters with tutors, NCOs and senior officers who if they didn't actually say 'Carry on' as they moved away might just as well have done. Lunch of soup, roast lamb and pear belle Hélène involved a lot of polite (and in Stella's case largely insincere) conversation with the other people on their table. She noticed that Will and his brother officers had all the respectful, gallant charm in the world, but that her brother, unlike some, had the looks to go with it; the table was his to command. He had always been of a fortunate disposition, but she couldn't remember him looking happier or more at ease. Her scepticism was tinged with envy. He had found his metier.

After lunch, Will was free until the evening's Commissioning Ball, to which the latest bird – Viv from Godalming, a photographic model with whom they had not been granted an audience – had been invited. Stella wondered if she had been one of the high-stepping beauties in the stands but decided not, as surely they would have been introduced. So not an item, yet. The icy wind had abated, and when he reappeared after some mysterious project involving the handing in of weapons and sorting of kit, he took them on a tour of the grounds in the spring sunshine: the cricket square, the rugby pitch, the assault course, the guardroom, the acres of manicured greensward and woodland. It would have been idyllic but for the cannon and tanks, and the clusters of firework stands like gun emplacements in front of the marquee. By the lake they saw a heron standing sentinel over the reedy shallows on the far side. As they watched, it rose into the air, unfeasibly slowly as if hoisted by strings, and flew away over the treetops with heavy, flopping wing beats.

'Off to raid the ornamental fishponds of Camberley,' observed Will.

'It's always a good day when you see a heron.' Kate was quoting a remark of their father's. Having kept silent on this subject thus far, Stella was not about to broach it, but Will said:

'Mum, thanks for coming. All this must make you think of Dad.'

'Yes, but then most things do. I don't mind, if that's what you mean. And I wouldn't have missed today for the world.'

They turned back towards the main building. Will shot a look at Stella.

'What about you, sis? Not too uncomfortable, I hope?'

'Not at all.'

'You made an impression on Guy Miller.'

'Guy who?'

'No false modesty, please,' said Kate. 'Tall, dark and handsome. We were introduced.'

'Oh yes.' They both seemed to be smiling at her as if something more were expected, so she said, 'I'm flattered.'

'You should be. He asked if you were coming to the ball.'

'I hope you told him I wasn't.'

'I did, and he claimed to be very disappointed.'

'Presumably he has someone lined up,' said Stella drily.

'He has, yes, but I thought you should know you scored a palpable hit.'

They were looking at her again.

'Well,' she shrugged non-committally, 'good.'

What else was there to say?

They made their farewells in the car park. Will would be going to join his unit in Catterick after the weekend. He would be in touch.

As they drove away, Stella looked in the rear-view mirror and saw him in conversation with a tall, slim woman in a black suit. Something about their demeanour, not touching, but standing close, spoke of intimacy.

'Yes,' said Kate, the mind-reader. 'I noticed her earlier, all on her own.'

Kate spent the night at Stella's Paddington flat, Stella's flatmate Judy having kindly agreed to visit her own parents in Hatfield for the weekend. For the jaunt to Sandhurst Stella had taken a day's holiday – in those days she was in personnel (as HR was then known) at Debenham's – and the following day was Saturday, so they were going to have lunch and a matinee before Kate got the train home. At lunch in a tratt behind the Palladium, they were joined by Angela, who was in town visiting her daughter and new-born grandson. They told her about the passing-out parade, and she reciprocated with her worries about her son-in-law's rough parish in Kilburn.

'The Rev adores it – I expect it makes him feel useful to have the challenge – but it must be hard on Bee,' she confided over the carbonara and a second splash of house red. 'There isn't a blade of grass within hailing distance, and the strangest people turn up at the back door.'

They agreed that it must be difficult. 'A nice rural living is what I'd like for them,' went on Angela, 'but I dare say that's not the point. *Mission*'s the word, I gather.' With a visible change of tack and tone, she turned to Stella. 'And Stella, how are things with you?'

'They're fine. Busy, you know.'

'Oh, I bet.' Angela pulled a sympathetic face. 'But not too busy for *some* fun, I hope?'

'No, no. Definitely not.'

'I wonder,' mused Kate, 'what exactly we mean by "fun" when we say it like that?'

'I didn't say it like anything,' protested Angela. 'I just meant that all work—'

'Presumably fun is whatever we happen to be doing at any given moment that makes us happy.'

There were times, and this was one of them, when Stella thought her mother almost perfect.

'Exactly!' agreed Angela, as if Kate had put her finger on precisely what she herself had meant to say. 'Different strokes for different folks.'

They laughed about that afterwards, but not for long. The afternoon's play was an unremittingly gloomy study of long-term marriage, the excellence of the acting doing full justice to the bleakness of the playwright's vision. Afterwards, as they shuffled towards the exit, Kate said: 'Was that my choice?'

'It was, actually, Ma.'

'What can I have been thinking of?'

An elderly gentleman behind them leaned forward. 'My sentiments exactly.'

Stella said, 'You wanted us to see an intelligent modern play, not another revival or a musical.'

'I must have been mad.'

'It was terribly good.'

'"Terribly" being the operative word. If we're at the station early, I shall have an enormous whisky.'

The man behind made a short barking sound. Stella wished he'd stop listening in; attracted to her mother, no doubt, as that friend of Will's had apparently been attracted to her, and rather more understandably, she couldn't help thinking.

They had half an hour to spare and Kate had her return ticket. In the cavernous, dingy station bar, Stella bought (with her mother's money, insistently pressed on her) the required large Scotch, and a brandy and Canada Dry for herself.

Kate closed her eyes, sipped and sighed. 'That's better ... You're right, it was utterly brilliant, but it didn't offer a spark of hope.'

'Not for marriage, no,' agreed Stella.

'I understand that that's his point of view, what the play was about, but he wasn't suggesting any alternative. He seemed to be saying here's what most dull, passionless, conventional people do, and it's a living death.'

'It probably is, for some of them.'

Kate shook her head. 'Anything is, for some people. There are those who just can't be happy. They don't know how to be. They don't know when they're well off.' As, a long time ago, I didn't, she thought and very nearly said. It takes one to know one.

'Well I – perhaps enjoyed isn't the right word, but I was completely gripped. Thank you.'

'My pleasure. It's good to try these things.'

With the play as it were picked over, an earlier image sneaked up on Stella.

'I keep thinking of that woman in the car park, the one with Will.'

'Yes ... a friend? The sister of a friend? I don't know.'

'But we don't think the great Viv?'

'No. As I say, I did notice her earlier. She stood out.'

'In what way?'

'Every way, really, in that company – very tall, all in black, glasses, hair up. Elegant in a donnish way.'

Stella considered this. 'Who on earth would Will know like that?'

'We can speculate till the cows come home,' Kate said, 'but we'll be no further forward. He has his own life now.'

Suddenly Stella was weary – of Will's irritating mysteries, of the two long days of putting on a good front, of the whole hard-work, happy-family shtick. She pushed her chair back from the table.

'It was just idle curiosity, Ma. I don't give a stuff who he sees.'

That wasn't true, and they both knew it. There were two Wills: the dashing, breezy subaltern with more front than Brighton, frugging the night away with Viv from Godalming; and the other Will, who was susceptible and secretive, who had been so moved by his father's funeral that he had decided there and then to join the army; the Will who far from being straightforward could be downright duplicitous.

Judy got back on Sunday night. 'How was your brother's army do?'

'Sovereign's Parade.'

'Is that what it's called? How was it?'

'Very military.'

'Super.' Judy looked enraptured. 'Were you shaken and stirred?'

'Look, Judy,' said Stella. 'It was square-bashing to music. I had to take my mama. Shall we leave it at that?'

'If you like,' said Judy. 'Only asking. I rather envy you.'

For some reason that she was unable and unwilling to fathom, Stella fretted late and long that night, and sleep, when it came, churned with disturbing dreams.

Chapter Eleven
1998

On bad days, Evie's life felt like a bunch of giant balloons that she had to carry in a high wind, the combined buoyancy tugging at her, threatening to sweep her away. She pictured herself beneath them, hanging on for dear life like an unfortunate character in a fairy story set some impossible and unending task. Not that she didn't enjoy her work, and her friends, and where Raff was concerned she could almost have burst with pride, but there was no escaping the fact that keeping the Flaherty show on the road, solo, was a struggle.

This year, on some long-since-forgotten impulse, she had offered to do Christmas. It would be a good one, she'd see to that – stylish and secular; they'd all have had quite enough myth, myrrh and magic by then, courtesy of Raff. Evie was organised, because she had to be. Her Christmas shopping had been completed by mid November and the presents were already wrapped in plain brown parcel paper with red and green tartan ribbon. Her cards, Japanese watercolours from the art gallery, were written and stamped and would be sent out in tranches from December the first according to destination. She had ordered the fillet of organic beef (a king's ransom, but no waste and no Jurassic carcass to be disposed of afterwards) and made Christmas pudding ice cream and tipsy plums. She had also ordered a two-pound wedge of Stilton and a small truckle of fierce, dry cheddar. Owen was supplying nibbles, crackers and chocolates; Kate had sweetly given her a cheque for booze. Holly, ivy and mistletoe she'd pick up from the market on Christmas Eve morning, and she had laid in a supply of creamy church candles and bought tiny tree fairings for everyone: that meant Kate, Stella, Dad (dream on), Raff, herself and Owen. This year Raff was going to his father for New Year, which was to be at a castle in Scotland, no less. Only a small castle, Mick had explained, rented out by the Landmark Trust, but still a bloody castle. At least that meant that Raff would be with her for next year's millennium – God knows what Mick would have lined up for that.

There was a move afoot for them all to go to Norfolk to the Rev and his wife, Uncle Joe's lot, on Boxing Day, but she was deferring the decision on that for as long as possible. She entertained a tempting mental picture of herself and Raff, when he was finally off duty, spending the day at home; a picture which didn't even include Owen, who would be going to visit his parents in Swansea. In her mind's eye she'd be wearing joggers and slippers (possibly new fluffy ones given to her the day before), and be curled up on the sofa with a good (again possibly new) book, a schooner of Bailey's on ice and the double-page spread of seasonal viewing to hand. Raff would be allowed to lie in long and sit up late and the two of them would have a wonderful day of slobby sybaritism doing just as they pleased and grazing on delicious leftovers.

But that – even if it happened – was still some way off. Right now, Evie was at the out-of-town superstore and approaching the end of her tether. Half the population of the city and its outlying villages seemed to be milling around in here, unable to make its mind up about the smallest bloody thing and determined to stand in the middle of the aisle while it did so. Still more infuriating was the fact that she herself had made her decisions before leaving the office and enshrined them in a list, taking the trouble as she always did to group them according to their position in the store – but had left the list in the car. So she was in effect – though not, she told herself, fundamentally – no better than the rest of them. The whole exercise was exacerbated by the natural tendency of people to clump. The moment she hove alongside, say, pasta and rice to check her mental inventory, at least a dozen other hunter-gatherers in an equally advanced state of irritation converged on her, jerking their trolleys and leaning across her to get what they wanted, snarling 'Excuse me' through gritted teeth. Evie had to fight to overcome the urge to batter them senseless with a can of chickpeas. A woman bumped – no, barged – into her, and she staggered and said 'Sorry' reflexively before thinking, *Hang on, who barged who?* But when she looked venomously over her shoulder at the perpetrator, it turned out to be someone she knew slightly and to whom, now they had caught each other's eye, she would have to be civil.

'Oh, hello!' Cynthia? Celia?

'Evie!' The woman blew at her fringe and rolled her eyes. 'Hades or what?'

'And I left my list in the car.'

'You know you'll spend a shedload on impulse buys.'

Evie smiled thinly. 'That's why I'm trying to audit from memory as I go along.'

'Right. Far be it from me to get between a woman and her audit,' said Cynthia/Celia, accelerating away. 'Happy Christmas!'

A child scooted past, pushing a trolley laden not only with shopping but also an excitedly shrieking toddler. The trolley wheel barked Evie's ankle painfully. A supervising adult, if there was one, was nowhere to be seen. Eyes watering, she rubbed her ankle and swore to stop herself from crying.

'That's not very nice.' A huge man in a Chelsea shirt was looming over her. She stared at him blankly. 'The kids are excited!' he said, his voice artificially high as if explaining to a simpleton. 'It's Christmas! Remember?'

Ankle still smarting, she watched his rolling gorilla gait as he caught up with the renegade trolley. They would be *his* ruddy children. She wanted to scream that Christmas was still two weeks off and that if he was so bloody keen on goodwill he should make the little bugger apologise for crashing into her and damaging her tights.

Back in the car, she consulted the list, found that there were four things she'd omitted to buy, and delivered herself of a few furious, full-belt expletives before reversing at speed.

It was Friday. Raff was sleeping over with a friend whose mother would take the boys into morning school next day, so he wouldn't be back till the following afternoon, after choir practice. This meant that Owen could spend the night. Their relationship had not yet reached the tipping point where she'd have felt comfortable with him staying while Raff was there. She wanted to be able to tell her son honestly that this was serious, committed, the real thing – and deal with the attendant flak – before that happened.

At the moment, the times when the two of them were in the house at the same time were a strain. Raff persisted wilfully in his view that Owen was thick, and Owen's well-meaning but clumsy attempts to ingratiate himself did nothing to help. Evie felt wounded on her man's behalf; he liked and admired Raff, was genuinely in awe of the whole chorister thing and not afraid to show it. Also, though he was very far from being thick, he was large, gentle and slow-spoken and could give that impression.

Being a policeman didn't help. Not CID, or Drug Squad, or Vice, nothing sexy as seen on TV; just a regular rozzer. She couldn't possibly explain to an eleven-year-old that Owen completely did it for her, that no one else – not even, she was afraid, Raff's father – came close; and that (uniquely in her experience) he combined this sexiness with being her rock. All he got for his considerable pains with Raff was the brush-off, the surface politeness of which served only to make it appear more considered. She didn't want to make an issue of this; when Owen commented on what a great kid Raff was, she always agreed but with a deprecating smile which allowed that he was no angel either, and left it at that.

She was almost certain that she loved Owen, with a proper, grown-up love, but she was super-wary of saying it, even to herself. After all, she had been head over heels with Mick, and much good it had done her. The thrilling quasi-lunacy of that relationship had in the end brought her to the brink of real madness; and the frenzied sex, which had left her chafed, swollen and light-headed, had transmuted, with marriage, into a terrible power to wound, as if the giving of pleasure had taught them how to inflict emotional pain in a hundred accurate, personal ways. She bitterly regretted the savagery, and the fact that she and Mick, who had so much going for them as individuals, had together joined the great ranks of the divorce statistics. And she was sad for Raff, who adored his father. But she didn't miss Mick, especially now. Peering back as it were through the smoke and flames, the crashing and burning, she felt only curious – incredulous, even. She knew what she'd been feeling, but what in God's name had she been *thinking*?

Jesus, she'd even made the first move! Though in public Evie derided the rules, at some deep, visceral level they still held sway; post-feminist pride notwithstanding, she believed a woman should not be too readily available. But all of that had gone out of the window when she spotted Mick Flaherty in a castle courtyard in the foothills of the Italian Alps.

The occasion had been a wedding the year she turned twenty. The only Italians involved were the caterers, waiting staff, musicians and florists. The bride was an Irish socialite, scion of a racehorse training dynasty, a tanned uber-babe in oyster lace with diamonds at neck and wrist and entwined in her hair. The groom, Calum, was a hippyish OB cameraman from the BBC eastern region whom Evie had known since she was seventeen and had always taken to be gay. How wrong could you be? On the day, somewhat overwhelmed by the rampant celebratory hordes of O'Flynns, he had chosen to behave as though there had been something significant between him and Evie in the past. Surfing on a smooth wave of Prosecco, Evie had gone along with this, or at least not openly denied it, which would have been both rude and unsporting.

Mick was leaning against the parapet, glass in hand, a cigarette between his fingers, in an attitude that proclaimed 'alone from choice'. Behind him the roofs of the picture-perfect medieval town glowed in the afternoon light, and beyond and around them the Ligurian fastness rose, the river valley slithering secretively between soaring olive-clad mountain walls to the sea. A backdrop to die for, as Mick must have known. He was dark-haired and blue-eyed, with a narrow, vivid face, the lower part of which, artfully shadowed, protruded slightly like the muzzle of an animal on the qui vive. Smart – foxy. Evie had asked to be introduced to him a) because he was fanciable, b) because inhibition had become a distant memory and c) to stop Calum using her as testosterone-cred. But she had still shamelessly worked the one-that-got-away impression to her advantage.

With Calum gone, Mick looked her up and down and gestured with his glass. 'Y'man kept quiet about you.'

She'd smiled, God help her, coquettishly. 'Calum's a dark horse.'

'You could have fooled me. Till now.'

'How do you know him?' she asked.

'Not the same way you do, evidently.' When she didn't react, he dropped his cigarette and trod on it before saying: 'I'm an independent film-maker – training films, promos, that kind of thing – he did some freelance work for me.'

'And has he been to *your* wedding?' Clever, that, she considered, but he wasn't falling for it.

'No,' he replied, answering the question but telling her nothing. 'Where are you sitting for dinner?'

'I haven't looked at the plan.'

'Let's look now, why don't we?' He held out his hand. 'Still time to make a few strategic alterations.'

She'd put her hand in his and – she remembered this so clearly – he held it very lightly, encircling her fingers with his and placing his thumb, also lightly, in the very centre of her palm. It was a touch that implied intimacy and collusion, like the coded handshake of a secret society.

They – or rather he – made the alterations and they sat next to each other at one of the long refectory tables for the Italian feast. They ate and drank prodigiously, danced like dervishes, and after the bride and groom had departed, took a taxi back to the large modern hotel on the outskirts of town where Mick was staying, and made whoopee till dawn.

To Evie's surprise and delight, Mick contacted her when they were back in England and they took things to the next level, and the one after that. Events escalated at hair-raising speed.

By the time they had their own wedding, Raff was on the way. They should have known that theirs was a union quite unsuited to the everyday rigours of marriage, and it began to go wrong almost at once. It didn't exactly turn sour, because sourness would have implied stasis, and what they had was turmoil. The beast, caged, wanted out.

In the months preceding Raff's arrival, Evie ballooned, and was nauseous and exhausted. She and Mick both disliked her pregnancy, squabbling and sulking their way through it and counting the days till the whole ghastly business would be over, ignoring the fact that with the pregnancy's end a whole other life would begin, theirs and another's. It would have been beyond the scope of even the most exemplary infant to fulfil so much hope, and it was certainly beyond that of little Raphael Flaherty. Instead of binding his parents together, his tiny presence drove a wedge like a battering ram between them.

They'd both loved him passionately in their separate ways. Mick had if anything taken to parenthood more readily than Evie;

in spite of or because of her youth, her urge to get on top of things was strong – she couldn't simply dive in, she needed time to catch her balance and get organised. Her father, highly delighted and a frequent visitor in those early days, was quick to point out that he'd been scarcely older than she was now when she herself was born.

'I may not have done much as a parent since, but I was there, I saw you make your entrance. Not very many men did that back then. I was ahead of my time.'

He was holding his week-old grandson quite confidently as he made this pronouncement, Raff's head with its patchy covering of black fluff tucked in the crook of his shoulder. It had, as usual, been all about him.

'Of course,' he went on, patting the baby's back absent-mindedly, 'I was very young to be a father, too young. No experience of life, hardly more than a boy myself. Your mother was probably quite right to take me out of the equation. Amazing,' here he grinned disarmingly, 'that you turned out as well as you did.'

He seemed to think that his benign emotional neglect of her was something to be proud of; that the legacy of his superior genes was and always had been enough.

'Look at you!' he'd exclaim. 'And you got it all from me.'

This attitude produced in Evie a fluttering white flame of something very like hatred. She was prepared to concede that her father had done at least one admirable thing in his time, but that had not been in the arena of family relationships. He may have qualified as a new man for attending his daughter's birth, but from that point on, as far as she was concerned, he had quite simply copped out. His line was that the two of them were better off without him.

Though her relationship with her mother had never been close – not cuddly and intimate like those some of her friends enjoyed – from her current perspective Evie admired Jacqueline. Hers had been a storming, and largely successful, model of single motherhood. Jacqueline had worked hard to provide for, entertain, educate and support her. If she hadn't been the warmest mother in the world, well – you couldn't have everything. There had been a succession of excellent (always British) nannies, but when she was around, she was available. Evie could not remember ever having been brushed aside, or not answered. She had never doubted that she was an important and valued individual, of whom much was expected. If something fuzzier was absent, she didn't miss it at the time, and only remarked its absence later, and dispassionately.

Raff was the beneficiary of these observations. Evie – driven, organised, disposed to be in control – recognised her likeness to her mother and realised, after the first embattled months of her son's life, that if he was not going to be deprived of emotional nourishment, she was going to have to make an effort. She loved him, her boy, with an almost frightening intensity, but unlike Jacqueline she was determined to show him, to step outside her natural reserve and demonstrate that love so that he would never, ever be in any doubt. Sometimes when Raff was busy – practising, nuking a pizza, doing homework – she'd descend on him and subject him to a fierce, unexpected embrace which he would invariably fight to escape.

'Mu-um! Get off! What's all that about?'

She never answered the question. One day, she told herself, he'd remember; and then he'd know.

When she was growing up, she had never been able to work out which of her parents was for real. Her father was a cavalier stranger; not uncaring exactly – he was always full of kisses, presents and endearments – but breezy, as though the limited time he had with her was just fine with him. Seeing him left Evie confused. Her mother, though undemonstrative, had the advantage of at least appearing straightforward. You knew where you were with her. She made it clear from the very first that she abhorred lying, and would never lie to anyone, most of all her only child.

Evie had been six and a half when she'd first asked about her father. Until then, she had simply accepted the way things were – his absence, his lack of any real involvement, her mother's slightly intimidating attitude towards him. But at the primary school she attended near their big flat in Bloomsbury, it had been brought to her attention that other little girls saw both their parents most days, and took their fathers for granted.

She had begun by asking Marian, the nanny of the day, and came up against a wall of pleasant but unbreachable discretion.

'He's a soldier, isn't he? He'll be abroad most of the time.'

'But Anne's daddy's a soldier.'

'Maybe he works here.'

She thought about this. There was something about the whole Daddy thing, but she couldn't put her finger on it enough to ask a second question. Marian, though, was quick to step in.

'You should talk to your mum about it. She'll know.'

It was just beginning to dawn on Evie that her mother, too, wasn't like the mothers of her contemporaries. There was about Jacqueline none of the early-seventies hippy vibe evident in even the poshest of the other mums. She was older, better dressed, cleverer, and when friends came to tea (every other Thursday, Marian's weekday afternoon off), she expected, and so got, proper conversation round the table. Haughtily ignorant of the fish finger and frozen waffle, she would produce pasta with a delicious sauce, unashamedly purchased from the Italian deli on the corner, followed by one of their many flavours of home-made ice cream.

Confronted with the Daddy question, she gazed calmly and intently over the *TLS* as if weighing up Evie's readiness for the straight answer she was about to give.

'He likes to see you, Evie, but not very often. Some people are like that.'

'Are they?'

'Yes. Everyone's different.'

'Why doesn't he live with us?'

Jacqueline removed her glasses and laid them on the arm of the chair. 'Has Marian been saying something?'

Evie was appalled. 'No!'

'That's all right. Because, Evie, when I had you, Daddy and I weren't married and we didn't want to be. Daddy was very young. So you stayed with me, and I look after you, and he comes to see us when he wants to.'

Evie considered this. It *seemed* clear, and yet somehow it didn't answer the deeper, more mysterious question that she felt turning darkly in her stomach like a worm. She tried again:

'Does he love us?'

'Of course he loves you!' Jacqueline laughed and came to sit next to Evie, her arm round her shoulders. 'If he didn't love you, he wouldn't come at all.' She gave her a brisk squeeze. 'Would he?'

'I don't know.'

Her mother released her with a pat. 'The next time he comes, you should ask him. He'll say the same thing.'

She did ask – in the spring, a few weeks after her birthday, when Will, on leave from Belfast, turned up with her present (a gonk with a Beatle haircut). Her mother was at work and they were taking a walk round the gardens in Russell Square, deciding which of the dogs they saw they'd like to own. Evie interrupted his enthusiastic running commentary on a boxer chasing squirrels.

'Why don't you live with us?'

'What?' He stopped and looked down at her. She tried to walk on, but he caught her shoulder. 'What was that, tuppence?'

'Why don't we all live together?'

'Come here.' He guided her to a bench with its back to the shrubbery and sat her down next to him. 'What brought this on?'

'I just wondered.'

'Fair enough, good question.' He stroked her hair and tilted his head, trying to catch her eye. 'Well obviously I agree, it's a shame that we don't, there's nothing I'd like more, but that's just not the way things have panned out.' She still didn't look at him, and he sighed. 'I adore you, tuppence, you know that, don't you? You're my girl.'

Now he tried to lift her, to sit her on his knee. Normally she would have liked this, but today she resisted and he let her go with a kiss on the temple.

'Sorry. Straight answer, eh?' She waited tensely, unhappily, while he got out a cigarette and lit it. 'Mummy's older than me. And a hell of a lot more grown-up.' The trace of a grim laugh came out of his mouth with the smoke. 'Anyway, long before you were born, we both realised I wasn't going to make much of a father, and we weren't going to get married, so we agreed that I'd – sort of – leave her to it. You're much better off with Mummy. But I'll always come to see you when I can. It would be more often, but soldiers have to go where they're put and I'm not around much.'

Now she did look at him. 'Can't you try and come a bit more?'

'God, you're so like her ...' he muttered, and then announced brightly, 'I will try, I promise. Hey.' He nudged her unresponsive shoulder. 'I *will*.'

After that, whatever his efforts, everything continued in exactly the same way. There was no denying that the answers given by both Jacqueline and Will were pretty much the same, but Evie remained unsatisfied. It would be years before she came close to understanding her parents, and long before that she'd grown tired of trying and forgiven the pair of them.

Now Christmas loomed, and she had responsibilities and decisions that she would make, as usual, on her own.

Chapter Twelve
1969

'*What?*'

Instinctively, Will turned so that his back was to the driveway where Stella's car was pulling slowly away in the direction of the Staff College gates. 'You're joking. I hope.'

'Scarcely. About something like this?'

'But ...' He felt dizzy, and laid a hand on the roof of the ice-blue Capri to steady himself. 'What's going on?'

Jacqueline was the mistress of fine-tuned hauteur; the eyebrow was only just raised, the sigh barely audible.

'Nature is taking its course.'

'There's no need to be bloody sarcastic.'

'I'm not. I'm being crystal clear.'

'Because, you know,' he went on as though she hadn't spoken, 'this is pretty terrible timing.'

'No, I don't know ...' She glanced around, not nervously as he had, but thoughtfully, then unlocked the Capri. 'Look, why don't we get in?'

'For Christ's sake, I haven't got time to sit about. I have to go.'

'Go whenever you like. I'm not kidnapping you, Will. I simply sense you'll be more comfortable out of the public gaze.'

With a flash of taut legs – legs made to get in and out of a sports car – she sank on to the driver's seat, and leaned across to unlock the passenger door. 'Hop in.'

He folded himself into the car, slamming the door and removing his cap. His forehead crept with sweat and his heart was racing. Around them in the car park little groups of people – new officers and their families and friends – were saying farewells, making plans, doing normal things. But to him, now, they seemed like aliens, and the stands on the parade ground, the stately college buildings, the marquee for the ball like spaceships, the vessels of another civilisation.

He said pathetically, 'I thought you were on the pill.'

'I was.'

'So what happened?'

She said calmly, 'I came off it.'

'Why the fuck didn't you tell me?'

'Because,' she lowered her voice as his rose, 'I suspected you'd react like this.'

He glared at her furiously. 'You wonder why?'

'Will. Come on.' She flipped open her cigarette case. 'Take one. These are my last for the duration, so you'll be doing me a favour.'

He took one, and she lit his, then hers, and they inhaled, gazing out at the slowly dispersing crowd of cars and supporters. After a moment, she said:

'You have absolutely nothing to worry about. My decision, my choice, my responsibility.'

'But my *child*!' He sounded like a child himself, and added nastily, 'I assume.'

'I'll pretend I didn't hear that.' She let a beat go by. 'Yes, your child.'

'But I'm just starting – just ...' He waved a hand at their surroundings, then placed it over his eyes, massaging fiercely. 'For Christ's sake!'

She said, more gently, 'I know. I understand. I don't want this to be any sort of burden. I'll do it all.'

Will gasped. 'But I'm going to be a father!' He was unable – and Jacqueline seemed unconcerned – to take in the sheer biological enormity of it. 'You've railroaded me into this, and I'm not ready.'

'I'm well aware of that, which is why I haven't railroaded you into anything. I've presented you with a fully fashioned fait accompli. Not the same thing at all. You're not listening, Will. You're free as air. I'm not asking for a thing. More than that, I don't *want* anything except to be left to get on with it.'

'*You* want – what about me, what about what *I* want?'

Too late he saw exactly where this was going to lead.

'All right, my love.' Jacqueline tapped her cigarette into the dashboard ashtray. 'What *do* you want?'

'I suppose ...' he mumbled desperately, 'a choice?'

'But you see, I've already made mine. I'm well over thirty, I don't want to marry, but this is an experience I want to have while I'm still young enough. My stake in the future. I wasn't about to be talked out of it.' She squashed down the remains of the cigarette. 'So you see, giving you a choice was sort of irrelevant.'

'It's my stake in the future too.'

He could hear in his voice that he was merely grumbling now, and knew that she would be able to hear it too. Without looking at him, she reached out and took his hand, holding it firmly between both of hers.

'This is what's happening, and I shall get on with it. I can afford it. I've made plans. You can have as much to do with the whole thing' (he noticed she hadn't said 'baby' once) 'as you like. Or as little.'

'And what will we say – I mean later – when we're asked?' He realised he'd fallen into the trap, too, the trap of not saying the word. He took a breath: 'When the child asks about us? About me?'

She looked at him with an expression of the purest astonishment, before releasing his hand.

'We'll tell the truth, of course. What else?'

That night at the ball, Will got well and truly plastered. He was not alone. Fortunately he was an affable and amusing drunk, but even if this had not been the case, his brother officers would have been disposed to forgive him because he was accompanied by Viv, who after achieving four O levels at Heathfield had appeared (so their girlfriends told them) in the fashion pages of *Honey*, *19* and a host of other publications. You could certainly see why. Viv had the longest legs, the briefest silver mini and the dewiest pout of any girl there; from beneath her blonde fringe her limpid eyes, fringed by sooty llama-lashes, gazed at the world with the serene confidence bestowed by beauty.

Her self-centredness (the one quality she shared with Jacqueline) made her the ideal partner for this particular evening. She was at the ball to drink, to dance and to be admired, and was completely oblivious to any emotional or psychological disturbance in Will. This, and the fact that he knew he was very far from being the only man in her life, was curiously restful. You didn't have to worry about Viv. She was, in the nicest sense, a good-time girl.

During the course of the night he became aware of a sea change in his feelings, and not only because of the booze. Hang on – he was going to be a father. And one with no responsibilities whatsoever. What had Jacqueline said? He could be involved as much or as little as he liked? In that case, whatever he chose to do would be a plus. He was in an opt-in situation. Now he came to think about it, there were worse ones to be in. At around one a.m., with the dance floor heaving to 'You Really Got Me', he experienced a tremendous urge to grab the microphone and announce at full blast: 'I'm going to be a daddy!' Fortunately there were just enough unpissed brain cells left to prevent him doing so. Instead he grabbed Viv and ground his pelvis into hers so she too could feel his sudden and tremendous elation.

'Well, hello,' she mouthed, her face close to his, her eyes huge.

He pushed a silken swag of hair back with his hand and placed his lips against her ear. She smelt fantastic. 'Come outside?'

'Good idea.'

For the night of the ball, the grounds were policed, but not officiously so. There was no reason why a couple shouldn't take a stroll. They went towards the lake and stepped behind a large tree. Viv was less passionate than Jacqueline but every bit as straightforward. Despite these uncomfortable circumstances, perhaps because of them, Will went off like a rocket and Viv seemed to have no complaints; they were walking back to the marquee within ten minutes to the band's strenuous rendition of 'Twist and Shout'. The moment they were back in the tent, Viv was on the dance floor, arms waving above her head, hips swivelling, hair flying round her face, the focus of every lustful male eye and every snitty female one. Will didn't even bother to join her, but got a last drink and sat at their table with a couple who were trying to lick each other's tonsils, feeling pleasantly melancholy and superior with his dark secret.

He was posted first to Catterick, then to Blandford. On weekends off he came to London, usually staying at Stella's flat. The first few times he rang Viv, but she had started seeing a much older man (married, Will inferred), who worked in films and was well placed to help her get on. She was happy to go out as always, and up for a shag, but he could sense that she was drifting off into the wider waters of self-advancement. When he finally contacted Jacqueline again, she behaved as if nothing had happened.

'Hello, have they let you out?'

'I'm down here till Sunday. How are you?'

'I'm extremely well.'

'Would you like, I don't know, dinner or something?'

'I choose dinner first, then something. I'll meet you at Rules, my treat.'

To his surprise, both he and Jacqueline found her pregnancy sexy. She didn't get huge, but she was narcissistic about the changes that did occur, parading her fuller breasts and swelling belly before him as if they were engaged in role play and she'd put on this new covering of flesh expressly to titillate. Afterwards she drank tonic water while he smoked. He was steeling himself to address the big question, but she got there first.

'I'll be going to St Mary's, Paddington. I'll let you know, of course, the moment things start, in case you're able to attend.'

'Really?' This hadn't occurred to him.

'Don't worry.' She patted his hand. 'Only if it's geographically possible and if you want to. Or would you rather I presented you with a fait accompli again?'

'No – no, I want to know.'

'UCL is a model employer. I'll be taking three months' maternity leave, and then going back to work. I've started interviewing for a nanny.'

'Oh, right.'

He felt rather than saw her look at him and smile. 'I'm extraordinarily fussy. I want British and traditional but young and nice.' She ticked the list off on her fingers. 'Queen's English, clean driving licence, steady boyfriend ...'

'Sounds like a tall order.'

'I shall get it, believe me.'

'Is there, um,' he reached for the ashtray and rested it on his midriff, 'is there anything you need?'

'Everything. I haven't bought a thing yet.'

He chose his words carefully. 'Only I'd sort of obviously like to make a contribution.'

'Thank you. How about a cot?'

'Okay. I don't know a thing about them, where do I ...?'

'I know where they are to be found. I'll take a look and let you know the price range.'

'Do you want me to come along?'

'Good heavens, no!' She was incredulous. 'We're not going to trail round baby shops together.'

Sensing he was safe, he said, 'I don't mind.'

'Well I do. It's not what we do, Will. But thank you for the offer, I shall take you up on it, subject to researches ...' Temporarily distracted, she put down her glass and placed a hand beneath each breast. 'Just look at these. Extraordinary ...'

As the months went by, her attitude didn't change. The cot – the price only just within his range, selected to flatter but not break the bank – arrived, and took its place in her flat's second bedroom, a receptacle for clothes, bedding, plastic mats and a mobile with stars (about the only whimsical purchase as far as Will could see). The other large items were a carry cot with collapsible wheels, and a small bouncy seat made of fabric stretched over a horse-shoe-shaped frame. Jacqueline subjected the room to a fresh coat of paint, but the decor remained unchanged, with no concessions to nursery status: three cream walls and one cinnamon-brown one, gold and white striped curtains and a spotless cream carpet. There was one picture, a Chagall print. Jacqueline showed him the cot and the room once, and then closed the door and did not do so again.

Over late dinner one night (she'd taken him to see *Equus*), he got just drunk enough to ask the question that was preying on his mind.

'Why do you want this?'

'Fillet of veal Holstein?'

'The baby. You said – when you first told me – that it was something you wanted. Why?'

As usual, she didn't skip a beat. 'Don't most people? Most women, whatever they may say to the contrary?'

He shrugged. 'You tell me.'

'It's an experience I don't want to miss out on.'

'What if you don't like it? The experience?'

'I shall.'

'But what if you don't? I'm not part of it, you'll be on your own.'

'Everything's organised, Will.'

A warning steeliness had crept into her look and her voice, but Will, on the outside of three glasses of Italian red, was not about to be deterred.

'I don't mean that. What if you don't love the baby?'

'I'm not necessarily expecting to, right away.'

He stifled his shock at this. 'And your work – your life's always been so unbelievably bloody neat and tidy ...'

'It still will be. I'm not going to disappear under a miasma of breast pads and Nappisan.'

'And,' he persisted, 'it's for ever. You'll be a mother for ever.'

To his relief, she didn't smack this one back at him, but replied equably, 'Biologically, yes.'

'In every way.'

'Will.' Her voice became quiet, glacial. 'Children fly the nest. Can we please change the record?'

He knew it was only a matter of time before Stella began to make enquiries. To be fair, she wasn't generally nosy about his social life, but her sisterly antennae must have picked something up, because not that long after the Sovereign's Parade, when he was still seeing Viv, she'd asked:

'By the way, who was that you were talking to in the car park as we were leaving?'

'God, I don't know, Stel, the whole place was heaving. It could have been anyone.'

'Rather tall and chic. You were deep in conversation.'

'Probably Durbridge's sister.'

She'd let it go there, but when he arrived one Friday night a few weeks later, she presented him with a copy of the *Evening Standard*, folded back to the diary page.

'Hey, look what I found – isn't this your Viv?'

'She's not my anything,' he said. But it certainly was Viv, adorning the arm of a thuggishly handsome man in black tie.

'Looks as if she's on her way,' said Stella drily.

'Good luck to her. Mind if I have a bath?'

'Feel free. Want anything to eat?'

'No thanks. We'll – no thanks.'

When he came back out, she was lying full-length on the sofa with a bowl of Twiglets to hand on the floor next to her. The television with its slightly stippled picture – the indoor aerial was temperamental – was showing a hospital drama, but she craned to look at him.

'Like the tie. Who are you seeing tonight, then?'

'Just this woman I know.'

'Lucky her. Who is she?'

'No one in particular.'

'The dark lady of the car park?'

Will made a lightning judgement. Stella was no fool. Better to tell part of the truth and keep her happy than to be secretive and arouse curiosity.

'Okay, yes. It's her.'

'Durbridge's sister, huh?'

'No.'

'Surprise, surprise. If not her, then who?'

'She's called Jacqueline and I met her in Cairo when I was travelling.'

'Will!' Stella got up, shedding Twiglet crumbs, and turned off the television. 'That was ages ago. Is it serious, then?'

'It might be.' He was being literal, but Stella wasn't to know that.

'Don't toy with me, I'm your sister.'

'I mean it. I don't know. She's quite a bit older than me. There are various things ...'

'Married?'

'No!'

'Thank God for that.' She looked at him, offered the Twiglets, and when he declined, picked up another one. 'But you're keen.'

'She is different,' he conceded, 'in all sorts of ways.'

'All right.' She gave a sardonic smile. 'I'll leave you in peace.'

In the tiny hall he put on his jacket, and then came back in. The television was on again.

'Stella.' She rolled her head to look at him. 'I'd appreciate it if you didn't tell Ma about any of this. About Jacqueline.'

'I won't.'

'It's private. And I've no idea where it's going.'

'I told you, my lips are sealed.'

'Thanks.' He knew she meant it. But just as he opened the door, she said:

'Keep me posted, though, won't you?'

Chapter Thirteen

1999

Stella was ambivalent about spring. Naturally it was nice to see things bursting and budding, to have milder weather and lengthening days, but the season had the vices of its virtues. Her domestic deficiencies were shown up by the sunlight that fought its way through smeary windows, the house seemed dingy and cluttered, and outside the robust weeds responded to the warmth far more readily than the plants she'd set herself. And then there was the vague sense that her own sap should be rising; that she should not only be laying about the house with a will and a solution of all-purpose cleaning fluid, but applying a feather duster to herself and her life, sprucing up her person and her ideas, casting about for dalliance. (On that front there had been nothing in the offing since she had given Paul his marching orders, and how very pleasant it had been, this uneventful interlude.)

Over Christmas she had settled quite happily into her usual seasonal role – easy-going, indulgent, sensible, prepared to help out, pitch in and go with the flow at all times. She took it upon herself to smooth over (largely by ignoring it) any friction attendant on the family celebrations.

After a slightly sticky start (Evie had been to Raff's Christmas Eve service with Mick, which well-intentioned encounter had left her out of sorts), the day itself had gone off splendidly. Because of Raff's choir commitments, they'd convened at two, dined at three and played games before Raff had to go back. Evie had laid on a delicious and stylish spread, Owen (whom Stella had decided was a Good Thing) had successfully trodden the tricky path between host and boyfriend, Kate had adorned the gathering with her customary elegance and vim, and they succeeded in restricting Raff to one weak Buck's Fizz. Owen and Raff had even managed to fit in a slice of M&S Christmas cake. Stella had driven Kate home at half past seven. As always, she'd invited her mother to stay for the night, an invitation she knew would be declined.

'Such a kind thought, darling,' said Kate, 'but I'd rather sleep in my own bed if that's all right.'

On the doorstep of number 3 Rectory Court, Stella said: 'I'll pick you up tomorrow at ten thirty, then.'

'I shall be ready.' Kate had scanned her face; though they'd both managed to retain neutral expressions, she added, 'We shall enjoy it when we get there.'

They always said this, thought Stella on the way home, rather in the way people said of their building projects, 'It'll be nice when it's finished', or of a war, 'It'll be over by Christmas.' And it was, generally speaking, true, because the event itself was never as difficult as they feared it might be. Sheer numbers helped: with sixteen present at the vicarage, Horton Benslowe, if a particular person was getting on your wick you could always transfer your attention to another in the melee. Not, Stella reminded herself, that any of the Norfolk contingent were unpleasant – *au contraire*, they were hospitable, sociable, couth and, well, altogether exemplary. In fact, therein lay the problem. Their own smaller, less orthodox and less obviously successful branch of the family was in danger of being swamped by this cohort of clean-cut high-achievers. In order to relax, it was necessary to cultivate a mindset that said: 'Their ways are not our ways; this is not a competition.'

On this occasion, all would have been well if Uncle Joe hadn't uttered the 'W' word.

'So – no Will then, in the end?' he'd asked as they all sat down round two tables pushed together in the vicarage's cavernous dining room to consume Bee's baked ham with Cumberland sauce. Stella found it hard to imagine a more stupid and unnecessary question. For crying out loud, she wanted to shriek, they could all *see* Will wasn't there, and it was common knowledge that neither she, Evie nor Kate would want to discuss it! But in the interests of harmony, she bit her lip.

'No, no Will,' said Kate equably. 'He's a long way away.'

'Of course he is,' said Angela, looking daggers at her husband. 'What a silly question.'

'Just checking.'

'Did you think he might be hiding under the table or something?' asked the Reverend, a muscular Christian well known for his sense of humour.

They all laughed immoderately at this feeble joke and Joe had the grace to look sheepish. But on the drive home, Stella had no longer been able to contain herself.

'Uncle Joe just had to mention Will, didn't he?'

'It honestly doesn't matter.'

'Does he really not know the score by now?'

'He doesn't mean anything by it.'

Stella seethed and braked a little too vigorously at a roundabout, causing Kate to lay a gloved hand on the dashboard.

'Sorry.'

'Not your fault – they come so fast.'

Stella started off again. 'Where is he anyway? I mean what *is* he doing?'

'Working, I suppose.'

'His grandson is. Mum, it's Christmas!'

'Besides, he has his own life.'

'Which we know nothing about!'

'No less than he knows about ours, darling.'

'And whose fault is that?'

Kate was silent, her head turned slightly away, as if there were something she simply had to look out for in the rushing rural darkness. Stella inferred the reproach and knew it to be justified. Her mother felt at least as awkward and unhappy as she did about the whole thing, but had agonisingly divided loyalties. It was neither fair nor productive to take it out on her.

'I'm sorry, Ma.'

'Somebody has to think the best of him.'

'I know.'

'Or not the worst, anyway.'

'I know that.'

'And I know how unfair it must seem to you,' said Kate. 'When you're here all the time, being part of the family, seeing Raff, doing family occasions, ferrying me about hither and yon ...'

'I *like* doing those things.'

'I dare say, but we all know you'd do them anyway, and Will

124

doesn't, because he's off wherever he is and we all talk about him. The prodigal son.'

'Except he hasn't come back yet.'

'No indeed. Not yet.'

Stella accelerated as they joined the motorway, glancing over her shoulder at the oncoming traffic. She was unable to keep the sarcasm out of her voice. 'And will you kill the fatted calf if he does?'

'Current circumstances don't allow for that. I suppose I might rise to a little poached salmon.'

They managed a forgiving chuckle. At Rectory Court, Stella saw her mother into the flat.

'Ma – sorry again.'

'Don't be. I understand, really I do.' They exchanged a kiss with their usual respectful affection. 'We understand each other, I hope.'

Stella thought about this on the drive home. Did they really understand each other? Or did family fondness and loyalty mean they cut each other some slack? A real falling-out would be too wounding and inflict irreparable damage. She always had the niggling feeling that though she was here, and did her bit, which, as her mother had said, did not go unappreciated, Will would always be closer to Kate, no matter how many miles he put between them. Was it just the obvious – that a single daughter, like a prophet, was without honour in her own country? That the bond between mother and son was particular and powerful? That the absent child could always be given the benefit of the doubt and so always romanticised? Their mother was no fool, but some things bypassed common sense.

Will! screamed Stella's internal voice. *Will, damn you – get your lazy, undeserving arse in gear and haul it back here before I start to hate you!*

Ted Guise returned in the New Year, and they soldiered on. She fancied him, but the teaching was hard work because of the perceived humiliation of having to learn skills that most schoolchildren possessed. The inherent intimacy of the situation didn't help, sitting as they did side by side at the table, heads bowed over the page, engaged in the slow struggle for comprehension. Stella always trod a delicate line between drawing the client out in order to boost his confidence, and straying into the realms of the personal, which in Ted's case, in any other circumstances, she would have done without a second thought. After all, though the flow of information was one way, they were two adults meeting on equal terms. She was being paid for what she did, and need not expect gratitude, admiration or even liking to be part of the bargain. Friendly professionalism was the key to success but was increasingly hard to maintain. Stella's nature was pragmatic; bedding Ted Guise was far from out of the question, and if things did not improve might well be justified.

He remained – the phrase inevitably sprang to mind – a closed book. As the weeks went by and no breakthrough was forthcoming, she told herself it was time to bend the rules a little.

'I wonder, Ted,' she asked towards the end of a session in mid-February, 'would you like a glass of wine?' She saw the demur rise on his face. 'Or I've got beer? Proper ale, Roosters?'

'Go on then, I'll have a Roosters. Just a half.'

Her turn to demur – or pretend to; she wanted him to make this decision, just as he was going to make the next, and the one after that. 'I don't want to hold you up, Ted.'

'No, you're all right.'

She brought the drinks to the table where they'd been sitting; no point in overdoing the change of gear.

'Cheers … Thanks for joining me. It's been a long day. I'll gladly give you a refund for the last ten minutes.'

He was concentrating on pouring the beer, and didn't smile. 'No worries. Thanks.'

Don't ask questions, she thought. *Tell him something.*

'At Easter,' she said, 'I'm doing something really interesting. I'm going to the First World War battlefields in northern France.'

'Right.' He licked foam from his upper lip. 'How come? Holiday?'

'Not exactly. My great-nephew's going there on a school trip and I'm tagging along as a helper.' She considered it best not to mention the posh chorister angle for the time being.

'Have you been before?'

She shook her head. 'Never. But like so many people I have lots of family connections, and it's something I've always wanted to do.'

'My grandad was there,' he said. 'With the Norfolks, at Passchendaele.'

'Did he ever talk about it to you?'

Ted shook his head. 'He died, shrapnel and gas gangrene. My mum was only two.'

'How terrible. Such a young marriage.'

Ted pursed his lips. He seemed to want to talk but to be hampered by his lack of information. 'There was a programme on telly about it, back in the autumn. Disgusting what they went through.'

'Is he buried over there?'

'Must be.' If Ted had been a blushing man, she sensed he would have blushed. 'To tell you the truth, I've got no idea. Don't remember anyone saying ...' He shook his head. 'Bad, that, isn't it?'

She shrugged a shoulder, aligning herself with his ignorance, a general ignorance. 'I'm afraid they were a lost generation.'

'Still bad, though – that we don't know. My nan died twenty-five years ago, and she went a bit ...' He circled a finger near his temple. 'Even if we'd asked, she wouldn't have remembered.'

'Do you have any siblings?' For a hotly embarrassing moment she thought he might not understand the word, but he replied at once:

'I've got an older sister.'

'She might know.'

'Haven't seen her since Nan's funeral. Not a rift, or anything, she lives in Scotland with her husband and we've lost touch. Not a close family.' He gave her a dark, cross grin. 'You'll have guessed.'

'Families are complicated.'

'Yeah.'

'You know ...' She turned her glass thoughtfully between her palms. 'The War Graves Commission has comprehensive records and information on this sort of thing.'

'I've heard that.'

'If you were able to provide a few basic facts, they could tell you where your grandfather's buried.'

This time she'd spoken in the full knowledge of what she was doing. She sipped her wine peaceably, conscious of Ted's discomfort.

'I dunno ...'

'I could go and take a look while I'm over there,' she added casually. 'Check he's all right.'

'Maybe.'

'Let me know.'

She'd sown the seed, and now she would let it lie.

At the end of the following week's session, she didn't offer him a drink – unwise to make that kind of thing a habit – but he still seemed in no hurry to go. He closed his notebook and stood it on end in front of him, like a small shield. Looking down at it, he said: 'I've been thinking about those War Graves people you mentioned ...'

'Oh, yes.' She made sure to sound as if she'd just been reminded.

'I wouldn't mind finding out a bit more. But you know – there's the obvious problem.'

'Sure, of course.' She spoke casually, collecting together her things. 'If you like, we could make it a project. You bring your grandfather's details along – your sister might be able to help – and we could spend one of these sessions on the computer seeing what we could find out.'

'Be great. That all right with you?'

'More than all right. It would be fascinating.'

Two weeks later, he brought along a few laborious, atrociously spelled notes, and they sat in front of the computer until eight o'clock, after which she made spaghetti with sauce from a jar, and one thing led quite naturally to another.

'Should you be doing this?' he asked when she brought two glasses of red upstairs afterwards.

'Should you?'

'No reason why not.'

'Nor me.' She got comfortably back into bed and took a mouthful of wine. 'I'm free, white and old enough to know better.'

He gave a funny little grunt, the laugh of a man not accustomed to laugh often. 'You're my teacher.'

'Correction, I'm a tutor.'

'There's a difference?'

'I'm not in a position of responsibility with regard to you.

You're here of your own free will. I mean here' – she patted the bed – 'as well as downstairs.'

He pursed his lips. 'You're a cool customer, you know that?'

She didn't answer, though she was flattered. Cool was the last thing she was, in her own opinion. But she was never less than straightforward – perhaps that made a woman cool?

'Understand,' she said, smoothing the hairs on his forearm with her finger. 'You only got laid so I could get some results out of you.'

That little grunt again. 'I'll give you results, you cheeky mare ...'

'Not yet, I'll spill!'

After that, the lessons got easier. Ted's reading began, slowly but surely, to improve. And the sex – the most string-free she'd ever enjoyed – made a very nice coda to their evenings together.

Chapter Fourteen

1921

Thea Kingsley, sitting on the veranda of the farmhouse in the heat of the afternoon, knew the letter by heart, but that didn't stop her picking it up and starting to read it yet again. Every time she did so, it was in the hope that the familiar words would suddenly reveal some hitherto unseen message that would shed light on the circumstances of the child's – Kate's – imminent arrival. Kate, a five-year-old individual with a name, and a developing personality of which some part, however small, would be inherited from her mother. Thea put on her glasses and for the umpteenth time studied the fussy, forward-leaning hand for clues.

Thea, ma plus chère ...

The use of French had a distancing effect, as Dulcie had doubtless intended. But Thea was always sad that it should have come to this. Whatever their differences as girls growing up in Kent, they had at least understood one another in the rough and ready visceral way of siblings. Whereas now Dulcie had erected a barrier of affectation that was as impermeable as it was gauzy. The rest of the letter was in English, but the tone had been set.

... she needs parents and a home and oh, all sorts of things which I am not in a position to give. And anyway, I should be no good at it, as you well know! How ironic that I, who never wanted children, should be asking this of you, whose dearest wish was to have a family, but perhaps there is a sort of poetic justice in it?

No, thought Thea, there was no justice in the situation, though it suited Dulcie to say so. Just like her to tweak the story so that what was expedient for her became a favour granted to someone else: the casually fecund woman offering motherhood to her childless older sister.

> She has been well brought up by my excellent nanny Mlle Paul, in fact rather more strictly than I should have done, though I dare say my temper would have been shorter! She is not a faddy eater and her health is good ...

She might have been talking about a dog, thought Thea, all these reassurances about training, diet and fitness. But no – she checked as she always did, in baffled disbelief – nothing about what the little girl was actually *like*, not even her appearance. From that, Thea inferred that Kate was plain; Dulcie had always set great store by looks, and if her daughter were a beauty she would certainly have mentioned it. So in that department at least, the poor little thing was a disappointment to her mother.

> As you know, Andrea Avery will be accompanying Kate on the journey. Mlle Paul will do the packing, so between the two of them you can be sure everything will be in apple-pie order! I shall send a money order to cover anything you need to buy for the climate, etc. Sadly I'm not able to give you any advice, as I have no experience! But knowing you, chère soeur, you will have the gift, as you do in so many things!

The exclamation marks popped up like hot springs, evidence of Dulcie's urgent need to get the matter sorted out, and the child off her plate.

> I am so happy that Kate is finding a new home with you and Jack. What a perfect solution! I have asked Andrea to send me a wire from Mombasa (I can hardly believe it) when they have linked up with Jack, and please write as soon as you can to let me know that all is well. As you know, I shall stay right out of things as far as Kate is concerned. She does not know me and that, I'm sure you'll agree, is how it should stay. This is a fresh start for her, and for us all ...

After the usual protestations of affection (again in French), Dulcie signed off. Try as she might, much as she wished to, Thea could never find any expression conveying gratitude, let alone the simple words 'thank you', anywhere on the two closely packed pages. There had been no 'please' in the first letter, with its guff about a 'war orphan', the one to which Jack had taken upon himself to respond. This was the second phase, fizzy with elation and relief. Kate was 'finding a new home', the arrangement was a 'perfect solution' and 'a fresh start' for them all. Thea disliked herself for feeling piqued – she had agreed willingly to take on this responsibility, and a display of (probably insincere) thanks was neither expected nor called for. It was just that ... oh dear! She removed her specs and laid them on top of the letter. The conduct of this whole thing was so *typical* of Dulcie. It would have been nice to be appreciated in a proper, grown-up way, not patted on the head and told that she would have the 'gift' of child-rearing, as though that automatically went with being a married woman who lived on a farm in the middle of nowhere.

Dulcie had enclosed a tiny snapshot of Kate, 'three years old, in her *plus belle robe*!', as the caption on the back said. The photograph was already soft and creased with handling; Thea smoothed it with her fingers. The child's small figure was in danger of being swamped by the '*belle robe*', but her beetling brows beneath twin explosions of hair ribbon made it perfectly clear that this was a picture taken on sufferance.

Thea rubbed her eyes with a small moan of anxiety. Her bull terrier, Brutus, who had been lying at the far corner of the veranda, lurched to his feet and approached with a rolling gait. He grinned sympathetically at her touch, dangling a pink and black tongue between fearsome teeth.

Admit it, she told herself as she stroked the dog's bullet head. You are absolutely terrified.

In all her conflicting feelings about her sister and the child, Thea had almost forgotten about Andrea. This old acquaintance, married but even more defiantly independent than Dulcie, would already have had several weeks in which to get to know her charge. The two of them might have become the best of friends on the journey, might even be dreading the imminent separation of which she, Thea, would be the agent. Thea had always admired Andrea's spirit, her willingness to roll her sleeves up and do her bit. But – well actually there were no buts, simply the fact that Andrea was tough, in body and mind. She would probably have done very well out here in East Africa, though she would have been impatient to impose order, a characteristic guaranteed to produce intransigence in the locals. And of course she would always have been smart, her clothes clean and pressed and her hair under control. Thea pushed absently at a straying grip. Andrea would stay with them for two weeks – how on earth would they fill them?

She stood heavily and went down the veranda steps, the dog in attendance. The two of them made their way across the area designated front garden in the direction of what she had learned to call 'the road', though it was no more than a dirt track winding away through the bush. The development of the garden was a three-forward-two-back process; Jack had his work cut out with the farm, so she and the garden boy Tamo had taken it on with more enthusiasm than expertise. The soil in the valley was rich but stubborn stuff, prepared to accommodate only what suited it. Some plants flourished exponentially; others withered or were stillborn. Thea had learned to roll with the punches, and the garden was at last beginning to take shape.

She reached the white five-bar gate and leaned on it. Brutus flopped down in the small patch of shade cast by the right-hand post, eyes slitted, panting. The gate had been an early purchase, extravagant perhaps in view of the fact that at the time, the boundaries of the farm, let alone its entrance, were a matter of the purest conjecture, but it had a symbolic significance for Thea. The gleam of the gate to the traveller meant home; to the insider, security.

Now she could see the swirl of dust, still over a mile away, that signalled the return of the ox cart with its terrifying cargo. Heart thudding, she turned and ran back to the house to prepare herself.

When she heard the cart draw up outside, she came out, walking slowly and, she hoped, calmly, wearing a welcoming smile. Not wanting to rush things, she waited by the gate.

Jesus began to unload the luggage. Andrea waved to Thea, jumped down and came running over. She embraced her, chattering about the journey, saying how she hadn't changed. Thea couldn't take in her words. Over Andrea's shoulder she saw Jack, his movements slow and heavy, alight and beat the dust from his hat, before lifting the other passenger down. The small figure looked stiff as a doll.

Andrea, still talking, had her arm linked through Thea's, but now Thea slipped free and walked forward on her own. In spite of the heat she felt as though she were wading through water; her anxiety weighed her down, each step was an effort.

'Hello, Jack.'

Even as she kissed him, his hand dropped on to the child's shoulder.

'This is she,' he said.

Thea was no expert on children, but she could tell that the silence that followed was not one of shyness but of willed and implacable hostility.

It was going to be a long haul.

'Oh *dear*,' said Andrea, giving Thea a pained smile over her glass, 'I do feel like the proverbial rat leaving the sinking ship.'

'Nonsense.'

On the night before her friend's departure, Thea's response was dictated by politeness; still, she had rarely seen anyone appear less troubled by conscience. Andrea's voice and expression held something approaching glee. The evening had not gone well. Kate was in bed. Jack had retired hurt. Before going to his office, he had poured them all a Scotch, accepting no demurs – 'God knows, we need it!'

Thea, who usually disliked whisky, took another large mouthful before adding: 'Why on earth should you feel responsible?'

'I've delivered you up to your fate. Or, more accurately, delivered it up to you.'

'Destiny,' said Thea, 'would be a better word.'

'You are a saint, you know.'

'I do hope not.'

Andrea tapped the rim of her glass below her pursed mouth. 'That – what happened earlier – that can't be allowed to go on.'

'We shall all shake down given time. She's not much more than a baby; she doesn't know if she's coming or going.'

'But still. Poor Jack.' Andrea couldn't quite hide the curl of a smile. 'That was a proper bite!'

'He's been bitten by worse things.'

'I dare say. But for heaven's sake, Thea, you should have let him give her that smack. He's no bully, and if ever a smack was justified ... well! Sometimes you have to fight fire with fire.'

Thea took another swig. 'I don't agree.'

Andrea gave a short, gusty sigh of exasperation. 'I'm not advocating regular beating and shutting her in the coalhole! But God knows, you of all people must have seen animals – when a smart swipe is required, they deliver it.'

'Yes, but we're not animals.'

'Indeed we are, but we won't argue about it. One can think too hard about these things. We neither of us have any experience of child-rearing, or I wouldn't venture an opinion, but in this case it seems to me that acting on instinct might be best.'

'I am doing,' protested Thea. 'It's just that my instinct is different.'

Brave words, but she could feel herself losing ground. They both knew that her enlightened views would be put to the test from tomorrow, when she would be on her own with Kate. She added, lamely: 'It's her circumstances she hates, not us.'

Andrea pulled a face. 'Try telling your husband that. The child drew blood!'

Kate could not be persuaded to come out and say goodbye.

'Don't worry about it,' said Andrea. 'I'm not.'

'It's not bad manners.' Thea glanced fretfully in the direction of the house. 'She's upset. I'm afraid she's going to miss you.'

'Not for very long.'

Jesus brought out the cases. This time Jack was taking the car, and he and Jesus stowed the smaller one in the boot, and strapped the larger to the rear luggage rack. Thea thought of the long, hot, bumpy miles her husband and her friend were going to endure alone together. What would they talk about, without the inhibiting presence of an African and a small girl? To stifle the unwelcome speculation, she put her arms round Andrea.

'Thank you so much. You've been an absolute brick.'

'Nonsense, I've enjoyed every moment. In a masochistic sort

of way. And it's not over yet!' Andrea opened the passenger door. 'Good luck.'

Jack, always reserved in front of others, kissed Thea briefly on the cheek. His forearm bore a fresh wad of lint, held on with surgical tape. 'Bye. Look after yourself and our unwilling guest.'

'I will.' She stepped back, already waving to both of them as he got in the car. 'Safe journey! Write soon!'

The engine started up. Andrea, laughing, pointed, and her lips framed the words: 'You first!'

Back in the house, all was quiet. Kate was not in her room, though her bedspread was dented. Brutus, whom departures made anxious, was shut in Jack's study. Thea let him out and he trotted on to the veranda. Turning back into the hall, she caught a flash of fox-coloured hair and a whisk of skirt darting from the direction of the kitchen.

'Kate? Kate!'

Karanja appeared, wearing his most clownishly lugubrious expression.

'Mrs Kingsley, she wanted some cake.'

'That's all right. Did you give it to her?'

'Yes, *bibi*, I did.' He nodded in the direction she had gone and repeated glumly: 'She taken it.'

'She's still settling in,' said Thea by way of explanation, and apology, for she caught real injury in the cook's tone. 'You shouldn't make such nice cakes, Karanja.'

He grew an inch. 'Victoria sponge.'

'Lovely. I shall have some myself later. And Karanja, I suggest you put the cake tin where Missie Kate can't reach it.'

Mollified by their conspiracy, he withdrew to the kitchen. Thea remained in the hall, uncertain what she should do. Hearing a small sound, she turned to see Brutus sitting in the veranda doorway, gazing at her expectantly.

'Sorry to disappoint you, old chap,' she said. 'I don't have the answer to this one.'

Kate remembered these things as she so often did these days, in a state somewhere between sleep and waking. The television was on, a documentary programme about awful things that had been done to children, and who was to blame (apart from the actual perpetrators, of course, who were terrible, twisted and without hope). She had turned it on for a cookery programme some time before and then gone into this trance. She hated to think what she looked like – body slumped, head tilted, mouth open, legs sagging apart. Even with no one there to see, she was glad she was wearing trousers. She pulled herself together, smoothed her hair and clothes and switched off the sad, cruel faces on the box.

Probably, she thought, her own childhood situation would now be thought of as 'dysfunctional' or 'deprived'. All those years brought up by a French nanny and then shipped off to Africa with someone she didn't know to take up residence with strangers. What had been going on? It was a wonder she had bitten Jack only once. In today's terms she'd have been entitled to rebellion on a massive scale, counselling and God knows what else. What she remembered about that day – the day Andrea left, the day her new life truly began – was the tension in the house.

She had rushed back to her room with the piece of cake Karanja had given her, and sat breathlessly on the floor at the end of the bed, waiting for Thea to follow. She didn't, or not at once. There followed a long moment of silence, and then approaching footsteps and a soft tap on the door.

'Kate? Kate, are you there? May I come in?'

She didn't answer. The door opened. Thea entered and stood in the middle of the room, looking down at her from a little distance away, arms folded.

'How's the cake?' Kate turned her head away. 'That one's one of Karanja's specialities. Victoria sponge. You must go and tell him how nice it was when you take your plate back. He'd like that.'

Kate could feel tears beginning to ooze, and her face tightening and bulging with the need to cry. She kept her face averted. Thea crouched down by her and touched her shoulder; she twitched it away fiercely.

'We're so glad you're here, Kate. We love you, you know. Both of us.'

She didn't understand that. How could they possibly both love her? Or she them? Could that just magically happen? She wanted – oh, how she wanted – to love Thea, and even (she supposed) Jack. But they were not what she was used to. Their strangeness, and the strangeness of this place, was overwhelming. She had only herself and her will that was familiar. If she was going to love, she would need to be shown why, and how.

Thea put a hand on her cheek and tried gently to turn her head, risking – even now Kate remembered the urge – another bite. When she resisted, Thea stood up.

'I'm going out into the garden to do a few jobs.' She pointed at the open window. 'I'll be just out there. Come and see me when you've had your cake.' She seemed to hesitate. 'Kate … I expect you miss Andrea.'

This was so wide of the mark that she was obliged to shake her head; the tiniest movement possible, but it seemed to satisfy Thea.

'I'll leave you to it, then, for now. But please come out – I'd like your company.'

The door closed, and there was the sound of footsteps retreating along the corridor, then out on the veranda, followed a couple of minutes later by the scrape and scratch of someone working in the dry soil outside.

She had been violently disappointed; *désolée*, as Tanty might have said (she'd been under orders not to speak French to her charge, but occasionally a few words slipped out). Left holding both her bad manners and the cake, she regretted the one and no longer wanted the other. She was miserable and paralysed. Every so often the scratching in the garden would stop, and she imagined that Thea was looking up at her window, hoping – for what? Something Kate couldn't provide.

They had neither of them known what to do, Kate reflected. The room was getting dark and she moved her foot stiffly to press the floor switch of the state-of-the-art reading lamp (a *Daily Telegraph* special offer bought by Stella) that stooped gawkily over her chair. They'd both been completely at sea, but it must have been hell for poor Thea. After all, she had no children of her own, but was suddenly responsible for a child, and a jolly difficult one too! She probably felt it incumbent on her to have things on an even keel by the time of Jack's return from Nairobi. The two of them were in the most frightful double bind.

The dog had sensed their difficulty, or perhaps it was his natural canine herding instinct that made him diplomatic. When the scratching outside the window had moved a little further away, Kate had a couple of mouthfuls of cake and crept to the door. Opening it, she saw Brutus lying in the hall, head on paws, gazing out over the garden. This was unusual. In the short time she had been there, she had noticed that he was never far from Thea. There were other dogs – noisy but generally unseen – who lived in kennels some distance from the house, and who went out with Jack on the back of the truck, but Brutus was Thea's pet and her familiar.

He raised his head and stared at her, ears lowered appeasingly. Kate had no personal experience of dogs, but based on her observation of them in the park in Paris, she wasn't frightened. She patted her knee encouragingly, as she'd seen people do. His tail moved in reply.

'Brutus!' she whispered. 'Good dog!'

His head went down and the movement of his tail speeded up, the very picture of divided loyalties. Kate had a sudden sense of a small, silent battle being waged, even if she was the only person who recognised it as such. She went back into the bedroom and fetched the plate with its largely untouched piece of cake. This she placed on the floor near the door.

'Brutus – here, boy.'

Without hesitation he got to his feet and trotted over. She moved the plate inside the room and closed the door. The cake disappeared in a couple of mighty, gulping mouthfuls, and he began licking up the crumbs vigorously with a slurping, clinking noise. She snatched up the plate and put it on the dressing table. Peeping outside, she saw Thea kneeling on the ground by the scrubby flower border. There was a fork in her hand and a pile of weeds next to her on an open newspaper, but she wasn't actually doing anything, just sitting back on her heels, gazing into space.

Brutus, with no further incentive to stay, was back at the door, scratching apologetically. Kate patted his broad, flat skull and let him out. Seconds later she saw him amble across the dry grass to Thea, who jumped, startled, as he licked her face, and then put her arm round him and kissed him back. Never mind: Kate had won her small victory.

*

Recollecting that now, she shook her head. Victory? Over whom? Her shameless bribery of the dog was hardly something to be proud of. But she had exercised a smidgen of power, and Thea hadn't known about it. In the days between then and Jack's return, she'd refused to eat at mealtimes, then plundered the kitchen and shared her booty with Brutus, who must have put on several pounds. Karanja had been beside himself, Thea anxiously tolerant. But, she reminded herself, thinking about the awful television programme she'd been watching, she had been only five. And in the end Thea had resorted to bribery too.

Before her arrival, they'd put all sorts of things in her bedroom to make her feel at home: a lovely set of brush, comb and mirror with shiny blue backs, a cuddly round-eyed lion with a woollen mane, books, a drawing pad and a tin of coloured pencils, a model farm with comforting European cows, sheep and pigs, and some slippers with multicoloured pom-poms. Looking back, Kate was deeply touched at the thought of Thea and Jack ordering these treats, making long trips to special shops where such items were to be found (not an easy thing in the East Africa of the day), deciding what would be just right for her – asking advice, probably, because how could they know?

She had not allowed herself to use the hairbrush, to play with the animals, to draw with the crayons, or to wear the slippers, because to do so would have been tantamount to an admission: an admission that she was staying; that this was her new home and accepted as such. She would rather have died of boredom than admit any such thing. But when, one evening, Thea brought in the chicken alarm clock – ah, that was different!

'Can you tell the time?' Thea had asked, a question which Kate did not dignify with an answer. She did not know then that one of the benefits of her solitary upbringing with Tanty was that she was advanced for her years. She could read well, do sums, speak some French, and, yes, tell the time.

'I bet you can, so we thought you'd like this. You have to wind it up every evening, like this ...' Thea turned the small key with a crisp rattling sound. 'And to set the alarm you make the red needle move like this – see?' Kate watched from the corner of her eye. 'And then pull up this button on the top. When the bell rings and you want to turn it off, you push the button down.' Thea put the clock on the bedside table. 'There. I'll leave it with you. When the chicken stops pecking, it needs winding – easy to remember.'

How she had loved that clock! Its busy mechanical life, the cheerful clangour of its twin-tongued alarm, its sunny farmyard face with the black and red chicken endlessly pecking, and the cockerel whose neck stretched when the bell rang!

In the doorway, Thea said: 'See if you can set the bell for seven o'clock tomorrow, in time for breakfast.'

She had done so, and had eaten what was provided, conscious of Karanja's animated approval, and of Thea's, more restrained. The clock had remained with her for years, until the movement simply wore away and the chicken rocked forward on its beak for the last time.

Kate was beginning to feel cold around the legs and feet – the heating had gone off. Time to get moving and go to bed. She knew from experience that by the time she'd done all those bedtime chores – put tea things ready for the morning, turned on the electric blanket, taken bloody pills, sorted out tomorrow's clothes, done her teeth and face – she would have got a second wind and be ready to read for an hour or two. A short and interrupted sleep pattern was one of the properties of old age, but she didn't mind. If you didn't need the sleep, why should you want it? Less sleep meant more time to read and listen to the radio. During the day she was a devotee of Radio 4, but in the small hours she favoured its brash 'live' younger brother, with its phone-ins and interviews with colourful, garrulous people from alien worlds: sport, pop music and stand-up comedy. Thinking – fretting, actually – was one of the activities she did not welcome in place of sleep and the one which she engaged in the others to avoid, but tonight her thoughts ranged restlessly around, sniffing out something to settle on and worry.

Thea, though inexperienced, had been surprisingly intuitive. In her own estimation Kate herself had never been a natural parent. There had been too much that was unresolved at the beginning of her marriage, things she didn't understand about herself or other people. She scarcely understood them now. Her love for Lawrence had never been in doubt – well, almost never ... her eyes moved to his photograph – but there had always been that turbulence on the edge of her life, waves and currents caused by the storms of the past. It made her feel quite ill to reflect how terribly close she had come to leaving her family, that bitter winter in Berlin. She closed her eyes and gave a little gasp, putting both hands over her mouth to stifle it. What would her life have been if she had gone with Bill? Where would she be now? And with whom? There would be no Lawrence and Stella, and no Will; no Evie and no Raff; widowhood possibly – probably, given Bill's age and habits – but of a very different order, without the comforting bulwark of respectability and honour.

Joe, perhaps, would have forgiven her; he liked to think of his older sister as 'wild as a hawk'. Lawrence, *in absentia*? Probably.

Would she have forgiven herself? Then, for what she had done in the heat of youth, yes. Now, for what had almost happened, she knew she never would.

It was very hard now to recall or recreate those feelings which had impelled her to leave the house in Berlin that Christmas Eve just after the war. Those were far-off times and she'd been a very different person. Did Stella, she wondered, at such a young age, have any inkling of trouble? Surely not. But sometimes she looked at her daughter, her determinedly single life and (in Kate's view) rather ramshackle independence, and wondered what influences were at work there. Long ago, had some tiny seed of doubt worked its way under Stella's emotional skin and taken root?

The main thing, she told herself, was that people – her children especially – should be happy. That they should make whatever decisions they made with confidence and for good reasons. That was what she hoped, and prayed for when given an opportunity to do so. She was an agnostic, but an optimistic one.

She was more hurt than she let on by Will's continued absence and thoughtlessness. He was a middle-aged man, entitled to live and work wherever he liked in the world, but he lacked any sense of responsibility, or of what constituted good behaviour. Her firm line with Stella on the subject was intended to steady her daughter, who she knew nursed a far greater sense of injury, and with some justification. An objective observer would have seen in Stella a textbook example of the single grown-up daughter bearing the brunt of family care. Kate didn't care to see herself as a brunt, and Lord knew she tried hard not to be, but as a widowed mother in her eighties, that's what she was.

And then of course there was Raff, who saw more of his great-aunt and great-grandmother than he did of his grandfather. And precious little of his father, as far as Kate knew. He was a child of his time, accustomed to dispersed, fractured and protean families; still, she couldn't help wondering what view of adults and adult life he was forming.

She had sternly to remind herself that she too had been within a heartbeat of ruining several lives, not through mere negligence but of her own free will. Loyalty, duty and yes, love, had thank God prevented her from taking the fatal step. But the impulse had been there.

She turned the light off and the radio on and let the clatter of distant talk fill up the anxious spaces in her head. But not before she had asked herself when, and how, Will, her shining boy, had become a black sheep.

Chapter Fifteen
1999 (1982)

With Christmas safely out of the way, Will, cruising down the Nile in order to write one of his amusing pieces for *The Worldwide Traveller*, was in no rush to go back. These days England was only 'home' in the sense of being a base he was obliged to touch now and again. He felt no great attachment to it, and the trouble with his family, whom he did occasionally miss in a vague, non-specific way, was that in their orisons (if his school *Hamlet* served him) were all his sins remembered.

His mother, God bless her, had been unreservedly pleased to see him the last time, but that went with the territory. It was in the job description of mothers that they opened their arms and welcomed one home. Everyone else had an axe to grind, even if for form's sake they kept it behind their backs. Joe and Angela regarded him with kindly amusement, transparently relieved that he was not theirs. Stella, though he never doubted her affection, plainly disapproved of him and had the most trouble concealing the fact (though God knows her own life was hardly a shining example of order and achievement, teaching no-hopers how to read and shagging everything that caught her eye).

Evie and Raff – well, yes, they were a real source of regret ... But she had always been an organised girl, and since she'd got divorced from that Irish twat, she was like a train, working and being a model mother; the resemblance to Jacqueline was striking. Will was in awe of his daughter. Almost without him noticing she had moved from being his child to being somehow older than him. When he saw her these days he felt like an unwieldy and inept teenager; she was proof against his charm. Raff was a terrific chap, fabulous. A shit-hot singer and smart with it; the devil only knew where that came from. Will would have liked to have played some larger part in his grandson's life but had now accepted – as he was damn sure everyone else had – that he must make the most of being a peripatetic figure, benign and a little mysterious, perhaps the instigator of some necessary adventures when Raff passed eighteen. More like a godfather than a grandfather – Will reckoned he'd have made a good godfather; it was the role to which in his opinion he was best suited, but no one had asked him, and anyone in the running was now past the age of needing one.

He stared at the smooth water unrolling behind the cruise boat as it hummed upriver towards Luxor. No, his family managed very well – a great deal better in fact – without him. Things had settled down. It would be a pity to disturb them.

Will had forgotten how many times he'd been on a cruise ship since starting his current job, but he'd always remember the first: seventeen years ago, bound for the South Atlantic. Embarkation at Southampton, that had been something! Crowds cheering, bands playing, a blizzard of waving flags and hankies and tossed hats reminiscent of a send-off in the great days of empire. Vivid, even now. He'd thought Margaret Thatcher a peculiar woman, but at that moment she'd seemed like Britannia herself, trident at the ready, ruling the waves. This should have been the Queen, of course. It was Her Majesty's sovereign territory they were fighting for, but Thatcher stepped into the ring and made it all her own. He'd often tried to remind himself that he'd joined up to defend Queen and country, but the 'conflict' (splendid euphemism) had been entirely Thatcher's.

Some of them had waited a long time for this, and their blood was up. He'd been old compared to most, in his mid-thirties, while the youngest were still in their teens – but he'd felt like a kid from the moment the great adventure had begun on the square at Tidworth, with the order 'To the Falklands! Quick, March!' And when the ship pulled away from the quay, it was impossible not to be infected by the young lads' simple excitement. They were going to give the Argies a lesson they wouldn't forget, and the whole of England was behind them!

But Jesus Christ – it was a long way.

There was that old song, *We joined the navy to see the world,*

And what did we see? We saw the sea ... And they hadn't even joined the bloody navy.

Eight thousand miles and all of it ocean, unless you counted the micro-dot of Ascension Island, which most of them had never heard of before. Bloody water, every heaving, droning, lurching, pitching knot of it. On and on they butted, through time zones and seasons and the equator, with only seagulls, flying fish and the occasional pod of whales for company.

It was great to begin with; morale was high after the send-off, and there was the novelty of being on board a big ship, which most of the younger men hadn't experienced before. Will, a major then, was a popular officer, but that wasn't always to his advantage. Popularity and the gaining of it came easily to him, but he'd come to recognise that others – his colleagues and superiors, certainly his family – saw it as a liability. He'd learned the hard way that the English didn't care for charm; it was a suspect quality. So he had to be careful, in dealing with the men, not to fall into the trap of trying to be their mate. Respect was more important than popularity in one who might well be responsible for giving orders of the harshest kind and expecting unquestioning obedience. He particularly bore in mind something the old boy on the dais had said in his speech at that long-ago Sovereign's Parade:

'If you do your job as you have been taught to do, and as all of us here know you can, your soldiers will give you their loyalty, their courage and, *in extremis*, their all.'

That had been the moment when a hot spot ran along the ranks of brand-new officers; when they all realised they were no longer a bunch of recruits to be bawled out and bullied into shape by NCOs who used 'sir' as if it were a term of opprobrium. From now on they were officers, with the power, and the responsibility, to demand a man's all. For many of them, Will included, that prospect was far more daunting than the risking of their own lives. To sacrifice something that was yours to sacrifice was one thing; to ask other, usually younger men to do the same was of another order entirely. For that, a different kind of courage was required; one that embraced clear-sightedness, confidence and humility, none of which he was sure he possessed.

He'd brought books with him for the voyage – as a symbol

of normality as much as anything; he didn't anticipate having much time to read. At Sandhurst, he'd enjoyed the course on international relations and written an essay the quality of which had surprised everyone, including himself. Visiting his mother on his twenty-four-hour pre-embarkation leave, he'd found a book about ancient explorations, his father's presumably, which included a few scattered paragraphs on the Falklands. The information he gleaned wasn't particularly encouraging. A passenger on the vessel of one Captain John Davis in 1592 had written in his diary:

> The 14th wee were driven in among certain Isles never before discovered … lying fiftie leagues or better from the shoare, in which place unlesse it had pleased God of his wonderful mercie to have ceased the wind, wee must of necessitie have perished.

A pretty typical example, Will discovered, of the kind of thing the early travellers, and most travellers since, had to say on the subject. The islands were generally characterised as bleak, remote, wet, foggy, freezing and blasted by Antarctic winds for eight months of the year. But the penguins liked them; penguins were often mentioned. Poor bloody penguins, he thought. Hope they're ready for this.

He tried to fill the men in on what to expect as best he could without depressing them unduly. 'Those of you from the north are going to feel right at home,' he told them. 'And for the rest of us, it won't be that different from the average British August bank holiday.'

They'd sniggered dutifully. They weren't stupid, they got the idea: the Falklands were inhospitable long before the Argentinians got there; the only mystery was why the fuck they should have wanted them back in the first place, and why the fuck the British would want to disagree.

The voyage out had three distinct phases: euphoria, which lasted till the Bay of Biscay, when seasickness put an abrupt stop to it; boredom when the seasickness subsided (for most – a few never got over it); and gradually increasing tension and trepidation after the halfway point of Ascension Island as they closed on their objective.

If he'd thought to disabuse his men of any illusions they might have about the islands, Will's own ideas and those of many of his fellow officers were put right a good deal less politely in successive briefings. The notion that there would be provisions for the asking and a landscape affording a certain amount of natural cover was quickly dispelled by the CO.

Briefings took place in the ballroom. Like everywhere else on board, the room had been stripped of fittings and soft furnishings and made serviceable, but its original identity was there in the sprung floor, the polished oak trims and the pleasant ambience of a place designed for leisure. Even the acoustics were benign, softening the CO's crisp delivery. He was a cool customer and a brainy one, good at chess; admired more than liked.

'Let me be clear. Every ounce of food and fresh water will be brought ashore by us – by the landing force. Outside Stanley, the islands have a scattered population, and currently a frightened one. It's not an agricultural economy, apart from sheep. Flowing with milk, honey and hospitality it ain't. A cup of tea is the most we can reasonably expect, and that only if we're doing our job efficiently and without fuss, with due regard for the sensibilities of the locals. Don't get the idea we'll automatically be seen as conquering heroes; that remains to be proved. The terrain's rough and open, no cover to speak of. If you've been on Dartmoor in winter you'll have the idea, but you'll need to multiply that by ten. Cover's here ...' He pointed directly to the ground at his feet. 'Everywhere above that line is the danger zone. Be under no illusion: the Argentine air force is technically advanced, well trained and highly motivated. We'll be sitting ducks.'

'Any good news, sir?' This got a muted chuckle.

'The good news, Major Drake, is that we're going to do what we've been trained for. And if we do it properly, we have every chance of success.'

Even that opportunity, they were warned, would not be granted until the naval battle had been won. There was no question of a landing until the surrounding seas were safe. So it appeared there would be strategic hanging about in mountainous waves. Will seemed to recall that some wag had likened war to film-making – days of tedium broken by occasional short bursts of excitement. It looked as if he'd been dead right; and also as if the senior service, so-called, might be in a position to take all the glory this show had to offer.

The war artist was at that briefing – over in the corner, sketching away. The only woman among three thousand men on board, quiet and small, always busy and focused in her workmanlike clothes. She never tried to be one of the lads, she was too dignified to play that card; her remarkable self-possession must surely have been a factor in her selection. The only change to her outfit of black trousers, biker boots and khaki sweater or parka came at dinner, when she topped the black pants with one of two coloured jackets: a pillar-box red with country-singer fringing, or a battered leather number in kingfisher blue, both of them a kind of Women's Lib take on mess kit. Will liked her – not that he knew her. Something about her reminded him of his sister – that air of slightly pig-headed independence.

He thought of Stella, but she was not one of those he wrote to. Those numbered just two – his mother and his daughter. Kate would pass on information to the family, and Evie (he hoped) would do the same with Jacqueline. The letters to his mother were easy to write; he'd been doing it all his life, and anyway he knew her to be an appreciative audience. In the case of Evie, it was trickier. The challenge was to find the right tone, which did not appear to take intimacy for granted, but which still conveyed the appropriate degree of parental love and interest on his part. He did certainly love her, but he had not showed enough interest over the years, he knew that. Jacqueline's attitude had conveyed not-wanted-on-voyage and he'd lazily taken advantage.

Evie was currently at boarding school in Somerset, an establishment selected by Jacqueline for having the highest academic standards and levels of Oxbridge entrance. He tried to keep his letters light; the poor girl had quite enough pressure coming from the other side. His second letter of the voyage was pretty typical:

My darling girl,

Your briny correspondent here, reporting on life on the ocean wave. The bad news is that most of the ship is hunched over the heads (not as complicated as it sounds; that's nautical for loos), revisiting its last meal. Huge seas for the past few days, and seasickness is the order of the day. I'm happy to say I haven't thrown up once and still have a disgustingly hearty appetite, annoying my shipmates by suggesting that bacon and eggs would do them the world of good.

How's things with you at St Dyspepsia's? (*It amused him, and he hoped his daughter, to make up different facetious names for the school.*) Any matches coming up? How is the play? Any dances with the lotharios of St Hayrick's? How are the smoking lessons coming along – no, forget that. Are you a mod or a rocker? Which Beatle is top in your set? (*References to his own teenage years were another affectation.*)

This is a very strange life we're leading on board. Imagine a whopping great hotel stripped of all its decorations and everything that made it comfortable, call it a barracks, load it with double the number (at least!) of passengers it would normally carry, plus mountains of ungainly equipment for seeing off the enemy in freezing conditions, and then call 'Carry on, men!' and shove it out to sea. We have to do drill, clean kit, attend briefings and keep fit just as we would on a base on land. Firing practice, can you imagine that below decks – deafening! It would be funny – it actually is sometimes. But then we remember we have a pretty important job to do when we get there and that wipes the silly smiles off our faces, I can tell you.

But we're all optimistic and ready for anything, so the atmosphere is good on board. At times it's how I imagine Butlins: all jolly bracing activity and home-made entertainment (I've been in a couple of those myself). Lots of parties, usually hosted by our naval chums. It's probably a bit like you and the other girls at Queen Amnesia's – banged up but kept busy and reasonably happy. The company your end is probably more couth, and certainly easier on the eye, but I wager our food's better. It's in a boarding school's job description to provide the most loathsome food possible so that pupils go out into the world able to eat anything it throws at them. One of the things that made the empire great, don't you know.

What are you reading? Apart from some research and the 5 Infantry Brigade QE2 news sheet (a barrel of laughs), I'm on the new Freddie Forsyth, and the *Oxford Book of Comic Verse*. Never say your father doesn't have wide-ranging cultural tastes.

I think of you a lot, Evie, and wish I could see you. That will be the first thing I do when we get back. Which won't be long. Till then, play up and play the game, be reasonably good and take care of yourself.

Lots and lots of love from your seafaring

Daddy xxx

He stuck with 'Daddy' instead of the more contemporary and democratic 'Dad' because Evie herself still used it. He did hope they weren't going round in polite circles, employing a usage that was causing his daughter intense embarrassment. She was at that sort of age. He might try 'Dad' some time and see if it provoked any comment, adverse or otherwise. That was almost certainly the kind of thing that those who saw more of their offspring would know instinctively.

His domestic circumstances, his 'private life', whatever you wanted to call it, set him apart from his colleagues. As far as they knew, he was a childless bachelor, which was unusual enough at his age and level. He was a good bloke and a good officer, but there was this little hint of mystery; he sensed their amiable curiosity but he had no intention of satisfying it. They would have been surprised – very surprised – had they known the facts. That he had a teenage daughter born out of wedlock to an older woman he'd met in a hotel bar in Cairo and who had wanted neither an abortion nor marriage; for his part he'd have welcomed the abortion, at the time, but had also not wanted marriage. They'd reached an accommodation. Jacqueline ran the show and he pitched in with such money (Evie would never want for shoes) and parental support as he was able and equipped to give. He was prepared to admit that wasn't much, but then Jacqueline was so formidable she often made him feel like a child, too. He might be a leader of men in the world's eyes, but to Jacqueline he was still the ardent, inexperienced, scruffy young man she'd picked up in the bar of the Bellingham. She was high-powered, often on the television and radio and reviewing books in the Sundays; she had written her own book, *The Romantics and the Romantic Delusion* (that said it all, really), which had been well received and had obviously done okay because it was still out there. On top of all that, she was always jetting off to symposia and conferences worldwide to make her unique contribution. Jacqueline was, he conceded, a star in her field.

She didn't need Will, that much was plain; she allowed him to do his bit because it was good for him, and good for Evie to know that he was doing it. Unfortunately (he recognised this), he had chosen to interpret this as permission to stand at ease ... and then to pretty much fall out. Jacqueline didn't just cope, she managed magnificently. Evie, the last time he'd looked, was flourishing – beautiful, brainy, personable. All that was required of Will was to service the standing order and dip in and out of Evie's life at regular intervals.

He sometimes wondered what she said about him at school – to Flick, and Rosie and Cath and the rest of the coterie whose names popped up all the time. Jacqueline had no qualms about the situation – she would have been frank, and encouraged Evie to be the same. But he couldn't help feeling – though God knew he was no expert – that it would be hard to come completely clean with one's posh boarding school friends, even in this spectacularly hard-boiled decade. He suspected that she had either woven some vague romantic fantasy about him, or depicted him as a ne'er-do-well whom she had to entertain for her mother's sake. Of the two, he knew which he preferred. And certainly the friends had not looked askance on the couple of occasions when he'd gone to take her out from school.

He was careful. The only photograph he carried with him was of his parents on their wedding day. Now *they'd* had something rare. Pity they hadn't passed it on. Maybe their capacity for enduring love was like a recessive gene, and had skipped a generation – him and Stella – to Evie. It would be nice to think so. He hoped she didn't think too badly of him or her mother, though it was unlikely she was critical of Jacqueline, the modern woman par excellence.

After Ascension Island, everything changed. That was the point from which the MoD had decreed that everyone should regard themselves as 'on active service'. Post, which had been pretty regular till then, became erratic. He missed Evie's brief letters; they made him want to cry, with their casual touch, light as a butterfly but with the power to sting.

Dear Daddy,

Lovely to hear from you. I'm glad you're having fun as well as going off to war, but of course I'd rather you weren't doing the latter. Flick's father is on Galahad so we exchange notes, though of course he's a bit further down than you. I find it very hard to imagine the scene with all of you marching about and waving your weaponry in the bars and lounges. Perhaps you could take a few snaps, or is that against regulations?

Yes, we had the first tennis match of the season. Bea and I are third couple, second team, but actually we did better than the first couple, which was pretty impressive! They must have been feeling the pressure. The play is Twelfth Night and I am Feste. No dance till the end of term, none of us really look forward to it as it will be horrendous. The boys are immature and the music's pathetic. Most of my reading is set books, though I did enjoy Fear of Flying, which Mum gave me (don't try it, please!). We're going to Athens at half-term. I am absolutely dreading telling her I don't want to go to university, she's going to go ape. You take care of yourself too.

Lots of love,

Evie x

He'd had a brief, guilty, hat-in-the-air moment when he read the sentence about not wanting to go to university. That was a long way off, but he was sure the topic would have been raised. It was quite gratifying to think of Evie rattling her mother's cage a bit, though he couldn't imagine Jacqueline going 'ape', as she put it. He hoped Evie stuck to her guns, Jacqueline was a tough customer with firm ideas on education, especially for women. As well, he reflected wistfully, as being the most historic lay north of Suez.

That was to be the last letter from her for some time, and after reading it he had the usual mixed feelings. But on balance, the evidence of his daughter's independence of mind was cheering, and he set off with a jaunty step for weapons drill in the Queen's Room with its Ginger Rogers staircase. En route he saw the Gurkhas out on deck, running flat out and blindfolded to the lifeboats against the time when the ship, stricken, would be without lights and full of smoke. Great little guys and tough as whipcord. Another of their regular exercises was to jump into the freezing outdoor pool in full kit. His father had been right – it felt bloody good to have them on your side.

There were worse things, he reflected happily, than doing the job you loved, with the nation's approval, on a luxury liner in the centre of one of the largest oceans on earth. No one could get at you.

An Egyptian waiter in a blue and white striped *jelaba* appeared at his side.

'Sir, may I get you a drink?' His voice was soft as honey.

'You know, I would adore a drink,' said Will, as though the thought had just occurred to him. 'I'll have a Manhattan.'

Chapter Sixteen
1999

Mick was incandescent.

'What the hell do you mean, he's on tour? He was going to spend time with me, Evie! We agreed, you expressly said—'

Evie, moving hastily away from the other coffee drinkers, transferred her phone to the other ear. 'Don't yell, Mick. I'm at a conference.'

'I don't give a tinker's fuck where you are!' Mick lowered his voice and added unnecessarily, 'I'm furious about this, Evie.'

'I'm sorry, but since nothing had actually been arranged—'

'What's that? I remember the conversation.'

She was getting angry back now. 'What *I* remember is that you suggested he spend a few days with you at Easter, and said you'd call me about it, but didn't. The ball was in your court.' She held the phone a little distance from her ear for a moment.

'... got a nerve! It takes two to come to an arrangement, and you knew fine well this was what I wanted. When this – this tour was mooted, why didn't you get in touch then, say to the school, Raff may be going to his father that week, I need to check? Why didn't you? Hm?'

'It was ages since we had that conversation, and I hadn't heard from you. And as *you* know "fine well"' – she parodied his lapse into Irishness – 'the tour isn't some optional jolly, it's a professional fixture, one of many that have been in the diary for months. We have a talented son, Mick, and this is the price we pay.'

She waited. Louise, one of the other delegates from her branch, was waving at her; they were going back for the next session. Evie held up her hand and mouthed, 'Just coming!'

'I know that, I know …' She heard his rage starting to ebb, calmed by pride and her diplomatic use of 'we'. 'I'm just so bloody disappointed, Evie.'

'I'm sorry. I really am. But to be honest, our crossed wires wouldn't have made much difference to the outcome. Raff's a senior chorister; this is a three-line whip for him.'

'I realise that. It would still have been nice to be in the loop.'

Evie closed her eyes, forbearing to remind him, now that he'd cooled down, that he could without bloodshed have made the effort to be in that loop. 'Look, Mick, I have to go, but let's talk when I get back and arrange something.' She allowed a careful laugh into her voice. 'Really arrange something – with diaries.'

'Sure, yes, let's do that.'

'I'll call in a few days. Bye, Mick.'

'Bye.'

She switched off the phone and ran along the corridor to the Harding Room. Louise swept her folder off the seat next to her.

'Catch your breath.' She handed Evie the folder. 'Nothing's happened yet.'

'Thanks.'

'All well?'

Evie rocked a hand, bobbed her head. 'Work in progress.'

Somewhere along the line Mick's emotional thermostat had gone haywire. There was no denying his devotion to his son, but he was still single and driven and seemed these days to be incapable of holding steady. There was nothing unusual in this latest over-reaction. She could have reminded him about the tour, had even considered it briefly, but then she'd thought sod it, let *him* follow through and do the planning, as she had to do with everything else the whole bloody time. He was never less than keen to see Raff, and was utterly reliable on short-term arrangements, but anything left open was up to her to fix and finalise. That was part of the deal, the down side of the contact arrangements that were not the result of some family judge's decision but of their own sweat-, blood- and tear-stained negotiations. Just this once she'd dug her heels in and not picked up the phone. Why should it all be down to her? Time he shaped up.

In Owen's universe, Mick might not have existed. He never mentioned him and in turn did not expect to be consulted. When, in the early days of their relationship, Evie had done so, she quickly recognised that this was a no-go area. She respected, and even approved of Owen's position, but it would have been nice sometimes when Mick was kicking off to be able to dump her resentment, to have some sympathy close to home.

That was never going to happen, because Owen's thermostat, unlike Mick's, was in perfect working order – correctly set and balanced. What was that prayer? *Give me the serenity to accept the things I cannot change, the courage to change the things I can, and the wisdom to know the difference.*

Owen had the courage (in his job on the mean streets of town and in his gentle persistence with Raff), and also the wisdom (he recognised when to leave well alone); there was no way he was stepping into the arena of her previous relationship, an arena that was of their making, hers and Mick's, and in which as far as he was concerned the two of them were welcome to scrap twenty-four seven provided no real injury was done to her or to Raff. Owen had made stability sexy.

After lunch and a quick woman-to-woman debrief with Louise, she went out into the garden and called him. He was on nights this week and would be sleeping, but he'd either pick up or he wouldn't, and if he did, he'd be nothing but chuffed to hear from her. There was a handset next to the bed and he answered after only a couple of rings.

'Yeah?'

'It's me.'

'Fantastic, how you doing, babes?'

'I'm good, but I'm missing you.'

'Glad to hear it.' She heard him heaving about, dragging the pillows and sitting up. Lighting a cigarette, possibly, but she'd let that go. 'How's the conference?'

'Useful. Interesting, and quite fun as a matter of fact. You know, not too demanding, nice place, nice people.'

Because it wasn't long since she'd spoken to Mick, she could almost hear him saying 'Not too nice, I hope', but Owen made no such comment.

'Where are you at the moment?'

'In the garden. We've just had lunch. It's lovely out here, quite warm ...' She began to walk across the lawn. 'They've left the grass long under the trees where the daffodils are growing, and there's blossom out, white and pink. It's a shame we have to sit indoors all afternoon.'

'I think it's sunny here too ...' His voice faded as he peered towards the window with its striped Roman blind. 'But I won't be seeing much of it either. Heard anything from Raff?'

'I've had a couple of texts, one from the ferry and one from the other side. Nothing to say except that he was alive and kicking and having a wicked time. Prompted by Stella, probably, bless her. She hasn't called yet, but she told me she would and that no news would be good news. Let's face it, they're working, and they're pretty intensively supervised when they're not.'

She heard the drag and exhalation of Owen's smoke.

'I'm looking forward to our couple of free days.'

'Me too. We ought to think of something nice to do.'

'I already have.'

'I mean apart from that. So we don't wind up going to Ikea or doing paperwork.'

'No problem. You'd be amazed how easily I can resist Ikea.'

'Or just loafing about.'

'Loafing about, bloody hell no.' He laughed, and then coughed. 'Can't have that. Don't worry. We'll have ourselves an outing.'

'I'll call again tomorrow, about now – you don't mind me waking you up, I take it.'

'Any time, babes. Any time. As it happens, you've woken me up good and proper now. Shame you're not here to enjoy it.'

Walking back over the grass, she directed her thoughts briefly – a little dutifully – to Raff, and his first concert, before letting them return to the prospect of home, and Owen.

Dinner was informal that night, pasta and ice cream accompanied by a 'pub quiz'. The wine flowed, and after the *frutti di bosca* Evie told Louise she was going to slip away.

'What do you mean? We're winning.'

'Then you definitely don't need me.'

'Yes we do, you're our current affairs expert.'

Dave, warmly flirtatious, the team's ladies' man, leaned in from the other side. 'Don't tell me she's going to bed?'

'Yes, tell her not to.'

'I wouldn't dare ... No – Evie! Don't go!'

She made a kissy mouth. 'I've got calls to make. Night, all. I'll see you at breakfast.'

She walked round the outside of the building to the covered walkway – a sort of cloister referred to in the brochure as The Orangery – and sat down in one of the steamer chairs. The spring night was chilly out here in the Fens, the sky teeming with beautiful stars. At half past nine it was perfectly possible that Stella had gone to bed after a gruelling day with the boys, but she dialled the hotel number anyway.

'Have I disturbed you?'

'Evie, hi there. Only dozing. I got your text.'

'I've been so thinking about you guys. On a scale of one to ten, just how shattered are you?'

'Oh golly, let's see – about nought point five? It's a doddle, honestly.'

'Really?' Evie was incredulous. 'The last time I went with them, we lost one of the little toerags in Exeter city centre. It was a complete nightmare.'

'Nothing like that at all. No wrecks and nobody drownded. And their singing is sublime, of course, so lots of added value.'

'Yes. I'm sorry to be missing that. What does tomorrow hold?'

'I have the itinerary here, I shall tell you ... Here we are. Arras. Reception at the Mairie, concert at the church in the evening.'

'What's your hotel like?'

'This one's kind of fun. Character rather than luxe, but then I don't want luxe.'

Evie laughed. 'Stella, you're a gem, do you know that?'

'I'm happy as a sandboy, I promise. And everyone's so nice. They're being very kind to me for some reason; they probably sense my lack of experience. I've been allotted some free time and I can take a whole day off on Wednesday if I want while they all go to Bayeux. I thought I might hire a car and explore.'

'What a good idea.'

'I've always wanted to visit this part of France, the war graves and so on. I shall pootle about and soak up the atmosphere.'

'As long as you don't get too depressed.'

'Steady on. Depressed? Moi? I don't, and anyway I'm on holiday.'

'Okay, if you say so. Where's Raff at the moment?'

'Watching television or playing on his Game Boy, I imagine. They're supposed to be asleep, but one has to be realistic.'

'I expect you're right. Just give him my love, will you?'

'I shall go and do it right now.'

'There's no rush, Stella, tomorrow's fine.'

'I know, but as one of the custodians of the flame, it will give me an opportunity to be firm about lights out. They have their performances to think of.'

'Good point. You tell them.'

'Don't worry about a thing, it's all going swimmingly and we're having a beezer time.'

'Night, Stella, and thank you *so* much.'

'Night-night. Pleasure.'

Evie put the phone down. Her mind's eye drifted fondly to Stella, and to Raff. Finally to Owen, which was where it stayed.

Thirty-six hours later, she got back as Owen was leaving for his shift. His embrace lifted her off her feet.

'Crap timing, as usual,' he said, coming up for air.

'I don't have to rush tomorrow. I'll be lying there when you come home, all warm and receptive under the duvet.'

'Reckon a fry-up will be out of the question?'

'Not entirely.'

'What a woman ... Better shoot. There's a message from your gran on the blower.'

Evie unpacked, changed and put a load in the washing machine before picking up the messages: a couple from the electrician about coming to put a timer on the outside light, one from a friend asking if she wanted to go the cinema, and the one from Kate.

'Evie darling, I know you're away, but when you're there, could you call me at some convenient moment? I know how busy you are and it's not urgent, but I'd really welcome your advice on a delicate matter.'

Evie rang at once. 'Gran, it's me. How are you?'

'Darling, thank you so much. You must scarcely have drawn breath.'

'No problem.'

'Stella's away too, or I'd have asked her.'

'Asked her what?'

'I've had the most extraordinary letter. I don't know what to make of it.'

Evie curled her legs up next to her on the sofa. 'Tell me.'

'Well!' She sensed that her grandmother would be curling her own legs up if stiffness allowed. 'I suppose it's slightly sinister, in a way. It purports to be from someone with something to tell me. But I've never heard of this person. Should I burn it, do you think?'

'No! No, Gran, don't do that. Not without showing it to someone else.'

'That's what I thought. I don't want to bother Joe, he'll only get in a tizz. Perhaps when you have a moment you could give me your opinion.'

Evie weighed up the pros and cons, but her curiosity was aroused.

'I'll have a sandwich and be with you in about half an hour.'

Kate replaced the phone. She was not, as Evie had imagined, sitting, but standing in the middle of her living room, with the letter in her hand. She wondered if she should be frightened or, at the very least, perturbed. But the truth was, she felt energised. Into her routine old lady's existence there had dropped this strange thing, like a message in a bottle or a bird that had flown down the chimney. The piece of paper in her hand seemed alive; waves of mysterious possibilities radiated from it. She was trembling, certainly, but with excitement rather than fear.

She answered the door with the letter still in her hand. Evie's kiss was perfunctory.

'Is that it?'

'Yes.'

'May I?'

'Of course.'

Evie took the letter and was already reading avidly as she sat down on the brocaded carriage chair in the corner. It was so rarely used that Kate had got in the habit of thinking of it as ornamental; to see her granddaughter sitting there in jeans and boots added to her slightly heady sense of dislocation.

'The signature's hard to read,' she said. 'But it doesn't ring any bells. Edith something?'

Evie didn't answer. It wasn't just the signature that took some deciphering; the handwriting was mad: fine and gawky and moving first forward and then back as if the writer kept moving the paper. Plus, whoever it was had been using a pen that was running out of ink. The paper was nice, though – thick, white and slightly textured; she rubbed it between her fingers, half expecting it to have a scent, something subtle and classy.

'The envelope was like that too,' said Kate, telepathic as ever.

'Hang on.'

'A drink? Why don't I get us both one?'

The letter was quite short – two thirds of one side and about halfway down the other. Evie was starting to get the hang of the writing; she went back to the beginning. The page was headed by an address, and the day before yesterday's date. The address was perfectly clear: 11 *Haig Mansions, Mansfield Avenue, London NW1*, and a two-oh-seven phone number.

Dear Mrs Drake (*she read*),

I hope you'll forgive me for writing like this out of the blue. We don't know each other, though I do know who you are, so to speak. The point is that I have in my possession some documents, left to me by an old friend, which contain information about you and your family. I am sure you would like to have them, and I in my turn would like to hand them over in person rather than entrust them to the Royal Mail. Perhaps you would care to ring me at the above address and we could arrange to meet? Or of course you could drop me a line giving a time and place – my diary is not that full! I'm afraid I'm a duffer about technology, and don't have a mobile phone or a computer – my secretary does, but this is a personal letter.

This reads rather like a bad spy novel, for which many apologies! I very much look forward to hearing from you.

Kind regards

And then the signature, which certainly might have been Edith or Erica something, but which she couldn't decipher.

Kate gave Evie her glass and sat down on the sofa, leaning forward with her own glass between both hands. Her hazel eyes looked green, large and bright.

'So. What do you think?'

'Hard to say, isn't it? Whether or not it's Edith, I do think it's a woman.'

'That's what I reckoned, too.'

'And quite old – wouldn't you say? No offence, Gran.'

'None taken. The style, you're right. I don't think I'd write a letter like that, but a certain sort of elderly party would.'

Evie looked back at the letter. 'She's enjoying it all, isn't she? Being the source of a little mystery.'

'I thought so. That's the aspect I don't care for – the *gleefulness*. The sense of power.'

'I wonder,' said Evie, unable to prevent a grin, 'what on earth she's on about.'

Kate held out her hand for the letter, and put her glasses on to examine it again, as if, subjected to enough scrutiny, it would yield up its secrets. She looked up, peering at Kate over the top of the glasses.

'What do you think I should do, darling?'

'I think you should ring up and make a date.'

'Really?' Kate sounded thrilled. 'You do?'

'And say you have to come at a weekend and you'll be bringing your granddaughter with you.'

'Or maybe not tell her that? It might look as if we were suspicious.'

'Which we are. Aren't we? I am.'

'Intrigued, perhaps. Yes, intrigued. But it would be lovely to have your company.'

'Why don't you do it now? While I'm here.'

Kate hesitated for only a second. 'Why don't I?'

Evie watched as her grandmother picked up the handset and dialled, checking the letter on her knee after each digit. While the number rang, she removed her glasses and sat back with her legs crossed, as if wanting to be seen at her best. An old-school telephone user.

'Yes, hello.' She pointed energetically at the handset, as if Evie might not have realised the call had been answered. 'May I speak to … Is it Edith? Never mind. This is Kate Drake. She wrote to me and suggested I call. Oh, right … yes …' She put her hand over the phone and mouthed, 'Not her – foreign!' There was a brief pause. 'Hello again. Oh, I've missed her, what a pity. When will she be back, do you know? I see. Yes. Yes, I see. Right. I'll do that. Would you be kind enough to tell her I called? Kate Drake. Drake. Like duck – no, don't worry! That's it. Thank you so much. Goodbye.'

'A charming lad, but not an English speaker,' she explained again. 'Eastern European? I'm a rotten judge of accents. Anyway, we had a spirited exchange in our respective languages.'

Evie found herself wishing she'd made the call. 'So how did you leave it?'

'You heard – I left a message. They'll get back to me.'

'How? You didn't leave a number.'

'Won't they have one of those little screen things? Or one-four-seven-one? I'm sure they'll manage.'

'Why "they"?'

'How do you mean?'

'You keep saying "they".'

'Do I?' Kate frowned. 'Well, I suppose I think the boy lives there.'

She told Owen about the letter in bed the next morning. An egg-streaked plate lay on the floor on his side. As she began, he was listening with only half an ear, felled by work, breakfast and sex, but it didn't take long for his police antennae to start waving.

'I hope your grandmother didn't do anything.'

'Of course she did, she rang while I was with her. Why shouldn't she?'

'Why shouldn't she?' Owen pulled himself up and scrabbled with one hand for a cigarette. She tapped his wrist reflexively but he ignored her and lit up, striking the match on his thumbnail with irritating facility. 'I'll tell you. Because this person could be a nutter, and she's an old lady living on her own with a lot of nice stuff.'

'Oh come on!' Evie rolled on her back and clapped her hands over her eyes in exasperation. 'For one thing I read the letter and the writer sounded a little eccentric, but not even remotely a nutter ...'

'What do you expect? Notepaper headed I. B.Villain?'

'... and for another, it would be an incredibly clunky way of casing the joint.'

'They'd have done that already, and when she goes to town to meet Person A, Person B, who might be Person A anyway, will be waiting round the corner with the Bedford van all ready to load up. We see it all the time, babes.'

Evie admitted she hadn't thought of that. 'I'd be absolutely mortified if anything happened, but I honestly don't think it will. It just doesn't feel like that. All the stuff about family papers?'

'Tricksters aren't stupid; they'd have a good story. I'm not saying it's anything nasty, just that your gran needs to develop a bit more of a defensive reflex.'

'You're right, shit, I know you're right. We were both so fascinated by the whole thing, we lost our presence of mind. And – oh bugger!'

'Don't worry.' He kissed her shoulder. 'We're on the case now.'

'No, no that! With all the excitement, I forgot to ring Raff!'

Half an hour later, Owen was dead to the world and Evie was on her way to work. Forgetting Raff's call was bad. With luck he'd be too busy to hold it against her. Evie despised unreliability in others, even more in herself. She'd so wanted to speak to him – but not, it appeared, quite enough.

That reminded her that she ought in all conscience to contact her grandmother and pass on the burden of Owen's song, however unnecessary it might turn out to be. She called, but the line was engaged and there was no way Kate would have her mobile switched on at home. At lunchtime she tried again, and this time Kate answered and was away before she could deliver Owen's warning.

'Darling, I spoke to that boy again, Stefan. He must be some sort of exchange student. I'm going up to town to meet this person next Saturday. Lunch at the National Portrait Gallery, which is not something I do every day. Will you come and keep an eye on me, make sure I don't do anything silly?'

'Yes,' said Evie. 'I definitely will.'

Chapter Seventeen
1999

Humming along a near-empty road through the wide, rolling expanse of French countryside, Stella appreciated the maxim that you never fully valued freedom until you'd experienced its loss or, in her case, curtailment. Not for the first time she felt boundless respect and admiration for parents, especially mothers, who from the moment they gave birth could never truly call their lives or hearts their own.

She hadn't been lying when she'd told Evie she was enjoying herself. She was devoted to Raff, and this was an experience she wouldn't have missed for the world. These boys of eight to thirteen might have been highly motivated professionals, but they were also the responsibility of the adults entrusted with their care and supervision. There had been one of those moments such as Evie had described when they appeared to be one short; thirty seconds' worth of escalating anxiety was ended by the discovery that he'd been in the coach's toilet – not strictly permitted when the vehicle was stationary, which was why he didn't emerge till the engine began running – but it had been enough to set her heart pounding. There were such strange people about these days, it only took a moment's lack of attention and the outcome could be unimaginably awful. And what if it had been Raff? Standing as she did *in loco parentis*, she bore a double responsibility.

The other adults, though, were a study … She smiled to herself. The musical director, John Dowd, was a fierce, dedicated perfectionist with a single focus, not inclined to engage with anyone except the members of the choir. Then there were three other members of staff: Peter Drage, the piano teacher, Marian Cook, RE, and Ralph Colquhoun, who taught French and was a useful interpreter when needed. There were two volunteers besides herself, a shy and serious father, Jonathan, who worked as a peripatetic private maths tutor and was therefore free in the holidays, and Prue, the Lumleyesque mother whom Stella had encountered from time to time at the school gate, and who turned out to be extremely good fun. She and Stella formed an instant friendship and even nipped off for a drink one night after dinner, to one of the narrow, brutally lit Formica-and-linoleum bars in which the provincial towns of Picardy abounded. Prue had been married for fifteen years and had not, as she put it, 'done a hand's turn' in all that time, though it quickly became apparent that she was one of those women without whom not just her family but the entire local community would probably have disintegrated. She had three other children, including six-year-old twins, all of whom had an impressive array of talents and interests, energetically fostered and serviced by her; she managed a Grade II-listed establishment in the country as well as 'a little house in Primrose Hill', was regional president of Riding for the Disabled, and ran an over sixties lunch club at the village hall. She was also ('for my sins') in line to be county high sheriff next year; largely ceremonial, she confided, but the principal-boy outfit was to die for. All this information had to be wrung from her and was vouchsafed with humorous self-deprecation.

'A stay-at-home like me has to fill her time somehow, Stella. Actually I feel as if I'm bunking off, doing this. My parents are holding the fort, God help them, while I swan around France listening to beautiful music and perching on bar stools.'

She was surprised to hear that Stella was Raff's great-aunt. 'That sounds *so* august. You don't look anything like old enough.'

'Thanks. I try not to think about it.'

'How great of you to come, though. I used to have a brace of great-aunts and I can't imagine either of them coming on a trip like this – not that I would have wanted them to. They were lovely women in their way, but not what you'd call child friendly. Raff's such a lucky boy.'

'He has a very hard-working mother. She's at a conference, which is why she couldn't come.'

'I know I've met her, but remind me?'

'Evie. Dark, fit-looking – always on the run.'

'Evie, of course! She's rather gorgeous. Enviably slim.'

'That's her. She is attractive, yes. And it's not surprising she's thin, she has no off switch.'

'Unlike me ...' Prue sank the last of her Calvados. '*Un autre, peut-être?*' She beamed at the saturnine barman in the open, ladylike way of one accustomed to expect, and receive, perfect service. '*Encore, s'il vous plaît.* And what about you, Stella? Who and what are you neglecting in order to be here with Raff?'

Stella took this to be a politely oblique enquiry about her marital status. 'I don't have children and I'm single, so I'm not neglecting anyone, really.'

'Maybe.' Prue gave her a sagacious sideways look. 'But I can't see you leaving anyone in the lurch. When you're away, I bet you're sorely missed.'

Stella experienced a warm glow not solely due to the brandy. 'Perhaps.'

'I've talked far too much,' said Prue when they got up to go. 'We must do this again and you must tell me more.'

The following night they sat next to each other in the splendour of the south transept in Amiens Cathedral – by far the largest and grandest venue thus far – listening to the boys perform the Britten *Missa Brevis*. In the interval, they agreed that the French audiences were different from those at home.

'It's an away friendly,' was how Prue put it.

'They seem extremely knowledgeable. But they're more impressed by the boys than people would be at home. I suppose it's something that's not in their tradition.'

'They think the British treat their young very oddly. Boarding school from seven, *quel horreur!* God knows what sort of regime they imagine goes into producing this – the artistic equivalent of sending the little dears up chimneys.'

They giggled, but Stella noted the assumption that all rightthinking Brits sent their children away to school. A given, in Prue's world. The choir school was a detour, albeit a desirable one; Jamie's name was down for Marlborough.

In the second half, she gave herself up completely to the beautiful, complex, humming subtleties of the Taverner; she let it wash over her, speak to her and soothe her. Prue's Jamie had a solo, and Stella glanced briefly at her to see what effect that had, but her expression of soft-eyed concentration didn't change. She was what Kate would have called a sweetie, but made of stern stuff, the product of generations of country-toughened breeding. Showing off, of even the most discreet and justifiable kind, was out of the question.

Supper after an evening concert was at nine, sandwiches having been provided beforehand. The hotel in Amiens was modern, and they ate their meals in a large airy annexe to the main dining room, looking out on the river. The menu was the ubiquitous *côtelette de porc frites* followed by *tarte aux pruneaux, sauce anglaise*; the management had done this before. Seating was on a rotating adult-per-table basis, and for the first time Stella found herself sitting next to Raff.

'Well done,' she said. 'That was wonderful.'

'There was a cock-up in the Gloria.'

'Nobody noticed.'

'Loads of people will have done.'

She took the point, that she wasn't knowledgeable enough to notice. 'Put it another way, it didn't spoil anyone's enjoyment.'

'Dowd gave us a bollocking.'

'Raff!' She glanced around. 'Keep it down!'

'Don't worry, he's not here.'

'Nor he is, why's that?'

'Lying down with a wet towel round his head?'

'You're lucky to have someone who cares that much,' she said, a touch sententiously. 'He's setting you up with standards for life.'

Raff let this piece of wisdom go. 'I saw you sitting with Jamie's mum. She's nice, isn't she?'

'Very nice. We've made friends.'

'Drage has got the hots for her.'

'Surely not,' said Stella, though it seemed perfectly likely.

'It's common knowledge. Poor Jamie.'

That, thought Stella, was a perfect example of the sublime self-centredness of youth. The agonising unspoken passion of a shy schoolmaster (one cruelly out of his league) for the married mother of a mate counted for nothing beside the embarrassment of the mate himself. Just wait – and it wouldn't be long – till Raff himself was the one with the crush, and let him see how it felt.

Changing the subject, she asked: 'Have you spoken to Mum?'

'Yes, she called before the concert.'

'How was she?'

'Fine. She was going somewhere with Great-Gran, London or something?'

'Good. That's nice of her.'

'She likes Great-Gran.'

'We all do,' said Stella quickly. 'But Mum's very busy with her own life to lead, and not everyone would make time for their grandmother the way she does.'

'You're here with me, which is giving her a bit of a break,' Raff pointed out, adding slyly, 'I expect Owen will be staying over.'

'Who knows?' Stella wasn't about to discuss this with Raff, but she certainly hoped Owen would be there. She knew there were tensions, and she worried that Evie, in trying to keep Raff happy, might not be giving enough time and attention to her chap. In her own estimation, and that of most of the family, Owen was a diamond. That was another reason why she was glad she had no children; if, as was so often the case these days, you were not with the father, even the nicest of them threw a spanner in the works by their mere existence. And if they chose to cut up rough, life might swiftly become a battle zone. This reminded her of something.

'Tomorrow,' she said, 'you guys are going to Bayeux and I've got time off for good behaviour. So I'll see you at dinner.'

Raff stared at her. 'What are you going to do?'

'I've hired a car from Gaston on the ring road, and I shall explore.'

'What sort of car?'

'Gosh, now you're asking ... A Ka, I think.'

'Will it be left-hand drive?'

'Naturally.'

'Are you okay with that?'

She'd wondered about this herself. 'That remains to be seen.'

Now it was hard to see why she'd worried. The advantage of these small adventures on one's own was that you were responsible for no one but yourself and consequently it didn't matter if you read the map incorrectly, took ten minutes finding reverse and performed mildly dangerous manoeuvres on the first two roundabouts. In fact it was all part of the fun when there were no passengers having the vapours, or alternatively sucking their teeth with annoyance in the seat next to you.

Her objective was the Newfoundlanders' memorial at Beaumont-Hamel. The place had no family associations, but was said to be one of the most complete and perfectly preserved areas of battlefield. En route she caught sight of Thiepval up on its hill in the middle distance but decided to give it a miss; it was simply too massive and imperious, too obligatory. Her mood required a place where she could immerse herself in what had gone on here. In her bag was the envelope containing a selection of photographs she'd borrowed from her mother – photos of Jack, Thea and Aubrey, and one of Primmy, the maid who had worked for the Tennants at Chilverton House before the First World War and gone on to be a nurse. Stella wanted this expedition to be personal; she was paying her respects to the past, and the photographs focused her mind.

Also in her bag was a carefully written note from Ted. They'd done some researches on the internet and she had the name and position of his grandfather's grave. She'd planned a circuit to take this in, but France was huge, the distances always greater than she imagined, and her car rental only covered her until six. Visiting the last resting place of Arnold Guise was important, but it might have to wait until another day.

The weather on this trip had been lovely till now, fresh and windy, with clouds scudding cheerfully in a blue sky. But over the course of her drive the day darkened, and by the time she reached Beaumont-Hamel it had begun to drizzle. As she got out of the car, it started to rain quite seriously. She sat sideways in the driver's seat with the door open to change into walking boots, and then pulled on her cagoule and put up the hood. There was something fitting about the change in the weather; one's mental picture of the trenches was that it was always cold and wet – the clinging, sucking mud, the trench foot, the polluted puddles, the sodden sandbags and slimy duckboards, the rain hammering like shellfire on the tin roofs of dugouts ... Looking round this place in a downpour might give her an idea of what that must have been like, a paltry gesture of solidarity.

*

She'd made the right decision, coming here. The Canadians had achieved something remarkable in this place, the preservation and reconstruction of an entire battlefield, including the German lines; a monument to the wasteful sacrifice of hundreds of Newfoundlanders. Just inside the entrance, rising majestically beyond the dark, dripping trees, was a man-made mountain of rock and plants, crowned by a bronze statue of an elk, its massively antlered head raised, its throat swollen with a silent bellow.

She joined a small party of about a dozen visitors – mostly Canadians but also American, French, Japanese and one other Brit – standing in the network of trenches under the tutelage of a first-class young Canadian guide. He'd not just given them the facts, which God knew were shocking enough, but had also painted a picture of the events, and the mind-map of those involved.

'Stand closer together – closer than that, much closer – until it's uncomfortable, until you can scarcely breathe. Then imagine standing like that for hours at a time, moving forward by inches, waiting to go over the top into a hail of fire. No possibility of charging, or of going back – just shuffling towards probable death.'

The faces of the group were solemn, chastened by his eloquence.

They emerged from the trenches into the solid, driving hiss of the rain. Stella was glad of her cagoule and boots. The Japanese girls were dressed only in T-shirts and Capri pants and the young man produced folding brollies and pac-a-macs from his rucksack.

They stood humbly, shivering, waiting to be told the worst. In front of them stretched a few hundred yards of tussocky grass, studded with black iron screws. This was no-man's-land, said their guide, where the majority of the men had been mown down, and the regularly placed screws had held the barbed wire in place. They were to imagine walking into a hailstorm – not a European one, he explained gently; an ice storm such as they got in Canada – only on that fateful day the hailstones would have been bullets. On the far side, he said, pointing, in that gully just before the rising ground, were the German trenches; they'd see those if they walked that far – he recommended that they did.

Silently, hunched and bent under the downpour, they followed him down a track that wound across no-man's-land to a wooded cemetery.

'These graves,' said the guide, 'are Canadian. A little way along, those are German. You might want to look at them too. I'm going to leave you now. Are there any questions?' He scanned their faces. They shook their heads. Their questions were too many and too big; they wouldn't know where to start.

The young man didn't press them; he'd seen that look before.

'Go wherever you like. Look at the German trenches; they're a bit different to ours. Take your time, think about it. When you've finished, make time for our museum. It's well worthwhile. I'll see you over there. Thank you.'

They mumbled their own inadequate thanks and he walked briskly away across no-man's-land in the direction of the visitors' centre. Hesitantly, their confidence shaken, the members of the group drifted towards the shelter of the small cemetery under the trees. Stella set off for the German lines. The others were all nice people, but she wanted to be on her own.

The guide was right, these trenches were better; deeper, wider and sturdily reinforced. She'd read that this was so, but gazing down into this mighty, safe ravine after the Canadians' huddled alley came as a shock. The rain thinned to a dribble, slowed and ceased. She pushed her hood back and walked slowly along the near rim of the trench. On the far side, beyond a post-and-wire fence, a small group of black-and-white cows gathered to watch her; they were young, their ears were like wings sticking out. At the end of the trench was a modest stone cairn, recording the numbers of fallen.

She heard voices and moved on, following the zigzag line of the reserve trench through the perimeter woods, her footsteps silent on a layer of pine needles.

The museum appeared to be empty but for their guide, smart in a green polo shirt with a maple leaf on the pocket. He was standing behind the counter consulting a computer screen.

'That was an excellent tour you gave us,' she said. 'Thank you.'

'My pleasure, ma'am. Take your time,' he said, for the second time. She liked that, his gentle insistence on leisureliness and reflection.

The word 'museum' didn't do the place justice, just as 'memorial' didn't convey the solemn reality and power of what they had seen outside. The room wasn't big, but it was spacious and well lit, and imaginatively divided up, so that you were drawn naturally from one exhibit to the next. Stella peered long and hard at the grainy black-and-white photographs of grinning check-shirted recruits back in St John's, then in uniform hanging out of the windows of a train. In next to no time the same young men were over here in France, still smiling, sitting on the ground out of doors, eating and drinking, in open-necked shirts, braces and puttees. Apart from the clothes, the only difference was the hair, now shorn to bristles up the sides, revealing vulnerable ears of all shapes and sizes. She walked slowly to the next photograph; oh God, it was film … Now they were marching, but there were still plenty of waves and smiles, and three local children in the foreground jumping up and down and making faces at the camera as children always do. A little further and they were constructing emplacements from hay bales and sandbags, positioning guns, goading and cajoling horses to work harder, pull further … And then, finally, they were here, or somewhere like it. They stood crammed into a trench, six men to every foot of wall, scores of tired, scared faces staring up into the lens, Enfields over their shoulders, one thin lad with a cigarette, one character jauntily tipping the edge of his tin hat.

Stella stood as close to the photograph as she dared, studying the faces, wondering how many of them had fallen just out there, where they'd been walking not an hour ago; walking, and grousing about the rain where these chaps had hurled themselves into a blizzard of bullets.

'Makes you think, doesn't it?'

The voice was quiet, but she stepped quickly back, conscious that she was blocking someone's view. 'Yes, it does.'

A man of about her own age and height took her place, peering intently at the photograph. 'I keep thinking I might see my great-uncle.'

'Did he take part in this …' she hesitated, not sure what to call it, 'this battle, then?'

'He did.' He nodded his head in the direction of the door. 'He's down among the trees. Private Douglas Muir, aged twenty-one.'

'Poor chap.'

'Sure.' He pulled a wry, rueful face. 'One of many.'

Stella studied him: a compact, nice-looking man, rimless glasses, grey flannel shirt, bomber jacket, chinos. Anywhere else she might, in her ignorance, have assumed he was American. She wished now that she had looked at the graves, that she could say she'd seen his great-uncle's name.

'I'm afraid I didn't go there. I wanted to get away from the group.'

'I can understand that.'

'I hope that didn't sound rude.' She frowned uncertainly. 'Were you with us? I was so gripped by the whole thing, I didn't really take in the other people.'

'Sure,' he said. 'No, I just got here, but I've been before. Yesterday, as a matter of fact.'

He moved slowly on to the next exhibit, a case containing uniform and kit laid out in the shape of a man. Stella wasn't sure whether to follow – it was a natural progression, after all – or out of politeness to let him get ahead so that a space opened up between them. If there had been other people in the museum it wouldn't have mattered, but she didn't want to appear to be dogging his footsteps in an otherwise empty room.

He solved her dilemma by remarking, 'Something eerie about the way they display this stuff, isn't there? Kind of an external skeleton.'

She joined him. 'And I suppose it will have belonged to what – a dozen different people? More?'

'A composite unknown soldier.' They studied the exhibits together. He clearly felt no awkwardness, and Stella relaxed. 'When I came yesterday,' he said, 'I spent so long outside I decided to do this separately, and I'm glad I did.'

'It's a lot to take in,' she agreed, 'Even for me – and you have a personal connection with the place.'

'I don't mind admitting I shed a manly tear.'

They continued to go round quietly and at their own pace, together and apart. The rest of her group arrived; she heard their voices, loud at first as they came into the warmth, and then respectfully muted. When they reached the end, she said: 'That was a terrific exhibition.'

'Would you care for a cup of coffee?'

'I'd love one.' She glanced around. 'Do they do it here?'

'Probably, but don't know about you, I'd prefer to keep things separate, go down to the village.'

'Good idea. I've got a car out there.'

'Me too. We could follow each other or I could give you a lift and drop you back.'

'Fine.'

'Alan Muir.'

She shook the proffered hand. 'Stella Drake.'

He went to the desk. 'Would it be all right if the lady left her car here for an hour?'

'No problem. By the way, sir, if you turn right in the village and go to the end, there's a little gas station with a café. Doesn't look much, but the coffee's great.'

'Thanks for the tip.'

Alan Muir's car was a Renault, a couple of sizes up from the Ka. She considered her impression of him as they drove down the hill: unshowy, but easy and confident.

The café was exactly as described. Monsieur manned the petrol pump (there was only one) and Madame made them a pot of coffee that redefined the term 'caffeine hit'.

After the first mouthful Alan smacked his lips. 'I needed that.'

'Are you on holiday?' she asked.

'Yes, I am. Or at least I'm doing this – not everyone's idea of a vacation, I can see that, but my chosen route. How about you?'

'I'm over here with my nephew.' Something made her leave out the 'great'. 'He's on tour with a choir.'

'Really? Is that from one of your great cathedrals?'

She told him the name of the college.

'Sure. I believe I've heard them.'

'I wouldn't be surprised.'

'So your nephew's famous.'

'Well – Raff isn't, but the choir is well known.'

'You bet.' He rubbed his hand over his head. 'That's really great.' His hair was greying and cut marine-short. Stella could tell (it took one to know one) that left to its own devices, it would have been riotously curly.

He was speaking again, asking when the tour ended.

'Another four days,' she said. 'It's very intensive. Expectations are high and the choirmaster's a martinet. They aim to turn in a superb performance every time.'

'And do they?'

'I think so, but then I'm shamelessly biased and not all that musical. Raff said they made a few mistakes the other night in Amiens, but I wouldn't have known. The choirmaster let them have it, I gather.'

He chuckled. 'Guess it's in the job description.'

A few minutes later he paid for the coffee and they drove back up the hill to the car park. There was a coach there now, a group of elderly men in blazers coming stiffly down the steps.

'That was a very nice interlude,' she said as they stood next to her car. 'Thank you.'

'I enjoyed it. Where are you off to next?'

'Like you, I have a grave to visit. Unlike you, I'm not sure exactly where it is.'

'They're marked on most large-scale maps.'

'I hope so, that would be helpful. Also, there's a place called High Wood I'd like to see if I can.'

'High Wood? That's just up the road – three, four miles.'

'You know it?'

'I know the location,' he said. 'There was a pretty rough encounter there on the first day of the Somme offensive.'

'That's right.' She was suddenly excited. 'My grandfather was there – my mother's father.'

'Did he make it?'

'He did. But she says he never forgot it. The casualties were simply frightful, it was carnage. Like here, but on an even bigger scale.'

'Okay, you need to see it.' He fished a pocket diary and a propelling pencil from his inside breast pocket. 'I'll write directions.'

He put the diary on the bonnet of the car and she watched as he first wrote, and then drew a sketch map with quick strokes and tore out the page.

'Here you go. It's not to scale. Turn left out of here and you'll be there inside ten minutes.'

She glanced down at the piece of paper. 'That's so kind of you, Alan.'

'Least I could do.' He held out his hand. 'Bye, Stella, good luck. It was a pleasure meeting you. I hope the choir blows their socks off.'

She would have waved as she left, but he was sitting behind the wheel consulting a book and didn't look up when she passed.

His instructions were clear, and he was right, with the rain easing off it didn't take her long. After a quarter of an hour and a couple of turnings that took her further off the beaten track, she came to one of the now familiar signs: *WW1 Cemetery L'Ecarme (High Wood)*.

She was on a narrow road that ran along a ridge. On her left was a dense stand of trees; on her right, a plantation of maize, falling away into a broad valley beyond which the wide, empty fields spread to the horizon; no other person, no other car, anywhere. Ahead of her she could see the arched entrance and low wall of the cemetery and opposite a cleared space at the edge of the wood. When she got to the space she found a war memorial there: *In memory of all the officers and men of the Public School Brigade who lost their lives here, June 1916*. It seemed disrespectful to park in front of it, so she pulled over on to the shallow grass bank near the cemetery entrance.

The sun was coming out now, and the air was full of the keen, poignant smell of damp earth and greenery. Birds cheeped in the trees across the road, and a kestrel hung motionless over the young green maize, some unsuspecting creature's nemesis. She had her camera with her – she wouldn't know anyone buried here, but she could take some pictures to show her mother and Joe.

She crossed the road again to photograph the entrance. As she did so, a car went by at a gentle pace, and she saw a hand raised briefly at the window: Alan, checking she'd got there safely. She waved at the receding car and he blinked his hazard lights in acknowledgement.

She didn't stay long in the cemetery, just long enough to locate and record a group of Kents' gravestones with their distinctive prancing horse emblem. The uniform arched stones looked as if they'd been erected only yesterday: creamy white, inscriptions perfectly legible, the concrete evidence that these men would not grow old as those that were left. Then she returned to the car, took the old cloth-bound battalion history and a Kit Kat out of her rucksack and leaned against the bonnet in the fresh sunshine to get her bearings. There were violets at her feet, blue and white, which she was careful not to tread on.

She ate the Kit Kat in four mouthfuls and brushed the crumbs off herself and the book. She opened the book at the chapter she'd marked with a yellow Post-it, and began reading, running her finger down the paragraphs to find the passage she was after, the part describing High Wood.

Glancing from the page to her surroundings, and back again, nothing was quite as she'd expected: the woods behind her were the site of the undiscovered German guns that had exacted such a toll that summer's morning in 1916; the attack had been launched from right to left, east–west across the valley where now there was maize wheat, a herd of distant cows mildly cropping the spring grass. That gentle view had absorbed and sealed in the savagery of battle. She lowered the book and closed her eyes, letting the silence and the sunshine, the twitter of the birds and the soft rustle of leaves enfold her. A cloud drifted past the sun and for a moment she shivered in the still wintry chill of mid April.

Further consultation of the road map persuaded her that it ought to be perfectly possible to get to Arnold Guise's resting place before she had to turn for home. She left the map open on the seat next to her and set off, heading due north-west towards the village of Luciere, which fortuitously, according to the guidebook, had a strong connection with Joan of Arc.

On returning the car, she enquired whether in principle she could book it for a further three days at the end of the week. Alfie's mother was coming to collect Raff after the final concert in Poitiers, she had nothing waiting for her at home until the following week, and she thirsted – yearned – for some more of this sweetly melancholy time on her own.

Chapter Eighteen

1999

Evie put the A to Z back in her bag.

'This is Mansfield Avenue. Haig Mansions must be somewhere further along.'

They had decided to take an earlier train and check out the address.

'I wonder,' said Kate doubtfully, 'are we being awfully childish, doing this?'

'No, we're being sensible. What's that thing you said Grandpa used to say?'

'"Time spent on reconnaissance is never wasted."'

'There you go then – we're reconnoitring.' They walked on. 'I didn't know it was so nice round here. I bet these don't shift for less than a million.'

'I should think that these days they're all flats, wouldn't you?'

As if in direct refutation of this remark, a skinny, high-performance blonde in sprayed-on jeans emerged from one of the front doors with a toddler by the hand, followed by a brown-skinned woman carrying a baby in one arm and a buggy over the other. The toddler, androgynously ringleted, wore a biker jacket. The baby, which could have fitted comfortably in its mother's red Mulberry handbag, was shod in tiny sparkling Converse high-tops. A black Porsche Cayenne with a this year's number plate, winked obligingly at the family's approach.

'Perhaps not,' murmured Kate.

In one of those social shifts that are only perceptible once they've happened, the end of the road where Haig Mansions was situated was considerably less grand. The Mansions themselves – an imposing red-brick Victorian block with white mouldings round the third storey, and a turret at each corner – were handsome enough, but there was a polystyrene takeaway casket in the gutter outside and several overloaded black bin bags by the main door which had attracted the attention of urban foxes and now spewed rubbish over the pavement.

'Fallen on hard times,' observed Kate. 'I bet they're lovely flats.'

'Big, anyway,' agreed Evie. 'I sort of imagined this, didn't you? Down-at-heel gentility, grand but a bit past it?'

'I'm not sure what I imagined,' said Kate. 'But now we've got the idea, I think we should go. It would be too awful if someone came out and we were standing here.'

'How would they know it was us?'

'I don't – oh look!' Kate stepped off the kerb and flung up an arm. 'Taxi! Here he comes, I haven't lost my touch.'

They arrived at the National Portrait Gallery a full ten minutes early, so it was slightly disconcerting to be told they were expected.

'I'm afraid we're not quite sure who it is we're meeting,' Evie explained while Kate went to the Ladies'.

'Mr Mallory is here already.'

'I'm sorry, who?'

The maître d' consulted her bookings. 'Ernest Mallory. Do you want to go to the table or …?'

'Thank you,' said Evie. 'I'll wait for my grandmother.'

She went into the Ladies' and found Kate dabbing her nose in front of the mirror. 'Gran, it's a bloke.'

'I beg your pardon?'

'Our host. A Mr Mallory.'

'No! Honestly? What a surprise.'

'Are you – you know – still happy to go ahead?'

'Of course. All the more interesting. Anyway,' Kate leaned in, 'I have you to protect me.'

They were shown to a table by the window. Their host was sitting with his back to them, and it was only when the waiter pulled back the chairs opposite that he saw them and rose to his feet.

'Mrs Drake? What an absolute treat this is, and how kind of you to come. And who have we here?'

'This is my granddaughter, Evie. I hope you don't mind.'

'Mind? How do you do, Evie, charming. Sit, sit, please. I'm

Ernest Mallory. Should we have champagne? Do you know, I think we will.'

During the ensuing small flurry – champagne being brought, checked, tasted and poured, menus being handed, specials noted and recommendations made – Kate did not dare look at Evie in case between them they were to do something inappropriate. Whatever she had expected, it was not this – this exemplar of male elegance and old-world gallantry. She saw now where that 'duffer' came from; it was all part of the charm offensive (an apt modern phrase) that was at once delightful and intended, ever so slightly, to dazzle and wrong-foot the person on the receiving end. There was something in Ernest Mallory – not much, but something – that reminded her of Will. But for the most part he was quite unique in her experience. He must have been her age at least, but so perfectly turned out that she wished she had spent longer in front of the mirror. Never had a shirt been whiter, a claret silk tie more luxurious, a suit more perfectly cut, gold cufflinks more discreetly engraved. His hair was luxuriant (a tad too much so), black streaked with gunmetal grey, and brushed back in smooth waves; his teeth small and white with pointed eye-teeth like an animal's; his nails manicured, though she noticed he had strange hands, broad, and with exceptionally long spatulate fingers, a hint of black hair showing below the gleaming shirt cuff. And they had been expecting hairy tweeds, a whiskery chin, pearls, kirby grips, a whiff of BO and cheap talc!

'I do hope you like it here,' he was saying to Evie, speaking as if she'd been expected. 'I debated with myself for ever, and then thought, I know! *I* know what your grandmother would like – somewhere simple and elegant, perched among these romantic London rooftops.' He waved a big hand, like a wing. 'And magnificent pictures to look at afterwards if you were to feel like it.'

'I've been before,' Evie's voice was cool, 'a couple of times.'

Kate lowered her menu. 'But I haven't. It couldn't be nicer.'

Mallory's eyebrows rose as he turned to her. He could scarcely have looked more enchanted if she had produced a bouquet of red roses from her sleeve.

'Have you not? Do you think so?'

'Well, let's say so far, so good.' She realised that she sounded almost flirtatious; she was entering into the game. 'I'll give you my full verdict when we've eaten.'

He tipped his head back and gave a boyish ha-ha-ha! laugh that made a couple of people near them look and smile.

'A challenge, I see! Then let's order, shall we?'

Their respective choices were telling, Kate thought. Evie asked for a tomato salad, 'lemon juice only', followed by another starter, the carpaccio of tuna; Kate, in her slightly reckless mood, ordered warm duck terrine and breast of pigeon with fondant potatoes.

'Delicious,' said Mallory. 'Now then. I shall join my guest with the terrine, but in the interests of variety I shall forswear the pigeon in favour of sea bream.' He handed back his menu. '*Beurre blanc*, if I may.'

When the waiter had gone, he surveyed the two of them, his fingertips resting lightly on the edge of the tablecloth.

'Yes,' he said, as if admiring his own handiwork, 'just right. If this were business, I'd have taken you to one of my own establishments, but given that it is the very opposite of business, I think this will do us all nicely.'

Kate sensed Evie's prickle of interest. 'When you say one of your own establishments …?'

'Restaurants, Evie. I'm in what is now known as the hospitality industry, but which I, who came up through the ranks, prefer to call the catering trade.'

'Would I have been to any of them?'

'You might have done. Let's see, which would suit you?' He mused, tapping his fingers on the cloth. 'Da Rufo in Charlotte Street? Bernadino's in Islington? The Spotted Duck—'

'The Duck?' Evie became animated for the first time. 'Not the Spotted Duck in Maida Vale – near Paddington Basin?'

'Ah, you know it!'

'I do, I used to go there with … I used to go there often.' Kate could hear her playing down the enthusiasm. Mick, she thought, she used to go there with Mick.

Their starters arrived. Before picking up his fork, Mallory engaged in a murmured exchange with the waiter over the wine list. That done, he said, 'You say you used to go, Evie; would it be impertinent to ask when?'

'Oh, I don't know – more than twelve years ago?'

'Before my time.' He smiled and shook his head. 'You should go again; you'd be very pleasantly surprised.'

'But I loved it then!' Evie's tone was a touch combative. 'I'm not sure I could bear any change; it was just the best pub.'

'Then you're right, don't go back.' Mallory sliced and speared a mouthful of terrine. 'It has changed.'

They started eating; the food was delicious, and their glasses were topped up.

'I do hope you're happy with champagne for the time being, Mrs Drake.'

'Kate, please.'

He inclined his head. 'I hope you're happy with the bubbly for now. I have taken the liberty of ordering us some wine; they have a very decent list.'

Evie's lips were pressed together, as if she would have taken issue with this.

'I would never complain about champagne,' said Kate. She was a little tipsy already; she was aware of cautionary glances from her left. She mustn't let the amusingness of it all, nor Mallory's cascade of charm, blind her to the fact that this was a meeting with a purpose, the weight of which he knew and they did not.

'I don't know what you think, Evie,' he said – he had an oddly random way of using names, as if to keep the two of them on their toes – 'but to my mind restaurant meals are a species of theatre. And for that reason I propose to give you your present after the second act, so to speak.'

'Deferred gratification,' said Evie. 'I see.' But if he noticed her sarcasm he didn't show it, adding:

'We can use the natural interval to let our stomachs decide whether we want pudding.'

He made a slight moue on the word 'pudding', prompting Kate to wonder whether 'Mallory' might be an anglicisation. That reminded her of something.

'Tell me, who was the young man who answered your phone?'

'Ah, Yannick – I take it you communicated successfully with each other, or you wouldn't be sitting here now.'

'We muddled through!' She laughed and he echoed the laugh, though Evie was unsmiling. 'I was trying to guess where he was from – Hungary?'

'Croatia, actually. A perfectly legal immigrant, learning English and doing gardening to pay his way. He has a gift: things grow for him, and in the right place, too.'

'Do you have a garden, then?' asked Evie, remembering Haig Mansions and trying not to catch her grandmother's eye.

'I do, and it's quite lovely, for which I can take no credit whatever. Before Yannick there was the redoubtable Jennifer, and before her, oh, some other nice energetic person who enjoyed grubbing about in the mud. I'm afraid, Kate, that I'm one of those people in the poem who says "Oh how beautiful!" while sitting in the shade. Preferably,' this time he leaned towards Evie, 'with a glass of chilled Montrachet to hand.'

Kate said carefully: 'Your address looked like a flat, but I suppose if you're on the ground floor ... aren't you lucky?'

'Ah, the address – no.' He waved his hands, erasing a false impression. 'I currently own a very pleasant flat in Haig Mansions – two flats on the top floor, actually, knocked through – and I use this as an office, and occasionally rent out the mansard room, or lend it to friends. Yannick in this case.'

'So where's home?' asked Evie. She was becoming impatient, and consequently blunt, but he didn't seem to mind.

'I have a house in the same road, not fifty yards away. I don't drive, you see, but since I can walk to work, what need?'

'Right. Very handy.' Evie sat back as their starter plates were removed, and then said abruptly, 'I don't know about you, Gran, but all this suspense is beginning to get to me. Couldn't you just cut to the chase and tell us why we're here?'

'I can, Evie, of course.' Still smiling, he turned away from her, blinking slowly, like a lizard. 'But Kate – this is for you to say.'

'Well, why don't you? There's probably no need for us to worry, but we have been, as I'm sure you can appreciate.'

'No need at all.' He picked up a slim leather case and unzipped it. Handing Kate a white A4 envelope he said, 'I am the bringer of good news.'

The envelope wasn't sealed. Inside were three letters, frail with age, one of them still in its own envelope with a faded foreign stamp.

'Good heavens.'

'May I look?' asked Evie.

'Of course.' Kate handed the envelope to her, adding quickly, 'But don't read them yet.'

'I wouldn't dream of it.' Evie was sharp.

'That's right, your grandmother should read them first,' said Mallory. 'But not now, perhaps. Ah!'

The main courses arrived, and wine – Bordeaux and Pinot – was produced, tasted and poured. With a face like thunder Evie passed the envelope back to Kate, who clasped it in her arms as if it might run away. She stared at Mallory.

'You've read what's in here. Obviously.'

'I have, yes, because I needed to know what they were and who should have them. Now they are all yours.'

Evie said, 'Food's here, Gran. Why don't you put that down on the floor.'

'Yes, why don't I.' Kate leaned the envelope against the wall.

Mallory picked up his knife and fork. 'Bon appétit.'

Evie was making it perfectly clear that eating was not top of her list. 'So since you do know what's in those letters, are you going to give us some idea? And before that, perhaps you'd tell us how you came by them.'

'It's quite a story… Mm,' he pointed at his plate, 'this is delicious.'

His good-natured self-satisfaction was, Kate realised, proof against any attempt to discomfort him – though God knew Evie was doing her best.

'The story,' he went on. 'Where to begin?'

What it came down to was this. Before and during the war, Mallory had had a male 'colleague' – Kate was sure the term must be a euphemism – who had a woman friend, beautiful but incomprehensibly single, who had died in a tragic accident abroad not long after the war. These two had enjoyed a true platonic love affair, said Ernest, and had been in constant communication – hence the letters. He and his colleague, Giles, had sadly parted company under a cloud and not seen each other for many years, but had been drawn together again by Giles's final illness. Ernest had been at his deathbed, over thirty years ago now, where they had been reconciled – 'quite wonderful, Evie' – and had become not only his major beneficiary, but also his executor.

'He left some incredible things, Kate. He was a collector, with a keen eye and excellent taste. Art nouveau was a special passion of his. I have one particular lamp, a dryad ... exquisite. And some beautiful pieces of Lalique ...'

But, as always, there had been the boxes of stuff one didn't like to throw away, but put in a cupboard and forgot about. It was Yannick who had obliquely been the cause of this recent discovery; soon after his arrival, before the gardening had taken off, Ernest had set him to some clearing out, going into the worst of the cupboards 'with a miner's lamp and gauntlets' and sorting the contents into piles for Ernest to check off – 'the three Rs – rubbish, retain, re-examine'. The letters had emerged from the third pile, comprising mainly boxes, files and folders full of old paperwork. Ernest and Yannick had spent a pleasant rainy afternoon going through them all. Most of it was dull, much needed only throwing away, but there had been some personal correspondence that Ernest had taken back with him to read in bed that night.

'And so, Kate,' he said, gazing at her, his eyes limpid with anticipation, 'we come to it.'

Evie pushed her nearly untouched plate away. 'Yes?'

His eyes remained on Kate. 'I think you knew someone called Dulcie? Dulcie Tennant?'

'I did,' said Kate. She felt oddly dizzy, and hesitated. 'She was my adoptive mother's sister.'

Mallory nodded. 'Mm-hm. Your adoptive mother, that would be ...?'

'Thea Kingsley.' She sensed that he knew, but was prompting her. It was part of his little production.

'You were fond of Dulcie, and she of you.'

'Oh yes – when I came to London, she was wonderful to me. A great beauty, I remember, when I was this gauche, rather contrary girl from the bush. Heaven knows what she made of me, but she was never less than generous.'

'And your real mother?'

Kate felt Evie's eyes on her. And his, this loathsome, creepy man opposite. 'She was— Thea was my mother, the one who brought me up.' Suddenly, from nowhere, her eyes stung of tears.

Evie said, 'We don't have to do this, Gran. We have the letters, let's go.'

'No – no, darling, I'm quite all right.'

'You're not.' Evie glared coldly at Mallory. 'You can see she's not.'

'Kate, you may go, of course, at any time. I apologise for keeping you waiting; it's my foolish desire to provide a little fanfare.'

She recovered herself. 'You've certainly done that.'

'Well then. What those letters make clear is that Dulcie Tennant, a pretty and fashionable woman, as you say, was not only Giles's close confidante, and a friend to you, Kate.' He leaned back, swollen with the weight of his superior knowledge. 'She was rather more than that, wasn't she?'

Chapter Nineteen

1952

Thea had never been sworn to secrecy, but after Dulcie's death it seemed too late for anything else. Secrecy was implicit in the pact she had made with her sister, and she feared that to breach it would be too damaging. That she had done so was a thorn in her side.

To soothe the persistent prick of conscience, she had raised the matter with Jack, once or twice over the years, though she could always predict what his reaction would be. On the most recent occasion they were sitting with their drinks in the drawing room, having just listened to the BBC World Service news. The brisk strains of 'Lillibulero' marked the cocktail hour for settlers. Jack's service revolver lay on the side table next to his glass as a precaution – there had been some worrying reports recently.

'No,' he said. 'No. Please, I beg of you, put that idea right out of your head. When we took Kate on, she became our daughter, though God knows it was hard fought.' He rubbed one finger over his forearm. 'I have the scars to prove it. As far as she and we are concerned, we're her parents.'

'You're right, I know you're right …'

'I can see no earthly point in stirring everything up.'

'But what about Dulcie?'

'What about her? She's no longer with us.'

'Do we owe it to her memory?'

'Owe?' Jack's voice took on the curl of bitterness that so often accompanied any discussion of Dulcie. 'We owe her nothing, Thea. Not a thing. We adopted Kate, at her request, and at that precise moment her daughter became ours. Your sister was always an opportunist, and I have to say that was her finest hour. I don't wish to sound harsh, but when she wrote you that letter she forfeited her rights as a parent.'

Thea couldn't contradict a word of this. It was the truth – just not the whole truth.

'She wasn't all bad, Jack.'

'Very few people are. But she was a foolish, self-indulgent, vain woman with no sense of responsibility.'

'She made her way in France during the war.'

'We all know how.'

'And she took care of Kate when she was little.'

'Correction. She paid someone else to do that.'

'Yes – but Jack!' Thea grew impassioned. 'Think what it must have been like for her, having a baby on her own, in a foreign city, with the war still on! And yet she never mentioned it at the time, she never complained, never asked anyone for help or money.'

Jack gave a sharp sound like the bark of a fox. 'She wouldn't have dared! Can you imagine your father's reaction? Or Aubrey's? And as for money – strangely, it appears not to have been a problem.'

'I still think she deserves credit for coping. Not just coping; for seeing that Kate was well looked after and nicely brought up.'

'Credit is due to the nanny, I grant you. Kate came to us with excellent teeth.' He smiled bleakly and held out an arm. 'Come here. We have splendid offspring, my darling, don't let's rock the boat.'

Thea rose and went to stand by him. His arm encircled her; he sighed, touched his face to her hip.

'I shouldn't be so hard on your sister.'

'But you are.' She stroked his head; her hand shook. 'And she's not here to defend herself.'

'You're right. It's caddish behaviour.'

'I only mentioned her because I've been fretting over whether Kate should know. Whether we owe it to her.'

'Fret no more.'

'I'll try not to.' Her voice broke slightly. He looked up at her. 'Please.'

'I'll try.'

She meant it, but experience had shown that Thea's efforts in this department would fail. She was born to fret, she carried guilt and anxiety as others did their skin.

She reminded herself the deed was done, long since and the world had not ended. But as a result of her deception the private and more precious world she shared with Jack showed a crack; a fault line he did not see, but that could never be repaired.

The worrying reports became more frequent. At lunch with their nearest neighbours, the Coltraynes, the Kingsleys heard one disturbing story at first hand. The Coltraynes' elderly neighbour on the other side had been murdered in his study two days ago. His wife had been staying with friends in Nairobi or she would certainly have met the same fate. Word had travelled via the farm workers, and their host, Fergus, had been at the scene not long after the police.

Fergus was an Ulsterman who didn't mince his words and believed that the best solution to any problem was the most swift and draconian.

'The ringleaders should be hunted down and shot,' he declared over coffee and cigarettes. 'If there's any doubt, round up the lot of them and bang them up somewhere extremely unpleasant until the alliances start to come apart and the scum floats to the top.'

'Might be counterproductive,' said Jack. He liked and respected Fergus, who was of a type he recognised from the first war – the sort of chap who made a first-class sergeant major, fiercely disciplinarian and rock-steady under fire, but a stranger to psychology of any kind. 'If the troops go charging in and are less than completely successful, we could face a ferocious second wave.'

'Then we'd be ready for them.'

Terri Coltrayne pushed her chair back. 'If you'll excuse us, I'm going to show Thea my rhododendrons.'

The men half rose as she and Thea left the room. Fergus fetched a decanter from the sideboard. 'Join me?'

'Thanks.'

'Did I scare the ladies, do you think?'

'Probably, but they're used to it.'

'And what the hell, they should be scared, Jack!' Fergus took a swig and another cigarette. 'We should all be bloody scared. I didn't want to say it in front of them, but those shits cut up poor old Jimmy Lloyd like a bush chicken. He was in pieces, blood everywhere. Brains and what have you smeared all over his desk, up the walls. I've been out here over thirty years but I damn near threw up. Whoever did it was in a frenzy. That wasn't a run-of-the-mill grudge killing, Jack, it was slaughter.'

Jack looked out of the window, to where the two women stood in the garden. The grass and leaves were green, the rhododendrons in pink and white flower; Thea wore a loose white dress, one he'd always liked, that seemed to shine in the sun. You could almost think you were in England, and yet only a few miles away this ghastly thing had happened.

He turned from the window and lifted his glass. 'What about the staff – the farm hands? Any suggestion it was them?'

'A couple of them have run away. Doesn't take a genius to work that one out.'

'What about your lot?' asked Jack. 'Are you confident they're loyal?'

'Are you?' Fergus thrust his face forward. 'About yours?'

'I've had no serious difficulties.'

'Nor me, but your Kikuyu is a natural turncoat. I'm not saying my boys haven't been loyal so far; they may even be loyal as we speak, but that doesn't mean I trust them as far as I can spit.'

Jack considered this. He was a strict employer, having learned early on and only too well that an inch of misplaced leniency could lead to a mile of genial exploitation. The reward for fairness was, he firmly believed, mutual trust. But even allowing for the difference in Fergus's modus operandi and his intemperate turn of phrase, there was a grain of truth in what he said. Life here was cheap, and easily bought.

'Do you ever wish,' he said, 'that you'd never brought your wife out here?'

'Brought her?' Fergus flicked a shower of ash over the table. 'I couldn't stop the woman!'

On the way back, Thea said, 'How perfectly awful about Jimmy Lloyd.'

'Shocking. And I'm afraid it has implications for all of us.'

She wasn't quite ready yet to face the implications, saying instead, 'Poor Fran. I should go and see her.'

'If she comes back from Nairobi.'

'I hadn't thought of that.' She looked at him. 'Do you think she will?'

'I agree it's hard to see what else she would do. She's lived in Kenya all her life, and the two of them have run that farm together for what, the best part of forty years?' He glanced at her. 'Even so, would you want to take up the reins again in the house where your husband had been hacked to death?'

'I don't know.' Thea felt cold and sick. Outside the window, the sighing bronze grassland, the wind-warped thorn trees and dry river brakes that she had tried so hard to love were full of a new threat. They and others like them might pretend they were a community, but it was an illusion. Each one of them was alone in a land that was becoming ever stranger; far from home, and outnumbered.

No, she thought. *No, I wouldn't.*

They made love only rarely these days, but that night they did. They locked and bolted every door and window as always, but with a new sense of what it was they might be shutting out. When Jack turned off the lamp by their bed, they turned to each other in the dark and wrapped their arms round each other in a tight embrace, clinging together for comfort and protection, kindling between them, like a spark between cupped hands, not just love, but hope.

The African night was always noisy. Thea had almost stopped hearing the sounds that made up its uneven chorus: the close ones of insects pattering on the mosquito net and window screens; those that were part of the farm – the outside dogs barking, the occasional voice from the shambas when there was rum about; and the sounds of the bush, the cries of animals hunting, and others dying, the resonant hollow cough of lion, which could be as much as five miles away. Tonight she heard every one. Long after Jack had fallen asleep, which he always did quickly and completely, as if tipped into a ravine, she lay awake, listening to the sounds, identifying them, straining to hear anything unfamiliar but dreading that she might.

When she did sleep, it was fitfully, and she dreamed about Dulcie. In her dream it was Dulcie who was outside in the dark

– thin, white and unprotected, but also unimaginably frightening: a demon, a fury, tapping on the window, pushing at doors, creeping light-footed along the veranda, calling in a high, thin voice. Thea woke in terror. The moment she fell asleep again, the dream repossessed her and Dulcie was there, scratching, crying, laughing—

'Thea!'

She crashed into consciousness, sweating and struggling in Jack's arms.

'That'll do … that'll do … Hey now, that'll do …'

They were the words he used to soothe horses and dogs. He was sitting up, holding her against him, one arm pinioning both of hers, the other gripping the back of her head so that her face was against his shoulder with only just room to breathe. His body felt cool and still, his hard-working muscles held her securely. Slowly, her breathing calmed and he eased his hold on her. She opened her eyes to meet his.

'Welcome back. That was a bad one.'

'God, Jack, it was absolutely horrible, terrifying!'

'I could tell.' He reached for the Thermos he always brought with him to bed to assist with his five a.m. start. 'Cup that cheers?'

'Thank you.'

They sat side by side against the pillows, nursing their twin plastic beakers. 'Look at us,' she said, closing her eyes as the hot, sweet tea crept through her system. 'Darby and Joan.'

'For all we know, they were the Hepburn and Tracy of their day.'

'Not us, then.'

He felt for his cigarettes and lit one. 'So what was the nightmare about?'

'Oh, you know – someone creeping about outside, wanting to get in.' She didn't want to say who.

'Hardly surprising after what we heard yesterday.'

'No.'

'I'm going to have a word with the boys today. And I'll get a couple more kennels knocked up so we can have the dogs better positioned around the house. There's no deterrent like a really good house dog. I might get another one; let's ask Dick Hall if he knows of any pups.' Dick was the vet in Gilgil, a man without whose unflappable expertise they might once or twice have gone to the wall.

'It'll take a long time to train a pup,' said Thea.

'You're right. A young adult would be better, but if you don't know what's happened to them in the past, they can be a liability. Anyway,' he stubbed out the partially smoked cigarette and swigged down the rest of his tea, 'if you're recovered, I'll get going.'

Jack had his spartan bath at the end of the day, before they had their sundowner. Thea listened to him shaving, scrubbing his face and chest vigorously at the basin, cleaning his teeth. It was a couple of years since she'd had a dog of her own, and she missed it. Pets meant nothing to Jack, who had always been unsentimental about animals and who had developed a farmer's utilitarian attitude since they came here. But under the circumstances, he would be disposed to indulge her.

He came back into the bedroom and began opening and closing drawers briskly; he wore clean clothes every day as a matter both of principle and of good business management. Boots were always buffed up, an old army habit. As he subjected his hair to a few brisk swipes with the hairbrush, Thea said:

'If you do speak to Dick, perhaps you'd ask about puppies anyway.'

'For you? Good idea. In fact why don't you call him? And if he's got anything I could use on the farm I'll get back to him, go and take a look.'

She put on her dressing gown and they breakfasted together. Jela produced poached eggs; since she'd taught him how to make the whirlpool in salted water with a little vinegar, and gently drop in the eggs (a skill, as she told him, that his venerable predecessor Karanja had never quite mastered), they'd become his *pièce de résistance*. He'd taken to standing and watching them try the first mouthful, anticipating their unqualified approval.

'Perfect as usual, Jela, thank you.'

'Very nice.' Jack waited till he'd left the room and lowered his voice. 'Will I ever see a fried egg again?'

'I'll mention it.'

'Do.' They smiled at one another, cheered by Jela's enthusiasm and the eternal poached eggs.

When Jack had gone and she was dressed, Thea felt much

better. The nightmare had receded, and although the horror at the Lloyds' farm lingered, and its implications must be considered, her own surroundings were peaceful. It was a shiningly beautiful day, the crowns of the Aberdares draped in mist, the bush gleaming green and gold, the garden fresh after the night. From the kitchen came the sound of Jela washing up and chatting to Nona the housemaid. Further away, some cheerful chi-iking from the shambas, and a burst of laughter. The morning chorus.

Terri Coltrayne had promised to give her some rhododendron cuttings in the autumn, and she went for a wander outside, snapping off deadheads and tweaking out weeds as she went, deciding where she would put the new shrubs. So she was lost in thought when Luke, the garden boy, materialised next to her, making her jump.

'Missus Kingsley, I cut the grass today?' She did her best not to appear startled.

'Oh! Luke, there you are.' He had the ability to appear from nowhere like a spirit of the vegetation. 'Yes, that would be a good idea, in about an hour, when it's quite dry.'

'I shall cut here, too?' He pointed to the ragged fringe of grass that protruded over the edge of the flower bed. He was only a youth, twenty at most; he gazed at her with big, heavy-lashed eyes and made scissoring movements and a little sound to accompany them, 'Whish! Whish!'

'Yes please.'

He strolled away on long, lean legs. The soles of his feet were thickly calloused but the whiteness of his singlet hurt her eyes. Luke was the son of Nona and her husband Jesus, who helped Jack on the farm and drove the wagon and now on occasion the car. It was something of a mystery why he remained here; times were changing, and most of the young men of ability were heading into the towns for better-paid work. Jack cited him as an example of family tradition, an indication of the family's pride in being part of a shared enterprise; Thea wasn't so sure. It was a rare instance of Jack taking the more romantic view. She considered Luke not so much lazy as insinuating. Those big, opaque eyes, the soft voice she had to strain to hear, that indolent walk, the sense she had that he crept up on her ... He always made her uneasy, and a little more so this morning.

Today was the day for her informal back-door surgery, when she set up a table outside the kitchen and dished out first aid and the very simplest forms of medication – plasters, antiseptic cream, analgesic tablets, kaolin and morphine – to the farm's employees and their friends and families. She had done so for years, with the local doctor's blessing, and there was always a queue. Anyone with a serious illness or injury she or Jesus would drive into Gilgil, but the farm surgery mopped up the smaller cases, many of whom needed sympathy and reassurance as much as medical attention.

Luke was standing by the back door. As Thea approached, Jela came out and handed him the kitchen knife-sharpener. Luke turned and would have walked past her with it in his hand, but she stopped him.

'What are you doing with that, Luke?'

'To sharpen the shears, *bibi*.'

'Surely there's a proper grinder for that with the garden tools in the shed.'

'No, *bibi*.' He shook his head. 'Not now. I can't find it.'

'You can't use that,' she said briskly. 'Let me look.'

The shed was to the side of a house, behind a trellis where she'd set climbers, clematis and honeysuckle, a profusion of Englishness. The door was open and she went in, her eyes taking a few seconds to adjust to the relative darkness. Luke, who had followed her at a slight distance, stood in the doorway, one hip cocked, arms folded, the sharpener swinging idly from his finger and thumb.

He was right, she couldn't see the grinder anywhere. On the other hand, that was nothing new. There was a lot of informal borrowing, which she and Jack tolerated provided things were put back next day, or as soon as they were asked for.

'I wonder who's got it?' she said to herself. Luke took a step back to let her pass. 'If the shears are really blunt, use that for now, but take it straight back, please. Jela will need it.'

'Yes.' The 's' was sibilant, suggestive.

When she got back to the kitchen, Nona and Jela had put out the folding table, with a bucket of hot water and Dettol on the ground next to it and her locked first-aid tin on top. Two or three people were already walking over towards the house from the farm buildings, slowly in the rising heat. She sat down at the table and unlocked the box. Jela brought her tea in the half-pint mug specially reserved for surgeries. She didn't mention the sharpener, which strictly speaking he should not have lent without her permission. Surgery was a sociable time.

She rang Dick just after midday, when surgery – hers and his – was over, and before he set off on his farm calls.

'Thea, what can I do for you?' She relayed Jack's enquiry. 'Nothing I can think of right now, but I'll keep a look out. I know what Jack's after. Best bet would be someone going back to the UK and offloading.'

'And Dick, I'm looking for a dog for myself. I've missed having one since we had to have Frost put down. Will you let me know if there are any litters?'

'There are some nice Labs due just up the road. I'll let you know when they arrive; you can take a look.' He coughed noisily. 'Did you hear about Jimmy Lloyd?'

'Yes.'

'Appalling business. You keep your wits about you, Mrs K, you hear?'

'Don't worry,' she said. 'We will.'

When she came off the phone, she fetched a glass of orange squash from the kitchen and went out on to the veranda. Luke had done a good job; the lawn was close-cut and smooth. Thea couldn't see him, but somewhere just out of sight she could hear him snipping the edges. *Whish! Whish!*

Chapter Twenty

1999

Stella wasn't altogether surprised to bump into Alan Muir in the interval of Raff's final concert in Poitiers. What did surprise her was how pleased she was to see him, standing at the foot of the cathedral steps with his jacket hooked over his shoulder, face uplifted as the stars began to come out.

'Hey, Stella!' He shook her hand and gave her a glancing kiss on the cheek. 'I hope you don't think I'm dogging your footsteps, but after meeting you, I guess I was sensitised to the publicity. In fact it was pretty hard to avoid, so I thought hell, I'll treat myself. And I have to say I'm glad I did.'

'It's great that you're here,' she said. 'Where are you sitting?'

'On the right, about halfway back. There's room in the row – you want to join me for the second half, or do you sit somewhere special?'

She experienced, then resisted, the temptation. 'Thanks, but I'm with a friend, the mother of one of the other choristers.'

An usher passed among them with the message that '*Le concert va recommencer*' and they joined the drift back into the cathedral.

'Have you had dinner?' he asked.

'Not really, but I'll be having supper with everyone afterwards; it's the last evening.'

'Okay. Well, it was really good to see you again.'

'Though as a matter of fact,' she said, quickly, before she could have second thoughts, 'Raff's going to stay with a friend in Brussels and I'm taking a long weekend over here, with a car, before I go back. Special dispensation. So if you're going to be about, dinner another night would be fun.'

'Terrific, let's do that. Give me your cell.'

'I don't have one,' she admitted.

'You don't? I'll give you mine, ring from where you are.'

They stepped to one side near the guidebook counter. As she scribbled in her diary, a passing usher threw them a look of the keenest disfavour.

'Done,' he whispered. 'Call me.'

Alfie's mother, Pam, was a vivacious, bustling woman whose husband was a private secretary at the European Parliament. Having attended the Poitiers concert – Vaughan Williams, Tippett, a dash of Lloyd Webber Senior – she joined them for supper at the hotel. After breakfast the next day, Stella accompanied Raff to the car park to see them off. She didn't attempt a kiss.

'Bye, champ,' she said. 'Have fun.'

'They will!' carolled Pam from the driver's seat. 'I guarantee it!'

'Thanks for coming, Stella.'

'That's okay. It was hard, lonely work, but someone had to do it.' She gave him a squeeze round the shoulders. 'Jump in.'

'See you when we get home.'

'You bet.' He got in and she leaned down so she could see both of them. 'Bye! Bye, Alfie! Pam, thank you so much – safe journey!'

She waved them off with a fond heart, but a light one. And it was even lighter when half an hour later the rest of the party, choir, staff and helpers, chattering and demob-happy, piled on to the coach and pulled away from the door of the hotel.

She called Alan from a small bar. She'd already spent a tranquil hour sitting on the pavement in the sunny village square, with her sunglasses on and a *pichet* of red in front of her, watching the locals and wondering whether it was possible to be any happier. The sound of his voice – hard-won after various adventures with the payphone – made her realise that it was.

'I'd have called sooner, but I was in the throes of farewells early on. But they're all gone now.'

'Where are you?'

'The bar's called Le Truc.'

'I get it. So you started the party without me.'

'Of course. Where are you?'

'In Vimauges. Near the Somme estuary. I'm sitting on a dune with a pair of binoculars, looking at seals on a sandbank.'

'That sounds really nice. I want to do that. How far away are you?'

'I don't know,' he said, deadpan. 'Because I don't know where you are any more than you do.'

'Correct!' She laughed. 'I can't be that far from Poitiers, I only drove for about half an hour. I'm going to come up and see those seals.'

'Why not? I tell you what' – his voice fluctuated as he cast about – 'there's a dodgy-looking snack bar in the car park by the beach. It's a caravan with a few chairs and tables, but it'll do. When you get to Vimauges, follow the signs for Parc Maritime and you'll wind up in the car park. I'll be the one with the pot of Lipton's and the day-old *Herald Tribune*.'

'What if it's raining?' she asked.

'Get outta here. I'll see you in an hour.'

An hour and a half later she arrived. He was, as promised, sitting at one of the rickety tables, tea tray in front of him, legs stretched out and ankles crossed, reading a paper; but he spotted her as she got out of the car and rose to greet her.

'Sorry,' she said. 'One or two elementary mistakes en route.'

'Bad luck.'

'Have you been here for ages?'

'I don't know, I've been reading. The time flies.' He pointed at the teapot. 'You want some, or shall we hit the beach?'

'Beach, or we might miss them.'

'We'll be fine, the tide's still going out.'

They joined a group of about thirty other people of all ages perched on top of the dunes and on an old Second World War pillbox, with binoculars trained on the sandbank about a quarter of a mile out.

'There are hundreds of them!'

'As the tide goes out they congregate. There were only about a dozen when you called.'

'What must it be like,' she mused, 'to have your every waking moment scrutinised by gawpers.'

'Lady Di?'

'Yes. Only they deal with it.' She handed back the binoculars. 'Not a lot of eating disorders and aberrant behaviour out there, I'll warrant.'

'Promiscuity, though, big time. Different partner every year.'

Stella had that wonderful feeling of a huge bubble of laughter – uncontrollable, funny-bone, pant-wetting laughter – rising up inside her, and as it burst out, she realised: *I want to sleep with this man.*

It was nearly two when they left the beach, and they went to find lunch in Vimauges.

'What do you want?' he asked. 'Mussels or mussels?'

'I'll go for the mussels.'

In the event they paid for having overlooked the French habit of set mealtimes, and met with a resounding *Non!* from all the establishments that caught their fancy. They wound up going to the supermarket and taking a carrier with bread, cheese, paté and a carton of rosé to a bench on the prom. Alan was impressed with Stella's penknife.

'If we'd bought a proper bottle you could have used the corkscrew.'

'If we had a horse we could clean its feet. But since we don't …' She opened a packet of Kleenex and put some spread slices on top. 'Voila! Next time you're up the Orinoco, be sure to take me with you.'

'I'll certainly do that.' He popped the top of the carton and poured wine into the plastic cups they'd blagged from a kiosk. 'Chin-chin.'

'*Salut.*'

They were starving, and hoovered up the picnic with almost indecent speed and thoroughness. Alan dusted his palms and waved the wine carton.

'We have a duty to finish this, otherwise it's only going to attract wasps in the garbage bin.'

'Too early in the year for wasps, but since you twist my arm …' She held out her cup. 'Tell you what, though, I shouldn't get back in that hire car any time soon.'

'No,' he said, 'you shouldn't.'

He was booked into a *pension* halfway up the hill between the prom and the old town. It was quite a trudge, and he offered her his arm.

'Don't get your hopes up,' he warned her when they paused for breath. 'It's cheap and cheerful.'

'Clean?' she gasped. 'Loo okay?'

'Absolutely.'

'That'll do me!'

There was no frenzied grappling and tugging as they undressed. They had plenty of time, and part of the pleasure was in mutual anticipation. When they'd drawn the curtains on the window overlooking the street, they took their clothes off quietly. Stella put hers on the wooden ladder-back chair; Alan dropped his on top of his suitcase.

'Jesus, Stella ...'

They still hadn't kissed. Together they rolled back the duvet. He took off his glasses and they lay at arm's length, the better to take each other in. His fingertips rested lightly on the mound of her hip; he was smiling.

'What a lady ...'

In a moment or two she moved a little closer and stroked him gently, watching as his eyes closed and his lips parted.

Then, they kissed.

Stella had often wondered whether it was possible for people to be both friends and lovers. Now she knew. When some hours later they were confronting the *moules frites* and aioli in a side-street restaurant she felt as if they'd always known each other, a phenomenon often referred to but which she had never before experienced. Though in fact, apart from a few bits of family history, they still knew almost nothing about one another. They had not yet, for instance, engaged in the ritual of exchanging the simplest background information, not from anxiety about their friendship's transience – because after all, who knew? – but out of a mutual wish to preserve the bubble of here-and-now-ness. They looked at their surroundings, and at other people, they ate and drank prodigiously (he never once commented on her appetite, for which she was grateful), they aired opinions (broadly similar but varying in detail) on matters of the day, and they laughed a good deal. They were also from time to time silent, without any awkwardness. It might be too soon to claim actual friendship, but Stella knew few people with whom she felt this at ease.

As to the sex, it had fulfilled her expectations. Her pragmatic attitude meant that she had had many experiences that were more explosive, more fevered – one or two where the furniture, if not the earth, had moved. Each encounter was for its own sake and nothing else; she had never seen anything wrong with wham-bang-thank-you-ma'am provided it was enjoyable. In this instance there had been a sense of time to spare, room for more – space for the mind and imagination to work on whatever might happen next. Which might prove optimistic, but was nonetheless pleasurable.

They didn't leave the table until after ten. She wanted to share the bill, and after some gentlemanly wrangling he let her, though she sensed it went against the grain. She appreciated that.

'I don't know about you,' he said as they emerged into the narrow street, 'but I could do with some exercise. Shall we go down to the beach?'

Her turn to humour him, by not mentioning the cardiovascular workout involved in returning to the *pension*. But hang on, she thought as they began to walk – who says I'm going back there?

Next morning as they lay next to one another he said: 'Got any plans for the day?' He touched and held her straying hand. 'Apart from that.'

'Not really. I can't remember if I had any. For some reason my plans are all awry.'

'Care to join in with mine?'

'Depends what they are.'

'Let's see …' He brought her hand up to his face and kissed the palm. 'Looks like a lovely day out there. Let's go somewhere we've neither of us seen before.'

'Machu Picchu's out, I take it?'

'Done that.'

They were silent for a moment, thinking.

'I know,' said Stella. 'I want to go to Agincourt.'

In Stella's only two relationships worthy of the name, there had come a point when she'd realised that she'd accumulated a few memories; when she found herself saying things like 'Yes we did, we saw her in that thing with Ewan McGregor', or 'I thought you said you didn't like Brie?' This creation of a hinterland was often, in her case, a premonitory sign that the end was nigh.

This morning as they set off, with (by mutual consent) her at the wheel and Alan armed with the map and the guidebook, she saw that once again things were a little different here. They were engaged in the deliberate creation of a memory, as if, were they never to see each other again after tomorrow, they would each take this away and keep it, like a polished pebble, as a reminder.

'We need to look for Azincourt,' he said. 'Z not G. And as a matter of fact, the site isn't exactly there.'

'It's near Tramecourt.'

'Exactly.' He glanced at her. 'You know more than you let on.'

'I've read up on it,' she explained. 'History was my favourite subject at school, and this is a bit of an obsession with me. It began with seeing Olivier's *Henry V* when I was thirteen, and went on from there. Since then I've seen several more productions and read everything I could lay my hands on.'

'I'm surprised you haven't been to the place before.'

'Bad, isn't it?' She pulled a self-mocking face. 'I'm lazy. But also, reality can spoil the image in your head.'

'Spoil? A battlefield?'

'Ah yes, but Agincourt isn't just a battlefield. Not like where we were before. For one thing, it was six hundred years ago; the world was a different place. For another, it's a story, a metaphor; it's attained mythical status.'

He shook his head. 'An English thing, perhaps?'

'Very.'

They drove a little way in silence, and then he said, 'You're ready to see it now, though?'

'Yes, because I'll be going there with you, and you'll be coming to it fresh, so there will be something added as well as something taken away.'

'Stella, I hope you realise I have only the sketchiest knowledge of what happened.'

'That's the point.'

'If you say so.' He smiled and looked out of the window, shaking his head. 'Glad to hear it.'

*

They saw the first wooden cut-out about a mile from the village – an English archer standing in the hedgerow at the side of the road, bow in hand.

'Oh no,' moaned Stella. 'I wish they hadn't done that.'

By the time they reached the village itself, they'd passed dozens of cut-outs of soldiers, French and English, one or two even on horseback. In the village itself there were signs to the visitors' centre displaying the Union Jack and at the entrance to the centre itself a flagpole bearing the same flag, barely moving on this fine morning. Stella drove past, fuming.

'I can't bear it. We should never have come.'

'Nonsense. Stella! Stella, hey – pull over.'

She did so, and turned off the engine. 'I'm sorry, Alan.'

'That's okay, I understand. This place means a lot to you.'

'It really does ...' She turned her head away so he wouldn't see her angry, disappointed tears. 'But it's a bloody tourist destination.'

'People want to come here,' he said gently. 'People like you.'

She shook her head, unable to speak.

'But there don't seem to be many around today,' he went on. 'There was only one car in that car park, and I don't see a crowd heading out of town. We've got the place to ourselves.'

Something in his tone – understanding, warmly supportive, a tad bracing – reminded her of someone, she couldn't remember who. She heard pages being turned as he consulted first the map, then the guidebook.

'If we carry on along this road we come to the battlefield in about a mile. We can get out and walk. I want to hear all about it. Don't rat on me, Stella.'

'Ratty!' She laughed and sniffed.

'You may be; not me, I promise you.'

'Yes you are. Like Ratty, in the book. *The Wind in the Willows*.'

'And – pardon me – that's good?'

'Very good.' She reached into the back seat for her handbag and retrieved one of the few clean tissues remaining after yesterday's picnic. 'He's the best friend in the whole of fiction.'

'Then for sure. Ready to drive on?'

'Ready.'

*

There was no one there; not a soul. Like High Wood, the field of Agincourt was so empty they could hear the birds singing. They parked the car on the grass and went to look at the plaque that was supposed to help them orientate.

Alan was delighted with the plaque, reading and pointing enthusiastically. 'So Henry and his guys were down there, to the right, and the French knights were kind of up there on the ridge. Makes sense, doesn't it?'

'I'm not sure,' she said. 'That's almost too simple and obvious. The layout of this land is quite different now; the campaign predates almost all these trees, for instance. The most authoritative expert I've read ...'

She held forth, and he was perfectly content to defer to her greater knowledge. The ground was pretty dry, and they set off to beat the bounds of the site as best they could, a walk of about a mile and a half, stumbling along edges of plough and the brambly outskirts of a wood. They were about halfway round when Stella suddenly stopped.

'Look. You can see from here.'

'What?' His shoulder was touching hers. She pointed and he squinted along her arm as if it were the barrel of a gun.

'The layout, this is right, I can see it all from here. I mean, I may be wrong – it was all so long ago and the topography's probably changed, especially the trees – but this makes sense ...'

She continued to talk excitedly, her earlier disappointment forgotten, outlining her picture of the battlefield, who had been where, how it must have felt, Henry's strategy, the bravery on both sides. She was elated, and moved, and Alan was a good listener; there was a pleasure in sharing her knowledge and speculation with him. And as to her emotional reaction, she sensed that he got it, just as – *mirabile dictu* – he got her.

As they walked back to the car, she paused and began casting about in the reddish soil.

'What are you after?' he asked.

'A memento.' She bent to pick up a stone. 'I take one back whenever I can, but especially where there's history.'

'Good idea.' He picked one up himself and turned it in his fingers. 'You think this stuff is old? It might just be builders' rubble.'

'That doesn't matter. Every time I look at mine, I'll think of Agincourt.'

'You're right.' He pocketed the stone. '"Some corner of a foreign field", that kind of thing.'

'Except in this case it will be some corner of your bookshelf which is forever France.'

How did she know, thought Alan, that there was a shelf in his study in Montreal where the books were pushed to the back to make room for a polyglot clutter of sentimental junk?

Having recovered her composure and thoroughly explored the area, Stella had no problem with going to the despised visitors' centre, and they went round it happily enough, not least because it reminded each of them – separately; it wasn't mentioned – of their meeting at Beaumont Hamel. Afterwards they had another picnic, this time sitting in the sun against the sheltering wall of a tiny First World War cemetery.

'What is it with us?' Alan asked. 'Anyone would think we were ghouls.'

'We're not, though – not at all.' She might have added that she'd never felt more burstingly alive. 'After all, both of us came here carrying a bit of family history, somewhere we wanted to see.'

'I did. You were with your nephew on that terrific tour.'

'Great-nephew actually.' She plucked at the grass.

'Whatever.'

'I was with Raff, but one of the reasons I volunteered was so that I could see northern France, where my grandfather fought. And I mustn't forget my grandmother – she was an ambulance driver.'

'That must have been tough. Did they meet over here?'

'No, I believe they knew each other already. They were slow burners.' She ran her hand over the grass next to her. 'Look at all these wild flowers.'

'You know what they are?'

'Violets ... celandines ... daisies, obviously ... I don't know this little pink one. Early in the year for so many. I suppose they're sheltered here.'

'I guess.' He placed his hand on her bowed head; her hair was warmed by the sun. 'You're something else, Stella, you know that?'

She shook her head without looking up, letting his hand rest there.

'Yes you are. I've never met anyone like you.'

Now she looked at him, and he let his hand fall, not sure if he'd said too much.

'I should think not,' she said, almost brusquely, 'since everyone's unique.'

'Some are uniquer than others.'

'So who are you, Alan?' She settled back against the wall, ankles crossed and arms folded. 'Tell me who you are.'

He was a doctor in Montreal, a paediatrician, with an ex-wife and a grown-up son, Pierre. His grandfather's family had emigrated from Glasgow to St John's at the turn of the century and the nine-teen-year-old Douglas had married a local girl not long before going off to war and swapping the ice storms of Newfoundland for the far deadlier ones of northern France. His father, their only son, had divorced his mother when the young Alan was fifteen. He'd moved with his mother to Montreal, where she still lived, a mile or so from him, in a modern apartment overlooking the park, with a great view of the Oratory perched on its hilltop. Mireille, his ex-wife, and he were on friendly terms, better now in many ways than when they'd been married, but they didn't see much of each other. Pierre now lived in France with his partner – that was another reason for this trip.

He had only a few close friends, one or two people he'd known during his marriage and who had stayed on his side of the divide. But he was solitary by nature, and after a day dealing with sick children and their worried, often worrisome, parents, he was gen-erally happy to spend the evening reading, listening to music or watching TV; he liked British costume drama, American sitcoms and sport – rugby when he could find it and hockey (she'd have called it ice hockey), a national obsession. A dog would have been nice – as a child his family had always owned one – but it wouldn't have been practical with his work, so he had a cat, Jules, a Bur-mese with whom he got along very nicely. Theatre he could take or leave – shameful to admit that the last time he'd been was to see *Miss Saigon* with Pierre. Film was his thing, especially MGM musicals and art-house stuff of the sixties, Buñuel, Fellini, Bergman. There had been one or two relationships in the decade since his marriage broke up, but he'd never felt inclined to get married again, and in the end the ladies had moved on and he had been left only a little sad, secretly relieved rather than broken-hearted. Travel was his passion; he was never so happy as when waking up in a strange place with all its intriguing possibilities. Every year he had one trip of three weeks when he did something adventurous – Nepal, northern India, the 'stans, Venezuela – and a couple of shorter ones with some sort of project: family history like this, or art, about which he knew shamefully little but was gradually learning.

At the end of all this he said, 'I have it in me to be a terribly dull stick. I reckon if I keep moving I can avoid that fate.'

'Neither of us could possibly be dull,' said Stella.

She noticed that he did not immediately ask her about herself. One of the many not-dull things about him was his unpredictability; there was nothing calculating in it, he wouldn't do anything purely for form's sake.

They got back to the *pension* at four, and spent the next three hours in bed, talking, sleeping, having sex and looking at the guidebook. Before dinner they decided not to worry about being tourists – that was, after all, what they were – and went for a drink in one of the bars on the promenade. Though neither of them said as much, their mood had changed; tomorrow Alan would be setting off for Pierre's house in the Dordogne, and they'd go their separate ways.

'Your evening fact,' she said. 'William the Conqueror set sail from near here.'

'For once,' he smiled, 'I know. I saw it in some old tapestry.'

'I'm ashamed to admit I've not done that. In fact, the day the boys went to Bayeux was the day I took off – when I met you.'

'Time well spent, then. But it is incredible, you should try and fit it in. You could go tomorrow,' he suggested.

'I might.'

'Stella.' He laid his hand briefly over hers. 'Your turn. What will you be going back to – when you do go back?'

'Let's see.'

She told him, ticking things off on her fingers, giving him almost as comprehensive a picture as he had given her (she thought; though of course she had no way of knowing what he had omitted).

'Holy cow!' he exclaimed when she'd finished. 'You fit a lot in.'

She gave a shrug. 'Not really. Other people's lives always sound busier, because they do different things.'

'You know what we should do?' he said. 'Before we part company we should fix another trip together. I haven't decided what to do with my September vacation, for instance.'

'That sounds nice,' she said. She could feel herself acting tough, distancing herself from the real distance that would soon intervene.

'It would mean a lot to me,' he said. 'A hell of a lot, to know we were going to do something like this again. Let's make sure we have all each other's contact details. Then we can call, too, and email – keep in touch.'

Over breakfast the next morning he gave her his card, and she tore a page from the back of her diary and wrote on that. When he'd settled up and they were outside, she said: '*Au revoir* then, Alan. And thank you, it's been great.'

'And it will be again.'

They kissed, quickly and softly.

'*Au revoir*, Stella,' he said. 'And do something for me. Get a cell.'

Chapter Twenty-One

1982

Colour Sergeant Linch was not a man to mince his words. He was never less than respectful in his address, but his was the token 'sir' that Will remembered from Sandhurst; a necessary evil when plain speaking was called for.

'I'll tell the men we're stopping here then, sir.' Without raising his voice, he was perfectly audible under the hiss and howl of the driving rain.

'Yes, Sergeant. Post the pickets. Permission to brew up.' It was a sort of joke, but Will was wasting his time.

'I'm sure they'll do their best.'

He snapped a salute and strode away into the maelstrom; for a small man he had a long stride. A whip-thin Brummie with seen-it-all eyes and a mouth like a trap, Linch had the mentality of a certain kind of hard-boiled, small-time entertainer: that trick with the voice, plus he was cynical to his bone marrow but programmed to put on the show no matter how inimical the conditions. And with precious little love for the management, whose fault the whole thing generally was.

It was seven a.m. Intelligence had gleaned via some glum locals that vehicles would be useless on the island terrain, so the jeeps had been left on board ship. (Vain to speculate how the sheep farmers managed to keep track of their flocks.) The company had been marching in the rain and dark for three hours and were now strewn over a heather-covered hillside – not quite a mountain, in spite of its name – without any natural features to provide shelter. A few miles back they'd yomped across a valley criss-crossed with shallow gulleys and ramparts of gorse, which was tough going in the dark but which meant that for a while at least they were shielded from the worst of the icy wind and rain. But they hadn't been able to call a halt there; they had to crack on. Now they were where they needed to be. The top of this hill was marked by an uneven, spreading outcrop of rocks, and beyond that, at the bottom of the far side, was the cluster of buildings that was their objective. According to the map, the total distance from here to there was no more than a couple of miles, but in their heads it was a hell of a lot further. Much had to happen in those two miles.

Head down, Will squelched across to where a couple of younger officers were directing operations, for their own satisfaction as much as the men's. The soldiers, hunkering down under the onslaught, had all but disappeared into the sodden heather.

'All right, Captain? Everything under control?'

'Yes, sir, getting there.'

The other young man, who had been crouched over a billycan, shielding it from the elements with his outspread cape, like a lapwing with its young, got to his feet and handed Will a tin mug.

'Brew, sir?'

'Thanks. And then try and get a bit of kip.' He tapped his watch. 'Work later.'

Will returned to his position and lay down. He tried to maintain the illusion that everything was routine. There was a balance to be struck between this 'part of the job' approach (the one favoured by Sergeant Linch), and acknowledging the unique and inevitable pressures of action under fire. Even if it had been desirable, it would have been impossible to tell a new man how real danger would feel, or how he would react to it, because his reaction would not be the same as yours, or anyone else's. No matter what a man's training, and the extent to which he'd been programmed as part of a team, his deepest response would be entirely personal and private.

Besides, Will was no expert, he conceded that. He'd done tours in Cyprus, and in Northern Ireland, but the peculiar terrors of those places could not be compared to this. The 'sitting duck' quotient, in Belfast especially, had been high – higher even than here – and the steady attrition of fear, without the antidote of adrenalin, was beyond anything he'd known. But what there had been – he ground his chattering teeth at the memory – was barracks. Hideous and grimly fortified, by no stretch of the imagination a home from home, but nonetheless places of safety to which you returned after nerve-jangling hours on patrol to find a roof, hot food and a dry bed.

The rain eased off a little, and he dozed.

The landing had been bloody awful as, historically, landings always were. They were packed like sardines into the landing craft, and like sardine tins the craft tilted and heaved on the South Atlantic swell and bobbed around wildly in the choppier waters near the beach. Everyone felt sick, and this time, even had they been able to move, they didn't have access to the facilities of a cruise liner. At least the Antarctic blast and the freezing water that eventually greeted them blew away the nausea and washed the vomit off their boots.

But even this dubious relief was some way off. They spent a full hour in the LCUs going round and round San Carlos Bay, bathed in clear moonlight, because the navy support ships were immobilised by the inevitable fog, further out. The language on board – Will was a keen student of army language – reached unprecedented levels of inventiveness. And when they were pitched out at last, fifty metres from the beach, the temperatures ratcheted it up again. They were all like turtles under the weight of their packs, scared shitless of falling over in the water in case they couldn't get up again. One of Will's lot did fall and it took four of them to drag him above the surface and upright, a dead weight, waterlogged and half frozen. On the beach he'd had to get sorted before he became hypothermic.

They'd been unopposed at that stage. On the beach they'd formed up into sections, the sections into platoons and the platoons into companies. The half-drowned soldier was supplied by his mates with two pairs of dry socks and a dry quilted jacket underneath his wet kit; no one had been sympathetic, the twat.

It was light on the mountain, and with the light came a dawn chorus of enemy air fire. Mirages, Skyhawks, you name it, snarling and flashing overhead at supersonic speeds, making the ground thud and explode. They'd dug in and taken pot shots when they could get a bead, which was almost hopeless. But a streak from a Stinger had gone up from the far side of the mountain about a mile away, and a Pucara had crashed in a spectacular tail spin, the pilot ejecting just in time and floating lazily to earth before the stricken plane burst into flames. That pilot beneath his fragile white canopy reminded Will of a drifting summer seed pod. From a distance; close to, he was probably screaming and shitting himself. Looking back, he could identify that moment as the one after which everything became a blur, and selective memory kicked in.

No such mental editing for Sergeant Linch, though; he kept a diary.

Chapter Twenty-Two
1999

Letters, thought Evie – they carried so much weight. Would modern means of communication ever speak across the years as urgently, as powerfully, as an old-fashioned letter? Emails, even deleted ones, could apparently orbit in cyberspace for ever, but who cared? A letter, especially a handwritten one, was organic: the paper, the ink, the smell, the minute traces of the writer's DNA that he or she had left behind ... She lifted a page to her face and inhaled. Eventually, like all things organic, even this letter would wither and die, but for the duration of its natural life it had a formidable presence.

She was in her grandmother's flat at Rectory Court. They had read the letters on the train, and again when they got back, with large G and Ts to hand. For Evie, there had been shock, disbelief and a sort of panic, followed by complete exhaustion. Strangely, no tears; Evie wouldn't have wept anyway, but Kate too had remained dry-eyed. She had protested when Evie announced her intention of staying, but had given up in the face of her own overwhelming need to sleep rather than argue.

'Will you be all right in here?'

'Fine, I'll use the sofa bed. I might even watch telly for a bit.'

'If I'm not stirring when you are, give me a shake.'

They'd exchanged a kiss, and Kate patted her cheek as she did so.

'Bless you. What a day.'

That had been two hours ago, and Evie had not watched television since. Nor, in spite of the fact that she was tucked up in the sofa bed in one of Kate's glamorous old-fashioned nightdresses, had she felt remotely like sleeping. The people from the past were with her – here, on the duvet and in her hands, and most of all in her head, their voices calling and tumbling in overlapping measures. She hadn't known them, or how they would have sounded – she was dependent on her imagination for that, and her imagination had caught fire.

Before getting into her borrowed dressing gown, she went outside to call Owen. He listened in respectful silence, with the occasional brief grunt and intake of breath.

'Bloody hell. That's a real facer. You do what's right, babes. Is she okay?'

'Well, it's been an extraordinary day, with a good deal of turbulence, as you can imagine, but she's tough. She says that Thea was right, that she had told her already, but that may be bravado. Perhaps she'd considered the possibility, had some idea in her heart of hearts, who knows? Anyway, she's asleep now.'

Evie heard him inhale. 'And you think it's true, do you?'

'Oh yes. Not the shadow of a doubt. He was a theatrical kind of guy, he was loving every minute of it, but the letters speak for themselves. Literally.'

'What sort of person makes such a production over a thing like this?'

'I told you, a drama queen. Gran was pretty damn splendid. I was proud of her.'

'Still … It's kind of none of his business and yet he set up this elaborate meet, dragged you and your gran to London … I don't get it.'

Twenty-four hours earlier, Evie hadn't got it either. Even earlier that same day, with Ernest Mallory in full flight, she had felt stroppy and mutinous. Now, listening to Owen, she realised that over the course of the evening her position had shifted.

'He wasn't so bad. He'd come by this life-changing stuff, more or less by accident, and he wanted to, I don't know, give it full value. I think he quite fancied Gran.'

Owen ignored this. 'It still sounds weird to me.'

'The whole thing is weird. But he didn't strike me as dangerous. Self-satisfied and manipulative, but not dangerous.'

'Right,' said Owen. 'Anyway, that's that, no one has to see him again.'

On the train, she and Kate had put the letters in date order before reading them. Kate went first, her hand covering her mouth. After she'd passed the first one over to Evie, she sat back, her hand still at her mouth, and stared unseeing out of the window while Evie read.

This was the one Evie returned to now. It was from Thea Kingsley in Gilgil, dated 1 May 1952.

Dear Mr Huxley,

Please forgive me for writing out of the blue like this. I am the older sister of Dulcie Tennant, to whom I believe you were a good and trusted friend for many years. After her dreadfully sad and untimely death over here a few years ago, I've been experiencing a great deal of soul-searching on a certain matter and have come to the conclusion that like King Midas I need to tell someone in order that that person – poor you! – can share the responsibility. You don't need to do anything about this letter, or act on it in any way, just keep it safe!

For only the second time in our whole married life, I am doing something that I know Jack wouldn't want. He doesn't even know that I'm writing, partly at least because things are very uncertain and troubling here, we're concerned for the future and I don't want to add to his worries. But we did discuss this and he made his view clear that we should leave well alone. He may be right. All I know is that my guilt and agonised indecision has become unbearable, so here goes.

Our daughter, Kate, was adopted. The adoption didn't take place till she was five, so she found it quite hard at first, but from that moment she has been as much ours as our son Joe, who was born a couple of years later. She's now happily married and has children of her own

The story we told her, and that she believed while growing up, was that she was a war orphan, and that a benefactress who had known her parents but wished to remain anonymous had seen to her welfare until now. This was a lie. (*Evie closed her eyes, and took a slow breath.*) Kate does now know that her mother is my younger sister, your old friend Dulcie Tennant. I told her against my husband's wishes and still have regrets about that. But I have long wanted to write to you, for Dulcie's sake, because I know

219

how much she admired and respected you, and how much your friendship meant to her (you were perhaps her only one). Please accept this rather rambling letter in that spirit!

When Kate travelled to Europe in 1936 with Joe, who was going to boarding school, she stayed with my father and brother for a while, and met Dulcie, who was very good to her. She had and still has a lot of her mother in her, so they got on famously! Kate got a job in London and stayed on, and they continued to see a lot of each other. I half thought the secret might come out at that point, but it never did until I chose to divulge it much later. Now I feel I owe it to my sister, to put these things on record.

They say that a letter written in the heat of the moment should be set aside for at least a week before you decide to post it. I'm not doing that – I've wanted to write this for a long time, and now I must send it straight away. The post office is five miles away and I'm going to drive like the wind!

I know how much Dulcie thought of you – I do hope you'll feel able to accept this in a spirit of love and respect for her, my late, darling sister and your true friend.

Yours determinedly

Thea Kingsley

PS Your address was in her pocket diary, and I'd heard her mention you often. I hope you don't mind.

Evie folded the page along its accustomed lines and replaced it in its envelope. Her hand trembled slightly, as though infected by the letter's urgent tone, its passionate anxiety and guilt.

She'd always considered her great-grandmother to be fairly distant, in family terms as well as in sheer miles; an ancestor, really. Although, she reminded herself, Kate was Raff's great-grandmother and he saw her often and thought nothing of it, so the distance wasn't always so great. Apparently she had met Thea Kingsley once; there was a picture of her as a baby in Thea's arms in the garden at Hallowfield – her grandfather, Lawrence, was in the corner of the picture, sitting in a deckchair. In that picture, as in others, Thea's warmly open nature, the quality everyone mentioned in connection with her, was plain to see; she'd been holding the nine-month-old Evie in such a way that they were looking into each other's eyes and laughing. It was odd now to reflect that there had been this moment of mutual delight of which she remembered nothing; and also that the lovely woman in the photograph was not all she had seemed. There had been a collusion – Evie tried not to think conspiracy. An anonymous hand had smudged and smeared the past, that precious part of it that she thought she knew.

Not for the first time with regard to family life, Evie felt cheated. And if she felt cheated, how much more shocking and painful must it be for Kate to have all this raised again now, and by that awful stranger? And for Stella, who didn't even know yet? And then there was Uncle Joe, and Raff ... Though actually Raff would take it in his stride; the young were pragmatic. His Kingsley forebears meant very little to him, and it would be a good story for him to tell when he was older.

And (she'd almost forgotten about him, and whose fault was that?), what about her father? As a small boy, Will would have met Thea and Jack. Perhaps – faint hope – this would be a wake-up call, reminding him that he had a family and that cracks in the fabric of a family, left unrepaired, could all too easily become unbridgeable fissures.

She turned to the second letter, which was brief. The handwriting was even and careful, as if to conceal (not always successfully) a certain shakiness, and something about the formation of the capital letters had told them at once that the writer was not English.

Dear M. Huxley

Thank you for your letter. I am glad that you have received news of Madame, whom I miss so much. I cared for her for many years from before the war and we knew each other well. I hope you will not be offended if I say no to your request to visit me. They look after me here but I am not in good health and like to be quiet. I do not wish to talk about Madame. I looked after her but her life was not my business. She was always kind to me and we had an understanding.

Please forgive me. I am very glad you are well.

Celine Hunt

So in spite of Thea's request, Giles Huxley had wanted to share the secret, and to discuss it, just as Thea had done. But this elderly, infirm French widow in her care home had manifested the cast-iron discretion of a lifetime in service.

The third enveloped turned out not to contain a letter at all, but a photograph. A snapshot of Kate as a young woman, mop of curls blown sideways by the wind, eyes narrowed against the sun, long legs in trousers planted firmly apart, hands in pockets. On the back, in a different hand, was written:

> Look at her, is she at all like me? Even the least little bit? No, you
> don't have to say. Dxx

The question – urgent, plaintive, slightly self-mocking – flew up at Evie. But she had no answers. How could she? She had quite enough unanswered questions of her own.

At two a.m. Kate woke up. In the tiny flat she could hear Evie's deep breathing, just short of a snore, from the next room, but the dear girl must have crept in earlier and turned the radio off. She hoped it hadn't been keeping her awake.

Kate pressed the button on her reading lamp and angled it away from the bed. On her dressing table opposite, the cluster of family photos that had been such a source of comfort over the years now confronted her in a smiling conspiracy. She felt no rancour towards the conspirators; they'd had their reasons and she herself had been the beneficiary, with parents whom she had loved and who could scarcely have loved her more.

But oh, it was so, so sad! Yet again the story of her life had been invaded. The first time she had been only five, she had understood nothing and the simplest way of dulling the pain was to hurt someone else – how had Jack not smacked her when she sank her teeth into his arm? Was her story never to be her own? Her sovereign territory? Age brought understanding, but the understanding brought precious little comfort.

She did, however, have an answer for Dulcie. She first thought, then spoke, it softly into the half-lit room:

'Yes,' she whispered. 'Yes, I am a lot like you. I am my mother's daughter.'

A summer's evening before the war, and she was walking in the park with Dulcie.

With her mother.

Regent's Park it must have been, because they had been able at one point to see over into the zoo, the Mappin Terrace, with a chamois perched improbably on one of the bare grey ledges. Dulcie had been wearing a hat, a tiny crescent-shaped confection of blue grosgrain that fitted snugly on the blonde ripples of her hair. Kate remembered that hat, and her shoes, in two shades of blue, with Louis Quinze heels. Walking on the grass was not (as Evie might have said) an option. God knew what she herself had been wearing – trousers, probably; it was when she was still working at the institute in Whitechapel.

They often met at this time, when Kate had either come off a shift or was about to start one, and before Dulcie went out for the evening. She always went out; her life was the sort of sparkling ceaseless social merry-go-round that Kate could scarcely imagine. But it was mysterious, too; Dulcie never discussed it, and mentioned it only in the briefest terms: 'Oh, show and supper with a friend', or 'a dreary gallery party' or, at weekends, 'driving out of town for lunch'. Knowing her as she did, Kate was sure that she was the life and soul of these events, exquisitely pretty, lively and amusing, and never less than perfectly turned out. She had once said to Kate: 'I'm very little use, so I try to be an ornament.'

Strange that Thea, in the letter, had referred to Kate being like her mother. On the face of it they could not have been more different, and yet it was true that she'd always sensed a kindred spirit under the differences. They were both people on the edge of the family, not quite conforming, both in their different ways bloody-minded. They had come together out of duty (though with hindsight, who knew what Dulcie's motives had been?) and stayed together as friends. If Kate had known then what she knew now, would that have been possible? How could it have been?

'Do you meet any young men in your work?'

Dulcie very rarely asked questions. Secretive about some things herself, she allowed others to provide such information as they chose. That was one reason why this occasion had remained so clear in Kate's memory.

'There are some men there, of course. But not in the way you mean.'

'And what's that?'

'Young men, who would take me out.' She glanced at Dulcie. 'I'm right, aren't I?'

Dulcie didn't bother to deny it. 'As long as you don't bury yourself in that dreary place and never have any fun.'

'I do have fun, and the institute's not dreary, it's exciting. No two days are the same, and it keeps me busy.'

'That,' said Dulcie, 'is what people say when they're trying to kill time.'

'Not me. The very last thing I want is a boyfriend.'

'You won't say that when the right one comes along.'

'In that case, I'll wait and see.'

'Kate, my dear.' Dulcie, the most untactile of women, paused and placed her hand on Kate's arm, just above the elbow. The light touch stopped Kate in her tracks.

'What is it?'

'I only want you to be happy.' Its work done, Dulcie removed her hand and gave instead her sweet, practised smile. 'I speak as your unmarried aunt *d'un certain age*, who thinks the world of you.'

Code, thought Kate – all her life everything had been in code, one it was never intended she should crack.

Celine had been a study, she remembered thinking so at the time, a cross between lady's maid, diplomat and palace guard. She was younger than her employer, but a life in service had left her looking ten years older. At a time when people increasingly – and quite rightly – wished to improve their situation and escape their place, Celine knew hers, and wanted no other. The devotion with which she kept clothes cleaned and pressed, shoes polished, the flat spotless, flowers changed, food prepared and unwanted boarders repelled was nothing short of heroic.

Kate was never sure if Celine liked her; possibly she didn't much care for anyone who occupied a regular place in her mistress's life, much less her affections. But after she'd left Dulcie's employ, and with Kate safely married, she'd fallen in love with Stella, who had elicited ecstasies of French.

'*Oh, la petite, comme elle est mignonne, regardez les belles cheveux! Tu as des très jolies cheveux, cherie, oui, oui, c'est ça! Viens avec Celine, viens trouver une madeleine, non?*'

Celine had reminded Kate a little of Tanty, though she was a great deal more emotional. Tanty had been a professional nanny, a hired gun to her bones; there was no doubt that after Kate's departure Tanty would quickly have found herself another job and another charge. But beneath the black costume Celine still wore always, there beat a heart that dreamed, even if the dreams were of, and for, Madame.

One day she had taken Stella to Dulcie's flat for tea. Celine had 'dropped in', though Kate secretly suspected she had been invited. She had slipped into her old routine, making tea, passing plates, all the time exclaiming over Stella and petting her. At one point Kate had gone out to the kitchen to find Celine, sitting at the small round kitchen table with her head in her hands, weeping silently. Kate pushed the door to behind her.

'Celine? What's the matter? Are you all right?'

She nodded dumbly, wiping her cheeks with her hands. Kate sat down. 'What is it? Tell me.'

A shake of the head this time. 'It is nothing.'

'I don't believe you. Are you ill? Has something happened to you? If so, you must tell someone, even if it's not me.'

'No, no …' Celine took a clean, ironed hankie from her pocket and wiped away the tears, giving a couple of brisk sniffs as she did so. 'It is Madame, and your …' she gestured towards the drawing room, from which overexcited shrieks and giggles could be heard, 'your little girl. They are so nice together, Madame is so happy.'

'She is,' said Kate. 'Which is good, surely.'

'There is not enough happiness for her.'

'For Dulcie, you mean?' Celine nodded briefly, trying to contain a second wave of tears. 'She strikes me as very happy, Celine. She has lots of friends, and this beautiful flat – and you. She has you!'

This was the moment that Stella chose to patter unsteadily along the corridor and push open the kitchen door. Both women jumped to their feet, Kate picked Stella up and Celine whisked past them and was gone; seconds later came the sound of the front door clunking shut behind her.

'Was that Celine?' said Dulcie in the drawing room. 'I thought she must have left half an hour ago.'

'She forgot something.' Kate put Stella down. 'And damn, sorry, after all that I forgot the hot water.'

Kate turned the lamp off again. She knew she should try to sleep. She had not, so far, shed a single tear. The unpleasant shock of the meeting with Mallory had sand-blasted her quite dry. But now, creeping out of the darkness, came all those memories, those people and events she believed she had long since come to terms with, those pieces of her jigsaw she had put in place – that she had made to fit. More than anything she thought of Thea, who had been a mother to her – when it mattered, she had known no other – and whose love, though sometimes sorely tried, had been constant and unconditional. She could not bear that others might think less of her.

She remembered the garden at the farm in Gilgil, walking between Thea and Jack, holding their hands; she must have been about six. It was early evening, just before sunset; they'd left their drinks on the veranda and were taking a turn so that Thea could talk about her new plants. Intermittently, contentedly, the adults spoke to one another over her head, but she was happy, she didn't feel left out. She wasn't interested in the plants; from time to time she put her weight on their hands and swung. They let her do this without complaint, continuing to laugh and talk together.

They took their stroll across the little path of stepping stones that Thea had made through the flowerbed. The path was flanked with spindly, fragile-looking flowers that always looked to Kate rather like the weeds that Thea and the gardener spent so much time pulling up. But Thea had told her they were English wild flowers, the most precious and important in the whole garden.

They paused, and Thea leaned forward to pick a sprig of something – nothing pretty, it had no flowers.

'Thyme,' she said. 'Smell!'

She rubbed it between her fingers and offered it to Jack first, then Kate. The smell was powerful and aromatic; it flooded Kate's head and hung round the three of them as the sun began its swift descent towards the Aberdares.

For ever after the scent of thyme would bring back her parents to her, and that moment when as a small child, happy to be ignored, content in their contentment, she had swung between their hands, between the English flowers, as the sun dropped below the hills.

Kate could smell it now, as she fell asleep. Her mother's daughter.

Chapter Twenty-Three

1999

'Other people's lives always seem busier because the things they're doing are different.' Flattered by admiration, Stella had said something of the sort to Alan.

Waiting for the London train in the drizzly half-light of Folkestone docks, her words came back to her as glib, sententious bollocks. The contrast between her surroundings and the broad, sunlit spaces of the past few days could not have been more stark. From her current, admittedly jaundiced perspective, the life to which she was returning appeared small, dull and uninviting.

On the other hand, there were lots of people she was looking forward to seeing and who, unaccountable as it seemed in her present mood, looked forward to seeing her. Pull yourself together, she thought, your life's of your own choosing; you're one of the fortunate ones.

Before boarding the train, furnished with a bacon roll and a cardboard beaker of coffee, she found a pay phone and rang her mother, whose day would have started some hours ago. After half a dozen rings the machine kicked in, the all-purpose voice that always prompted Stella to redial in case she left a message on the wrong number.

'Hi, Ma, it's me, I'm back. I'll call later in the day and tell you all about it. We had a super time. Take care, see you soon.'

Once on the train, she stared out of the window, her cheek resting on the back of the seat. Kent, the garden of England and now its increasingly built-up gateway, rocketed past the window. Suddenly there was green space, a field of hops, an oast house – delighted, she lifted her head to look and half raised her hand to point them out, before realising her mistake – that he wasn't with her.

Generally speaking, she wasn't someone who missed people, but that seemed to have changed.

She was exhausted when she got home, and disgruntled because of it. Good lord, she hadn't been hitch-hiking from Namibia; the journey she'd just done would have counted as scarcely more than a commute for some people! The house felt small and stuffy and she stumped about opening windows, turning on the hot water, gathering up sheaves of mostly junk mail and pushing a load of clothes into the washing machine. She hadn't even worn half of them, but it was simpler to process the lot than to sort through her hastily packed suitcase.

She wasn't quite ready to face the mail, or the winking answering machine, or the computer, so she took a bottle of Roosters (reminder of something else that must be dealt with) and a packet of crisps out into the garden and wiped the rain off a plastic chair. The garden was a fright; in her absence it had been romping unchecked through the season's riot of new growth. A week from now and the patch where she was sitting would be swamped by a tsunami of weeds. She supposed, without any enthusiasm, that she was going to have to get out here and do something. In the past, one or two of her male friends had been keen to help on the gardening/DIY front; she interpreted their keenness as a sort of display mechanism by which they hoped to present themselves as suitable mates. If so, they'd picked the wrong woman. Their offers (and, worse, the efforts of one of them, who'd actually turned up early one morning and 'made a start', as he put it) had the opposite effect on Stella. On those rare occasions when she imagined togetherness, sweated labour was not part of the deal. When the garden, the paintwork or the clutter became intolerable, she'd deal with it herself – some of it anyway – and not worry about the rest. What she didn't need was someone 'getting everything ship-shape' (in one bloke's artery-thickening phrase), and expecting to be thought more manly as a result. At least Ted didn't do that, she thought, and then wished she hadn't.

She finished the crisps, drained the beer and put both packet and bottle into the general rubbish bin, cocking a mutinous snook at recycling.

Back inside, there was a psychological game to be played. She needed to prioritise those things that demanded her attention, then list them in inverse ratio to their attractiveness, and work through them in that order, saving the least unappealing till last. On this basis she began with the remaining unpacking; she put everything if not exactly away, then at least in the place where she'd last found it, and hoisted her case on to the top of the wardrobe. It would be nice to think she wouldn't have to blow the dust off it next time, but she wasn't holding her breath.

She pressed the button on the answering machine – not as much as expected. She listened to the most recent one, from Evie. 'Welcome home, Stella, call when you get back, need to talk about something.' This was an exemplar of the vice of modern communications: an indication that something was afoot, but not what.

She deferred responding to that message and sat down at the table, where she opened the post and started a shopping list on one of the discarded envelopes. Apart from the junk mail, there were a couple of bills, a postcard from a friend in Thailand, and an admirably prompt letter of thanks from the Head of External Studies at Raff's school. She stuffed the envelopes and the junk into the organic bin, at the same time retrieving the beer bottle and crisp packet and dropping them into the box with their kind, where they would be happier.

Moving up the list, she switched on the computer. She was relatively new to the process, but lo! she 'had mail'. Ten emails to be precise, most of them selling something, or indicating ways in which she could improve her sex life. When she'd deleted those, she was left with one from Child Friendly about quarterly supervision and one from a client asking when 'term' started. A third was from Alan Muir, with the words 'French leave' in the subject box.

I'm writing this at the end of Pierre and Ben's garden; there's a hot spot where you can pick up an internet signal, and I'm hogging it. Hate to madden you with envy and lust, but it's seventy-plus here and I'm in T-shirt and shorts. I miss you, Stella. The boys are great and this is a stunning place, but we had such a good time together, didn't we? In every way. After we said goodbye, I wanted to rewind and do it again, even better. I really didn't want to go. If you're reading this, you'll be home confronting that busy schedule of yours – hope you had a good journey back and that all's well your end. I'm going to put you in an opt-out situation and keep in touch unless expressly told not to – that trip in September is still live as far as I'm concerned, so let me have your thoughts.

Q: What becomes lighter the fuller it gets?

A: A heart.

Alan xx

She replied to the other two, but put off writing Alan an answer until later, not to make him wait, to appear cool, but on deferred-gratification principles.

The other phone messages were from Shannon, saying Toyah was sick but it would be lovely if she could pop round as usual for a natter; from one of her literacy clients who thought, rightly, that she'd like to know he'd had a breakthrough and was reading *Jurassic Park*; and from Alan, sounding convivial with voices in the background.

'Thought I'd use all the systems while I was at it. Welcome home. I wish you were here to help me road-test all this local wine. It's hell, I tell you, hell … I'll call again.'

Stella was glad he was in convivial company. Buoyed up by his messages, she sailed through the remainder of the afternoon, winding up with clean sheets, a full fridge and a quieter mind.

Until six, that was, when Evie turned up, agitated.

'Stella – have you spoken to Gran?'

'No, I was just about to. I left a message earlier.'

'Then don't, not yet.' Evie walked straight into the living room and stood in the middle with her hands thrust in her jacket pockets, thumbs sticking out like six-guns. 'There's something you need to know before you do.'

Fortunately for Stella, she came straight to the point, in a couple of sentences.

'That's the gist of it. This awful man, thinking he was bringing bad news to her door. Thank God he wasn't, but it threw me, I can tell you.'

'Bloody hell.' Stella put a hand to her brow. 'How is she?'

'Pretty well, on the face of it. I stayed there last night and she slept all right, or so she said.'

'Sit down,' said Stella. 'I think we should both have a drink.'

When she came back, she said: 'What about you?'

'Me? I'm fine, doesn't really affect me. But it's a biggie for you guys.'

'I'll say.'

Evie gulped her wine and fished cigarettes from her bag. 'I've officially given up, but mind if I …?'

'Carry on.'

'No, to be honest, I am a bit shocked.' She blew smoke towards the fireplace. 'Sorry to dump this on you so abruptly.'

'Best way. Besides, it's not the end of the world; they were sisters, after all. I gather it used to happen a lot with young unmarried mothers – the child was brought up believing its mother was an older sister. Not so very different.'

'Yes,' Evie tapped her cigarette on the hearth, 'but Stella, that's social history. This is *us*.'

'You're right. Tell me a bit more about this Mallory man.'

Evie gave a lively description of him, and of her own reaction, which had altered a little over the course of the day.

'He was too ingratiating for my taste, but Gran was quite taken to begin with, I think. Or at least he was very gallant towards her, and she was obviously flattered. Until he started on this "something you ought to know" stuff.'

'Creepy.'

'Then she got quite grand. Said thank you and changed the subject.'

'Who's got the letters now?' asked Stella. 'Ma?'

'Yes. She's not precious about it, you must read them. Talk about a blast from the past – I didn't know Thea, but you can sort of hear her talking.'

'But nothing from Dulcie?'

'A photo of Gran, looking like Katharine Hepburn. She'd scribbled on the back.' She glanced at Stella; her hand shook, the wine slopped dangerously. 'You should see that.'

They sat for a moment, silent with their respective thoughts.

An awful thought occurred to Stella. 'He's not after money, is he?'

'Stella, he's a millionaire, he owns restaurants!'

'So he says.'

'He does, I googled him.'

'He must want *something*.'

'Power? Influence? I think he liked having that bit of power over us.'

'As long as he doesn't continue to exercise it in some way or other.'

Evie shrugged and threw her fag end into the hearth. 'What can we do?'

After Evie had gone Stella was felled by a delayed reaction, the force of which frightened her. After all, nothing so very terrible had happened. 'No wrecks and nobody drowned,' as her father used to say. A meddling stranger had put his foot in the door, but had not been allowed over the threshold. So why was she shivering? Why were her hands and face cold, and her stomach fluttering?

Sinking down on the sofa she put her hands over her face and tried to breathe deeply. The past, the bloody past! It was always with you, always there, shadowing you. Ready to bite you in the bum, just when things were starting to look up.

Half an hour later, still lightheaded and queasy, she sat down to reply to Alan's email. She considered telling him about the seismic shift in her family, but decided against. Whatever her feelings, she didn't know him well enough to give details, and to mention it without details would be to provoke curiosity, as Evie's phone message had done earlier. But she wanted to tell him, she couldn't believe how much. She yearned to confide in him, to watch his face as he listened, to elicit his opinion. This yearning, she realised, was something else new.

'Dad, one for you.'

Pierre carried the laptop up the steep garden to where Alan was lying on a lounger with a paperback in his hand. He sat up and swung his legs over the side, dropping the book on the grass.

'Thanks.'

Pierre bobbed his head towards the laptop as he handed it over. 'Who's Stella?'

'None of your business.'

'Ah, go on.'

'The lady I met last week, before I came down here.'

'She's English, right?'

'That's right ...' Alan opened the message. 'Did you read this?'

'Would I?'

'Yes.'

'As it happens, I didn't. You like her?'

'Yup.' Alan glanced up, distracted. 'Look, mind if I read this?'

'Hey,' Pierre raised his hands, 'sorry.'

In the kitchen, Ben was making salad dressing, shaking a jam jar like a maraca. 'Ay-ay-ay-ay-ay I like you ve-ree much!'

'I think Dad may have a lady friend.'

'Great.' Ben wiped the jar with a tea towel. 'On what do you base this observation?'

'Straws in the wind ... Phone messages, emails. A son knows.'

'Excellent.' Ben put a board on the table, and six scarlet mis-shapen tomatoes on the board. 'He's an attractive guy, your father, I've always thought so. Chop-chop.'

'Get outta here.'

They cuffed each other, the cuffing turned into horseplay, and the tomatoes lay forgotten on the board.

Stella spoke to her mother and arranged to visit the following morning. When she arrived, the gentleman admirer was already there. He got to his feet as she entered, and held out his hand.

'Hello! Stella? Ian Macky.'

'Yes, I know, hello, Ian. Ma.' She kissed Kate warily. 'How are you?'

'I'll be off, now that you're here,' said Macky. He seemed to have appointed himself Kate's *ex officio* minder. Stella bristled slightly.

'There's no need,' she said politely, but Kate began to move in the direction of the door.

'Ian, thanks so much for dropping in. I shall look forward to Tuesday.'

'Me too.' He followed her into the tiny hallway and they touched cheeks, but with kiss-shaped mouths. 'Bye, Kate. You know where I am.'

'See you soon.'

Kate came back into the room and put her arms round Stella.

A full-on hug wasn't in their usual repertoire; Stella responded cautiously. Her mother's tall frame felt bony and fragile. They sat down in their customary chairs. Normality restored, Stella asked:

'You all right?'

'Bloody but unbowed, as your father would have said.'

'Not too bloody, I hope?'

'I was joking, darling.'

'Did Ian Macky come round for any particular reason?'

'He was very sweetly asking me out to a pub lunch next week. We generally do these days, but we observe the formalities.'

'Only he seemed, you know – solicitous. As though he was concerned about you.'

'Darling, he always is concerned about me.' Kate adjusted the cushion behind her back. 'And I'm not complaining about that. No, when he came round, I was feeling a bit blue. I probably looked peaky. We're all so ancient here, we're pretty quick to read the runes.'

Stella said, 'You didn't mention anything about what's happened?'

'Good heavens, of course not, he'd have been most alarmed.'

'Too much information?'

'That's it. We're a more discreet generation.' They must both have thought the same thing simultaneously, because they caught one another's eye and Kate added, 'And our parents were even worse than us.'

This allowed Stella to burst out:

'Ma – what is all this about? How on earth does it feel to have your roots moved like this?'

'How does it feel …?' Kate steepled her fingers and laid them against her mouth. 'Very odd, to have someone I don't know and have never heard of – a complete stranger – stake some sort of claim on my life. And sad, because of what people put themselves through. But not terrible. Not *traumatising*. Not for me. For you, darling – well, I'm so sorry.'

'No need. I'm pleased you're all right, of course, but—'

'See for yourself.' Kate waved a hand. 'The letters and whatnot are on the desk in that white envelope – take them away and read them.'

235

'Are you sure?'

'Never more so. I doubt that I'll ever look at them again.'

'I'll bring them back anyway.' Stella fetched the envelope and tucked it under her bag on the floor. 'What about this man, this Mallory, who gave them to you? Evie didn't like him.'

'He overdid the old-fashioned charm a bit for her taste, I dare say. But he bought us a very nice lunch, and he hasn't been in touch since, which I regard as a good thing. In other words, he's not a pest.'

'Evie thought he was smitten with you.'

'That is sweet, but utter nonsense!' Kate laughed. 'He wasn't taken with either of us in that way. He was queer as a coot.'

Half an hour later Stella left, with the envelope. She invited Kate to come out to lunch, but she said she had things to do. Her mother's calm was disconcerting, especially when compared with Evie's feverish excitement and anxiety of the previous evening. If Kate wasn't taking it all in her stride, she was making a good job of appearing to do so. Though of course there had been the matter of Macky's obvious concern, and he was no fool. Stella reminded herself that she was fortunate to have a parent who was still fighting fit in her eighties, but that she mustn't take Kate's rude health for granted. A person's systems were bound to be more friable in the ninth decade; it only took a fall, or a bug – or a shock – and everything could change.

When she got back, she put the envelope to one side. Evening was the time for that, she told herself; it wasn't as if she didn't know what they contained. But that was bollocks. She was putting off reading them because she was afraid. Creeped out, as Raff would have said.

She found the photographs she'd had developed before leaving France. Some of them she'd forgotten about – early ones with Raff and his mates on the coach, the choir in their striped blazers at the first concert, her and the other helpers having dinner, her and Prue in a bar ... Then suddenly she was on her own, Beaumont Hamel in the rain, followed by open fields, patchy sunlight, white graves, the secretive wall of trees that was High Wood.

She continued to riffle through until she found what she was after: her photo of the cemetery where Arnold Guise was buried, and his grave. She separated these from the others and put them aside for Ted.

Doing so, she felt a pang of guilt. There was going to be awkwardness in that quarter, and she had brought it on herself. Not that she expected a scene, or anything she couldn't handle; after all, they weren't in a relationship, let alone in love – they were just a couple of adults thrown together in an inherently intimate situation, who had gone with the flow. And it had done the trick, too – an easier atmosphere and a little positive reinforcement had brought Ted's literacy skills on by leaps and bounds.

She hoped he wouldn't cut up rough and abandon the course; she would have to be very diplomatic. But there was no question in her mind that – no matter what the future held – this must end.

Later that evening, Alan called.

'What are you doing?' he asked.

'Reading.' She cleared her throat. 'Old letters. Very old ones.'

'That sounds romantic,' he said. 'And a little sad.' There was a pause, in which she sensed he was weighing his next words.

'Alan?'

'Like me, actually.'

Stella fell into bed, heavy with tiredness. In the swooping interval between waking and sleeping she felt herself to be at the centre of a web, the fine filaments stretching from person to person, past and present. The web trembled, disturbed by an invisible movement, light as a breath.

But it didn't break. And she slept.

Thea was calm now that the monkey of indecision was off her back. Once sent, the letter to Giles Huxley, written in such a ferment of anxiety, had assumed for her the character of a will: true evidence of her loyalties and affections, and of her sister's. She had not betrayed Jack, either then or now; she had simply taken steps to preserve her peace of mind and, by association, his.

Also, there were more pressing matters to occupy her attention. The Lloyd murder was no longer, it appeared, a random atrocity but part of something bigger, an organised rebellion about land. There had been another killing, the horrific slaughter of a young couple at Eldoret. Any one of them might be next.

The rebel movement had an official title, the KCA, but the Kikuyu words 'Mau Mau' had been borne on the hot wind from farm to farm, and stuck.

Jack was flatly realistic. 'This was bound to happen sometime. We had it coming.'

'But we've done so much for them,' Thea protested. 'Work, and housing, education – modern medicine. How can that be wrong?'

'We took what was theirs.' He made a sharp chopping gesture. 'And then hung on to it and kept them in their place by looking after them. I'm not saying we deserve it, just that it's human nature.'

'Are we safe here, Jack? Can we stay?'

'The authorities are mobilising. And we,' he took her hand, 'will go on making ourselves as secure as possible, being as vigilant as we can, until this thing is put down.'

In other words, they weren't safe, but he at least was going to stay and see it through. Unspoken but equally clear was Jack's view that whatever happened now, change was inevitable.

Joe, Angela and the children were supposed to be coming to stay – Thea and Jack hadn't even seen their littlest grandchild – but now they booked a trunk call and told them not to come, their voices raised harshly over the crackling waves of static. Two minutes wasn't enough – Jack told them to read the papers, and she'd had to shout 'I'll write! I'll write!' just as they were cut off. It was appalling. Afterwards she was wretched to think of the disappointment and worry that the call had caused. Kate and her family were no longer in Berlin but were still with BAOR; Thea wrote to them and Kate called at once, and they had to go through it all over again. They tried not to communicate their fears, but stories were beginning to appear in the English papers and their offspring were justifiably anxious.

Homesickness and a longing to be with them all broke over Thea as it hadn't done for years, and Jack was helpless in the face of it, unable to comfort her.

'This isn't going to last, Thea. A few weeks – months at most – and we'll have them to stay. Or you could go back and see them. How about that? You're long overdue for a visit home.'

'No ...' She shook her head frantically, like a trapped animal. 'I don't want to leave!'

She didn't say 'leave you', but they both knew that was what she meant. Fran Lloyd had returned to the farm and was soldiering on out of respect for her husband and in his memory – even, it was said, for the sake of the employees, who might well be harbouring a viper in their collective bosom. But this was Fran's country, her home. If Thea were to go back to England, there was a possibility she would find it hard to return soon; and if anything happened in her absence ... The thought made her ill.

For several weeks after the atrocity at Eldoret, nothing happened. The paper was full of suspects being rounded up, pictures of rows of sullen Africans with their hands on their heads or lying prone on the ground with guards standing over them, guns trained on their backs. Whatever his bullish words to Thea, Jack was not optimistic. The feelings he tried to keep to himself were scored on his face. Pared to the bone by worry, he became gaunt; he aged visibly. The widow's peak that in his red-headed youth had contributed towards an attractively foxy appearance was now exaggerated by a receding hairline. His thin face resembled a tribal mask. There were times at the end of the day when that face scared Thea.

Over the drinks following Jimmy Lloyd's funeral, Fergus Coltrayne had given full vent to his opinion that nothing short of Roman-style decimation of the suspects would do the trick.

'I've told my boys that one whiff of anything going on and I shan't wait to find out any more,' he said. 'And they know I mean it. I'd be doing us all a favour. I hope you'll do the same, Jack.' He banged the side of his hand repeatedly into the opposite palm: 'Toughness, clarity, swift action – they're what the Kikuyu understands. You know it as well as I do.'

Did he? Thea glanced at Jack, who declined to rise to the bait. 'What we face here is a genuine grievance, and in many cases divided loyalties. I'm not sure a pre-emptive strike will help either of those.'

'I'm not talking about help, Jack!' Fergus scooped up a fistful of the small sandwiches being passed round by an impassive black waiter. 'I'm talking about stamping out this blasted menace. Once and for all. Right now.'

'The authorities are wading in.'

'They are, and a bloody good thing. But that shouldn't stop us doing it for ourselves, on our own land.'

Thea, listening to this exchange, was secretly appalled. She thought of the people who came to her surgery: the old, baffled and dignified, offering up their corns and cataracts as if *bibi* had the power to cure both; the children with their cuts, stings and jiggers, shyly smiling and almost always stoical; the sad-eyed women carrying beautiful babies suffering from tummy upsets or sticky eyes; the frightened girls with infections caused by roughly executed circumcisions, who had to be calmed and comforted before being driven to the local hospital. The common factor in all those faces was trust. There might be pain, fear and impatience, irritable or wheedling, but that trust was a given. How could such trust, built up over more than thirty years, be simply wiped out?

Regular air letters came from Kate, concerned about the situation and asking how they were.

I keep thinking of you both and the farm, and trying to imagine what it must be like to have this hanging over you. I spoke to Joe and we both thought we ought to be there, helping, I don't quite know how! Is life going on as usual or are you confined to quarters? Lawrence says, and I agree with him, that it's hard to see how things can ever quite go back to normal after this. It's awful and we're dreadfully worried ...

There was more, in a similar vein. The responsibility of shouldering the load, not shifting too much of it on to the family, weighed heavy on Thea. Such emotional self-sufficiency came easily to Jack, but she yearned to pour out her fears to someone else. Her hitherto tenuous friendship with other wives in the area assumed a new importance; she and Terri Coltrayne took turns to undertake the long drive between their respective farms, a gun on the seat next to them, to drink and talk. Where the drink might once have been coffee, it was now, as often as not, scotch or a G and T; in Terri's case several – Fergus had always been a prodigious drinker, and under pressure, she was following in his footsteps. Sometimes they'd go together to visit Fran. At the Lloyd place there would be no alcohol; Fran no longer kept it in the house. They sensed that without Jimmy, the farm was marking time rather than flourishing, and the house itself, though spotless as ever, seemed desolate – and if that was how it seemed to them, how must it feel to Fran? The Lloyds had no children, and the place was devoid of those photographs and mementos that represented a stake in another life and place, the future. Once Fran went, that would be that. She was hanging on.

She was a neat, pale woman, who habitually wore the sort of print dress that looked like a pinny (never trousers), and shoes with socks. She must have been in her late sixties, but her hair had been grey for as long as Thea had known her. The most striking thing about her was her hands, which were as large and weathered as a man's – hands that could turn to anything.

She was always pleased rather than grateful to see them, and they in their turn were careful never to characterise their visits as errands of mercy. She rarely referred to her husband or the manner of his death, but confined herself to the present and how things could be managed.

'I make sure there's no one else in the house after six,' she told them in her flat, wispy voice that sounded as if all the energy had been leached out of it by sun and hard work. 'And I keep two of the dogs by the kitchen door.'

'No one else at all?' Terri frowned. 'Not your house boy?'

'Especially not my house boy.'

'Why's that?' asked Thea.

'He knows a little too much about my habits.'

Terri shook her head. 'I do admire you, Fran.'

This was precisely the sort of remark to which their hostess was never likely to respond. But in the car afterwards Terri said, 'She's a tough old bird. And nobody's fool – she could be right about the house boy.'

'How do you mean?'

'They know a lot about us, don't they? Ours must know just about everything. He's always around, in the background, eyes wide open and mouth shut.'

'We can't start thinking like that,' said Thea. 'We'll go mad.'

'Perhaps we have to. It's not enough for Fergus to try and scare everyone. In fact, scared people could be even more dangerous.'

This accorded with the Kingsleys' view, but Thea had never cared to express it to Terri, and she didn't do so now.

'I suppose,' she said carefully, 'we shouldn't assume that the people closest to us are automatically the most reliable. But I'd hate to feel we were under siege.'

'But Thea!' Terri swerved to avoid a particularly savage rut. 'That's exactly what we are.'

The following day, Thea accompanied Jack into Gilgil to fetch the new farm dog and her ten-week-old black Labrador puppy, Sweep. They collected the young Alsatian first and tied him up in the back of the Land Rover. When Thea brought the puppy into the cab with her, the Alsatian became agitated and whined and scratched on the panel between them; Jack banged the panel with his fist and shouted, and the dog, a well-trained animal that knew its place, went quiet. The puppy, trembling and leaking gently on to the newspaper in the footwell, Jack ignored, but he did smile at Thea and say, 'Nice little dog – happy?'

She was happy, and not just with Sweep himself, who was ador-ing and adorable from the first, but with the diversion that his training created. Jela and Nona were entranced, though Nona in particular was a little afraid of the puppy's needle-sharp teeth, only used in play but capable of puncturing the skin. She would shriek and back away, her hands alternately lifted high in the air or flapping at him, all of which he interpreted as an encouragement to leap up and down, snapping delightedly.

'He bites! He bites!' she screamed.

'Treat him quietly, Nona,' Thea explained, stroking him, 'and he'll be quiet with you. We want to teach him to be gentle.'

'Oooh!' Nona touched his head with a cautious finger. 'He is fierce for a baby.'

'He isn't really – he's young and excitable.'

Nona couldn't quite get the hang of it, but she learned to like Sweep because of Thea's obvious pleasure in him, and the way she had with him.

The same could not be said of Luke. The first time Thea took the puppy into the garden when Luke was there he simply ignored him – something Nona could never be persuaded to do – with the result that the puppy did the same and each of them went about his business as though the other didn't exist. This in itself Thea considered to be no bad thing, but a few days later she witnessed a much less obliging little scene.

She was in the drawing room, writing a letter to Joe. Her desk was near the window, with a view of the garden, and Sweep lay dozing beside her on the window seat. When Luke appeared, pushing the wheelbarrow with a sheaf of tools balanced across it, he bounced up and began barking excitely. If Luke heard the barking he didn't show it. After a moment, when there was still no let-up in the racket, Thea tucked the puppy under her arm and pushed the window further open.

'Luke!'

There was a second's pause before he turned. His expression was sullen, not enough to be insubordinate, but noticeable. He may have spoken; she saw his lips move but couldn't hear.

'I'm going to put the puppy out on the grass; he's frightened of the wheelbarrow. He'll calm down when he's taken a proper look at it.'

Another movement of the lips, this time accompanied by a slight inclination of the head.

'Would you take him, please? He can't manage the veranda steps.'

Luke propped his hoe against the barrow and came up on to the veranda. He took Sweep in one hand and carried him down on to the lawn, putting him on the grass immediately and returning to his work. Thea watched as the puppy lolloped, still barking, towards the wheelbarrow and bounced up and down at a safe distance. Luke took no notice; gradually Sweep ran out of steam and began sniffing around, tail wagging. Thea returned to her letter. Problem solved; they'd run a temporary chicken-wire fence round this part of the garden to make it escape-proof.

When she looked up a couple of minutes later, Sweep had transferred his attention to Luke, and was in the flower bed, digging. She was just about to lean out and remonstrate when he made a couple of excited passes at the shaft of the hoe. Quickly – so fast that for a moment she couldn't believe she'd seen it – Luke swiped the puppy on to the grass as if hitting a golf ball. Sweep yelped and rolled over a couple of times, before sitting up dazedly, shocked but apparently unhurt.

Thea dashed out of the house and on to the lawn. Luke didn't look at her but continued his chop-chopping movements with the blade of the hoe.

'Luke!' She picked up Sweep. 'You mustn't do that!'

He turned. 'Sorry, *bibi*. Snake.'

'What?'

He pointed to the shrubs at the back of the border. 'Snake there.'

'Are you sure?' She joined him and peered, not expecting to see anything; if there had been a snake, which she doubted, it would long since have disappeared in the commotion.

Luke pointed again – a rigid, precise gesture, brooking no argument. She had no alternative but to accept the explanation. Under her arm she could feel Sweep's tail wagging cheerily at his tormentor.

'All the same, you only had to pick him up.'

Luke shook his head – was she mad? '*Bibi*, it was very big snake!'

It was his word against her suspicions.

'There was no need to be quite so rough. I'll take him inside now.' Luke resumed his hoeing. 'Be careful of the snake,' she added pointedly, but he was immune to sarcasm.

When she told Jack about this, he said: 'The pup won't do that again.'

'Jack!' She was hurt, and a little shocked. 'He could just have yelled at him.'

'I agree. Still, no harm done and a useful lesson learned.'

She wanted to explain that the problem lay not simply in Luke's hitting the dog, but in his whole demeanour, which in any school report would have been summed up in the phrase 'dumb insolence'. It was kept low level and fine-tuned, but she didn't care for it, and told Jack as much.

He said she was oversensitive; the puppy was fine and Luke a conscientious worker. 'It's just his manner. You have to learn to ignore it.'

'I can't. It's so – I don't know – so pointed.'

'I'm sure he's not trying to needle you, and if he is, then the worst thing you can do is give him the satisfaction of showing it. Don't start hovering round him when he's doing his job, let him get on with it.' To mollify her, he leaned down and fondled the puppy's ears. 'You're all right, aren't you? Damn sight better than being bitten by a snake.'

What could she say? That she didn't believe there had been a snake? She could already hear herself sounding neurotic, and a neurotic wife was the last thing Jack needed at the moment. On the scale of things to worry about, an insolent gardener barely registered. She didn't mention it again.

The annual gymkhana was really no more than a pretext for a party, an excuse for the scattered locals to get together, eat prodigiously and dilute any troubles with alcohol and talk. There was a programme of events, ranging from pony and horse races to family sports and a tug o' war, and support for these competitions was enthusiastic and vociferous, but a year was judged less on its winners than on its plucky participants and the entertainment they provided.

Using those criteria, 1952 was a vintage year: daredevils of all ages rode their mounts like the wind and turned them on a sixpence; the under fives' egg-and-spoon lasted for a record time, with several participants leaving the course altogether and having to be retrieved by their parents; and in a famous victory, the civil servants beat the farmers in the final of the tug o' war. Thea came second in the slow-bicycle race, wishing, as she tottered and weaved over the finishing line to tumultuous applause, that her family could have been there to witness her triumph.

But beneath the cheers and clapping, the clink of glasses and drift of cigarette smoke and dust, the atmosphere was sombre, and all the talk of Mau Mau. Its centre of operations had moved to Nairobi, from where it exercised more and better-organised control. They'd designated themselves a pro-independence party, standing for freedom as well as the reclamation of land. Most worryingly of all, it was rumoured that the KCA had infiltrated the formerly loyalist Kenyan African Union, and that their central committee had instigated a campaign of blood oaths throughout the city. The draconian measures taken by the colonial police had gone some way to containing the uprising, but where it remained, it flourished with even greater vigour.

Jack rarely drank much, but the gymkhana was an annual exception. On the way home that night, they twice came off the road in the pitch blackness, and Thea had to stand arcing a torch back and forth like a lighthouse, shivering, while he put sacking under the wheels and gunned the engine irritably till they were back on course.

They reached the farm just before midnight. Jack got out to close the gate behind them. Back in his seat he said, 'I'm going to take a look round, no particular reason. I'll drop you off.'

'That's all right, I'll come with you.'

'There's no need, you go on in.'

'But I'd like to.'

He didn't argue with her. The truth was, she didn't relish the idea of entering the house alone. They drove down past the side of the house and the nearest outbuildings to the shambas – the scattering of smallholdings worked by Africans in return for their labour. As they passed the kennels, the dogs started up, a terrific racket in the stillness, and Jack leaned out and yelled at them to be quiet.

'Doing a good job, though,' he commented. 'Funny the ones near the house didn't bark; must have recognised the car.'

They were going to remember that.

They drove slowly along the dirt track between the wooden houses. A man was sitting on his step, smoking; they could see the red spark glowing and dimming like Morse code.

'Twelve of the clock and all's clear.'

Just beyond the end of the shacks, Jack stopped and wound the wheel slowly, to turn round. As they reversed to the right, the headlights showed something on the ground ahead of them, about ten yards from the side wall of the nearest building.

'Hello, what's that?'

'A dead animal,' said Thea. 'Don't let's look.'

'No ... No, hang on a second. Stay there.' Jack left the engine running and got out. Thea watched him walk away from her in the pale glare of artificial light, and lean down, hands on knees, to examine the object on the ground. A second later, he took his handkerchief from his pocket and placed it over his nose and mouth; then abruptly turned away, out of the light. When he reappeared, he walked briskly to the car and was already turning the wheel with one hand as he closed the door with the other. He brought a bitter smell with him.

'Jack?'

'They've been up to their tricks.' He was curt. 'Let's get back inside and I'll telephone the police.'

The house was empty. The guard dogs had been killed and cut up with a *panga* and the back door forced. Blood had been smeared over the walls of the office and the dining room, and used to write the words 'MAU MAU' across the glass of the veranda door. They found Sweep trembling in his own mess in the cupboard beneath the sink.

The police, when they arrived, left one officer with Thea and accompanied Jack down to the shambas. After half an hour's rough encouragement, Nona and one of the other women identified the headless torso (further damaged by animals that Jack must have surprised with his headlights) as that of Nona's son Luke, the garden boy. About a hundred yards from where the torso was found, in the edge of the bush, they came across a trampled clearing, damp with blood; strings of animal viscera hung on the surrounding branches.

There followed a loud, brutal search of the shambas, during which it was quickly established that Jela, the cook, had gone. The police sergeant was in no doubt what had happened.

'Looks like you've lost two boys here, sir,' he told Jack. 'One who's taken the oath – you don't want to see him again – and one who wouldn't' – he indicated the torso – 'who you never will.'

Chapter Twenty-Five

1999

When Kate had come to Mansfield Avenue before, with Evie, they had taken the tube and walked up the road, admiring the million-pound houses en route to Haig Mansions. This time, wanting to arrive fresh and uncrumpled, she took a taxi from the station and was deposited at the foot of the steps of number 23. Someone must have been looking out for her, because she was still down on the pavement putting away her change when the front door opened. A woman in a plain blue shirtwaister was standing in the doorway.

'Good afternoon,' said Kate, smiling as she went up the steps. 'I'm Kate Drake.'

'Welcome, Mrs Drake, please come in. May I take your coat?'

Kate relinquished her jacket, which was spirited away. The hall where she was standing was light and high-ceilinged, with a gleaming floor of blond wood. An elegant but uncomfortable-looking chaise longue stood against the left-hand wall, beneath one of the biggest paintings she had ever seen, an expanse several metres square of unframed canvas covered in overlapping red, black and orange circles.

'Mr Mallory's in the conservatory,' said the woman. 'Won't you come through?'

The conservatory was at least as big as the hall, with doors on the far side open on to a garden which for its size and lushness might have been miles from anywhere, not in built-up north London. Ernest Mallory was sitting in a chair near the garden door, his hands on his knees, but the moment he saw her he got to his feet and came to greet her.

'Kate, what a treat this is! Thank you, Jean, tea when you're ready? Come and sit down; this must have been quite a journey for you.'

'Only an hour on the train,' she said, 'and then a taxi. Not exactly intrepid.'

'But a great effort, and so sweet of you to come.'

'It was my idea,' she reminded him. 'I wanted to.'

He ignored this. 'Please, sit!' He extended an arm to take in the enormous space, with its tinkling water, carved teak screens, and jardinières spilling over with lush giant ferns. 'Where would you like to be? In the sun? In the shade?'

Having seized the initiative by inviting herself, Kate was determined to retain it.

'What *I* should like,' she said, moving to the French window, 'is to have a look at your beautiful garden.'

'Do, do ... come!'

She went out on to the terrace and stood leaning on the stone balustrade. The garden was sheltered on all sides and the sun struck warm on her face. Ernest came and stood next to her. She noticed for the first time that he walked stiffly – arthritic hips, she surmised – and so was much less confident out here. She moved away from him again and went down on to the lawn, which was smooth, even and firm as a well-sprung mattress, not a daisy or plantain in sight. This time he didn't follow her.

'You say Yannick does all this?' she asked, over her shoulder.

'Not all, no, no. There is a company near here who do the donkey work, Jean organises that. But Yannick likes to plant and have fun. He is creative, he likes to play. Talented people should be allowed to play.'

Kate made a non-committal sound of agreement and drifted further away. It was now clear that Ernest was staying put, and this tour of the garden would be taken on her own.

She went right to the end of the lawn and in amongst the trees, stopping there to look back at the house and her host, standing on the terrace gazing after her. It was naughty of her, she knew, but also fun to discomfort him a little as he had discomforted her and Evie. When she saw the nice woman Jean appear again, this time with a loaded tray, she set off back across the lawn, returning his wave.

The tea itself was sumptuous. Jean hovered, asked what sort and how she liked it, and took the covers off a plate of sandwiches and another of cakes. Kate exclaimed.

'Heavens, it's years since I saw Eccles cakes!'

Ernest leaned across the low table, waving a hand in Jean's direction. 'She makes them. I'm telling you because she's too modest.'

'You made these?' Kate picked one up and eyed it appreciatively. 'I can hardly believe it.'

'I can't make complicated dinner dishes, but I learned to bake at my granny's knee.' For the first time Kate noticed the hint of a Scottish accent.

'Delicious. Thank you so much.'

Munching her first flaky, sticky, feather-light mouthful, Kate wondered exactly what role this paragon performed in Mallory's household, but he saved her the trouble of asking.

'Jean runs my life,' he explained. 'She's not a housekeeper, and she's not a secretary, she's much more than either of those. I don't know what you'd call her! She's Jean!' He stirred sugar into his tea. 'I don't like titles and demarcation; I like people about me who have talents and abilities that I lack, that I can call upon. I've been very lucky, Kate, that all through my life such people have come my way.'

She dusted away crumbs. 'Like Yannick?'

'Exactly.' He beamed. 'You have the idea.'

'He's where – at your office in the mansion flat?'

'As a matter of fact, he's out today, tending someone else's garden, down in Chelsea.' He tapped the side of his nose. 'Word gets about.'

They talked gardens for a little while – or at least Ernest did, and Kate responded, Eccles cake permitting – and then she broached the reason for her visit.

'I wanted to thank you,' she said warmly, appreciatively, 'for giving me those letters.'

'But they're yours. They were always yours.'

'They're not addressed to me.' She interrupted his demur. 'They're not. But I'm awfully glad to have them.'

'Of course.'

'I hope,' she went on, 'that we – either of us, Evie or I – didn't appear rude when we met you the other day. You appreciate how nervous we were: you were a complete stranger and there was all that mystery – you could have made it simpler for us all by simply putting the letters in the post.'

'But not so much fun.' He allowed a little space round each word, as though placing sweets one by one into a child's hand.

'Oh, we could tell *you* were having fun. You were playing, but we were on tenterhooks.'

'Was it naughty of me?' He affected a downcast look. 'I do apologise.'

'Anyway, that's over and done with and my family is coming to terms with this new angle on their forebears.'

'You've told everyone?'

'Not yet, one step at a time. They've all thought one thing for so long that it won't do anyone any harm to go on thinking it a bit longer.'

'A fine philosophy!' He cut short a chuckle. 'Quite right.'

Kate continued coolly. 'But I've found that one of the consequences of what's happened is that I think a great deal about the past. I do that anyway these days if I'm not careful, and this has made me remember all kinds of things – inconsequential things that I thought nothing of at the time – and look at them, study them, in a different light.'

'I know what you mean.'

'No. No, Ernest, I'm sorry, but you don't.'

'No?'

'Look.' She spread her hands on her knees, moving and turning her wedding ring with her thumb, as if touching a talisman. 'Not to beat about the bush – I do I know who you are.'

'But Kate!' He beamed. 'It's no secret.'

'I should say, know who you *were*.'

His expression didn't alter by so much as a blink. 'Were?'

'Your name isn't Mallory, is it?'

'I beg your pardon, I have no other. And there is any amount of business documentation to prove it.'

'You used to be Ernest Marx, didn't you?'

This time his expression of smiling interest froze for a second.

'Ah, that – I see.'

This time it was Kate whose face didn't alter, and who didn't speak either. She was not going to help him. He lifted the teapot.

'Another cup?' She shook her head. 'I will, I think.'

He poured, added sugar and stirred with a steady hand; took

a slow sip and replaced the cup on its saucer. When he spoke, his tone was airy.

'Yes, I changed my surname long ago. I wanted to change my whole life, Kate, and that seemed like a good start – to sail under a different flag. Not an uncommon impulse, I think, especially at that time. We all like to reinvent ourselves now and again ...' His gaze drifted to the garden as he spoke, so she couldn't be sure if, as she suspected, the words had contained any needle.

'Of course, anyone can change their name if they want to,' she said. 'My worry is about your motives in giving me those letters.' She tilted her head to draw his eyes back to her. 'That's what bothers me.'

'My motives were utterly straightforward: that you should have what was yours, or at least what concerned you. My only regret is that I didn't find them sooner.' He gave a little sigh as he picked up his cup.

'Let's not beat about the bush. You and Giles weren't colleagues, were you? You were close.'

'Lovers is the word you're after, Kate. We were lovers.' He spoke the two syllables in a slow, salacious stage whisper, mocking what he took to be her prudery.

'Yes. I knew that, even then.'

'No flies on you.'

She ignored this. 'I didn't exactly meet you, but I have seen you before; I remembered after we met you the other day. And Dulcie – Dulcie spoke about you, in connection with Giles. She didn't trust you. She said you were jealous and vindictive and that Giles had been too good to you for too long.' The heat had risen to her face; her cheeks were burning. Ernest's eyebrows rose in faux astonishment.

'Did she say that? That makes me sad.'

'I came here today to make one or two things perfectly clear.'

'Continue, Kate, please.'

'If all this was some sort of revenge – on my mother, or her sister, on all of us – I want you to know that it hasn't worked. I loved her then and I still do, just as I love my adoptive parents. We were always all one family. A family to which I am proud to belong.'

'Which is exactly what I hoped.' He inclined his head, but his manner had undergone a subtle change. The exuberant gallantry had been replaced by something careful and insinuating.

'I want you to know,' Kate went on briskly, longing now to escape, 'that I'm genuinely grateful to you for giving me the letters. By doing so, you've enriched our lives immeasurably.'

'Good, good.'

'And finally, we'd all be most grateful if you didn't get in touch again. For any reason. We want no more to do with you.'

'I'm sure I don't need to remind you, Kate, that it was you who came here, to see me.'

'I realise that.' She stood up, but he didn't follow suit.

'A note would have sufficed. Even an email would have found me, eventually.'

'Face to face is always preferable. For absolutely clarity.'

'Oh, I do so agree.' Now he got slowly to his feet. 'You're going?'

'Yes. Thank you for the tea, by the way.'

He waved away her thanks. 'Would you like us to call a car for you?'

'No. Thank you.'

She wondered whether he had some sort of buzzer in his pocket, because as if by magic Jean appeared. 'Jean, will you show Mrs Drake out?'

'Goodbye, then.'

'Goodbye, Kate.'

Neither of them made a move to shake hands, and as she followed Jean into the hall, she saw him start to walk heavily towards the garden, holding the backs of chairs for support.

She had gone about three hundred yards, almost back to the main road, before she found a cab. Seated in its blessed privacy, she found she was trembling with tiredness and relief and her head was aching. As a young woman she'd had the habit of frankness – to a fault, some said; it had got her into trouble more than once. Perhaps it was an example of the reversals that went with old age: some people shrank, others grew fat; some became cantankerous, others compliant; some, with grandchildren, turned into the understanding parents they had never been. In her case, she had mellowed and learned the value of diplomacy, so this return to her old, sharp-tongued self had been both exhilarating and exhausting.

On the whole, though – she touched her regimental brooch and noticed the jubilation of blossom in the park – she felt better for it.

The occasion had come back to her two nights ago. She was sleeping deeply, dreamlessly, but the memory, like a sharp nudge from the subconscious, had woken her. Her eyes flew open in the darkness and she thought: *Yes*.

She had been at the launch of an exhibition of pictures by an acquaintance of Dulcie's; the sort of event that left to her own devices she would have sought most strenuously to avoid. To be fair, the paintings themselves, of country people with their horses and dogs, were more to her taste than Dulcie's, which was why she had been invited ('At least you'll be able to appreciate the animals'), but it wasn't the paintings that were the problem. The large room was packed with smart, pretentious people and their loudly expressed opinions. Dulcie had been drawn aside by one excitable group; she had introduced Kate, who had brusquely – indeed rather rudely – extricated herself. Once she'd elbowed her way round the room and looked at all the pictures, which at least looked like what they were supposed to be, she had gone into self-imposed exile against a wall near the entrance. From time to time, if she sensed someone moving towards her, she consulted her watch and stared impatiently over the heads of the crowd, as if the only thing delaying her departure were the non-appearance of another. Which was true in a way – she'd been here now for twenty minutes and longed for Dulcie to get a move on and rescue her. Five minutes more, she told herself, and she would go anyway – pin a note on the door and leave.

Two men, late arrivals, came in and stood near her, drinks in hand, surveying the room. She could tell at a glance that they did not share her sense of alienation; they had the air of people born to be at such occasions, completely at ease, idly conferring about where first to make an incursion into the melee. The older man was the shorter, but broad-shouldered and handsome, with thick greying hair and a face that radiated good humour. His companion was slim and dark, with large eyes and a sensuous, petulant mouth. He seemed to Kate to be full of a spoiled, demanding energy, like an overindulged child. She heard him say, 'Don't let's bother, animals are so dull!' and the older man's reply, 'We should admire his technique …' before they set off, wrangling amiably, into the mob. Someone was already waving.

A little vignette, more interesting than most. And that might have been that. But a few minutes later, just as she was preparing to go, she saw Dulcie coming through the crowd. She paused, waiting for her, but Dulcie was waylaid by the older of the two men. Plainly delighted, he took her by the shoulders and kissed her three times on the cheeks – right, left, right. Kate saw how warmly her face lit up, not the practised social smile that she so brilliantly switched on and off, but the glow of something deeper, evidence of real feeling. They talked and laughed animatedly, his hand still resting lightly on her shoulder. They didn't see the younger man approach, but Kate did, and never till then had she felt the full force of the expression 'a face like thunder'. The sultry androgynous features lost their beauty, the eyes turned cold and the soft, sensuous mouth mean. Kate was shocked. When the older man did notice him and extended an arm in welcome, he simply turned sulkily away and disappeared, shouldering roughly through the crowd, leaving a wake of inclined heads and raised eyebrows. The older man kissed Dulcie once more before following, and a moment later she was at Kate's side.

'Poor Kate! I do apologise for abandoning you.'

'You didn't. I abandoned you.'

'That's true. Have you been bored senseless?'

'No. I enjoyed the pictures.'

'You looked at the pictures?' Dulcie sparkled with amusement.

'I jolly well did. And then at the people.'

'I bet that was *much* more interesting.' Dulcie took her arm and they moved towards the door. 'Anyone in particular?'

'Your friend – the one you were talking to just now.'

'Giles, he is my absolute favourite! It was so lovely bumping into him.'

Kate said, as they waited for their coats, 'His friend wasn't all that thrilled to see you, though.'

'Who? Oh, little Mr Marx – no, he wouldn't be. But who cares what he thinks?' She sent Kate a sidelong mischievous smile. 'After all, I was there first.'

In spite of this remark, Kate had never imagined Giles to be one of Dulcie's lovers. She had met a couple of those, and Dulcie's manner with them was altogether different – managed, enhanced, self-aware. What she had seen in the gallery was the unaffected pleasure of true mutual friendship. And its opposite, an instinctive and visceral enmity, on the face of Ernest Marx.

A man like that, she reflected, could turn the bearing of a grudge into an art form. No time was too long, and no means too devious, to exact stone-cold revenge.

Will was sure he could not be the only one who knew that courage was in the eye of the beholder. There must be hundreds – thousands – of men out there, some honoured, most unacknowledged, who had experienced the unthinking out-of-body experience, the species of madness, that constituted valour under fire. Of those, perhaps one in a hundred consciously thought, *Now then, let's see. Here's an appallingly dangerous situation that requires immediate action if lives are to be saved and the enemy cheated. Honour dictates that I risk my life for my brothers-in-arms and our dubious cause, even though I'm highly likely to wind up dead. So here goes! Cry God for Maggie, England and St George!*

A more likely and credible scenario would have gone something like, at the time: *Shit!*

And now, in his case at the investiture: *How the fuck did I get away with that?*

But as Will ascended the staircase at Buck House, flanked by his mother and sister, there remained the ever-present, niggling fear that he might yet be found out, that someone in today's cohort of good eggs would rise to his or her feet and shout, 'Stay your hand, ma'am – that one's a fraud!'

If deeds were all, then he was a hero. There were witnesses. What had happened on that sodden Falklands peninsula was beyond dispute. Sergeant Linch owed him his life, and had said as much, in spite of the fact that his diary for the preceding weeks expressed with spare, cryptic credibility his disdain for all 'Ruperts', and Will in particular ('grinning' and 'Goldilocks' were two of the more flattering epithets applied to him). No one was going to question the testimony of someone as irredeemably hardbitten and ill-disposed as Linch. Except Will himself, in whom it would appear only as the becoming modesty of a true hero.

The barn, stuffed with enemy ordnance, had gone up like a torch. There was a moment, a split second, when it seemed to swell; they could see a thin line of red, like a pulsing vein, round the rim of the door and then there was the crump and roar of the explosion and the roof flew off, sending timbers and sheet metal spiralling into the air in a shuddering torrent of flame. A cohort of rats shot out in all directions; one of them ran over Will's boot. At the same time, Linch and the two Argentinian prisoners, the picket they'd captured only an hour ago, came round from the back of the barn, out of the adjoining lean-to, Linch driving the prisoners in front of him. He was bawling at them: *RUN, YOU STUPID FUCKERS, RUN!* Will could see the black hole of his mouth stretched wide. The next second the fire broke through the side of the lean-to. The Argentinians were out of range – they hurtled into the embrace of the troopers – but the flames licked the side of Linch's arm and he whirled round, beating at himself, a flickering dervish. The success of the first shell had drawn others; the ground to right and left erupted violently, spouting debris and smoke. For an instant Will caught sight of the colour sergeant's screaming face, huge and clear as if it were feet away, and he began to run towards him, gaining speed with every step, like a train. There were two men ahead of him, but he barged them roughly aside and almost trampled them underfoot. The noise of the shelling deafened him. He couldn't hear his feet pounding the ground, or his own shouts – he might not even have been breathing; he'd become a hurtling, weightless automaton. In a heartbeat he was on Linch, embracing him, stifling the flames, then they were rolling over and over like playful lovers, screaming and swearing. He felt the crack and crumble of his arm beneath their combined weight.

And then the others were there and there were voices, hands, orders, action that cut through the pandemonium. He and Linch were separated; men crowded round, bending over to minister to them. Will was lurching, nauseous, in and out of consciousness, until finally there was the jolting, lurching rush to safety, agonising pain and the slow dawn of satisfaction.

*

At the top of the staircase, a discreet steward indicated that they should turn left. They were now proceeding along a gallery flanked by enormous paintings (probably famous and of immense value, Will had no idea), one small element in an evenly spaced procession of guests, moving, by instinct or design, at the same pace – a sort of purposeful stroll. Immediately in front of them was a Sikh in a black Nehru suit and a grey silk turban, accompanied by his wife in a pink and silver sari; behind them, a famous jockey with his leggy thoroughbred girlfriend.

Stella said drily, 'Here's something you don't do every day.'

'Like it?'

'It's not bad.' She threw him a sardonic glance.

'Okay, Ma?'

Kate nodded. 'Just drinking it all in so I don't forget anything.'

'I'm afraid I have to peel off in a minute.'

'I'm sure they'll tell us where to go.'

'Oh, shame,' said Stella. 'You mean we shan't get lost? I had visions of stumbling across her Maj powdering her nose in some distant corridor.'

Kate shushed her, laughing, but Will sensed his sister's – what, exactly? Disapproval was the closest he could get: a knee-jerk leftie rebelliousness combined with an underlying disapproval that he of all people was about to be decorated for courage. Because of course Stella knew him too well – his vanity, his susceptibility, his moral cowardice – and no amount of public *puja* could wipe the slate clean.

They came to a parting of the ways – Stella and Kate were directed to seats in the ballroom, he to join the rest of the soon-to-be-honoured ones in an antechamber – and Stella, as if she'd been thinking the same thing and wished to make amends, gave him a peck on the cheek.

'Good luck. See you in there.'

'Thanks.'

He exchanged a gentler kiss with his mother. 'We're so proud, Will.'

The jockey's girlfriend sashayed by; he couldn't stop his eyes from flicking her way, the merest glance, but Stella noticed, and he saw the corner of her mouth tweak and tighten.

*

The thing was, it *had* to be him. He didn't want anyone else to rescue Linch; he'd bloody nearly stamped on the others' faces to get there first. It was spite, not selflessness, that propelled him forward. If he hadn't caught that look, that screaming glare of pain and scorn, the final insult flung at him *in extremis* because it no longer mattered – if he hadn't seen that, some other guy would have saved Linch's life, and been in his place today, picking up his gong.

The incident was instantly mythologised. Major Drake had not only saved his Colour Sergean but had led from the front, taken sole responsibility and physically prevented younger men under his command from risking their lives. Colonel H was gone, killed in the moment of his glory, but Will had emerged pretty well unscathed. His action was just what was needed: a boost to morale in the hitherto dour, cold campaign of yomping and hunkering down. A couple of weeks later and the Goose Green peninsula was theirs. Linch would be fine given time, though his pretty face (said the smirking squaddies) would never be the same. He was repatriated to a specialist burns unit in the UK.

The equerry called Will's name and he walked forward. Supporters on their ranks of chairs to his right, dais to his left. He stopped, turned, saw the familiar, once pretty face stamped by lines of duty; the gobsmacking pearls with a sapphire clasp lying on the upper slopes of a comfortably cut cream brocade shift; the steady hands – slightly weathered, he noticed – bearing his medal, placing it carefully on the ready-positioned hook on his left lapel, giving it a little pat. She said that he had done a remarkable thing and was to be congratulated. There was a polite query about his injuries, he didn't recall his reply. He thanked her; bowed; stepped back; saluted. Walked off. Major Will Drake MC.

When it was all over, the Falklands regained and the Union flag fluttering once more over Stanley, Will had gone to visit Linch, who was back in barracks at Tidworth. They had about half an hour in the sergeants' mess, mostly discussing the forthcoming victory parade, in which Linch hoped to take part. The burns on his face were hideous to look at, but doing well; the more severe ones were on his right arm and upper thigh – 'getting there', he said. Will had a few on his neck and hand, the pain had been unimaginable – worse than the broken arm and still visible. He tried not to think what Linch must have been through.

In the softer light of peacetime, Will could see that this was a tough, solitary man who had joined the military at sixteen and for whom the army had provided all human contact ever since. But the insight did nothing to lessen his dislike.

The meeting was excruciating, the conversation stilted and the atmosphere edgy and guarded. No mention was made of the incident until the very last moment, when Will stood to leave.

'Thank you, sir.'

'No trouble. I'm glad you're doing so well.'

'I meant thanks for doing what you did.'

Will brushed this aside. 'Anyone would have done the same.'

'Ah, but they didn't, sir, did they?' Linch's eyes narrowed. 'It had to be you.'

This was open to more than one interpretation, but they both knew exactly what he meant.

In Palace Yard they posed for the official photographer, and then took some of their own. It was a windy day, but Kate remained magnificently unruffled, like an officer herself, very upright in a narrow dark suit and a snap-brimmed hat with a feather. Stella wore no hat and her hair, coiffed for the occasion, flew about and got plastered over her face.

Over a celebration lunch at the Rag – Lawrence's club, to which Kate still had membership – conversation turned to Evie, not a topic with which Will was comfortable, and one that today of all days he would have been much happier to avoid. But Stella was always on his case, suggesting – no, telling him – that he should ring his daughter before they sat down. Stella had (officiously in his view) 'taken the liberty' of informing the school about what he was doing today and asking if Evie could take a call around midday. She even gave him the number of the school secretary's office. This meant leaving them with their G and Ts – and his – and trooping down to the phone in the foyer. When the secretary fetched Evie, she was cool and in a hurry.

'Oh – hello.'

'I wanted to ring,' he lied, 'because we've just got back from the Palace.'

'Right, did you get your medal?'

'Fortunately yes, they hadn't lost it.'

She didn't laugh. 'What's she like?'

'If you mean the Queen, she's exactly like her photographs. It's like meeting a five-pound note.'

'I'll tell her you said that. Congratulations, anyway.'

'Thanks. I'm just about to have lunch with Gran and Stella; they send their love.'

'Give them mine. See you soon.'

'I hope so, cupcake. You all right?'

'Fine. Look, Dad – I've got to go.'

'Course you have. Off you go. Lots of love.'

'Cheers, and you. Well done on the medal. Bye.'

When he got back upstairs, Stella and Kate had been shown into the dining room. His drink had been removed, he hoped to the table.

'How was our splendid girl?' asked Stella. He found her proprietorial tone irritating, though he knew he'd forfeited the right to that particular irritation.

'Rushing as always – stuff to do, friends to keep up with.'

'I bet she was pleased to hear from you,' said his mother, closing her menu. 'I shall have the paté and the lamb.'

Once they'd all chosen and ordered, Will selected with a flourish one of the club's most distinguished red wines. Stella said, 'Gosh. I do hope we're going to be able to appreciate that.'

'It's not a test,' he said pointedly. For God's sake, this was his day and his celebration; she could be a little less crusty. 'Tell you what, why don't you taste it for a change? If you don't like it, we can have something else.'

'Come on, you two,' said Kate. '*I* can't wait.'

The wine when it came was wonderful, and Stella mellowed under its influence. They discussed the day's events and agreed that the occasion had been dignified and moving. Stella asked to hold the medal, and he unhooked it and handed it to her. She let it lie in her palm and gazed down as though it were a small living thing – a bird or a butterfly. She passed it to Kate, who did the same, stroking its surface gently with her finger.

'You must take that down and show Evie sometime,' said Stella.

'I will in due course. In the nicest possible way, she's not that interested.'

'The young are self-centred,' agreed Kate, 'as they should be. But this' – she tapped the medal and handed it back – 'will be part of her family history. Don't let her exclude herself, Will. She won't thank you for it.'

Will actually saw Stella press her lips together, biting back what she might have said. He knew very well what it was; he could have said it himself: that he'd better garner what thanks he could, because there were precious few due to him, now or later.

That evening, after he'd seen his mother and sister on to their train home, he returned to his hotel, showered and changed into civvies. Then he cracked open the minibar and poured himself a stiff one to make up for the one he'd missed earlier. Sitting in the tightly upholstered chair, he examined for himself the small piece of metal with which he'd been honoured: a silver cross, its arms ending in four crowns, with the Royal Cypher at the intersection, hanging from a purple and white ribbon; an extremely pretty thing, elegant and unshowy. He took a clean handkerchief out of his case, wrapped the medal in it and put it in his jacket pocket, before setting out for Knightsbridge to meet Jacqueline.

The venue for this meeting was the cocktail bar of a large hotel. Her choice – she knew what suited her, and much preferred bars to restaurants; you could go a long time in Jacqueline's company before you saw a square meal. The moment he arrived at the hotel, Will could tell that she was also playing a little game, recreating the mood and setting of their first meeting. This place was the London equivalent of the Bellingham in Cairo – opulent and retro, and with the kind of silky, extra-mile service that was rapidly becoming a thing of the past. The bar, he was told, was on the mezzanine floor, overlooking Kensington Gardens. Rather than take the lift, he walked up the wide, curving staircase.

She was, just as he'd expected, sitting at the bar with her back to the door. He stopped to admire that straight, narrow back, so perfectly poised, the neat backside perched just so, the long, lean legs that seemed made for a bar stool, elegantly crossed. Amongst the big hair and technicolour clothes of the rest of the clientele, her sleek head and white shirt, and her stillness, stood out like a lily in an amusement arcade.

He was standing right next to her before she turned to look at him, and then, typically, she spoke as if she'd seen him coming.

'You have to try the Manhattan.'

'Is that what you've got?'

'It is.' She knocked back the last mouthful and put down her glass in front of him. 'And I shall soon have another, thank you for asking.'

'Another and one more, please ...' He kissed her cheek. 'How are you?'

'Fighting fit.'

'You look wonderful. As usual.'

'As usual, hm.' She glanced down at herself. 'You know me; I can't be bothered with fashion.'

'That's what's I like.'

She took out a cigarette case (her abstemiousness had lasted only as long as her pregnancy) and offered him one; he shook his head, and she lit up with swift, snappy movements. 'So come on then – tell me all about your visit to the Palace.'

Unlike her daughter, Jacqueline was a good listener, attentive and appreciative. She took off her glasses as if removing a barrier, and her eyes were sometimes on his eyes, sometimes on his mouth, reading between the lines, her expression mirroring his words. Talking to her like this, he remembered how quickly and completely she turned him on. They were probably the least devoted couple either of them knew, but their very lack of commitment had kept the spark alive, for him anyway, and each time he saw her, everything in him leapt.

'Well,' she said slowly when he'd finished, 'it sounds quite something. Congratulations on all that. Now tell me how you got it.'

For a second, though he knew it was just her way, his face went cold and his scalp crawled, before he realised that right now, with Jacqueline, nothing would serve him like the truth.

'You don't want to know.'

She raised an eyebrow.

'I saved my stroppy colour sergeant from a fire because I knew how bloody furious it would make him.'

Both eyebrows went up for a moment, before she realised he

wasn't joking. Then she tipped her head back and laughed aloud.

'And did it?'

'Oh, yes.'

'That's outrageous, Will!' She was still laughing, shaking her head in disbelief as she looked into his eyes. 'Why didn't he want to be rescued?'

'Being rescued wasn't the problem. I was. Anyone but me.'

'He didn't like you?'

'You could say that. He thought I was a prat.'

She began laughing again. 'And were you?'

'In his eyes, yes.'

'Oh, Will!' She rested her cigarette on the edge of the ashtray and put down her drink, the better to lean her face in her hands. Her shoulders shook with mirth. They would definitely have sex tonight.

She looked up again, and replaced her glasses. 'Would this stroppy chap have died if you hadn't got there?'

'He would if somebody hadn't.'

'So – that you saved his life isn't in dispute?'

'No.' He glanced away for a second. 'Joking apart, I suppose it depends how much importance you attach to motive.'

She shrugged. 'Speaking personally, none at all. The outcome's the thing.'

Considerably later, they ordered omelettes Arnold Bennett and a bottle of hock from room service and ate sitting up in bed. Once presented with food, Jacqueline ate voraciously, as though she forgot about the need for calories until they were right in front of her and instinct kicked in. They'd been pretty plastered when they first came up, and their lovemaking had been quick, clumsy and explosive, like teenage sex. Her body had scarcely changed, and Will was grateful to the army for keeping him fit, if a stone or so heavier. He looked forward to the watches of the night, when they'd eaten, and slept a little, and would come together again.

They got rid of the trays, and she lit a cigarette, asking 'Do you mind?' as she did so.

'I'd much rather you didn't for your own sake – but that's your business.'

'It is, isn't it?'

Will rested his glass on his midriff. 'I spoke to Evie earlier. I thought I should tell her that I'd been duly decorated.'

'Hm.' Jacqueline gave a little grunting laugh. 'I hope she was civil.'

'Reasonably.'

'She isn't always. She reserves the right to withhold her favours.'

'Well put. So it's not just me, then?'

'Honestly?' Jacqueline rolled her head to look at him. 'It's mostly you, Will.'

He felt that familiar lurch of unhappiness and resentment. 'I suppose I have to expect that.'

'Yes, you do.'

To say 'Like mother, like daughter' would be a cheap shot, he decided.

'Is she well? She sounded sparky enough.'

'She's flourishing like the green bay, though you do know she wants to leave after O levels.' She shot him a sideways glance. 'You're aware of that?'

'I believe so.'

'You either are or you aren't.'

'I am.'

'You know I'm against it.'

He said carefully, 'She mentioned a disagreement.'

'I bet.'

He sighed. 'I do want to see her more of her, you know.'

'Go ahead. What's stopping you?'

Hard to explain his shame, his sense of self-banishment. She broke the silence by tapping his arm. 'You're a war hero now. Make the most of it.'

Chapter Twenty-Seven

1999

Alan rang Stella to say he was flying back via Heathrow and had extended his trip by a few days. Was there any chance of them meeting up? Or he could always come to her and check into a hotel; he'd be happy to see her at odd moments when she was free. 'I'm good at amusing myself, as you know.'

Her heart was flapping like a flag, but she told him that would be best, she didn't want to let down her clients or, more importantly, Shannon, who was having a worrying time with Toyah, still having tests for an as-yet-undiagnosed lameness. She booked him into the Hat and Feathers, not the most attractive pub, but the nearest one that had rooms. She had considered having him to stay with her, but decided against. Togetherness on holiday was one thing, domesticity, even for a short time, quite another. It was too soon, in Stella's opinion, for toothbrushes and toast.

Ted had listened to her announcement in silence. His first remark was to express doubt about continuing the course.

'That's that, then, isn't it?'

'I don't see why,' she said.

'Get away.' He was sharp. 'We've been doing this – getting together – it's made a difference, you know?'

She nodded. He was right. His literacy, duly rewarded, had improved. That had been the idea – her idea – and it had worked, and been enjoyable for both of them. But now she could see how selfish and naïve she had been to suppose Ted would take this new development on the chin.

'I've been really looking forward to coming here, Stella. To seeing you.'

'And I've liked it too, Ted,' she said gently. 'I still do. But we can't go on as we have been.'

'Why?'

She didn't want to tell him the truth, that she might be in love, because to do so would be to imply that this was all just a question of degree, that there had been more to her and Ted's pragmatic sex than had been (for her) the case. Instead she fell back on that last resort of the scoundrel, form.

'It's inappropriate.'

'Don't give me that. You came on to me.'

'I'm sorry.'

'Not half as sorry as I am.' The words were grumpy, but there was no disguising the real hurt in his voice.

'Ted, I am. I mean it.'

'Sure.' He began collecting up his things. 'Thanks for taking that photo.'

'It was my pleasure. You must go yourself, one of these days.'

'Yeah, well!' He jerked his head sceptically.

'Ted ...' She followed him into the hall. 'I will see you next week, won't I?'

'I doubt it.'

'But you've been making amazing progress over the past couple of months.'

'Haven't I just?'

'Please. Don't chuck it all in because of this.'

'You know what?' He stood with his hand on the latch, looking at her with a bitter, puzzled expression. 'I agree. It was really inappropriate.'

She wanted to say something – anything – to restore his dignity and salve her conscience. But she couldn't, and he was gone.

A palpable hit. Ted had turned her own words against her and slipped them like a blade between the plates of her emotional armour. For the rest of that evening and over the ensuing days, Stella was restless, unable to concentrate and close to tears. It wasn't just her words Ted had thrown back at her, but a dismaying reflection of herself. She'd always been proud of her independence of mind and heart, her ability to conduct relationships on her own terms and be the first to extricate herself. Suddenly all that looked pointless and shabby. From start to finish she had not treated Ted well. She was ashamed.

Alan arrived during this period. She met him at the station in the late afternoon and brought him home to show him where she lived. Picking up on her mood, he did not, the moment they entered, seek to lure her upstairs, but accepted the suggestion of tea and followed her into the kitchen while she made it.

Into her fraught silence he said, gently, 'I love your house, Stella. It's exactly how I pictured it.'

'Hm.' She cleared her throat. 'A mess?'

'Lived in. Full of you.'

She grimaced as she handed him his mug. 'That's one way of putting it.' She made to go past him to the other room, but he laid a hand on her shoulder.

'What's the matter, Stella?'

Her struggle not to weep must have communicated itself.

'Hey ...' Without further questions he led her into the living room and swept the newspapers off the sofa. 'Sit down.'

'Stupid, stupid ...'

'You are not.'

He waited quietly, tea in one hand, the other on her knee, while the tears finally flowed.

'I don't seem to have the time-honoured well-pressed hankie ...'

'It's okay, I've got tissues.'

When she was done, he nodded towards her mug. 'Want me to freshen that up for you?'

'No, it's okay, I don't mind it tepid.'

'Really?' He raised his eyebrows. 'Not the impression I got.'

She managed a watery laugh. 'Alan, I am so, *so* glad to see you.'

'Now that is a relief.'

'Really. I've missed you.'

'Me too. Like hell.' He tweaked aside her hair where it had stuck to her damp cheek. 'So what's up?'

She hesitated. If she chose to say 'Nothing', she was sure he wouldn't press her. On the other hand, talking to one man about another, no matter what the terms of engagement ... She compromised.

'I don't like myself much at the moment.'

He lifted a shoulder. 'It happens. Trust me, I can make up the shortfall.'

'I'm sorry you had to see me like this. I like to think of myself as confident and self-sufficient, not a weeping self-doubter.'

'Show me someone with no self-doubt and I'll show you an insufferable prig. If it's any consolation, one ... two of the things that first attracted me to you were your confidence and self-sufficiency.'

She smiled, reassured. 'Get away.'

'It's true. You have' – he wafted a hand – 'an air about you.'

'You say the nicest things.'

'Ah, but there's a quid pro quo ...' He drew her into his arms, pushing his fingers into her hair and holding her head steady under his kiss. 'Right now. Okay?'

'Okay.'

The following day, Alan took himself off to look round the colleges. Stella had another literacy student in the morning, and was due to visit Shannon and Toyah in the afternoon.

She was touched by the welcome she received. Shannon fell on her neck.

'It's so great to see you, Stel! Toyah, look who it is, it's Auntie Stella! We've missed you, haven't we, Toy?'

She kissed Shannon, then Toyah, and sat with the latter on her lap while Shannon made tea. Silent cartoons flickered frenetically on the television. Toyah played with a small plastic mobile phone, alternately pressing it to her own ear and Stella's, chirruping 'Hello? Hello?'

Shannon brought in the tea. To Stella's relief, and in the face of Toyah's noisy protest, she turned the television off.

'She doesn't watch it, you know, she just likes it on.'

'I can see that.' Stella stroked the baby's feathery curls. 'How is she?'

'She's all right in herself, but she's still got this bad foot.'

Stella, miming a phone conversation, reproached herself for not having asked about that. 'Remind me which one?'

'The left, you take a look. See, it's sort of turned in? And she's got a limp.' Shannon's eyes were suspiciously bright, but her voice was steady. 'So, you know, when she's been walking for a bit, it hurts because it's all bent over. And she's always waking up in the night and crying; she's never done that, she sleeps like a dream usually.'

Stella held the small, round foot in its stripy sock; it sat curved in her palm like a warm shell. 'What do they think it is?'

'Arthritis.'

'At her age?'

'It's not good, Stel. They've got her on anti-inflammatories and painkillers, which upset her little tum, so that's not very nice, and when they've got the results, we've got to go back in.'

'What are the options?'

'It can be one of two kinds, a kiddy one which is quite rare but not serious. The other one's rheumatoid arthritis.' Shannon stopped and took a gulp of tea.

'How horrible, Shannon. I'm so sorry.'

'If it's rheumatoid, she could be poorly her whole life.'

'Don't say that.' The phone was pressed to the side of her head. 'Hello? Is that Toyah? Hello there. They can always manage these things.'

'Yes, but I don't want my daughter to be ill and have all that pain, and have to take pills for ever!' Shannon's voice had risen. 'Sorry, Stel.'

'Don't apologise, you've every right to be angry.' Stella helped Toyah clamber down and set off for the toy box. She'd been walking, running, for almost six months, but now, after a couple of hobbling steps, she dropped to all fours and crawled. 'I can see she's not comfortable.'

'It's been a whole month like that.'

'You know what I think,' said Stella. 'Let's hear what they've got to say, and then if it's not such good news you and I will put our shoulders to the wheel and make sure we understand everything about it, and that she gets the very best treatment going.'

'That's nice of you, Stel. But the best's going to cost.'

'Not necessarily. We'll work the system.'

'Cheers.' Shannon smiled wanly. 'Would you be able to come with us – when we go for the results?'

'I want to. I'll give you a lift and wait with you. Let me know the minute you hear when your appointment is.'

After leaving Shannon, she went to call on her mother. There was no answer to her ring, so she used her key. They had a tacit agreement that she would never simply let herself in as a matter of course – this was Kate's home, after all – but a second key was a sensible precaution.

'Ma?'

Kate was asleep in her chair. She wore her reading glasses, and Anne Tyler's *Ladder of Years* was just about to slip off her lap. Stella retrieved the book and put it on the side table. Knowing how annoyed her mother would be if she found out she'd been here and not woken her, she gave her arm a gentle shake.

'Ma..? Ma, it's Stella.'

'What?' Kate's eyes flew open; there was that tiny flash of disorientation and alarm. 'Hello, darling – was I asleep?'

'You were. I hope you don't mind me waking you.'

'I'd have been very cross if you hadn't.'

'I've been round at my young mum's.'

Kate took off her glasses and put a hand to her hair. 'So you thought you'd drop in on the old one.'

'Exactly.'

'Would you care for a drop?'

'Um …' Stella looked at her watch: five thirty, but Kate had probably lunched at twelve. 'Good idea.'

'Why not get us both one. The usual things are in the usual places.'

When Stella came back, Kate said, 'Raff comes home tomorrow.'

'Of course. That's nice, I'll look forward to hearing his tales of high life among the Eurocrats.' She was about to add: 'What have you been up to?' when Kate forestalled her.

'I expect you've been rushing about since you got back.'

'Oh, just the usual.' Suddenly, in the sequestered comfort of this small room, she longed to unburden herself, to tell her mother everything.

'Be that as it may,' Kate was studying her, 'you're looking very pretty, Stella. And very well.'

'Am I?'

'I like the turquoise scarf.'

'It was a present.' Stella touched the warm silk. 'From a new friend, actually.'

'Whoever it is knows what suits you.'

'He does.'

Kate didn't miss a beat. 'And does he suit you?'

'Yes. Yes, he does.'

'Come here. Give me a kiss. I do like to see you happy.'

Stella stepped over and leaned into her mother's embrace, not resisting it but not quite returning it either. This was uncharted territory and she might already have strayed too far.

'Don't get too excited, Ma. We're not talking wedding bells.'

'I didn't suppose we were. Anyway, I don't know him – he might be a complete thug whom I should dislike on sight.'

Stella laughed. 'I assure you he's not. He's a Canadian doctor I met in France.'

'Whereabouts in Canada?'

'Montreal.'

'I believe it's a lovely city. So is he in general practice there?' Throughout this mild, formulaic exchange, Stella could feel her mother watching her, reading her face rather than her words. Useless to dissemble – there were no flies on Kate.

She told her a little more about Alan's work – not, she realised, that she knew a great deal – and then said, 'As a matter of fact, he's over here at the moment.'

'Is he? Is that work or holiday?'

'He was staying with his son in France, and decided to go back to Canada this way. To see me.'

'What a good idea.' This time Kate's response was carefully managed. 'Have you been able to squeeze in some free time?'

'We're going to Norfolk for the day tomorrow. Then he goes home.'

'He'll like that, it's such a lovely part of the world. And coming from Montreal, those northern blasts won't bother him.'

'I'd have introduced you,' said Stella, 'but this is a flying visit and there hasn't been time.'

'Best not anyway,' said Kate. 'Relatives at an early stage aren't a good idea.'

This reminded Stella of something and she asked, cautiously, 'How are you feeling now, Ma – about the family thing? About Mallory.'

'Do you know, I'm absolutely AOK. In fact a lot of things have fallen into place as a result. And it was all such a very, very long time ago, the principal players have been dead for years.'

'Except you.'

'True. But I'm old; I'm more interested in the people ahead of me than the ones in the past. I do so hope that none of you feel – I don't know – cheated. Kept in the dark.'

There were only two options here, and Stella took the simplest. 'We're fine, Ma.'

'And there's no reason for everyone to know.'

'Don't worry. I understand.' She leaned over and pressed her mother's hand. 'Mallory hasn't been in touch again, I hope.'

'No, he hasn't. All clear on that front, I'm happy to say.'

'Ma!' Stella raised her glass. 'You are such a realist.'

'Maybe,' said Kate as they clinked, 'but then what's the alternative?'

Stella considered this as she cooked rice to go with the Indian takeaway that she had ordered and Alan was picking up. The alternative to being a realist, she supposed, was to be a fantasist. But no, that was the opposite – there were many alternatives occupying the middle ground: optimist, pessimist, risk-taker, cynic … Was there a word for what she had been, and felt that she no longer was? Pragmatist came closest, but even that flattered her … She didn't want to go there. Over the past couple of weeks she'd outgrown that skin and sloughed it off.

When Alan arrived, she took the fat, rustling carrier bag off him and put it on the kitchen table before wrapping her arms round him and kissing him till he gasped.

'Wow, Stella …' She felt him pull at his belt buckle. 'Will this stuff stay hot?'

'You bet,' she said. 'Come up and I'll show you.'

The next day, Alan's third and last, she had free, and they were going to drive up to the north Norfolk coast, where he'd never been and which she'd promised would remind him of the Bay of the Somme. When she came downstairs early, in her dressing gown, there was a note on the mat – hand-delivered; the postman didn't come till ten. She picked it up and opened it, still standing in the hall.

Dear Stella, so you now I did learn some thing. Ted. X

Forgiven, she pressed her lips, briefly, to the 'X'.

By eleven o'clock the next morning they were at the coast. Both agreed that the first thing to do in these circumstances was to walk to the beach and, if possible, get their feet wet in the sea. They parked the car in a sandy layby with a windmill to the west of them and a great grey church on a hill to the east, and set off over the marshes towards the shingle bank that kept the tide at bay.

It was a fine, windy day of flashing sunshine and trundling white cloud. On either side of the path the rippling expanse of reeds, grass and water was covered in a shifting population of birds – geese, curlews, lapwings, gulls, ducks and swans, a sentinel heron and even a stop-out barn owl, chided by the other birds as he drifted home to the safety of the village. Occasionally a cacophonous flock would take off, rise and wheel as one, their wings glinting as they turned. Two hares leapt up as if they'd burst from the ground, and raced away, vanishing in seconds.

Alan stopped and put his arm round her. 'This is amazing.'

'I hoped you'd like it.'

'Like it? It's an earthly paradise.'

They climbed over a stile, crossed a low wooden bridge and a run of duckboards, and scaled the shingle bank, holding hands for mutual support as their footsteps slithered and smashed on the cascading stones. Then there below them was the sea – glittering green, brown and grey – and the unchecked northern wind charging across it, making them stagger, snatching their breath.

Alan was the first to whoop and run helter-skelter down the other side, arms flailing. He hopped about as he pulled off his shoes and socks and hobbled warily, jeans rolled, over the last of the pebbles to where the waves pounced and sucked on gritty sand. Stella followed, and they both howled with shock as the icy water rushed round their ankles, shrieking and laughing at themselves as they jumped from foot to foot. Another walker appeared at the top of the bank and released a bounding black dog, who charged past them, crashing exuberantly into the water and swimming back and forth for the sheer hell of it.

Within a couple of minutes their feet were numb and they clambered out and put their things back on. They walked along the beach, heads down in the thudding wind, for half a mile or so, and then turned inland, back over the natural rampart and along a raised path parallel to the first.

Stella pointed to the big grey church, moored like a ship above the village. 'That's where I want to go.'

'Let's do it, lead on.'

Once they'd crossed the coast road and were climbing the narrow lane that led to the church, they were out of the wind; warmed by the exercise, they took off their coats and paused for breath to look back the way they'd come, at the shining bird-strewn marshes and the sea, tranquil from this distance. Tucked under the brow of the hill, they could no longer see their objective, until they passed through a rickety gate in a wall of ivy and were suddenly in the open churchyard. The grass hadn't yet been mown and was like a meadow, shaggy and scattered with cheerful flowering weeds; any new graves must have been in a far corner, because here the stones were old, some of them at crazy angles, the elaborate epitaphs weathered and scabbed with lichen.

Stella and Alan wandered separately among the graves, pausing, peering, reading – sometimes calling to one another to look at this or that curious or poignant story. The church door was open and they went in.

Alan whistled softly. 'Did they used to fill this place?'

'At one time, I suppose.'

'Maybe it was the church for several villages.'

'No.' She shook her head. 'There's one in each village, but not all quite as big as this.'

'Incredible …'

Stella took a leaflet from the back and sat down in a pew to read, while he walked slowly round and then came to join her.

'Do you ever go to church?' he asked when she closed the leaflet. 'I mean, to services?'

'Only to hear Raff, I'm not a believer. But I do like them for their history. For bearing witness.'

'Me neither. I don't believe, and unlike you, I don't have any other reason to go. Right now, I think I may be missing something.'

She felt for his hand and they sat quietly for a few minutes in the stillness, the colours of the east window brightening and fading in the changeable spring sunshine so that the boat in which Jesus and his followers sat seemed to rock on the water.

They left the churchyard by a different gate and found, in the corner, the ruins of an even older chapel, now scarcely more than a dark tent of tangled ivy and a tumble of mossy stones – and a beer can, which Alan crushed with his foot and picked up to throw away.

'Great little hideaway, I can see that.'

'That's the charitable view.'

'Hey – look where we are.'

A narrow footpath took them back down to the village, and to the pub, where they had a pint in the garden overlooking the sea and retreated to a sheltered courtyard for fresh crab sandwiches.

'I wish we were staying over,' said Alan.

'Me too.' She was going to add something but stopped herself. In the event, he said it for her.

'Maybe next time.'

After lunch the sky clouded over and they drove west along the coast road with raindrops pattering on the windscreen. In Blakeney they parked and walked round the harbour and back through the town. Alan went into a gallery and bought a print, a watercolour by a local artist. Privately, Stella thought it a rip-off; the gallery was no more than a gift shop with pretensions and the artist probably turned out her seascapes by the yard.

'I wouldn't do this at home,' he said. 'But hey, here I'm a tourist, and I need a souvenir.'

On the drive home, the weather worsened and that and Alan's impending departure dampened their mood. To dispel the blues, Stella found a golden oldies channel on the radio and they greeted favourites with loud whoops, singing along to 'Eight Days a Week' and 'The Mighty Quinn' and a string of others to which they still knew all the words. Alan, a couple of years older, waited in vain for Buddy Holly.

'Nothing dates us like popular music.'

'Records are like tree rings,' she agreed.

'Records!' He teased her and himself. 'Shellac!'

'Remember those – remember listening booths?'

'And seventy-eights. I had the whole of *The Lone Ranger* on seventy-eights – all together now …'

'Hi-ho, Silver!'

By the time they got back, the golden oldies were long over, and they were quiet again. The house felt chilly, and Stella turned the heating on before putting her arms round Alan's neck.

'You will stay tonight, won't you?'

'I was kind of planning to.'

'It'll be eggs or eggs.'

'Eggs is fine.'

She tilted her head back to look at him. 'This may sound odd, but what I want is a nice hot bath.'

'Don't let me stand between a woman and her bathtub,' he said. But when she'd run the hot water and was undressing, he came in.

'Mind if I join you?'

'What – in the bath?'

'That okay? I could soap your back.'

'Why not?' she said, asking the same question of herself, surprised at being so thoroughly taken aback. All these years and she'd done most things with many men, but this was a level of intimacy too far, even now. The bathroom was the last bastion of Stella the singleton.

He studied her. 'Are you sure?'

'Honestly?'

'Honestly.'

'Then honestly, no, I'm not sure. I don't know why. You've managed to uncover my inner prude.'

He laughed. 'That'll be the day! Anyway, it's not prudish to want some peace and quiet. I'll leave you to it. Enjoy.'

He stepped forward and kissed her, and for the first time she was conscious of her naked body next to his clothed one, and crossed her arms over her breasts. When he'd gone downstairs, she went into the bathroom and lay down in the steaming water with her eyes closed. The door wasn't locked, but he didn't come up, and she heard the burble of the television news in the sitting room below.

With the slight sadness, she also felt relief. Slowly, she relaxed. There was so much she wasn't ready for.

Chapter Twenty-Eight

1999

Evie encountered Prue at the school gate on the boys' first day back. They knew each other only slightly, so she was surprised when Prue came over to her, smiling broadly.

'It is Evie, isn't it? I'm Jamie's mum.'

'I know, I mean I've seen you with him. Hello.'

'I had to tell you, I went on the tour to France, and your – aunt, is it? Stella? She was completely wonderful.'

Evie suppressed a twinge of jealousy. 'You don't need to tell me.'

'I'm quite sure Raff would rather have had you there,' said Prue, whose interpersonal antennae were perfectly tuned. 'But it was brilliant for me, we became drinking partners.'

'I was very sorry not to make it – bad timing.'

'For heaven's sake, Evie, unlike me, you're a working woman.' There was no getting round it, Prue was super-nice. 'I was thinking maybe you and I could have a coffee or a drink some time?'

'I'd like that.'

'Then it's a deal. Do you have a card or something? I bet you do.'

'Actually, yes ...' Evie fished one out and passed it to her.

'Excellent. I shall give you a ring.'

'Jamie's mother's nice,' she said to Raff later, as they were loading the dishwasher.

'Yes, she's okay. Drage fancies her.'

'I wouldn't know about that. But I wouldn't blame him if he did.'

'Her and Auntie Stella were getting on really well.'

'She said – I'm pleased Stella found a kindred spirit.'

Raff leaned against the fridge, disposed to talk. 'She wasn't the only one.'

'How do you mean?'

'The only kindred spirit.'

'Oh?' Evie closed the door and pressed the 'On' button.

'When we were in Amiens she met this bloke.'

'Who did? Prue?'

'No, Stella.'

To disguise her curiosity, Evie filled the kettle with the tap on full, so the water splashed out. 'Probably someone she knew, on holiday.'

Raff wasn't interested in such tame explanations. 'Alfie was on the bench for that concert. He said they were talking outside in the interval and then exchanging phone numbers.'

'Well I never,' said Evie. 'Have you finished that history?'

Later on, when Owen was there and they were entwined in the sofa, she told him about the mystery man, allowing herself the speculation she hadn't liked to voice with Raff.

'I bet that was why she stayed on.'

'Let's hope so. She deserves some fun, your auntie.'

Evie nudged him. 'She's no charity case, you know.'

'I realise that. She's a sexy lady.'

'Too much information.'

'No pleasing you, is there?' He pulled her over. 'Give us a proper kiss.'

'Sorry to break things up.' Raff's voice came from the doorway, where he stood in blue boxers and a Simpsons T-shirt. 'Mum, did you fill in that form for cricket coaching?'

'Hi there,' said Owen.

'I haven't forgotten about it.'

'I need it tomorrow morning.'

'And you'll have it.'

Owen stood up. 'If you ever fancy going to the nets, I could do with some practice.'

'I shan't have time,' said Raff rudely.

'Just as well, you'd be too good for me.'

Raff didn't deny this.

'Night then, love,' said Evie pointedly.

He disappeared and went up the stairs with long strides, two at a time. Evie waited until they heard his door close before saying, 'I'm sorry.'

'Not a problem.'

'Well – it is.'

'Only if we let it be one.'

'But he's so horrible. And he's not actually horrible.'

'I know that. He's a super lad at heart.'

Evie grimaced. 'You're very forbearing.'

'Not really. This is an awkward situation for him. He's eleven, I'm forty-two. It's down to me to put the hours and the effort in.'

'Some people would say he's young, he ought to show you some respect and be polite.'

Owen chuckled silently. 'Then some people need to get real. Mind you,' he added, 'it'd need sorting if we got hitched.'

She pulled back to get a better look at his face. 'What's that supposed to mean?'

'Raff. If we wanted to get married. We'd have to decide how to play it.'

'We certainly would.' Evie narrowed her eyes. 'Was that a proposal?'

'I was just thinking, that's all.'

'I see.' She held his gaze for a second or two, then stood up. 'Well – let me know when you've done deliberating.'

'Evie? Don't be like that.'

'I'm not being like anything. Actually, I'm wiped, it's my bedtime.'

'Fair enough.' He rose, but she moved away before he had time to embrace her. In the hall, he lowered his voice and asked, 'When's Raff going to see his dad?'

'Half-term. A few weeks. I can't remember.'

'We should go away.'

'I'll think about it.'

'Okay, point taken.'

She opened the door. 'I wasn't making a point.'

'Right.' He put his hand on her upper arm, holding her quite firmly, and placed a kiss on her mouth. 'Night. See you soon.'

She closed the door and went quickly into the kitchen at the back of the house. She didn't know why she was so angry. Angry and let down. She was accustomed to Owen's calmness, his steadiness, his solidly confident outlook, his different-from-Mick-ness; they were qualities that she found not only a comfort, but sexy. His big frame and strong, unflappable presence allowed her to be feminine in a way she couldn't be at other times and with other people. But just now she'd seen the flip side of those qualities. She'd sensed that she – and Raff – were under consideration, and she hadn't appreciated it. For the first time she could envisage the possibility of a straight choice, and she was by no means sure that she wished to make it. But then of course – she turned the key in the back door and switched the kitchen light off – a straight choice might turn out to be no choice at all.

As she reached the top of the stairs, she heard a quiet voice: 'Mum!'

She opened his door. 'Hiya. You should be asleep.'

'Has he gone?'

'Just now.' She didn't, as she might usually have done, suggest he use Owen's name. 'I'm going to bed.'

'You won't forget that form?'

'Of course not. I'll do it first thing.'

'Night.'

She went over and stooped to kiss him. He lay on his side, but she could see his eyes shining, wide open in the darkness. 'Night, love.'

In her own bed, with the light off, she thought, *No – there's no choice at all*. And the enormity of it made her catch her breath.

Such a consideration – such a realisation – had never been part of her own parents' experience. Their course in life, together and severally, had been taken for reasons that had nothing to do with her, or only by default. The criteria they'd applied were entirely selfish. Her interests and welfare had been taken into account, but were not of primary importance.

Evie's judgement was dispassionate, meted out equally to both parents, which was perhaps a little unfair to her mother, who had brought her up and released her, well educated, confident and with state-of-the-art orthodontistry, into the adult world. Jacqueline had taken on motherhood as she took on almost everything else, with committed professionalism. She could never have been accused of lack of effort. Nothing was too much trouble, and she could make things fun, too – tennis, skiing, shows and exhibitions, trips abroad. Whether with friends or just the two of them, to all these activities Jacqueline brought the added value of her energy and expertise. Evie's contemporaries thought she was great – a really cool mum. What they didn't realise was that there was no other, private Jacqueline; no off-duty, gentler, less out-there mother in whom to confide, and for whom one was the sole focus of attention, even perhaps the repository for hopes and dreams. Jacqueline was the star of her own life, and her natural habitat was in the spotlight, centre stage.

Evie had not held this against her – after all, she had no other experience of mothering, and by the time she was old enough to make comparisons, she was used to it and on her way – but these days she did occasionally feel a little hard done by. The irony was that her father was so much the opposite – all heart but no head, and certainly no organisational ability – so there was scant consolation to be gleaned there. Each parent could have done with a little of what the other one had. Evie tried to redress the balance; she punished her mother by not going to university and her father by withholding her filial favours, but neither of them reacted satisfactorily. Her mother told her it was her decision and went off on a lecture tour, and her father, instead of renewing his efforts to win her over, simply made himself more and more scarce until he dwindled to a dot.

Had she, Evie wondered, cut off her nose to spite her face? She'd not been dealt that bad a hand, not by comparison with some girls she knew whose loyalties were torn apart by their parents' rancorous divorces, or who were vilely misunderstood, or wilfully abandoned to dull, lonely lives. Evie had always been supported and encouraged to do well and have fun, and provided with the means to do both. The role model provided by her mother was impeccably independent and high-achieving. Her father, when she saw him, was handsome and charming (something else her friends commented on), but looks and charm were a matter of luck; they required no effort and so deserved no admiration, and certainly no respect.

Still, it was Will's love she sought; or evidence of his love, because she didn't doubt its existence. Why had he simply allowed her mother to take over? Why, when he was a soldier – an officer, even, a commander of men – could he not have played a bigger part in both their lives? Why, when she had spent time with him, had the girlfriends always been there, and somehow standing in for what he seemed congenitally unable to provide?

The result was that as often as not, when Will did make a paternal effort, she spurned it. Painfully typical was that time when he'd turned up unannounced at school. She'd been in the study doing a French plait for Juno to the accompaniment of Culture Club when a third-former knocked on the door. Kaye, the only one not wired for sound, answered the knock and flapped a hand to indicate that the message was for her.

'Mrs Dornay says please can you go down to the front hall, your father's here.'

'Okay, thanks.'

She closed the door. The other two were looking at her, eyebrows raised, approving smiles in place.

'Jammy,' said Kaye. 'Were you expecting him?'

'Definitely not.'

Juno began teasing out the unfinished plait. 'I reckon I can forget about this.'

'I'll do it another time, promise.'

'Go on then! What are you waiting for?'

When she got to the hall, the door of Mrs Dornay's drawing room stood open, and she could see the head and her father in conversation by the bay window. Will wore a blazer over a white shirt and faded pink chinos, and brown loafers without socks; his ankles were tanned. He did actually look quite cool. Doorway was very sparkly and smiley; when she spotted Evie hovering, she was all over her.

'Evie! Come on in. Here's a nice surprise for you.'

'Hello, Dad.'

'Hello, love.' Thank *God* he hadn't come out with 'tuppence' or 'cupcake'. 'Hope you don't mind me dropping in out of the blue.'

'No, of course not.' They exchanged a kiss, and he left his arm around her shoulders, knowing, perhaps, that she wouldn't shrug it off in front of Doorway.

'Mrs Dornay has graciously given permission for me to take you out for lunch.'

'Thanks, Mrs Dornay.'

'Do you want to run up and change, Evie?'

'All right, thanks, Mrs Dornay.'

As she left, she could hear them laughing together indulgently.

Trying strenuously to please (and having, Evie was sure, consulted her mother), Will took her to Beni's in Brighton, a chic pizza palace with charm-farm waiters, the eatery *du jour* of her year. Will suggested they work their way through the card, and ordered a bottle of Prosecco to get them 'in the mood' – for what, she wasn't sure. Under its influence, she was at least able to ask him why he was there.

'Do I need a reason? To see you.'

'You could've let me know.'

'Yes, sorry about that – it was a spur-of-the-moment thing.'

They both knew perfectly well why he hadn't let her know – because he couldn't be sure that his resolve would hold, and because she might have told him not to come anyway – but she wasn't going to let him off the hook that easily.

'So, what – you just happened to be passing?'

'Sort of.'

'I see.'

'How's your mother?'

'She's in Oslo.'

'Oslo?' He pulled a jokey, oversurprised face. 'What's she doing there?'

'I can't remember.'

'She does get about,' he said. 'Become an academic and see the world.'

Evie couldn't quite get the weight of this remark, which seemed to hover somewhere between a compliment and mild sarcasm, and anyway, he wasn't going to change the subject that easily.

'So have you got the day off?'

'Well I wouldn't go AWOL, tuppence, even for you.' When she didn't return his smile, he went on, 'Actually, I wanted to show you something.'

'Oh, right.'

Their mixed antipasti arrived and he surveyed it with relish, shooting his cuffs and wiggling his fingers like a conjuror. 'But first things first. Dig in.'

It was almost impossible to dislike her father, which made it hard work being off with him. Over the antipasti and the pizza, during which he moved on to the house red and she cut the remaining Prosecco with orange juice, they engaged in reasonably affable mutual interrogation, with Will pretending, as usual, that everything about school was bafflingly arcane.

'I wonder,' he mused, 'what prompts a glamorous woman like your Mrs Dornay to become a headmistress.'

'Dad – she is not glamorous!'

'Forgive me, tuppence, but you're not in a position to say. She is, rather. In the same way that Mrs Thatcher is glamorous.'

'Oh, please.'

'Booted and spurred. Brisk. We public-school chaps find that quite sexy, you know.'

She didn't want to hear about what her father found sexy, especially as she could see that in her own way her mother was of this 'brisk' type.

'Do we know if there's a Mr Dornay?' asked Will. 'Or does she keep him in the attic?'

This made her laugh in spite of herself, and he joined in, pleased with his small success. In the slipstream of their laughter he fished something out of his inside breast pocket and laid it on the table.

'There you go.'

It was a flat black leather box of the sort that usually contained jewellery, or an expensive watch. Evie could not suppress a flutter of thrilled anticipation.

'What's this?'

'Take a dekko.'

She picked up the box and pushed up the lid. For a moment she was confused – for her? But what ...? She stared at the object, feeling her father staring at her.

'I said I'd show you.'

Her heart subsided and sank. 'Oh, yes.'

'I wanted to keep my promise for once.'

'Thanks.' Disappointment bleached every trace of feeling from her voice, and she said again, 'Really, thanks, Dad.'

'Pleasure.' He leaned forward. 'Quite a pretty thing, isn't it?'

'Yes. Yes, it is.' She picked up the box and inspected the silver cross closely – unseeingly – before handing it back to him. 'Congratulations.'

'Hey-ho.' He slipped the box back in his pocket. 'I won't say it was nothing, exactly, but honours of this kind are a bit dodgy.'

'Dodgy?' She had been thrown a bone and pounced on it fiercely. 'Why's that?'

'Oh, I don't know ... Heat of battle, adrenalin, general overexcitement ... Sheer slog against the odds is far more deserving.'

'Anyway,' she wasn't prepared to bolster him up, 'you got it.'

'I did, didn't I. Fancy a *gelato*?'

After that, she couldn't wait to get away from him, and back to the normality of school with her friends. As so often, her father's vanity had won. The great surprise visit had been all about him, as usual. And almost as bad had been her own inability to enter into the spirit of the occasion, to take pleasure in his pleasure. An MC (she had looked it up) was no small thing. When she'd told Juno, her friend's reaction was one of awed respect: 'God, Eves ... he's a hero!' But one outstanding act in the heat of battle didn't make a person heroic, as Will himself – to his credit, she supposed – had as good as admitted. Colonel H had got a posthumous VC, and there were still those who thought he was bonkers.

At school he saw her to the door and put his arms round her quickly before she could escape.

'Thanks for indulging me.'

'That's okay.'

She felt the quiver of his laugh, and then he let her go. 'Let's not leave it so long next time.'

'That's up to you.'

'You're absolutely right. I'll be in touch again very soon. Bye, tuppence.'

At the doorway she glanced back, and he was already in the car, one hand on the ignition, the other raised in a cheery wave. It was nearly a year before she saw him again, by which time he was out of the army and she realised she hadn't known when she was well off.

All of this meant that now, as a parent herself, Evie took a fierce pride in recognising instinctively and beyond doubt that her first loyalty was and always would be to her son. The knowledge wasn't comfortable; as well as responsibility, it brought a worrying whiff of self-sacrifice. Of course she hoped it wouldn't come to that, but the exchange with Owen had forced her to confront the possibility.

The following day he rang her – stumbling and hasty; they were both at work.

'Evie – I want to apologise. I was out of order.'

'Don't worry about it.'

'But I have been. Look, I can't be long ...'

'Nor me.'

'Can I drop in tonight?'

'If you think you can face us.'

'Of course I can.'

'All right then. Owen, I have to go.'

'See you later, babes.'

She hadn't meant to be so sharp with him – he was apologising, after all – and regretted it afterwards. Her reaction was involuntary, as if all her rejection and resentment antennae had been activated by the previous evening's exchange, and stood to quivering attention again the moment she heard his voice. Her eyes were smarting as she put the phone down.

That night Owen came round late, long after Raff was asleep and she had gone to bed, and they made it up to one another with fierce, quiet intensity. Afterwards, lying in the warm, relaxed, man-smelling cradle of his arms, Evie saw all too clearly that reconciliation, however sweet, did not necessarily bring resolution.

Chapter Twenty-Nine

1999

Will liked Egypt for all kinds of reasons, and *The Worldwide Traveller* liked the way he wrote about it. They'd sent him back now, in June and with the temperature soaring, to bring his particular perspective to bear on Luxor and Aswan. The temperature was creeping up by the day, but he didn't mind the heat, and he was always at his most comfortable on the more exotic work assignments; they made him feel further removed, and therefore safer. Between Christmas and now his work had taken him to cleaner, quieter, cooler places – Denmark, Bruges, Boston – all of which had been enjoyable, but which had not quite done it for him in those terms.

Outside the hotel in Luxor a foal was tethered on the dusty verge. Every day of Will's stay, and no matter what time he went out (admittedly he was not an early riser), the foal was there, skittering about on the end of its rope or standing, quivering, looking up the road towards town. Will liked everything about Arabs and their culture except their attitude to animals. The piece he was due to write here was about another aspect of the culture – badgering for business, *baksheesh* and how to deal with it – but he was beginning to think he might touch on the animal thing. Brits had delicate sensibilities in this area and might need warning.

On his third morning he broke an unwritten rule and went over to the foal. It started nervously away from him, and a boy of about ten materialised out of nowhere, grabbing the rope and pulling the animal roughly towards him.

'Nice horse, sir – you pet, come, you pet!'

He should have known better. The whole story was there – the foal's mother out between the shafts of a *gharri*, the foal itself an inconvenience, the brainwave of leaving it somewhere where it would attract tender-hearted tourists, and the equally sweet-looking boy stationed nearby to relieve them of a few bob.

The boy jerked the rope so that the neck of the still resisting foal was stretched taut, and its little hooves sledged unwillingly through the yellow grass.

'See him, sir, you stroke him.'

'No thanks.' Will put his hands in his pockets – a counterintuitive gesture because he would have loved to touch the plushy coat and soft, trembling muzzle, but wanted more for the boy to stop pulling on the rope. 'How old is he?'

The boy held up four fingers. 'Months.'

Weeks, more like. 'He should have some water.'

'He has water.' The boy gestured vaguely. 'Have water.'

'It should be here.' Will pointed at the ground in front of him. 'Where he can get at it.'

The boy nodded and smiled. Will fished a note out of his pocket and glanced at it briefly before returning it. 'Fetch the water, bring it over here.'

'Okay.'

The boy dropped the rope and disappeared in the direction of the shrubbery. The foal retreated to the furthest extent of its rope, flanks pumping; he and Will surveyed each other as a small off-stage drama was enacted – the boy's voice, then a man's, peremptory, raised in irritation, then the boy again, jabbering excitedly; a pause.

A moment later an elderly man hobbled over on thin, bowed legs.

'We have water.'

'Good.'

'The boy is fetching.'

'Splendid.'

Now there were the three of them, the equidistant points of a triangle, staring each other out. In the road behind Will, tourists, cars and *gharris* went about their morning business. One woman came over and took a photograph of the foal, and the old man was instantly all smiles, suggesting a shot containing himself, a picturesque local to complete the picture. Will was pleased that the woman's husband whisked her away without money changing hands.

Wherever the water came from, it had not been standing ready – it was several minutes before the boy returned, staggering under the weight of a plastic washing-up bowl, its contents sloshing over the sides. The old man emitted a volley of furious Arabic, indicating where the boy should put the bowl, and then turned to Will.

'Water, sir – very fresh!'

Will now faced a dilemma. The bribe, tacitly agreed, was for the boy, but now this unpleasant old git had got in on the act. So much for warning his readers – he'd been stung by experts. The foal, however, was drinking, its front knees drawn together as it bent down to the bowl. Quickly, ungraciously, Will took two notes from his pocket and gave one to each of them. As he walked away, he could hear the old man's obligatory protestations that it was not enough, and suspected that the perceived shortfall would be made up with the boy's share.

He'd decided to buy one or two presents. His motives weren't wholly altruistic; he wanted an up-to-date 'shopping experience' for his piece. He knew only too well that the whole haggling thing was a sham – the average tourist had got the idea and either plucked up his courage or opted out, and the canny vendors of Luxor made generous provision for tyro hagglers in their pricing system. There was no place on earth where the warning *caveat emptor* was more apposite.

Walking the mile or so into town, he made a mental note of the number of times he was pestered to purchase goods, rides, food, tours – one driver even had the gall to suggest he was going the wrong way, that the historic sites and the souk were in the opposite direction; Will smiled benignly, said oh well, he'd decided to take this route anyway, and got a volley of abuse for his pains. But at least the pesterer gave up. This was the technique he would recommend: to be pleasant and ostensibly grateful, while sadly declaring the absolute impossibility of a transaction. And then not to look back or get trapped into an argument. Perfectly polite, utterly immovable.

He went first to the museum shop and bought a self-assembly cedar-wood model of a pharaoh's boat for Raff. The transaction was straightforward, but in the hushed, spacious elegance of the museum itself, one of the stewards asked him repeatedly in an urgent whisper whether he would like a 'very knowledge-able' guide, an offer he declined. As he gazed intently at the shriv-elled beauty of a four-thousand-year-old mummy in its casket, he thought that for this sort of thing you needed only the most basic information, plus a vigorous imagination.

In the souk, he had it in mind to find something for Evie, and possibly for his mother. He saw Jacqueline only rarely these days, and she had always been a poor receiver of presents, accepting them brusquely as if duty-bound to indulge the giver. He'd settled on the idea of a scarf for Evie – jewellery and bags were a tricky area, but most women liked a beautiful scarf. He favoured the sort worn by belly dancers around their hips, in gorgeous col-ours, spangled with paillettes and gold and silver thread, the edges adorned with glossy tassels. If she didn't like it, he reasoned, she could always hang it on the wall.

In his straw hat and pale linen jacket Will might as well have had 'this is a live one' branded on his forehead, but this morn-ing that didn't bother him – it was the idea, really. He strolled the length of the market's main drag with what he hoped was 'an independent air', like the man who broke the bank at Monte Carlo, maintaining a serene, other-worldly detachment in the face of all blandishments and covertly selecting a stallholder to target on the way back. The man was puffed up with his suc-cess at having – in his view – reeled in this particular punter, and laid out about a dozen shawls and scarves for Will's scru-tiny. He chose one in brilliant kingfisher blue, shot with green and gold and with a long, rippling fringe like a horse's mane of turquoise and gold. He could see Evie, with her dark hair, cutting a dash in it, but that was not the whole object of the exercise. Negotiations took a full twenty minutes (including two attempted walkouts), and the price he eventually paid was three quarters of the one being asked, an outcome with which the stallholder, in spite of his glum head-shakes and rueful pout, must have been delighted.

At the very last stall he bought a pretty tooled-leather spectacle case for his mother, handing over the asking price without demur and walking away with his purchase in seconds, to both parties' complete satisfaction. The message he would pass on in his article, he decided, would be to haggle only if you enjoyed it – souvenirs in all parts of the world tended to be overpriced, and if you were going to shop in tourist traps, you might as opt for a quiet life and embrace your fate.

In the interests of further commercial research, he went to a popular bar in the centre, where he paid an arm and a leg for his G and T and 'free' olives, and then to lunch in a small back-street restaurant that he remembered from a previous visit. The cleanliness and ambience (no women allowed) left something to be desired, but the food was delicious and good value. He felt pleasantly at ease, and smoked a water pipe after his coffee. Not a lot of point in recommending this specific place because of the no-women thing, but it would serve to illustrate the enormous range of prices and quality. Also, one had eternally to emphasise the importance of not eating anything uncooked, and of washing one's hands at regular intervals – this was the country that had given gyppy tummy to the world and worked at maintaining its reputation. After many visits he considered himself largely immune – had never in fact been that susceptible – but he had seen whole coach parties laid low by a few ill-judged salad garnishes. The stuff he wrote was subjective and observational, not a litany of ill-disguised puff copy and name-dropping, but certain basic travel rules bore repetition.

After lunch he strolled gently through the pressing heat of the back streets, found a seat in the dimmest recesses of a café bar, ordered tea and another water pipe and dozed the afternoon away. At five thirty he emerged on to the street, walked to the nearest thoroughfare and hailed a cab to take him back to the Phoenix Oriental. Several *gharris* were parked in the private road ready to pounce on the early-evening cocktail trade, and he couldn't see whether the foal was still there.

He had a leisurely swim, enjoying the sensation of the pool and its surroundings emptying of people as the sun set over the Nile. A flock of ibises flew overhead, heading for their nocturnal roosting ground upstream; the waiters came and began folding down the parasols and securing them so they looked like tall, pale-robed monks; others lit lanterns on the poolside tables; on the narrow quayside below the pool the handsome Arab boatman licensed to the Phoenix returned one romantic couple, handed them courteously on to dry land and stood in the stern of his felucca, leaning on the long paddle, waiting with magnificent patience for his next customers.

By the time Will got out of the pool, the shift from day to evening was complete, and the first spruced-up drinkers had taken up residence on the terrace. They smiled and exchanged a 'Hi!' as he slapped past in his robe and flip-flops. Back in his room, he watched half an hour's CNN and part of a local talent show before getting showered and changed and going down to the bar.

He wasn't surprised when the woman hit on him. He had spotted her the moment her coach arrived the previous evening, part of an organised tour but on her own: fiftyish, well presented; nails, highlights and waxing (he was prepared to bet) freshly done in honour of the holiday; vivacious to a fault; almost certainly newly single and up for it. She was on her way to join others of her group at a table outside, but paused by where he sat at the bar as though she'd suddenly spotted him.

'Excuse me, do you mind if I ask you something?'

'Please.' Will turned towards her, smiling. She was elegant in an ankle-length black cotton dress; a gold torque around her tanned arm, above the elbow.

'It's just that you look like someone who knows the ropes – a proper traveller.'

'You do me too much honour.'

'I'm right, though, aren't I? You've been here before?'

'I like Egypt. How about a drink?'

'Ooh …' She patted her hands together in a small and unconvincing show of hesitation. 'Why not? I'd love a Bellini.'

The barman was already hovering. 'Thanks, and another of these for me. So, what's the question?'

'I'm with a tour group – you've probably spotted us, with a certain amount of dread.'

'Not at all. I bet you're having a whale of a time.'

'We are, but a few of us thought it would be fun to go off piste one evening. Is there somewhere in Luxor you could recommend – a bit off the beaten track but not life-threatening?'

'No problem.' Their drinks arrived, and Will raised his glass. 'Cheers. I'm Will Drake, by the way.'

'Gina Jump.' She caught his eye. 'No, really. I only got married to take someone else's name.'

'So why didn't you?'

'Divorced, done and dusted.' She waved a hand. 'So I've reverted to Jump.'

The first piece of information confirmed what Will already knew – that he was on a promise. The second, that this lady's seaside-postcard surname meant that she stood a chance (uniquely) of being remembered. The bar pick-up that had so spectacularly initiated his sexual awakening had, he reflected wryly, become all too commonplace in his life.

Fortunately, the following day was his last in Luxor – he was returning to London for a few days before flying to Atlanta. Gina Jump, having lived up to her name, left his room at one a.m., and he made a point of breakfasting early to avoid any coy eye contact over the buffet.

As he waited for his taxi, he walked the thirty or so yards to where the hotel's forecourt gave way to the stretch of private road. The foal was tethered in the usual place, still with nothing to drink but with the boy in alert attendance – waiting, no doubt, for him to come along and pay for another washing-up bowl to be filled. He waited till the boy spotted him, before pointedly ignoring his broad grin and gesturing hand, and returning to the cool of the hotel lobby.

Being in London these days was a strange experience. He was after all a displaced person, of no fixed abode. Abroad, this was an ideal state; he liked the role of elective gypsy, footloose and fancy free. Back on British soil, things were rather different. Whatever he did, no matter how quietly he slipped in and out, and kept his head down in between, there was always the nagging awareness that this was a small country and his relatives were never far away. The sensation was the same as one he used to get when as a child he'd prevaricated over some piece of schoolwork for so long that in his mind it had assumed monstrous proportions. The intervals between seeing his family had been growing longer and longer, and this one he had somehow allowed to extend to over a year.

He could well imagine what they said about him, what their different takes were on his absenteeism. While he had no doubt that he would be welcomed if he showed up, albeit a little gruffly in some quarters, the simple act of showing up had, with time, become an insuperable obstacle. After the welcome there would be the questions, the needing-to-talk, the eliciting of an explanation. And there was no explanation. Just accidie, slip-sliding away, hoping not to be noticed ... He didn't worry much about responsibilites – he'd abrogated those long ago. Thanks to Jacqueline's genes and her own upbringing, Evie was set; the ex was paying his dues and the bush telegraph indicated that there was another chap in the offing. Stella was on hand to keep an eye on Kate, who was anyway fit for her age and not hard up. It was only Raff, really, over whom he felt the odd tweak of conscience; and of regret, because he reckoned he had the makings of a good grandfather, indulgent and agreeably subversive. The trouble was, he didn't know what impression the boy had of him from other people's attitude and remarks; it could go either way, and Will was frankly wary of finding out.

So in London, when not meeting up with his editorial masters, he stuck to his small service flat in Dolphin Square, and his club, Pinks, off High Holborn. He walked a lot, looking at London with his travel journo's eye, taking his home city's changing temperature. The year before last he'd gone to see the Diana tributes in Kensington Gardens, and found the whole thing queasy – the sobbing people, the candles, the mounds of dying flowers with their sweet, rotting smell. The English had undergone a sea change. Not all of it for the worse – if there was a show or a rock concert that took his fancy, he'd go along; it was never difficult getting a single ticket. He ate in Chinatown or Camden and saw one or two old friends who knew almost nothing about his domestic situation.

One of these was a former fellow officer in the regiment, Crispin Hambury. Crispin was the social equivalent of beans on toast – comforting and good value. He had stayed in the army for longer than Will, and had done rather better since, being now in charge of transport for the Thames Valley Police. Just as well, because he had a nice wife and three pony-mad daughters to maintain near Westerham. The most uxorious of men himself, Crispin regarded Will as a bit of a dark horse, an image that Will did nothing whatsoever to dispel.

To their immense satisfaction they managed to get a couple of returned tickets for Tina Turner at Wembley Arena and spent the best part of three exhilarating hours drinking Southern Comfort and working up a sweat to 'Steamy Windows', 'Nutbush City Limits' and the rest of the hallowed oeuvre. Emerging bedraggled but happy, they agreed that after these excesses curry was the only meal in town, and got the tube back to Baker Street, home of several reliable establishments, including the British Raj. They placed their order of chicken dansak, taka dahl, lamb bhuna, stuffed paratha and pilau rice pretty much on autopilot and glided happily into the second round of Kingfisher.

'To Tina!' Crispin raised his glass. 'What a woman!'

'Fucking incredible,' agreed Will. 'Legs like nutcrackers, at what age?'

'Older than us, mate,' said Crispin solemnly. 'Even older than us.'

'Glorious …' Will momentarily lost himself in contemplation of the legs, something Tina had in common with Jacqueline. 'But a survivor, you see? Got out from under that bastard, and who's crying now?'

'I heard she married a millionaire. Lives in France, surrounded by priceless antiques and liveried lackeys.'

'Good luck to her. A millionaire with good taste, obviously.'

Somewhere towards the last shards of poppadom the euphoria began to evaporate. Will was conscious of feeling tired; his legs ached from all the standing (even if you had a seat at a rock concert, it was a matter of honour not to sit on it), his head throbbed with the first premonitory beats of a real corker. To make matters worse, Crispin was beaming away opposite, a beacon of bourgeois Anglican rectitude shining through the accumulated smog of booze.

'How's Pauline?' Will asked grimly. 'And the family?'

'She's very well, she sent her love – told me to tell you not to, er …'

'Lead you astray?'

'Something like that. God knows what she imagines we get up to.' Crispin shook his head fondly. 'And the kids, well they aren't kids any more, of course …'

Will's mood deteriorated as his friend continued enthusiastically to recite the usual litany of universities, gap years, changes of direction, spots of bother, relationships failed and fulfilled, and, inevitably, a brace of 'cracking' grandchildren born out of wed-lock but soon to be legitimised. Will was used to it all, bored by it and well practised at not responding in kind. He was accustomed to easing others over that awkward moment when the reciprocal question had to be asked.

'So how about you, Will? Still globetrotting? I see your name in the Sundays from time to time.'

'That's right. I just got back from ten days in Egypt. Off to the States the day after tomorrow.'

'Jammy sod.'

This was the game they played, although Will knew that Crispin wouldn't have swapped places for all the tea in China, and prob-ably pitied him into the bargain. He had no idea whether any of the very few people he called friends speculated about him, and if so what they said. He kept them all separate, never saw any of them together, but presumably they went back to their wives and worked him over. For a brief moment Will contemplated unbur-dening himself, simply ordering more beer, or something stronger, and dumping the lot on this nice, loyal man, but he still had enough of his wits about him to see how disastrous, and how rude, this would be. You made your bed, you had to lie on it. Whining was the last resort of the desperate.

Three quarters of an hour later they emerged unsteadily into the street. Crispin announced his intention of getting a taxi to Victoria for the last train, and they shook hands, long and hard, on the pavement.

'You know, Will, if you ever want to come and doss down in our spare room you'd be more than welcome – we'd be delighted, in fact.'

'That's very kind.'

'I mean it. Only forty minutes on the train, and handy for Gatwick.'

'I know.'

'As long as – taxi! As long as you do. Pauline would be thrilled to see you.'

'Do give her my love.'

'Of course. Night, Will. See you next time.'

Will mumbled something non-committal and stooped to wave as the taxi pulled away. A ripple of nausea flowed over him, and he felt the blood drain from his face. He felt awful. He staggered back across the pavement and just made it to the window of the British Raj before falling to his knees and vomiting a scorching torrent of semi-digested curry, then passing out.

It was only the following morning that he realised he was not just hung-over but properly unwell. The gentlemanly head waiter of the Raj had been a good Samaritan, sitting him up with his head between his knees, encouraging him to drink some water, putting his ruined, rolled-up jacket in a plastic carrier and calling a mini-cab. He had to stop and heave a couple of times on the way home, and was overwhelmingly glad that he didn't encounter anyone else on his way up in the lift.

During the night he was sick again, and started to run a temperature. That was when he realised that what ailed him was in all probability the legacy not of Wembley and the Raj, but of Luxor. The irony of this would almost have been funny if he hadn't felt so bloody terrible. He was tottering, head throbbing and stomach churning, to the tiny kitchen to fetch water when the phone rang at – Jesus! – eight a.m. He considered not answering. But it rang a second time and he hauled the handset to the side of his head.

'Yes?'

'Will? It's Crispin.'

'Hi …'

'Just wanted to say, great night, I couldn't have liked it more. And also – are you okay? I thought you looked a bit groggy as I left, but I was in no position to turn back.'

'No, I'm shite. Thanks for asking.'

'What a bugger. Can you afford to take some time in bed?'

'No option. Actually, I can't talk now.'

'Sorry …'

'Bye.' He dropped the handset and headed for the bathroom. Back in bed, in the interval before the next wave hit, he switched off his mobile and took the phone off the hook.

He had a robust constitution and had forgotten what illness felt like – the sense of being cut off from normal human society, the weakness, the indignity, the plain physical suffering from which it was impossible to get any relief. In the army he'd suffered a few injuries and minor wounds, but the army looked after its own

– they had a lot invested. During that interminable, humiliating twenty-four hours, Will could have cried for sheer loneliness.

The next day, still light-headed and weak at the knees, he packed up and headed for Heathrow. He called Evie over a brandy and ginger in Departures.

'Dad?'

'That's right.'

'Where are you?'

'In transit. Just off to the States.'

'So – you're in England?'

'That's right. Only passing through, so I thought I'd—'

But she'd hung up.

Chapter Thirty

1999

Midsummer's night, and the four of them – Kate, Raff, Stella and Evie – sat in a row on a grassy bank, Kate on the end in her folding chair, the rest of them on rugs, with the picnic and drinks. At eight o'clock the sun was still high, but was just moving behind the highest gable of the college – its sharp shadow lay across the middle rows of the hundred-strong audience, but long rays lit the stately roofs and chimneys opposite, the twisted willows by the river, and the little stage, no more than a wooden gazebo hung with greenery, flags and props.

This was a *Dream* with a jazz-age vibe, the cast young, cool and beautiful: Titania lithe and languid, swathed in bias-cut satin; Oberon in white tie, tails and plimsolls; the lovers the maddest of bright young things, all loud checks and flapper fringes; and Puck sly and decadent in bowler and black stockings. Bottom and his timeless team could have come straight off the site of a dozen conservatory extensions in the posher suburbs of the city. A piano, sax and percussion combo were perched on a trailer to the left of the stage, playing up a storm against the random counterpoint of passing ducks.

There was a sense among the audience, on this most beautiful of English summer evenings, that they too were part of the performance. All were conscious of their good fortune in being here, of the luckiness of their lives, the happy and intelligent choice they had made for their evening's entertainment back in chilly March when the advance booking had opened. As well as the age range, of which Kate and her family were the embodiment, the crowd spread over the grass represented the people who filled the city's streets and squares at this time of year, but (thought Stella) with the bad bits taken out. Here were students, pensioners, schoolchildren, young professionals, tourists, academics, the conjugally blissful and the carefree single; the sorted, the slackers, the driven and the don't-knows; all brought together by the pleasing genius of a four-hundred-year-old provincial playwright. The locals wore attractive light clothing as befitted a fine evening in late June, but with sweaters and socks at the ready; visitors from abroad wore the tourist uniform of fleeces, cotton-mix separates and trainers. Degrees of formality among the Brits ranged from cargo shorts to linen suits, from miniskirts to flowing dresses; each wearer was pleased with his or her choice, but also entertained by the surrounding diversity. The atmosphere in this green, sequestered quadrangle was wholly benign.

Raff wasn't mad about Shakespeare. They were reading *Twelfth Night* at school and it was well boring. The language was mad, the jokes crap and the characters a pain. He'd learnt the song 'O Mistress Mine' and that was okay, but the rest you could keep. So this family cultural outing hadn't been on his to-do list, but Stella had got the tickets and his mother, perhaps making a point, had asked him ahead of Owen. She may have been expecting the answer no, but (also to make a point) he'd accepted, so he couldn't really complain.

Actually it wasn't bad. Even if you couldn't keep up with the words, there was plenty to look at – the girls were fit – and the musicians knew what they were doing. There was a younger boy from school in the audience and Raff had decided that it was cooler to appear on top of things than bored. Also, Stella and his mother had laid on a world-class picnic, so there were compensations. The combination of barbecued sausages, virtuoso keyboards and Puck's suspenders was slowly but steadily winning him over.

Evie, accustomed to picking up and interpreting the small visual signals, observed this conversion with relief; the evening was going down well. Stella's invitation had been to her and Owen, but after consultation with both parties, it was agreed she should ask Raff first. She'd been a little sceptical of his ready acceptance, but at least now he was here he seemed to be enjoying himself. It would have been infuriating if he'd been bored and fidgety when Owen, who could have done with a night out, was kicking his heels at home.

She was tired. It had been a long, hard day at the workface, exacerbated by tricky customers, fractious, overheated staff and a glitch on the computer system. At five o'clock there had been nothing she'd been looking forward to less than an evening spent sitting on the ground in the company of her family, and the bloody bard. She had come home via the posh supermarket, to buy fruit and cheese, her designated contribution to the refreshments, where it appeared the town's entire middle-class population was planning to dine al fresco. Having whizzed round, she found herself with a choice of queues ranging from long to interminable, full of self-satisfied people, their trolleys laden with olives, Brie, Pimms and paté, genially explaining their choices to the checkout girl. By the time she'd got home, showered, changed, encouraged Raff to do the same, put things into cold bags and spent twenty minutes hunting down the tickets (disseminated by Stella in case anyone should be held up), the evening's entertainment had assumed the character of a necessary evil, to be got through with all the stoicism at her disposal.

But she had to admit that like Raff, she was disarmed. The perfect evening, the music, the grassy fragrance of the garden, the wit and charm of the performance, the timelessness of it and, yes, the nostalgia (she had played Quince at school) all combined to cast their soothing spell. She could actually feel herself unwinding, particular muscles in her neck, back and legs, even her face, unfurling a bit at a time, like spring leaves. And Raff's being here instead of Owen made it family-only, which seemed right, and therefore relaxing. From this tranquil perspective she could appreciate Owen's generosity – he had stood down not just for Raff's sake, but to make her a gift of all this, knowing it would be balm to her soul. If there had been a smidgen of self-interest in his wanting to please her, she readily forgave him. Forgiveness was always easier in absentia, especially with a glass of chilled Pinot Blush and a Brie and grape sandwich to hand.

Stella could not have been more delighted with how it had all turned out. Owen, in her view, deserved a medal. In all probability Shakespeare meant even less in his life than in Raff's, but he had still sacrificed time with Evie on the loveliest night of the year in the interests of family harmony. She vowed to make a point of expressing appreciation when next she saw him.

But, oh – forget Owen, how she wished Alan was here! She

longed to share this with him, the sweet, warm air, the droll band and the ducks, the poetry and laughter, the beauty of the people and the place, the quintessential Englishness of the whole thing, of which (you could sense) they were all proud, but which they were all sending up a little too. Look at us, the assembled company seemed to say – we may be at best quixotic, at worst barking mad to organise these outdoor events with our weather, but when it all comes together, how sublime is this? She could picture Alan's reaction, his warm, intelligent interest in the play, his fascination with the surroundings, his tickled-pink laugh. Afterwards they could have talked about it over a nightcap. A whole part of her – the main part, so she supposed it was her heart – strained and swelled to bursting point with the simple yearning for his company.

Kate allowed her glass to be filled by Raff; one of the advantages of giving up her car. But her eyes barely left the stage – the play was such a delight. She and Lawrence had not been great theatre-goers, but she had seen *A Midsummer Night's Dream* once before and this was far more fun. The energy and enthusiasm with which these sexy young people performed, and managed to rattle off the difficult verse in such a way that you got the sense even if you didn't catch the words – it was exhilarating! She was bowled over by the whole thing.

And of course Shakespeare was full of lines you recognised, that kept popping up, a series of small, happy surprises along the way. She had already spotted 'the course of true love never did run smooth', 'ill-met by moonlight', and 'put a girdle round about the earth'.

Now the saucily dressed Puck had returned to Oberon with the magic flower, the one that was going to cause all the mayhem, and Oberon was stretching out an imperious hand.

    ... I pray thee, give it me.
    I know a bank whereon the wild thyme blows,
    Where oxlips and the nodding violet grows
    Quite over-canopied with luscious woodbine ...

This, too, Kate recognised – a speech they'd been made to learn at school, perhaps. Learnt in Kenya, purporting to be Greece, but really England, as English a woodland bank as it was possible to imagine. And the wild flowers, the thyme … oh, yes. She closed her eyes, and the pungent remembered scent filled her head, and she could feel again the heat beating on her head, her hands in her parents' hands, Thea rubbing the pale green leaves between sun-burnt fingers. Kate was transported, and sat still with closed eyes for a moment, allowing the actor's low, sensuous voice simply to flow through her.

So odd that you could be absolutely in the moment, concen-trating, watching and listening closely, and then in the space of a second be so far away and long ago. All the worlds one carried around in one's head – every person here had those worlds, and a single word or line could transport them to any one of them. This notion, like thinking too hard about the universe and the infinity of space, made her feel weightless, detached. A burst of laughter brought her back, and there were the rude mechanicals lined up to receive directions. She glanced down at Raff, who was smiling in spite of himself. She thought she might simply float away for happiness.

Dulcie, she thought, *your family is doing fine*.

By ten o'clock the air had turned cool, and the grass was damp. The little stage was like a brightly lit boat floating in the dark-ness. Here and there among the audience smaller lights flick-ered – torches, tea lights and Zippos brought into play as people passed flasks and bottles to ward off the chill. The faces of the trio were in shadow, their music stands like candelabra in front of them. The play-within-a-play ended in noisy hilarity, the court characters laughed, and kissed, and drifted gracefully en-twined away, the lights going with them one by one. Titania and Oberon cast their spell, and now even the musicians' stands were doused until finally there was only Puck left, perched on a high stool beneath a single lantern, eyes shining slyly beneath the brim of the bowler. The audience waited, with breath held, to be dismissed.

If we shadows have offended,
Think but this, and all is mended,
That you have but slumbered here
While these visions did appear …

Here, each one felt, was a charm just for them, an invitation to collude, and to forgive. They needed no second bidding.

> ... So, good night unto you all.
> Give me your hands if we be friends,
> And Robin shall restore amends.

Puck disappeared, plunging them into two seconds of disorientating blackness before the noisy exuberance of the curtain calls – the band giving it all they'd got, the cast dancing and waving, off to the pub. And then the party was over and the audience were suddenly returned to their everyday selves, mortal and messy, getting stiffly to their feet in the chilly darkness, folding chairs and rugs and collecting up their clutter.

They were ready to go home now, but feeling anticlimactic too, and sad that it was over. Kate, Raff, Evie and Stella joined the queue that wound out of the garden, through an arch, along a cloister and out of the college's imposing main gate into the street. The play-goers in their slightly dazed state created a nuisance, blocking the pavement, causing other pedestrians to swerve ostentatiously or simply barge their way through. On the far side of the road the pizza restaurant was doing a roaring trade, and next to that a throng of smokers stood outside a pub, another hazard for those going about their business.

Stella said, 'Ma, you stay here, I'll go and get the car.'

'Where is it?'

'In the multi-storey.'

'That's not far, I'd much rather come with you. The walk'll do me good.'

'If you're sure.' She looked at Evie. 'Where are you parked?'

'Same as you.'

They parted company by the talking pay-machine, with its voice like the Muppets' Swedish chef, and exchanged kisses, and promises to do this sort of thing more often. Stella and Kate had a place at ground level, and in a couple of minutes they were on their way.

'Thank you so much for organising all that,' said Kate as they headed out into the one-way system

'Pleasure. Wasn't it great?'

'Oh, I did enjoy it! And Raff, did you see?'

'Yes. I'm glad of that, for Evie's sake.'

'Is all not well there?'

'Lots of friction potential,' said Stella. 'Male egos. But she has to be on Raff's side.'

'Of course. I do hope they see it through.'

Evie popped her ticket, and glanced at her son as the barrier rose.

'So – honestly. Was that fun?'

'Yes, it was really good. Thanks, Mum.'

Evie tasted pure pleasure. 'No need to thank me. Text Stella, she got the tickets.'

'I will, but, you know …'

'What?' She wound the wheel and turned into the stream of traffic.

'Thanks for asking me.'

'That's all right.' She kept her eyes on the road. 'You were the man for the job, as far as I was concerned.'

There was a brief silence before Raff said, 'We ought to show Owen the programme.'

'Yes,' she said calmly, her heart leaping. 'Why don't you?'

Stella saw Kate in and picked up the message when she got back to the car.

When she arrived home, she curled up in the corner of the sofa, with the Agincourt stone in one hand, the phone in the other. She'd learnt Alan's routines – he'd still be in early-evening surgery – but if she left a message, he'd always ring back within the next hour.

'Hi, honey, I'm home. We had such a wonderful evening, I can't wait to tell you about it, and I *so* wished you were there with me. Raff was the only man on the island, outnumbered three to one, but he didn't seem to mind. Beautiful setting, stunning production, ace picnic though I say so myself. It's all left me feeling up in the air. Not sure I can wait till September to see you. What do you think?'

In fact he rang back almost at once. 'I finished early, long story – never mind, here I am and all yours.'

'What do you think?' she asked. 'About my suggestion?'

'You need to ask? Let's do it.'

'How?' She smoothed the stone with her thumb.

'The trouble is, I can't get away for at least another six weeks.'

'I might be able to, though. My life's more flexible, I can move things around.'

'You don't want to let anyone down.'

'Alan – I won't.'

There was a short silence; she could hear him thinking. 'Summer flights will be expensive at short notice. Can we split this?'

'Might as well be practical.'

'Is that a yes?'

'Yes.'

'I'll be working a lot of the time.'

'You amused yourself in my town, I can do the same in yours.'

'Of course you can.' He gave his confiding laugh that was – almost – as good as a kiss. 'And on weekends I'll show you a good time.'

'Believe me,' she said, laying the stone against her cheek, 'I'm counting on it.'

Kate left her bedroom curtains open, so that when she turned out the light she could see the triangle of sky between her patio fence and the sloping roof of the rectory. Tonight there were stars and a perfect half-moon. Her head was still full of the play, and with it the powerful, poignant remembered scent of wild thyme. She would get some, she decided. She'd ask Ian if he could take her to the garden centre; she would have it in a tub by the French window.

One moment she was wide awake, stargazing. The next she was deep and dreamlessly asleep.

Chapter Thirty-One

1963

Nineteen sixty-three was a vintage summer, and the year of the Kingsleys' last visit to England. They were over for just three weeks; Jack didn't care to leave the farm for longer, and Thea wouldn't stay on without him. When they arrived, it was pretty clear why.

'Dad's dying,' said Kate to Lawrence. Her voice was hard; she was making herself face it.

'He does look older.'

They were sitting in the garden at Hallowfield, but they spoke softly. Thea and Jack had not long gone up to bed. It was nine thirty, and still light.

'Worse than that,' she said.

'It's not surprising. He's had a hard life, and they've been through some pretty tough times over recent years. And actually your father's never carried much weight.'

'No, but he's always been fit,' she protested. 'Wiry and strong.'

'Yes.' Lawrence knew her too well to try and soothe her on this one. 'He does seem frail.'

'Thea did say he'd been run-down, that's why she made him take this trip, but it's much more than that. I don't know whether to ask, or to say something ...'

'I wouldn't. They'll tell you if they want to, Katie. If there's anything to tell.'

'Oh, God.' Lawrence's use of the affectionate diminutive signalled more clearly than anything else could have that he shared her opinion. She got up and took a few steps, arms folded. 'I do wish they weren't so far away!'

'I know, me too – but it's been their home now for far longer than England ever was, and that was the life they wanted.'

'The one Dad wanted. I've never been sure about Thea. She went to be with him.'

'Of course,' he said softly. 'That's who she is, your mother.' He had never got used to her saying 'Thea'. 'She made her choice, and for the best possible reasons.'

'I still wish ...' She clasped her arms tighter around herself, looked down at the ground. 'Oh, I just *wish*.'

'I know.' He got up and came to her side. She felt his hand on her waist, guiding her gently forward until they fell in step. Anyone looking down from an upstairs window would have seen a contented middle-aged couple strolling around their garden. 'I know.'

Thea let the curtain drop. It was barely dusk, but at an hour when they were used to equatorial darkness. Jack, exhausted, had fallen asleep at once. The spare room at Hallowfield had twin beds, so she couldn't creep close and put her arms round him; probably as well, because the impulse was entirely selfish. He would be all but unconscious for an hour or two, and then the long, fretful watches of the night would begin, with tossing and turning, sitting up, drinking water, the not exactly complaining, but cursing and groaning. There would be very little she could do, and anyway he was a hard man to help. It was almost as if no one else, least of all his wife, was supposed to acknowledge the illness that was eating him from the inside. He would say, 'I feel terrible!' as if that were an affront, an indignity that had been visited on him and which he could scarcely believe. But however she responded, it wasn't right. Sympathy was brushed aside, practicality treated as fussiness. Once, infuriated, she had snapped back, 'Of course you feel bloody terrible!' and that had been the closest she'd come to getting it right. He had looked startled – even, briefly, amused – but perhaps such a straightforward acknowledgement of his condition had been too close for comfort, because the next second he changed the subject, cutting off any possibility of discussion.

What Thea hated was the sense of him moving away from her. If, as she feared (she was a realist), the physical Jack was unravelling, then it was all the more important that the other lines of communication stay open. Instead of which he seemed to have retreated behind a barrier of downright grumpiness, deliberately keeping her at arm's length for reasons she suspected had less to do with protecting her than with his own pig-headed pride. She veered wildly between fury at her exclusion and panic that something might happen while they were stranded in this de facto separation.

His withdrawal had begun a while ago, during the worst year of the emergency, when they'd been living with an ever-present danger, the dread exacerbated by not knowing who to trust. Following Luke's murder, there had been no further atrocities on the farm, though two more men had followed Jela's defection and some wilful damage was inflicted on the coffee crop. But the fear and tension had taken their toll, especially on Jack, whose responsibility everything was.

Fergus's crowing notwithstanding, they had taken no satisfaction from the reprisals, which had been horrific and disproportionate. Even when the uprising had been put down, with tens of thousands of Africans dead or in camps, there was no escaping the fact that change was inevitable. The carefree assumption of a way of life and a given order was no more; they could pretend, and keep the pretence going for a while, but the old certainties had gone, along with any idea the settlers might have had that this was their country, and the farms a shared enterprise. The sleeping beast had stirred; they were there on sufferance. Thea knew that Jack's sense of responsibility did not rest solely on the farm and its profits. He believed that he had dragged her here, and that she still hankered for England. The first was not true – she had come willingly, enthusiastically even; but the second, well, though she could not deny it, she longed to tell him exactly how it stood with her: that while she might still pine for certain people and things, her home would always be with him. But whenever she found an opportunity and began, he would stare at her so hard that her tumultuous feelings took on the flavour of common sentimentality in her mouth. He had always been the reserved one, and it had never mattered. Now she often found him unapproachable, and it hurt her heart.

She sat down on the edge of her own bed, facing his. He lay on his back, with one arm across his forehead. His once handsome aquiline profile was sharp, and with his mouth open his lower jaw had dropped back slightly, which gave him the appearance of a much older man. Or a dead one. Frightened, she leaned forward and gave his shoulder a little push. The bones were close to the surface and felt loose, almost uncoupled, beneath her hand; but at her touch he turned with a sigh and lay with his back to her. Now, there was just room ... She eased herself on to the bed behind him. She resisted the temptation to put her arm round him in case its warm, robust weight woke him up. Instead she made herself small, folding her arms in front of her and laying her cheek against his back, feeling through cotton and skin the worn machinery of his body still going, still stumbling along. Just.

Their itinerary was simple. It was really only family, as Thea said, that they wanted to see. They would spend a week with Kate and Lawrence, who would then drive them over to Joe and Angela, then living in St Albans. From there they were all linking up for a long weekend by the seaside in Aldeburgh, with the children having a couple of days off school, after which they'd come back to Hallowfield for the remainder of their stay. She had told their few friends the dates when they would be over, and one or two visits had been arranged.

The one important and slightly daunting day trip that had to be made was to London to see Iris Tennant, now a widow. Aubrey, having never experienced a day's illness in his life, suffered a bad fall down the garden steps at Mapleton Road, broke his pelvis, and contracted pneumonia while in hospital. He had always seemed indestructible, so his death had come as a terrible shock, especially to Iris, who had been his housekeeper long before she became his wife. She was bereft, not only of the husband upon whom she'd doted, but of her *raison d'être*. For years, she had looked after Aubrey, his welfare, house and possessions, and now she was a lost soul. More than that, without him at her side she could no longer quite see herself as one of the family. It plainly worried her that apart from a few specific bequests, Aubrey had left her everything, including the house, and that as a result she might be seen as a gold-digger. No one who knew her would have thought any such thing, but she had adopted a slightly formal, self-conscious manner with them all which no one had yet been able to breach.

'We don't have to go, you know,' Kate told Thea in the kitchen after breakfast. 'It will probably be a bit sticky.' But Thea was adamant.

'No, we should. I'd like to. We couldn't be at their wedding, and I feel we owe it to Aubrey. I remember how happy she made him.'

'It will be hugely appreciated, Mum, I promise you.'

In the end, Jack remained at home. Lawrence had taken a few days' leave from SSAFA to be with his in-laws, so he would have company. On the drive to Lewisham, Kate reflected that this would make it easier all round – nice for the men to have a quiet day together, and far less for Iris to worry about. Kate had rung her that morning to explain that they would be only two (Iris was not a person on whom one sprung surprises), and had heard the relief in her voice.

'I'm sorry to hear that. Is Mr Kingsley all right?'

'He's a little under the weather and rather tired. So we thought we'd make it a ladies-only occasion.'

'Yes – well, it's a shame, but it will be very nice to see you both.'

Useless to tell her not to go to too much trouble. Kate's earlier suggestion that they take her out to a local restaurant had been met with something approaching horror – they couldn't possibly come all that way and then go out! – and the concept of a light cold lunch would also be considered inhospitable. Without Aubrey's mediation Iris had reverted to type; telling her not to take trouble was tantamount to patronage.

Thea had turned down the offer of going to see Chilverton House. Whether it had changed out of all recognition, or scarcely changed at all, it would be overwhelming. The house in Mapleton Road had no such power – Ralph's move there had more or less coincided with the Kingsleys' departure for East Africa, so the place held no memories.

For Kate, though, it was redolent of that strange time when her whole life had changed: the return to England; meeting her family and, later, Dulcie; the start of that long and bumpy road to self-discovery. She made the journey about once a year these days, and it was getting increasingly hard to find a parking space, but she was glad to leave the car further up the street – the short walk gave her time to adjust.

Thea closed the car door and looked around. 'You know, at the time I couldn't understand why Father made such a drastic change – from Chilverton to this – but now I think I know. He was making a clean break – going back to what he was before he married.'

Kate locked up and they began to walk. 'What was that?'

'Oh, you know, a townie, an industrialist, a plain man.'

'He did seem to suit the place. It was a bit of a bachelor pad, with him and Aubrey on their own.'

'Until you and Joe came along!' Thea smiled ruefully. 'Poor Kate, talk about a baptism of fire.'

'For them too – Joe was good as gold, but I wasn't an easy customer.'

'You were extremely brave, both of you.'

'But they were saints!'

This made them both laugh, and they were still smiling as they reached the house. The door opened and Iris was there to greet them.

'Hello. Oh, Kate.' She accepted a kiss, and another from Thea, who ignored her outstretched hand. 'And Mrs Kingsley.'

'Thea, please. Hello, Iris.'

'Come on in, do, and have a glass of sherry. Lunch'll be ready in half an hour.'

They followed her into what was now very definitely the front room, to the right of the hall overlooking the street. Apart from it being if anything even cleaner and more orderly than before, Kate noticed one or two small reorientations of the house since her uncle's death. This room, which had once been Ralph's study – more of a snug, really, packed with books and papers, the windows rarely opened – was now unmistakably a parlour, kept for best. The first-floor drawing room had been made into Iris's room, with her sewing machine, television and radio. On the other side of the hall was still the dining room, more or less unchanged, the furniture polished to a high shine and the sideboard gleaming with unused Sheffield plate. Kate could see the table laid up for three, though the basement kitchen was now light and pleasant with a Habitat table and a French window on to the garden; since Aubrey's death the perilous outside staircase from the first floor had gone and the cinder path had been replaced by a neat crazy-paving patio. It would have been nice to eat down there, and on the last occasion Kate had visited they had done so, but

Iris would never have countenanced such informality with Thea present.

The room in which they drank their very good but wintry Oloroso was immaculate, the familiar furniture gussied up with scatter cushions, and with nicely arranged fresh flowers in front of the fire screen. Most of the books had gone, or been stashed away, and those remaining were neatly bestowed on shelves on either side of the hearth, hardbacks top and bottom, paperbacks in between. The tall bay window wore half-nets, pristine white with a lace edging.

'Isn't this nice!' exclaimed Thea. 'So much prettier than before.'

'Everything's still here,' Iris assured her. 'I just moved things round a bit. I'd never get rid of anything without consulting the family.'

'Iris, you *are* family. These are your things to do what you want with. I don't know about Kate, but I certainly don't have a sentimental attachment to anything.'

Kate shook her head. 'No. If there's old stuff you're dying to get rid of, you must go ahead. You'd be doing us a favour.'

'It's a big house,' observed Iris. 'It takes quite a bit to furnish it, and too many modern things wouldn't look right.'

Thea said, 'A bit later on you must give me the guided tour. Remember, I hardly knew this place. No sooner had my father moved in than Jack and I were off to Kenya.'

Watching her mother put Iris at ease, Kate saw that she need not have worried. Thea liked people and consequently they liked her. In fact, warmed by her flattering attention, they very often fell in love with her; Kate could see it happening now. Slowly but surely Iris discarded her Sunday-best manner, relaxed and became the friendly, down-to-earth woman Aubrey had married. Not that there would be any slackening of standards – lunch would still be taken in the dining room – but the vague sense of an old order was gone. They all three began to enjoy each other's company. Out of respect to Iris's widowhood and Jack's illness, no one ventured a comment along rather-nice-without-the-men lines, but that was how it felt.

Lunch, though larger and hotter than they might have chosen, was delicious – roast chicken, new potatoes and garden peas, followed by rhubarb pie – and they did it justice.

'It feels like Sunday,' said Thea. 'I shall go to sleep in the car. That was an absolute treat, Iris.'

'It's nice to have someone to cook for.'

'Not many leftovers, either.'

'I'm pleased you enjoyed it.'

After coffee – taken in the front room – Iris gave them the conducted tour. Kate got as far as the garden and sat down on a bench.

'Do you mind if I stay here and soak up the sun?'

'Please do. The garden's a bit wasted on me – I like the sun but it doesn't like me.'

Kate watched as the two older women perambulated gently round the long, narrow plot – how suffocated she had felt as a young girl from Kenya by these walled strips of city garden. Iris had confessed, somewhat shamefacedly, to having help out here, and it was every bit as neat and orderly as the inside of the house. Against the wall at the end, the small prefab shed that housed the tools was screened from view by a beaverboard fence. If there was a compost heap or rubbish tip they were also hidden. The lawn was smooth as a billiard table, the edges sharply defined, and the herbaceous border that undulated along the south wall was weed-free, each shrub and plant standing proudly in its own space. Kate remembered coming out here and hauling on ramparts of convolvulus, jabbing at the stubborn weeds with the hoe and fork, anything to use up her furious homesick energy. Now, there would have been nothing for her to do.

Thea pointed, asked a question, listened carefully to the answer. Iris drew her attention to something else; they moved on a little way ... paused again, came together, peered, discussed, nodded in mutual respect and agreement ... It was, Kate thought, nothing short of miraculous, the Thea effect.

As they went up the stairs to the first floor, Thea experienced her first tremor of something like recognition – a couple of familiar paintings on the wall were like a half-heard tune, or an old acquaintance glimpsed from a window; they made her catch her breath.

'There's a lot of stairs,' said Iris. 'They keep me fit.'

'They must do.'

'Let's go all the way to the top and work our way down.'

'Good idea.'

On the top floor was a box room, and a wide, low bedroom with a dormer window overlooking the garden. Thea went instinctively to the window.

'This is nice.'

Iris smoothed the bedspread and adjusted the runner on the chest of drawers before coming to join her. 'Yes, it's a pleasant room for someone who doesn't mind the climb. This is where Kate was when she first came over, Aubrey told me. Before my time, of course.'

'I remember she said she was at the top of the house. The sense of space appealed to her, I think ... London must have felt very alien after what she was used to.'

They both looked down to where Kate sat on the garden bench, her arms stretched out, face turned upward.

'Still a sunflower, I see,' said Iris, 'in spite of that red hair.'

'I know. We tried to protect her when she – as a small child, but she was a tomboy and it was hopeless.'

'She looks very well and happy.'

'She is. A lot of that wild restlessness has gone. Thanks to Lawrence, I think.'

'I never asked, how is the Colonel?'

'Very well. Taking a day off to keep Jack company.'

'That's good.'

They went down to the next floor, and Iris showed Thea the main bedroom, the one that had been hers and Aubrey's, and where she had changed the rust-coloured brocade curtains and bedspread for something a little lighter and more feminine. The other room was smaller, and here Thea at once recognised various less distinguished relics from Chilverton House: the mahogany chest of drawers, the shield-shaped mirror and dressing stand on top, the watercolour of the Kentish hop fields, the high single bed with its twisted corner posts, the bentwood chair with the threadbare tapestry seat.

'This is the guest bedroom,' said Iris. 'I think it needs some attention.'

Thea sat on the edge of the bed. 'Do you have many people to stay?'

Iris shook her head. 'Very few.' From this Thea inferred probably none, but then Iris added: 'Dulcie came once or twice. And I
believe your cousin Maurice, before he died.'

'Oh ... Poor Maurice ...'

Thea rose and walked round the room – it wasn't large, but she
moved slowly, as though it were a museum or gallery, here and
there touching familiar things with her fingertips.

'You didn't know him, but he was a sweetheart.'

Iris shook her head. 'It was ever so difficult for Aubrey, all that
– he couldn't understand it.'

'But he did in the end. I'm sure he did.'

Iris was quiet, and Thea turned to look at her. 'You don't believe
that.'

'I don't know. They were chalk and cheese, weren't they? Aubrey
had spent all that time in a prisoner of war camp; he found it hard
to sympathise with pacifists.' She blushed a little. 'But I wasn't
around. I feel sorry for the poor chap, especially going with the flu
after all those struggles.'

Yes, thought Thea, Maurice may have been the bravest of us
all. And much good it did him – there's been another world war
since then; everything's changed, and those of us who are left
are going to die in our beds after long and mostly happy lives.
Whereas poor Maurice – she could see him now, slender and pale,
nervously wringing his hands, his large, intelligent eyes wavering
behind spectacles, that abrupt way of speaking as if every blurted
sentence meant screwing his courage to the sticking point.

And Dulcie had never been kind to him.

'My sister must have hated it in here,' she said, without thinking. 'Too many reminders of Chilverton House.'

'She never complained,' said Iris, with a hint of her former
prickliness.

'I'm glad to hear it. She could be the least tactful person in the
world.' Thinking of Dulcie, Thea tilted the mirror as if she might
catch a glimpse of the past. But it was her own, shockingly old
face that she saw, weathered and lined by the African sun, surrounded by a halo of iron-grey hair.

'Hell's bells,' she said cheerfully. 'If she could see me now, Dulcie
would have a fit.'

*

When they got home and were sitting under the tree in the garden, Thea said to Jack:

'That house reminded me of Dulcie – the one room in particular. Iris said she used to sleep there when she needed to.'

'When there was absolutely no alternative, I take it.'

'She never liked it there. She never liked anywhere that was to do with the past. She was a creature of the moment.'

'That's a polite way of putting it. No,' he caught her expression, 'I didn't mean that. It was a reflex, and not a kind one, I'm sorry.'

'That's all right.' She stroked his hand, absolving him. 'She wasn't easy and she was selfish, but she was plucky.'

'I accept that.'

Dulcie and Maurice both, thought Thea. Who would ever have thought their names would be linked, let alone under the banner of courage? Time was the only truthful historian.

Kate was rinsing lettuce at the sink under the window. Behind her, Lawrence was putting bottled beer, lime juice and glasses on a tray. She turned to him, pointing.

'Look.'

He joined her, one hand on her shoulder. 'Picture of a happily married couple, eh?' He dropped a kiss on her neck. 'Must be where we get it from.'

Chapter Thirty-Two

1999

Stella, still in her dressing gown, coffee mug in hand, stood gazing out over the St Lawrence. Jules the cat, lolling in the depths of a threadbare tapestry sofa, watched her, as he had done from the first. She had decided to ignore him. Though not a cat owner herself, she instinctively understood cat behaviour. Occupancy was nine tenths of the law, and petting (unless accompanied by the promise of food) was weakness. Old yellow-eyes would not catch her arguing with either of these rules. Even when – as would undoubtedly happen later on – he began writhing round her ankles in an ecstasy of cupboard love, he'd get no change out of her. She had her orders: feeding time was when Alan got back in the evening, and to mess with that would be to throw out the balance of their shared bachelor life. The cleaner, Kim, came once a week on a Friday; he hoped she didn't mind.

Mind? She had assured him she did not. This was Alan's patch, and she had no desire to leave her mark, or to add or subtract anything from what seemed an almost perfect existence. She was free.

His apartment was on the second floor of a shabby-grand brownstone block overlooking the quay. The area was still quite rough, but she could see why he loved it and could well understand the encroaching gentrification. She was awestruck by the scale of the river and everything on it. A container vessel the size of several football pitches came into view, nudging majestically upriver, dwarfing the rest of the traffic. You could easily linger here all day, watching the world's shipping go by.

There was only one thing more fascinating than the view, and that was the apartment itself. She turned round and surveyed it. Jules stretched, his long legs extending like chewing gum, his mouth opening in a pink, heart-shaped yawn. The movement may have been drowsy, but it displayed a delicate armoury of claws and teeth.

The moment she'd arrived here, the day before yesterday, Stella had felt at ease. On the flight over, it had occurred to her that Alan had seen her own domestic set-up, warts and all, before she had very much idea about his. Though he might, now, have been a single man, he had once been a married one, with a French wife and a home that was doubtless *tout propre*, if not by her own hand then at least under her regimen. If the apartment turned out to be dauntingly chic, or simply too ordered for comfort, if he was a man who ironed his socks or arranged his books in height order – well, all would not be lost, but it might require a little recalibration.

What she found was a place where the tenor of life, its pace and pleasures, was similar to hers, but where the demands of work called for a slightly greater degree of organisation. He had too many books, CDs and films – especially books – and the available shelving had run out, so there were piles on tables and even forming tables next to the two large, unmatched sofas, the one Jules was occupying and a chestnut leather one that converted into a bed. This was a corner apartment, and by the smaller window at the side of the building was a dining table and chairs, glass and wicker – they'd been the garden set, he told her, from the house he shared with Mireille, but he'd liked them so much he'd brought them indoors here. The living room was huge – not much smaller than the whole of Stella's ground floor – but the kitchen was a well-appointed galley, and the second bedroom, which Alan used as a study, was tiny. The bathroom wasn't big either, and the only structural difference he'd made when he moved here was to convert it into a Japanese-style wet room, just slate tiles and a power shower that rattled your brain.

There were no fitted carpets – the apartment had parquet flooring, not all of it in good condition, covered with an eclectic patchwork of rugs ranging from an ancient family rag-weave dating from Newfoundland to a small but beautiful hand-made Turkish carpet between the sofas. There were masses of pictures, haphazardly hung, which again seemed to have been accumulated rather than carefully selected, and allowed to jostle for attention on the crowded walls. She liked the place enormously.

'Are you going to be all right?' he'd asked on her first morning, arriving at the bedside in a crisp short-sleeved shirt and bearing a cup of tea.

'More than all right – as happy as anything.'

'Make yourself at home. I expect to be back around six. I've arranged some back-up.'

'Don't change anything for me, I'll be fine.'

He stooped to kiss her, holding his tie with one hand. He smelt of shower gel, something fresh and coconutty. 'I can't tell you,' he said, 'what this means to me. See you later.'

She couldn't quite believe it herself – that she had put everything in place so quickly, and was here! If you wanted something enough, it was this easy – you just wriggled out of your self-imposed restraints and did whatever it was, and then wondered why you hadn't done this, or something like it, before.

The only small cloud on the horizon was Toyah. Stella had accompanied Shannon to the hospital for yet more tests, which had taken place over two lengthy and trying appointments. The results when they came were apparently inconclusive and might, they said, have to be done again, only this time she wouldn't be there to lend moral support.

Shannon, uniquely for her, had been a little weepy at Stella's departure, but also touchingly keen that she should go. Maybe it was the younger woman's instinctive understanding of how important this trip was that made her sad – that it might very well mean a sea change in Stella's life, a change that would have implications and consequences for both of them. Shannon wasn't daft.

'You have an amazing time now, Stel.'

'I will, and I'll tell you all about it.'

'Lots of photos, yeah?'

'Don't worry.'

'I tell you what.' Shannon blinked and waved an apologetic girlie hand in front of imagined tears. 'I hope this bloke appreciates you.'

'He does, and it's mutual.' Stella hugged and released her. 'But I am coming back, you know. This is only a holiday.'

'Sure. Here – we got you something for the flight.' She lifted Toyah, who held out a small, beautifully wrapped parcel, decorated with a butterfly on a wire. 'Don't open it now, put it in your handbag.'

After take-off, with a tumbler of white wine to hand, Stella took out the package. Inside was a perfume stick, an expensive brand in an enamelled case. She dabbed it on her wrists and throat and breathed in her own aura of White Lily as the plane rose above the clouds.

The first thing he said to her after their long embrace in the arrivals hall was:

'You smell great. What is that?'

'A bon voyage present.'

'Anyone I know?'

'Oh, just a friend.'

'They have good taste.'

'She does.'

'You don't know,' he said as he began pushing the trolley, 'how relieved that makes me feel. I got you one, too. It's in the car.'

When they were in the car, he opened the glove compartment and handed her a store carrier bag containing a box.

'Self-interest. It's a Canadian cell to use while you're here. All set up. So we can be like normal people and talk to each other whenever we want.'

The sex was even better than she remembered, because it had become lovemaking. Now what they did together was about affirmation, exploration – celebration, even – and without the (admittedly agreeable) tension of novelty they were relaxed and able to take their time. They continued to surprise each other, as well. Like the childhood game where you put your hand into a bag and tried to guess the contents, the likes and dislikes, the tricks and treats that they noticed in each other, and whose provenance they still didn't know, were both mysterious and fun – part of conversations they would have, and memories in the making.

What she had forgotten – or perhaps never considered – was that there were other people in Alan's life. Pierre might be in France, but there were friends, and colleagues, and the team of people who helped him run his life, from Kim the cleaner to Franco, the doorman. Someone rang on her first day; a crisp female voice asked: 'Who's that?'

She had no idea whether she had been mentioned, and if she had been, how described. 'Stella Drake – I'm a friend from England.'

'Oh, hi, Stella, is he at the clinic?'

'I believe so. He's at work.'

'Could you give him a message? Tell him Marie can't make the meeting on Tuesday, but I'll email him the notes.'

'Hang on …' Stella scribbled it down. 'Does he have your number?'

Marie – if Marie it was – laughed heartily at this. 'He certainly does!'

A parcel arrived from Amazon (it turned out to be a book she'd recommended); Franco knocked on the door with a second key he'd had cut on Alan's instructions. A formal invitation lay on Alan's desk; the door was open and there was no indication that anything was private.

Dr Alan Muir
The Directors of Blackwood Northfield
request the pleasure of your company at a dinner
to mark the company's fiftieth anniversary
The Hotel Montclere, Avenue Labec
6 p.m. drinks
11 p.m. carriages
Black tie
RSVP Sheila Laverne slaverne@videotron.ca

The date, she noted, was three weeks away, when she would no longer be here. He had not mentioned the event and she wondered who he would be laughing and talking with.

She spent the first few days sightseeing, learning the metro system, walking for miles, even going by train to Quebec for the day. She went up the mountain in the middle of the city, where the people-watching beat even the view; she listened to lunchtime jazz at a café-bar on the docks, she looked at art, she mooched around the upmarket areas with their vast mansions and gardens cut from the ancient forest; she went to see the memorial to the Irish famine immigrants and visited museums and shopped for presents for the young and the old – native American rabbit-skin boots for Toyah, a T-shirt for Raff, and a fur scarf for her mother. It took her a while to get used to the heat; her mental picture of Canada was of frozen wastes and snow, but Montreal was closer to the equator than London and in late summer you knew it. Moving between thirty-five degrees plus in the streets to the near-arctic air-conditioning of the stores and galleries, she promptly got a cold and spent her fourth day in the apartment snuffling and nursing an inflamed throat. The arrival of Kim, a plump Chinese girl with a permanent smile and a machine-gun vocal delivery, was to begin with unwelcome, but she soon rediscovered the pleasure of lying in bed ('staying out of the way', as Kate would have put it), feeling only slightly unwell, listening to the purr of the Hoover and the sharp hiss of the spray polish and accepting occasional refreshments. Kim in her turn had clearly been primed about her employer's house guest, and if she did feel any surprise at finding Stella in Dr Muir's bed, she didn't show it. She had even brought an offering of strange glutinous sweets, akin to Turkish delight with a filling of nuts. When she was finished, she tapped on the door.

'All done, miss, I go now.'

'Kim, thanks so much. I'm sorry to have been lying around here when you've been busy, but better than under your feet.'

Kim chattered with laughter. 'Okay, okay! I see you next week!'

'Probably – I hope so.'

She felt rather better after Kim's departure, and the apartment had that stroked and soothed appearance that only a professional cleaner could achieve – she suspected it had as much to do with plumping cushions and straightening books as actual cleaning, but it was very pleasant. In the kitchen a couple of empty product bottles had been left out, presumably to show that more was needed, and under one was a note, written on a sheet torn from the telephone pad: NOT IN BEDROOM TODAY, YOUR GUEST SICK. NEXT TIME.

She wondered how long Kim had lived in Canada, and whether her just-off-the-boat Chinee character was assumed or carefully maintained for the benefit of people she worked for.

'I think she's for real,' said Alan. 'A branch of her family run the

Dewdrop restaurant in Chinatown and that's where they live, so they speak Chinese most of the time. She doesn't need to assimilate that much.' They were in bed, and he pulled his head back a little to look at her. 'Speaking of assimilation, would you mind meeting my mother?'

She didn't miss a beat. 'I'd love to.'

'Sure? No agenda, you understand.'

'I don't mind if there is.'

She said it quickly, casually, and he didn't react. 'I'm her only family; she likes to see new faces. And I hesitate to say this, but I think you'd get along.'

'Take me to her.'

'Thanks.' They kissed and were quiet for a moment. 'I appreciate it.'

'You forget,' she said, stroking his face in the dark, 'I'd have introduced you to my mother if there'd been a bit more time. And I wanted to keep you to myself for a while.'

'Yeah, well,' he said, 'I've cracked. I want to show you off.'

Barbara Muir lived only a mile away from her son, on the twentieth floor of a modern apartment block. The building was on the corner of a broad residential avenue and a bustling shopping street. Barbara's flat was at the back, with a view over a park, towards the Oratory in the middle distance. The main entrance was on the avenue, but when Stella and Alan went on Saturday morning he took her through the back, via a busy bakery and coffee shop. He bought three doughnuts and a couple of cappuccinos at the counter and they went up in the small service lift. As they got out, he said: 'By the way, you'll find her very direct, and she likes others to be the same.'

'Fine.' She sensed his slight trepidation, his wanting everything to go well. 'I get it.'

The most surprising thing about Barbara Muir was her size. She was tiny, barely five foot in her trainers, with smartly cropped white hair, sharp eyes and a throaty, still sexy voice. Her handshake was firm.

'Hello, hello, what a treat, he brought you to see me! And doughnuts too. I put plates ready, ever the optimist!' The accent was Canadian, but Stella thought she could still detect the Scottish burr underlying it. 'Sit down, Stella – you carry on with your frothy nonsense, I'm going to make a cup of tea.'

Stella half rose, but Alan waved a hand. 'Let her, she likes to.'

'I do – if I once get out of the habit, I may never move again. Kettle's boiled.'

Alan seemed completely relaxed and at home, sitting back with his coffee and picking up a local paper. The apartment was very far from being the musty old person's nest that Stella had half expected; it was bright, modern and tidy, the home of someone determined to live in the present. When Barbara came back in, Stella said, 'I love your flat – it's so airy and full of light.'

'That's why I bought it. I must have light, Stella. Not just old age, I've always wanted it. What's your place like in England?'

While Stella told her, Barbara sat forward on her chair, sipping her tea, her eyes over the mug never leaving Stella's face. She suspected that the description of her house was far less important to this perspicacious woman than the impression she was making.

'And is he looking after you while you're here? Keeping you entertained?'

'I'm working, Mom,' Alan protested.

'I knew he would be,' said Stella. 'I like exploring on my own.'

'Quite right,' said Barbara. 'It's the best way. You can't go where the mood takes you when you're with someone else. Or change your mind. There's much to be said for wandering lonely as a cloud.'

'That's what I think.'

Alan put the paper down. 'Anything need doing while I'm here?'

'The washer on the bathroom tap, and the light bulb in the hall, son. Would you mind?'

'It'd be a pleasure.'

'You might need a bulb.'

'I'll see.'

He left the room and Barbara nodded in the direction he'd gone. 'I don't know what I'd do without him. He's a wonderful son.'

'He obviously thinks the world of you.'

'Oh, well ...' Barbara picked up her doughnut. 'This looks gorgeous. Do you have parents living near you?'

'My mother. My father died a long time ago.'

She nodded. 'I'm not a widow, you know. I'm a divorcee – a

wronged woman. Not a good thing to be when we first came here, when Alan was young.'

Alan appeared in the doorway. 'There's one or two things you need. I'm going to pop down to the street.'

'Bless you.'

'We'll keep our hands off your doughnut,' said Stella.

'I shan't answer that.'

Barbara continued. 'All the women thought I was after their husbands, and all the men thought I was available. Tells you how long ago it was.'

'That must have been tough.'

'It was. But then *I* was tough.'

'I can imagine.'

'A tough cookie, is that what you're thinking?'

'Let's say a strong woman.'

Barbara chuckled. 'Very diplomatic.'

They were eating the doughnuts and getting sticky. Barbara fetched paper towel from the kitchen.

'I'm so glad you're having one too. They're a weakness of mine.'

'These are especially good,' agreed Stella, licking the sugar off her lips.

'You'd better believe it.' Barbara adopted a TV commercial voice: 'You're in the land of the doughnut now, sister!'

'You won't hear any arguments from me.'

Barbara put down her plate and dusted her palms. 'So, Stella – are you keen on him?'

Stella remembered Alan's admonition about directness. 'I am rather.'

'Because he's very keen on you.'

'I hope so.'

'Oh yes.'

'You do understand, Barbara, we haven't known each other very long.'

'It doesn't take long, though, does it – the real thing?'

Stella's face grew warm. 'Perhaps not.'

'Don't worry, I'm not a hovering mother. He and I are both far too old for that. And I never have been anyway.' Barbara got up. 'Care to join me on the balcony? I'm due the first of my three per day.' She made her way to the sliding glass door, taking a small box off a side table on her way. Stella followed her out, and they sat down on two green plastic armchairs. It was already very warm, but the sky was overcast.

'I hope we have a really tremendous storm later on.' Barbara lit up, shook out the match and dropped it in a plant pot. 'The thunder and lightning are wonderful up here. Rude of me, would you like one?'

Stella shook her head. 'I bet Alan takes a dim view of that.'

'He does, but it's almost my only vice, the weed. That and the odd whisky. And when I look at some other clean-living people my age, I realise I'm not doing badly.' She tapped ash into the same pot. 'Don't you start, though. I'm not proud of it.'

'And I'm not criticising.'

'I should think not, coming here and trying to make a good impression on the old dear.'

'I deny that.'

'Hah! You know,' said Barbara, 'you'll be a tough cookie one day too.'

'I certainly hope so.'

They talked about general stuff – the practicalities of life, families, books, television – and while they talked, Stella considered that it was a long time since she had liked a new acquaintance so much. A little part of her issued a warning – however she currently felt about Alan, this was early days; they led separate lives on either side of the Atlantic. They might have some sort of future, or none at all. Friendship with his mother might be just too complicated.

Alan returned, ate his doughnut and went to fix the tap and check the bulbs. They came in from the balcony and the cigarette box was returned to its place. When they left, Barbara urged her to visit again.

'You know where I am now, Stella. I have a life of sorts, so call me first. But if you're at a loose end, nothing would give me more pleasure than to share a doughnut with you.'

'Okay.' Stella glanced at Alan, who was standing back. 'Okay, I will.'

In the lift, she said, 'What a lady.'

'Pretty good, isn't she? I need to be reminded of that when she drives me up the wall, which she does with increasing frequency.'

'Why?'

They reached the ground floor, and Alan made a snorting sound as they stepped out into the lobby. 'You have to ask? She's old and she lives on her own.'

Stella didn't point out that both of them did too. 'So does my mother.'

'And – don't tell me – she's a saint.'

She was surprised by the venom in his voice. 'No. I was just going to say it can't be easy.'

'For who?' The automatic glass door opened to let them out on the street. The heat flopped over them. In the lobby behind them, the pale thumbprint of the porter's face was still turned their way.

'For her,' she said, trying not to raise her voice as he moved away. 'For both of them. For any intelligent woman whose world has become smaller and duller than it used to be and who no longer has the resources to change things.'

'Point taken,' he said, but more, she sensed, to shut her up than to concede the argument. They walked swiftly and in silence to where the car was parked.

'Let's go find a drink.'

'Suits me.'

I'm seeing another side of him, she thought. *We may be having our first row. There was bound to be one. It's not the end of the world.*

They went to a bar by the docks, and ordered beers – two for Alan; he knocked back the first one immediately and poured the second. His face looked pinched. Stella half wanted to apologise, but then asked herself what for? He was behaving badly. About time he did, it had to happen sometime, but she wasn't going to give him a hand up. She'd been here before; she could sit this out. If she'd had a book with her she'd have read; instead she got out her new phone and studied it, her face calm, concealing the uproar within.

After about five minutes he said coldly, 'Okay, I'm sorry.'

She put down the phone. 'What exactly was the issue?'

He looked away for a second, lips pursed. She saw that he was truly angry, though not, she suspected, with her.

'What?' she said again.

'She's not always wonderful, you know.'

'Who is? She appreciates you, though.'

He looked at her sharply. 'Is that what she said?'

'Yes. And she has your interests at heart.'

'I'm sure she thinks she has, but she has precious little idea what those interests are.'

'Not specifically, maybe, but your happiness is important to her.'

He took a long swig of beer and put the glass down heavily. 'You know what would make me happy?' She shook her head. 'To be free.'

'But you are, surely.'

'I mean, free of my mother.' She was shocked, and it must have showed. 'Damn, have I blown it?'

'This isn't us we're talking about,' she said, though in a sense she knew it was. 'Go on.'

'I don't mean I want her dead ...'

'I realise that.'

'... but I do wish there was someone else to take the strain occasionally.'

'Is there much strain?' asked Stella. 'She's pretty self-starting, isn't she?'

'Yes, but look – how many in your family? Your kin?'

'Not that many – five or six?'

'But you all live within a hundred miles of each other, right?'

'With the exception of my errant brother.'

'Forget him, but the rest.'

'Yes.'

'Here, there is literally only me. My mother's been on her own, no husband, for over fifty years. Half a century, Stella, without a mate, can you believe it? She loved the bastard and he left her. Left the both of us. She brought me here and worked, and put up with all my teenage shit, and watched me screw up with Mireille, and waved Pierre off to his gay life in Europe, and now there's just her and me again. Whatever she says, she doesn't have much of a life; she's not good with all the old widows, and the old widowers are a bit scared of her. I couldn't just move if I wanted to – to the States, to England, not even to Toronto, for heaven's sake.'

'How do you know?' asked Stella.

'Because she's eighty-six and I've left it too late.'

'I think you underestimate her.' Stella pushed aside her beer glass. 'I'd like a glass of wine. What's yours?'

She came back with a large white wine and a Jack Daniel's.

'I really do,' she went on. 'If you ever had a good reason to go, she'd wish you luck and get on with it.'

'I do a lot for her,' said Alan. 'Don't get me wrong, I want to, it's right and proper. I only mention it because the result is that if I weren't here, she'd definitely notice.'

'She would, naturally, and she'd miss you. I'm just saying that you can't allow your life to be conditioned by what might or might not happen if you had to go. She'd hate that. I know I've only just met her, but unless I'm a really lousy judge of character, I bet she'd rather be here on her own with the support systems in place, knowing you were happy, than feeling she was tying you down.'

'Maybe.' He rubbed a hand over his eyes; his mouth looked uncertain, vulnerable. 'The very old are like the very young – selfish because they have to be. Remember, I see plenty of both. If you're helpless, you grab the help where you can get it and hang on like grim death.'

'But Barbara's not helpless.'

'Not at the moment, no. She has good genes, and she has me.'

Stella watched him, this man with whom she was falling in love, and tried to calibrate her feelings. She sensed that this conversation was a turning point of sorts. His loss of composure and dignity was going to haunt him, and there was nothing she could say or do to prevent that. Over the last little while she'd seen the petulance and resentment of the only child, as well as his devotion and loyalty. Who was ever truly grown up? Did the child ever leave any of them? Or were some people just better at keeping the child in its place?

'So she's very lucky,' she said. 'I'm not denying that. But from where I'm standing, you're letting a hypothesis spoil everything.'

'Yup.' He snatched a mouthful of bourbon, avoiding her eye. 'I wonder why that is, all of a sudden?' When she ignored this, he added, 'Anyway, here we are, both in the second half of our lives, both with aged parents who depend on us.'

'But who love us, too.'

'Sure, sure, let's take that as a given.'

'No, Alan, don't let's – if there's love and goodwill, all things are possible.'

'That's a counsel of perfection, if I may say so.'

Stella didn't want to get angry. She wanted to see this through, but a determination to look on the bright side and persuade him to do the same wasn't going to get them anywhere, no matter how much she believed in what she was saying. He had let down his guard, allowed her to look in one of the messy corners of his life; she should do the same.

'Just now,' she said, 'I mentioned my brother, the absentee. You said forget about him. Well I can't.'

'Out of sight not out of mind, then?'

'The opposite.' She had his attention now. 'The more he's away, the less he does, the more I obsess about him. He's become my whipping boy, the one I blame when I feel like hell.'

'He brought it on himself, I guess.'

'He did. But here's the thing. He's the prodigal; if he came back – I'd like to say *when* he comes back, but there are no guarantees – we'd all welcome him with open arms. There's no point in chastising someone when they finally do the right thing.'

'That's true.'

'But you know what? I'm going to be spitting tacks – remember the other brother, the one who stayed behind and kept the show on the road?'

'I'm not good on the Bible.'

'Well, he was pissed off when the prodigal came home and the fatted calf was slain, and I bloody well don't blame him. I know who *I* blame.'

For what seemed like the first time that day, Alan smiled. 'Poor old – what's his name?'

'Will.'

'What exactly did he do wrong, apart from not be around?'

'How long have you got?' Sensing that the crisis was past, she was beginning to enjoy herself. 'He split from his partner and child and has been around only intermittently since. He barely knows his grandson. He's the original moving target, never in one place long enough to pin down. Our mother always sticks up for him but she knows he's behaved like a shit. Everyone knows, but no one says it in so many words.'

'Self-protective behaviour,' he suggested. 'Pretend and make it so.'

'Very *English* behaviour,' she said. 'Very evasive and dysfunctional.'

'You're too hard on yourself, Stella.'

She cocked her head on one side and stared at him. 'QED.'

He downed his drink. 'Let's drive out of town.'

It took them a while to find their way back to where they'd been before, and they both knew that when they did, the landscape, like the one outside the car window, would be different. Gradually, as they drove, and walked in the woods, and had lunch at a pleasant, touristy inn, the equilibrium between them was restored. But the exchanges of the day had left a legacy of unanswered questions. In bed that night they did not make love, but lay spooned together, facing the same way, lost in their own thoughts before falling asleep.

The next day, Sunday, they collected Barbara, and all three of them spent the day at a barbecue given by a colleague of Alan's, Dick Klavitz, and his wife Sandy. The Klavitzes lived out in the suburbs in a low-rise family house with a rumpus room in the basement, a big garden, two handsome, boisterous sub-teenage kids and a golden retriever. It was going to be a party of sorts, their hosts told them; there would be about twenty people of all ages. In the car on the way, Barbara asked, 'What's the occasion?'

'Nothing in particular,' said Alan. 'I think they wanted to meet Stella.'

'What?' Stella was taken aback. 'Why?'

'Only joking. But they knew I had a house guest from England and they're very sociable people.'

This much was certainly true. A sign on the front door told them to go straight round to the back of the house, where Dick immediately spotted them and came across, a striped apron over his Lacoste polo, waving a fork as big as a trident.

'Alan! Welcome – and this must be Stella, welcome to Montreal! Barbara, gorgeous as ever … Sandy's in the kitchen. What can I get you guys?'

The barbecue was a shiny, gas-fuelled giant, and there were

three striped gazebos put up in the garden, the largest of which contained a plastic barrel full of bottled beer and white wine on ice, and a table groaning with salads of every configuration and baskets of bread. Chairs and small tables stood about in the other gazebos and under parasols on the lawn. At the far end was an upright plunge pool, where several children were already leaping and shrieking. Another family with teenage boys in cargo shorts came round the corner, and Dick waved at the bar tent and went to greet them.

When they had their drinks, Alan linked arms with Barbara and Stella. 'Let me take you in to meet Sandy.'

Their hostess, a trim, fortyish blonde in white shirt and Bermudas, was mixing potato salad in a bowl the size of a washbasin.

'Sandy – you remember my mom, Barbara?'

'I should hope she does.'

'Why certainly I do. Hi, Barbara! No touching, I'm greasy.'

'And this is my friend Stella, from England.'

'Stella, it's a pleasure. Excuse me, up to my elbows in mayo.'

'Can I help?' asked Stella, glancing round at the kitchen – the fridge alone was about the size of her downstairs cloakroom at home.

'Yes.' Sandy made a shooing gesture. 'You can get out of here and enjoy yourselves. There's only this left to do, I'll be right out.'

A couple of the older people were sitting taking it easy in the shade of the living room, drinks in hand.

'Hey,' said Barbara, 'this'll do me. May I join you?'

'Sure, sure, take a seat, this is the cool place to be.'

They left her there and went back out into the garden. The glare and the heat broke over them. At the end of the garden, spouts of water rose from the giant blue tub of the pool.

'That looks so nice.'

'You want a dip?'

'I didn't bring a cozzie.'

'You want bathers, Sandy can lend you some. She's got everything.'

'I'll see.' She smiled at him. 'I am hot. You go and mix, I'm going to admire the pool for a moment, then I'll join you.'

'Promise? They all want to meet you.'

'I'll be over. Go on.'

She walked past the pool and stood on the far side. There was a little shade from the trees by the back fence, and she had the benefit of the occasional shower of cool drops from the children larking about. Here, she thought, was another side of Alan's life, the part that wasn't at all like hers. His flat might feel like a home from home, but this was another world. She was suddenly a little homesick – dazed by the heat, and dazzled by the glare. The exuberant sociability of these strangers in their sun-baked garden was almost overpowering, and the acrid smell of the barbecue only served to remind her that she had no appetite. She was like a timid, sickly English mouse, cowering in the undergrowth. But hell – she pressed her lips together and closed her eyes for a second – she was not a mouse! She *would* not be. Whatever role these people thought she had in Alan's life, the most important thing was for her to get out there and be her own person.

A shout, followed by a sudden lull in the splashing and shrieking, made her open her eyes. The children had run off to get food. But she was not alone. A slim dark woman in a black linen shift stood leaning against a tree. Big sunglasses made her inscrutable, but her stance – face tilted upwards, arms folded, her glass resting lightly against her chin – suggested a reverie. The clearness of her voice, therefore, came as a slight surprise.

'Isn't this corner just delightful? Away from the fray.'

'Yes. I'm afraid I'm not used to the heat.'

'Are you not?' The woman pushed her glasses to the top of her head. Her sleek black bob, Stella noticed, seemed naturally to re-adjust to this arrangement. 'Where are you from?'

'England.'

'And you thought Canada was a chilly spot.'

'Ridiculous, isn't it?'

'We get forty degrees on a regular basis through July and August,' said the woman. 'And humidity from hell. Why anyone would do this' – she gestured in the direction of the party – 'in these temperatures, is beyond me.'

Stella laughed. 'In the UK we pray for fine weather so we can get the barbie out. And if we don't get it, we go ahead anyway. So I don't know why I'm complaining.'

'Because it's too extreme.' The woman fanned herself and placed her glass against her forehead. 'Everything's too extreme.'

Stella liked her – her amusing languor, her untypical take on things; a fellow sufferer.

'How do you know our hosts?' she asked.

'We're all members of the opera society. Not' – she lifted her forefinger – 'amateur operatics. Opera buffs. First-nighters.'

'I know absolutely nothing about opera, I'm afraid.'

'It's a free country last time I looked. What's your connection?'

'I'm here with a friend. Alan Muir? He's a colleague of Dick's.'

'I know Alan.' The woman pushed herself away from the tree and stood straight. 'Actually, I'm his ex-wife. Should I leave you in peace?'

'There's no need.' Stella managed not to miss a beat. 'So you're Mireille.'

'That's right.'

'I'm Stella Drake.'

'Hi, Stella, nice to meet you.' Mireille extended a pleasantly cool hand and they shook. 'I didn't see Alan when I arrived. I'm afraid I grabbed a glass and sought shelter.'

'Me too. He's in the thick of it somewhere.'

The strangeness of the encounter, and its suddenness, should have shocked her, but instead she felt refreshed and invigorated, as if someone had pressed a cold damp cloth to her temples. If this had to happen, best it should happen by chance, and without Alan.

'So,' said Mireille. 'Are you staying with Jules *et* Alan?' She made the names sound French.

'Yes.'

'And are you and he – pardon me – an item?'

'I hate – pardon me – that expression.'

Mireille tipped her head back in a soundless laugh, exposing her long, pale neck. She was not exactly a beauty, but perfectly, purely elegant. 'Let me try again. Are you in love?'

'You mean the two of us, or just me?'

'For you to say.'

'I believe we are.'

'You believe? You don't know?'

'I am. I think Alan is. But we haven't known each other very long.'

'Long enough to come all the way to Canada to stay with him.'

'It's all part of the learning experience.'

'But quite extreme – wouldn't you say? Like this climate?'

Stella declined to answer. She didn't have to, and the oddness of the situation was beginning to make itself felt. A man, one of the other guests, appeared round the side of the pool, carrying a heaped plate.

'Ladies! Food's being served – when it's gone, it's gone!'

'Thanks, we're coming.' Mireille looked at her. 'Have I intruded?'

'Not in the least. I'm pleased to have met you.'

'Then shall we …?'

'Wait a minute. Mireille – does Alan know you're here?'

She shook her head. 'I doubt it. I wasn't sure whether to come myself, because I thought he might be here. Not that there's any hostility between us. But for simplicity's sake.'

'Do you see much of each other?' Stella hesitated. 'Not that it's any of my business.'

'But it's a fair question, and the answer is no. The next time may well be at the civil partnership ceremony. You know about Pierre?'

'Just a little.'

'I think,' said Mireille, 'I shall go.'

'Not because of me, I hope?'

'Of course because of you! Tell me, did you bring Barbara?'

'She's in the house.'

'I'll see her on the way out, then. Goodbye, Stella.'

'Goodbye.'

She followed Mireille out into the fierce sunshine. More people were sitting down now, eating and drinking, the young in a kind of encampment in the middle of the dry grass. Mireille skirted the edge of the lawn and disappeared into the house.

'Are you okay?' It was Alan, beer bottle in one hand, steak sandwich in the other. 'We sent Paulo to find you.'

'He did find us.'

'Us?' He led her towards the barbecue. 'There was another party going on over there?'

'No, but I met someone else and we got talking.'

'Good.' He kissed her. 'Great. Now eat, and come and meet the others.'

*

They dropped Barbara home at about six. They took her up in the lift and saw her in. While Alan was in the bathroom, Stella made a pot of tea. It was only now that Barbara said:

'You must have met her, then? Mireille.'

'Yes.'

'I hope that wasn't awkward for you.'

'Not in the least. I liked her.'

'She's a strange girl,' said Barbara. 'But still quite good to me, you know, and she doesn't have to be.'

'That doesn't surprise me.'

'Well done.' Barbara pumped her fist. 'Very well done.'

It was so rare for Evie's father to get in touch these days that she found herself unable to respond in any sensible way to his overtures; she was out of practice. By the time she'd got over the shock of hearing his voice, he'd be blarneying away and though part of her, the rational part, wanted to tear into him tooth, nail and razor tongue, the moment would pass.

He never seemed conscious of his monstrous sins of omission, or if he was, appeared unconcerned about them. He was always casually affable and affectionate, rattling on as though it were only days since they'd last spoken, usually mentioning a present he'd bought, a treat he had planned. Evie could never quite bring herself to tell him to stuff his blandishments. Besides, if she did, he might take that as 'permission to fall out' (one of his phrases), and that would be that. He'd never bother to show up again, and Raff would be devastated.

She sometimes wondered if her father suffered from some pathological condition, if he was congenitally unable to empathise or feel remorse. She had mentioned this once to Stella, who had nearly choked over her glass of wine.

'You what? Don't make excuses for him!'

'I can't see how else he can be like this.'

'Because he's a lazy, cowardly—'

'He got a medal, Stella!'

'That was different. Rescuing someone from a firestorm is one thing. Facing up to your responsibilities is a bloody sight harder.'

'Now who's making excuses?'

They'd wound up laughing, but it was no laughing matter. Evie didn't see her mother very often either, but Jacqueline was at least dutiful, or perhaps conscientious would have been a better word;

she was not a woman who would want to be accused of backsliding. So it was that well-chosen presents arrived on time, regular calls were made and visits and outings arranged. These were only ever directed at Evie and Raff – the rest of Will's family, Jacqueline's attitude made plain, was not her concern; any duty towards it was fully discharged through her relationship with her daughter and grandson. It was curious – Jacqueline was on the case, and even if no one's idea of a typical grandmother, she was proactive in maintaining contact, but if there was a wellspring of love there, Evie had never experienced it. She didn't mind – it was after all what she was used to – but now that she had Raff and knew what real, complicated, painful, albeit imperfect maternal love felt like, she could see the gap. Whereas her father – her bloody useless, never-there father – could do the warm fuzzies as to the manner born.

His latest approach was typical. He was going to be in London for a regimental reunion in early September; it would absolutely make his day if they could come up the evening before, do a show, have dinner, they could choose – how about it?

As ever, she had to take a couple of deep breaths, slow her heartbeat before answering. It was his casual assumption that he could ring up out of the blue – after, what, a year? More? – and suggest this jaunt with no thought of what they might be doing, or the increasingly stiff demands of Raff's schedule.

'I'll have to check with the school,' she said.

'Won't it still be holiday?'

'Yes, just, but' – she tried to keep her exasperation in check – 'term begins that week, and there may be choir rehearsals, or services he's got to be at.'

'Surely he can have a special dispensation to see his grandfather? Time off for good behaviour?'

'I told you, I'll have to see.'

'And anyway, what about you?' he went on. 'It's equally important that I see you, my darling girl.'

If it was that important, she thought, you'd have seen me months ago – but yet again she didn't say it. Why not? Why couldn't she come right out and blame him, fair and square, give him the roasting he deserved? Perhaps because she feared that once she started she might never stop and the bile would just go on and on, spewing out until it enveloped them both.

'I might be able to; it depends on work and what Raff's doing.'

'I understand, sweetheart. I do. I know how much you have on your plate.'

'It's not that,' she said snappishly, batting aside his faux understanding of her life, 'but you haven't given me much notice and a night in town during the working week needs a bit of organising.'

'Of course, I understand. I shall await developments.'

In a normal world he, or she, might have suggested he come out here and spend the evening with them, but they both knew that wasn't the deal. It suited her father to be the busy, passing-through person, the giver of treats, waiting for her to find time to accept.

'Let me know when you've decided,' he said, 'and I'll book tickets and an eatery. Bye, darling. Give Raff a manly hug from me.'

As it turned out, Raff came into the kitchen at that moment, but she didn't bother passing on the hug – why should she act as her father's agent?

'Was that Grandad?'

'Yes, it was.'

'Great.' Raff went to the breadbin and began assembling a cream cheese and marmite sandwich in a flurry of greasy crumbs. 'Will we see him?'

He made it sound like a safari: *Will we see lions?*

'He was asking if we'd like to meet him in London in a couple of weeks.'

'Yay! I'm well up for that.'

'I'm sure you are, but we need to look at the date and make sure we haven't got anything happening. It's just before the start of term.'

'Oh come on!' Raff headed for the door, sandwich in hand. 'We must! We never see him!'

No, thought Evie. 'Plate, please.'

Of course that was the plain fact of the matter – they did almost never see him, so when the summons came they were supposed to jump for joy. And not, as she was doing at this moment, be left picking the tacks from between her teeth.

*

Generally speaking she wouldn't have mentioned this to her mother – since Evie's twenty-first birthday Jacqueline had not concerned herself with how much she saw of Will – but on this occasion it so happened that they had arranged to meet. Jacqueline was due to give a lecture at Summerby Hall, a manor house turned adult education centre outside town, and Evie was going there for a drink straight from work.

Whenever she saw her mother, she had the vague and uncomfortable sense that Jacqueline was, if not actually getting younger, at least marking time, while she herself was ageing in the normal way and therefore in danger of catching up. Jacqueline had the lean figure, the classic style and the healthy income to maintain a timeless appearance. Her hair, these days cut in a short, swept-back style, was now snow white, but apart from this, sitting ramrod straight, legs crossed, in a wing-back chair, she looked as she had always done – a smart, grown-up woman who even when completely still, reading a book, hummed with purposeful energy. She glanced up as Evie approached, and set the book aside, rising to greet her.

'Hello, my love. How are you?'

There was nothing the matter with the greeting, or the light kiss that accompanied it, but Evie had, as always, the sense of being subjected to portion control where maternal demonstrativeness was concerned – just enough and no more.

They sat down and an elderly waitress (probably the same age as Jacqueline) brought two glasses of Kir Normand.

'I hope this is all right – you've got to drive and I've got to sing for my supper. This light cider is rather delicious.'

'It looks lovely,' said Evie. 'Cheers.'

'To us. How's Raff?'

'At a choir practice, but he sends his love.'

Jacqueline reached down into her handbag and took out an envelope. 'A little something for him.'

'That's so kind, you shouldn't.'

'A crisp tenner won't endanger his immortal soul.'

'He'll be delighted.'

'Tell him to email. I like getting emails and his are surprisingly witty.'

Evie let the 'surprisingly' go. Just for once, she decided, she was going to dive straight in and say what was on her mind.

'Dad rang up the other night.'

'Oh yes?' Jacqueline tilted her head enquiringly. 'And how was he?'

'How would I know?'

'I mean, how did he sound?'

'The same as usual – lots of chat and charm. But we all know he could be in traction and still sound like that.'

'I haven't seen him for months,' mused Jacqueline, as though something might have changed in that time.

'Nor have we,' said Evie. 'In fact I can't remember the last time. And now he's asking me and Raff to go for a night out in London. Do you think we should? Or would that be simply playing along with him, letting him feel good when it suits him?'

'Goodness, Evie.' Jacqueline raised her eyebrows. 'I'm in no position to give advice on the subject. And anyway, it sounds to me as though you've already made up your mind and want me to endorse the decision.'

Evie wished her mother would be a little less clear about everything. 'I'm angry with him,' she said, 'but who isn't?' Jacqueline raised a hand. 'All right, so you're not.'

'Sorry about that,' said Jacqueline unapologetically. 'I gave him a long leash and he made the most of it.'

'Fine, that's your prerogative. Never mind about the advice, I'd just like your unbiased opinion. Raff would love to go, but there's part of me that says if we do, we're telling him it's fine with us if he goes AWOL for years at a time and then rocks up expecting to make everything okay with a pizza.'

Jacqueline waited for a moment as if asking *All done?* and then gave a slow, expressive shrug. 'I suppose it depends on how much you want to punish him.'

'Quite a lot, actually. But not at the expense of Raff's relationship with him.'

'There's your solution, then. Let Raff go by himself.'

Evie thought about this. 'I suppose I could.'

'Who knows?' said Jacqueline. 'They'd probably have more fun on their own.'

If this exchange told Evie anything, it was that she didn't know what she wanted. Certainly she could show her displeasure by not going, but if Will and Raff were more likely to have fun without her, where was the satisfaction in that? She would in all likelihood spend the evening chewing the carpet, wondering what was going on and wishing she was there. In the end, even she could see the contrariness in that. Time for her to make her feelings plain but let Raff have his fun. She spoke to him that evening.

'Raff, I must call Grandad back. I'm afraid I can't make it, but if it could be managed during the day, would you like to go on your own?'

'*Really?*' This one word gave her her answer before the politeness reflex kicked in. 'But you want to come, don't you, Mum?'

'To be honest with you, love, I've got such a lot on at the moment, I'd welcome some space. So it'll have to be during the day, but if you don't mind, it might be the best answer.'

'Okay, yeah! Cheers, Mum.'

She rang Will and told him. She was determined, when talking to him, to make herself plain. 'Dad, I'd prefer not to come, but Raff would love to if it could be during the day. I could put him on the fast direct train in the morning and you could do the same your end at about five.'

'I'll be very disappointed not to see you, tuppence. Is there no way you can get away?'

'I'm afraid not.' It was too much to hope that he'd got the message first time – that she didn't want to come – and she couldn't repeat herself.

He sighed wistfully. 'You work too hard. But I'm sure Raff and I can contrive to have a good time together.'

'I'm sure you can too.'

Whatever he and her mother might say, she knew he would prefer her to be there. For one thing, evenings were Will's natural time, when he was at his best and could shine and squire the two of them around for a strictly limited period. A day with Raff, no matter how much they enjoyed themselves, would feel a lot longer, and there would be none of the natural checks and balances of a threesome. He would have to shape up, not drink too much – if at all – at lunch, and keep the conversation going unaided. He might even, God help him, find that he was having to explain himself.

Well, she thought with delicious malice – let him get on with it.

The agreed day was a Saturday, and she wasn't working. There was paperwork that needed doing, but under the circumstances, that would be a lost cause; she wouldn't be able to concentrate. She persuaded Owen to come for a walk by the river. He regarded walks as utterly pointless unless they represented a challenge of some sort, so she incentivised the expedition by proposing lunch at the Bridge Inn.

She called for him after seeing Raff on to the train.

'Just us?' he asked as he got into the car.

'Raff's going to London for the day to see his grandfather.'

'Whoa! Bit of a result?'

'I expect they'll have fun,' she said primly.

She'd already started the engine, but he placed a hand on her arm. 'Hang on.'

'What?'

'That's good, right?'

'Good for who?'

'Raff.'

'I suppose. Yes.'

'And we've got a day to ourselves, so everyone's happy.' He leaned across and kissed her on the lips. 'Let them get on with it, darlin', and we'll do the same.'

They parked the car on the edge of town and set off upriver in a southerly direction. The weather had been overcast but dry for the past week, so they were able to take the lower path, along the riverbank right beside the water. As they walked, the sky cleared for the first time in days and the sun came out. The colour returned to the water meadows, the bent willows and hedges were suddenly full of birdsong, the water shone and the air was warm and sweet on their faces. Childishly happy with this change in the weather, they discarded their jackets and strode along hand in hand, hopping over cowpats, stopping to count minnows and watching some children swing and splash on a rope tied to an overhanging branch. By unspoken agreement they kept things simple and talked about nothing except what they could see; no more heavy topics today.

Evie had taken the precaution of booking a table at the Bridge Inn, which was just as well because the sun had brought everyone out. They sat in the garden, near the water, and had chicken and ham pie, with salad for her, chips for Owen. A couple of swans with a flotilla of teenage cygnets patrolled back and forth near the bank.

'Will I start a riot if I throw them a chip?'

'Don't anyway,' she said. 'It's not good for them.'

'You're right.' He popped the chip in his mouth. 'It's my cholesterol and I'm keeping it.'

She did worry about that, but now was not the moment to preach. He was potentially a classic case: a big man with a thickening waistline, stressful work and unsocial hours, who ate, drank and smoked as unthinkingly as he breathed. *I don't want to lose him*, she thought, surprising herself. *I don't want him to kill himself.*

Of course it wasn't her responsibility – Evie believed firmly in people looking after themselves and not being nannied and chivvied by others. But looking at Owen sitting opposite her, downing his second pint, his broad, kind face catching the sun, she recognised in herself the other side of that particular coin: that she cared enough about him to try and make him stop. But then you couldn't change someone – could you? That was what foolish, deluded women did, and she was neither.

He lit a cigarette and leaned his elbows on the table. 'What's up?'

'Nothing.'

'Yeah, but what?'

'I wish you wouldn't smoke.'

'I know,' he said unapologetically.

'This may come as a surprise to you,' she said, 'but I don't want to lose you.'

'Is that right?' He stubbed out the cigarette. 'In that case ...'

She laughed. 'What's this, a grand gesture?'

'Why not? You deserve one.'

'You're mad.'

'And there's me thinking I was Mr Overcautious.'

'Was that a dig?'

'Might be. Want the other half?'

She had a coffee while he downed a third pint and then they set off back along the bank. It was now a gloriously hot afternoon.

The torpor of picnickers was broken by the occasional wasp-related shriek; children paddled on the little beaches of silky brown mud beneath the overhanging riverbank; the odd punt glided past, passengers lolling indolently beneath hats and sunglasses. Into this scene of riparian peace a great hairy dog charged down the meadow and took a flying leap into the water, paddling about joyfully with grinning jaws, ears spread on the surface. A small child of about three, wearing a green inflated vest, yelped with delight and began scooping up handfuls of mud and water to throw at the dog.

They hadn't walked more than twenty yards past this little scene when they heard a scream, harsh with terror, from somewhere behind them. At once everything happened so fast Evie could scarcely keep track. After the scream, there was a split second of quiet, followed by a panicky crescendo of voices. Owen was gone, away from her side, racing back the way they'd come, feet flying, arms pumping, shirt leaving his waistband; she'd never seen him move so fast, she pictured his heart pounding, pumping. Next thing he was in the river, his body smashing the surface and sending up spouts of spray. People were standing on the edge, uncertain what to do; there was a commotion in the water. A punt was drawn up a little distance away, the passengers sitting up in attitudes of shocked attention, the boatman holding the pole braced in front of him.

Evie began to move towards the commotion; a woman was racing from the opposite direction, running awkwardly in flip-flops with a baby in her arms, screaming in terror. Owen was waist-deep in the river, there was the flash of the child's green vest, the big dog jumping and snapping, a completely different animal from the genial giant of moments ago. The child was crying now, choking and wailing with fear and pain, but he was under Owen's arm and Owen was hauling himself towards the bank, fending off the dog. The water was no more than three feet deep, but she knew what the bottom was like, thick with mud and weeds; it was hard to get one's footing. Owen was bellowing in a huge voice, 'Take him! Someone take him! For fuck's sake, someone!' and then there was another person, a lad in a football shirt, at the edge of the water and he took the child and dumped it unceremoniously on the bank, falling over himself as he did so, to be swept up by its hysterical mother. The boatman swung at the dog with his pole, making the punt rock dangerously, but diverting the dog just long enough to allow Owen to scramble out. A moment later the dog too exploded on to the bank, barking and scattering the spectators, shaking itself violently. Owen made a grab at its collar but it was too quick for him and charged off, wild and excited, along the bank. The woman, clutching her children, continued to scream like a fire alarm, over and over.

'Who owns the dog?' Owen was no longer shouting, but Evie could hear him quite clearly. 'Whose dog is that? Anyone know?'

They didn't. Owen set off purposefully in the direction the dog had taken. Evie knew herself to be forgotten, and rightly so. A couple of other women were comforting the mother; the rest of the people were talking amongst themselves, the initial shock over, no serious harm done, but circulation was returning, and with it their sense of occasion, of having witnessed something frightening that might have become really nasty. The punt moved off again, its chastened, white-faced passengers murmuring to each other.

Evie considered following Owen, but decided to stay where she was. There was no knowing when, or even if, he'd catch up with the dog's owner. There was a small lopsided bench beneath the nearest tree and she sat down to wait. She'd only been there a moment when an elderly man detached himself from the little crowd and came over to her.

'You all right, love?'

'I'm fine – how's the little boy?'

'Scared half to death, but no bites. That jacket was in tatters, though, he could have drowned.'

'How absolutely terrifying. For him and for his poor mother.'

'Shocking thing.' They both looked respectfully at the scene. The family was now sitting on a picnic rug, the boy wrapped in another; a Thermos had been brought; the kindness of strangers had kicked in.

'You mind?' The man indicated the bench next to Evie. She moved slightly.

'Not at all.'

'Silly, but I'm quite shaky ...'

'Me too – I think we all are.'

He took a hankie from his pocket and patted his brow. When he'd put it away again he said, 'That your husband? That big feller?'

She shook her head. 'No.'

'Well whoever he is, you be sure and tell him he's a hero.'

'I will.' Evie experienced a hot rush of pride that made her eyes smart. 'He's a policeman, actually.'

'Is that right? We'd expect nothing less, then.' He gave her knee a fatherly pat. 'He was in there while the rest of us were still making up our minds.'

'I didn't know he could run that fast,' she admitted.

'It's training, isn't it?' said the old man sagely. 'Training, instinct … Put the rest of us to shame.' He glanced around. 'Where did he go?'

'To find the owners of the dog, I think.'

'Good luck to him. Stupid bastards. Where were they, anyway? That kiddie could have been killed.'

They sat there for another couple of minutes, during which time the crowd began to disperse, the woman and her children accompanied in the direction of the car park at the top of the hill.

'Right.' Evie's companion slapped his hands down on his knees. 'Panic over, best be going. You going to wait for him here?'

'For a little while, then I'll go back to the car. I haven't got my mobile on me.'

'Ah, the mobile phone, I see the sense of that now.' He held out his hand. 'Bye-bye, pass on my congratulations to your copper.'

'Thank you. I will.'

Over the next ten minutes the scene reverted to its former tranquillity. The churned water began to clear, a flotilla of ducks bobbed upstream, and a fresh wave of walkers passed by who had no idea of the drama they had just missed.

Almost as suddenly as he'd gone, Owen was back, coming up behind her from a different direction.

'Job done.' He sat down heavily on the bench. His chest was heaving, his face shone with sweat, and his trousers and shoes were wet and sticky with mud. Evie grabbed his hand but he fidgeted it away from her.

'You found them?' she asked.

'I did. I caught the dog, and met someone who knew where it

lived. The owners had only just realised it had got out and were on their way to look for it. Nice people' – he shook his head – 'but they've got some facing up to do. I told them I'd got to report the incident. They took it on the chin.'

'The little boy seemed to be all right.'

'Scared shitless – but yeah, he was lucky. He wasn't the only one. Frankly, it could have been a bloody sight worse.'

'*You*,' she beat his hand gently up and down, 'were brilliant. I've been told to tell you you're a hero.'

'Another five seconds and someone else would have been. Programmed to react quickly.'

'Another five seconds and that child would have been mauled – it doesn't bear thinking about.'

'Nope.' He rubbed his face with both hands. 'Christ, I could do with another pint!'

She laughed. 'If ever a man was entitled! Come on – come back to mine and have a hot bath and a proper drink.' She smoothed the damp hair off his forehead and kissed the corner of his mouth. 'Who knows, there may even be some other way I can show my undying admiration.'

'Now you're talking.' He put his arm round her and they stood up together. 'But don't get your hopes up.'

Owen was on duty the next day; she dropped him at his place on her way to collect Raff from the station. He dropped her a quick kiss before getting out, and said through the open window, 'Say hi to Raff for me.'

'I will.'

'And don't – you know – go telling him some big story about this afternoon.'

'Why not? It is a big story.'

'I'd appreciate it, Evie.' The use of her name told her how serious he was.

'Okay then.'

'Thanks.' He tapped the roof. 'See you later.'

Standing on the station platform, it suddenly struck her – she mustn't forget that a long time ago her father had been a hero too, and equally self-deprecating. But then, with him, she'd taken the self-deprecation at face value.

These reflections settled over her so that she was hardly aware of the people leaving the train, and only noticed Raff when she heard him call 'Mum!' and saw his face, shiny with the happiness of the day.

Chapter Thirty-Four

1999

Will strolled down Sloane Street with his suit jacket over his shoulder and his regimental tie loosened, cool as a cucumber in the heat, at peace with himself and the world.

The day with Raff had gone astonishingly well. More than that, it had been an absolute pleasure. He'd been looking forward, naturally, to seeing his grandson, but there were long intervals during which boys of that age could change out of all recognition, and each time he half expected to find that they'd lost the knack of talking to each other. He'd been particularly worried about Evie not being there – these were generally circumstances in which three was not a crowd but an advantage. Evie's slightly censorious manner was tempered by Raff's presence, and she acted as a social intermediary. Also, no getting away from it, he'd planned an evening outing because that was what he preferred; you knew where you were with dinner and a show, there was a natural rhythm to the thing. The prospect of having Raff for several hours, just the two of them, had made him a little nervous. But he need not have worried – the day had been an unqualified success.

The weather had helped. They'd taken a short bus ride up to Regent's Park and walked across to Marylebone, where they'd wound up in an excellent noodle bar. In the afternoon they'd gone to one of the many must-see holiday blockbusters, some brilliantly clever superhero twaddle that Raff had to keep explaining to him. After that, they'd gone back to the station and he'd kept Raff's strength up with a doughnut and hot chocolate before putting him on the train near a couple of ladies who were getting off at the same place.

And now here he was, at six fifteen on a golden Chelsea evening, with further delights ahead. About twenty yards short of the Duke of York's Barracks, he paused to put on his jacket and do up his collar and tie. His back straightened as he did so. He experienced that familiar thrill that was both anticipation and nostalgia. The moment he entered the building, he felt right at home – at blood temperature. There was the name of his regiment on the board, and here was a smart-as-paint NCO advancing to direct him to the room where the reunion was being held. At the door, an attractive girl soldier (one of the big improvements since his day, that) took his name and gave him a lapel badge. That was two 'sir's, two snappy, morale-boosting salutes; there was nowhere, he reflected, that he would rather be at this moment.

The room was already heaving – this was not an occasion at which the guests arrived politely late. One glance showed him at least half a dozen familiar faces, flushed and animated by plentiful infusions of the house bubbly. Another good-looking young woman in uniform, plus white gloves (rather sexy, he considered), advanced with a tray; he took a glass and considered his options.

'Will! Is that Will? Get over here!'

In seconds he was in amongst everyone, part of the throng, the centre of a group. It was heady stuff; he'd have to be careful not to get too plastered. In recent years, due to circumstances that he appreciated were his own fault, this annual reunion had become the one occasion when he could really shine, throw his shoulders back and walk tall. He didn't simply belong; he was respected and admired – his presence made a difference.

The talk here was unashamedly of the past; that was what bound them all together, what they were here to celebrate and remember. Ten years ago, the regiment itself had been swallowed up; it no longer existed in the form and with the name that they who were left had known, so they were the custodians of the flame, and this was their moment, when they could continue the process of turning stories and memories into history.

Will was in his element. The team of white-gloved handmaidens brought round trays of eats – more substantial than mere canapés; people had travelled some distance for this – but he couldn't be bothered with them. After fifteen minutes he was in the zone, that exhilarating first stage of inebriation when he knew himself to be the most amusing, the most popular, the most sought-after man in the room.

He wasn't even fazed when he bumped into Colour Sergeant Linch – the one person present who hadn't signed up for the Will Drake admiration society. Successive reunions had worn the corners off this particular encounter. Also, Linch had married a sympathetic older lady and had mellowed as a result.

'Sergeant! Good to see you.'

'And you, Colonel.' They stuck to handles these days, which preserved a sort of neutrality – rank without deference.

'How's life treating you?'

'Superb,' said Linch. 'We've got a lovely pub down near Selsey.'

'A pub? Good for you.'

'Yes. You should drop in if you're passing. The Royal Oak. Beautiful place – lovely old beams, inglenook fireplace, all the trimmings.' There was something defiant, almost challenging, in his pride. 'Sandra and I have got the freehold, it's all ours.'

'Tremendous, I'll remember that. How's business?'

'Superb,' said Linch again. 'We've got a nice bunch of regulars, and it's a holiday area so there's plenty of passing trade. Great chef, garden for the kids, people love it.'

Will had the strong sense that Linch was making a point. That was then, this was now, and he was doing bloody well, thanks very much.

'Do you have a family?' he asked. 'I can't remember.'

Linch shook his head. 'Never missed it, either. Too busy!'

'I know what you mean.' Will cast about. 'Is your wife here with you?'

'No, she's minding the shop.'

'Of course.'

Linch continued to enlarge on the splendours of the Royal Oak, and why they'd finally taken the plunge from management into ownership. Will had never met Sandra, but considered she must be a woman of iron. His colour sergeant had been no daisy before his injury, and looked downright unsettling now, in spite of successive operations. He wondered what the 'passing trade' made of the face behind the bar. Perhaps there were pictures of the Falklands all over the place, the Simon Weston effect; perhaps they came knowing the landlord was a veteran of the conflict, and wanted to shake him by the hand. Was he himself, he wondered, the hero of the hour, ever mentioned? He somehow doubted it. Will experienced a warm tingle of satisfaction thinking of Linch working his way round the facts, making a good story without parting from all the credit.

'I shall definitely look in next time I'm down there,' he said, meaning it – that'd put the bugger on the spot.

'How about you, Colonel?' asked Linch. 'How's life treating you?'

'Very well.'

'Still travelling? Sandra sees your name in the paper now and again.'

'Oh yes,' said Will. 'I'm very lucky.' This was the point when he began casting about for an escape route, and happily one presented itself.

'Will? I'm so sorry to interrupt – Will Drake?'

'Yes?' The woman was looking up at him with a sweet, pleased smile. Linch stepped politely aside. She reached out a hand.

'Please, don't go, I didn't mean to break up your conversation.'

'No, no, that's all right,' said Linch. 'There's a lot more I want to talk to. Catch you later, Colonel.'

'Nice talking to you! Hello …'

Will looked down at the woman, his mind whirring. Charming, but who the devil was she? This was the only trouble with the re-union: sometimes people hove in view who for some reason knew and remembered you, but whose name the filing system failed to throw up.

'Don't worry,' she said, 'you're not supposed to recognise me.'

'I can't imagine why not. I'm terribly ashamed.'

She laughed. 'Don't be. I'm Felicity Bradburn.'

'Yes!' He clicked his fingers, remembering now. 'How very nice to see you. Is Tony with you?'

'Actually, Tony died.'

Oh, God! 'Oh, God. I'm so sorry.'

'Will, you couldn't possibly have known,' she said. 'It was in the newsletter, but honestly, who reads that?'

'I'm afraid – I'm away such a lot, I don't always get to read the newsletter, mea culpa … Felicity, that's awful, really. Tony was a terrific chap.'

'Indeed he was. My special chap.' Her eyes shone, but everything was under control. When she went on, her voice was perfectly steady. 'Do you know, I almost never came to these things, I used to think he'd have more fun reminiscing without the ball and chain, but this year I thought I would attend to sort of represent him.'

'What a very good idea. I'm so glad you did. Tell me – I'm shamefully out of touch – was his death, you know, in any way expected?'

'A long illness bravely borne, yes.' She went on to tell him, straightforwardly, about the harrowing events of the past year. Will looked as he listened. She was a very pretty woman of about his own age or a little younger, with a rounded figure, a fresh complexion and a silky ash-blonde bob; nicely dressed in a timeless country-casuals way but with a few discreet diamonds. What she exuded, along with a delightful scent, was utter, unaffected niceness. Army wives of his generation tended to be good eggs, but Fliss he recalled had always been a real sweetie. With Tony's sad story out of the way, she changed the subject gently but firmly, accustomed to soothing the discomfort of others.

'But I want to hear about you, Will. You look marvellous.'

'Thank you.' This was the aspect of reunions he didn't relish, the polite enquiries. He suddenly spotted the cavalry in the form of Crispin, weaving through the crush towards them, glass aloft, expression like a billboard. 'Here comes Cris Hambury.'

'I'll leave you to it.'

'No, please …'

'I live near Cris and Pauline, so no novelty there, we talk to each other all the time.'

'I take your point.' Crispin, accosted by somebody else, had paused, was gesturing with his glass in their direction. Will pressed his advantage. 'Would you like a spot of dinner after this? We could catch up properly.'

'How sweet of you, but I must get back for my train. I've got an early start tomorrow; my grandchildren are coming to stay.'

'What station do you go from?'

'Victoria.'

'Let's share a taxi. My treat.'

'All right, that would be lovely.' She glanced at her watch. 'About three quarters of an hour by the main entrance?'

'I'll be there.'

She moved away, exchanging a greeting and a quick kiss on the cheek with Crispin en route. Will swapped his empty glass for a full one off a passing tray, then Crispin was upon him, pumping his hand.

'Greetings!'

'Greetings. I understand you and Felicity Bradburn are neighbours.'

'We are. I saw the two of you deep in conversation.'

'I haven't seen her for years,' said Will, 'so I had no idea about poor Tony. I felt pretty bad.'

'I'm quite sure you didn't need to. Fliss is *such* a great girl.' Crispin's expression became solemn. 'They went through complete hell, the two of them. Seemed to go on for ever. She was absolutely bloody marvellous throughout.'

'I can imagine.'

'It's a bit of a cliché, I know, but Pauline and I were genuinely relieved when Tony died. It was a blessing all round – most of all for him. Grim seeing such a great chap suffering and dwindling like that. You could tell he'd had enough. We were half expecting Fliss to go to pieces sometime after the funeral – you know, when the reality kicked in – but if she did, it wasn't in front of us. She's a gem.'

For some reason he didn't care to examine, Will did not want to go any further down the road of discussing Felicity with his friend. He suspected he was experiencing a kind of pre-emptive jealousy; he wanted to find out all about her for himself. When after a few minutes' conversation it was time to move on, Crispin said:

'You know, you really should come down and stay – especially now you've seen Fliss.'

'I might well take you up on that.'

'This time I'm holding you to it.'

By the time he met up with Felicity in the hall, he was pleasantly pissed. But then so was everyone else, so he didn't feel bad about it.

'Right,' he said, holding out his arm. 'Lock on, and we'll hail ourselves a hackney carriage.'

She laughed warmly and tucked her hand into his arm. 'You don't change, Will. I'm happy to say.'

This casual and entirely friendly remark caused him to wonder, briefly, why she seemed to know him better than he knew her. She must have gleaned something from other people. A quotation came to mind: *There's more know Tom fool than Tom fool knows*. He didn't dwell on it.

It was that time in the evening when people had left work some time ago and were now at home, eating in or out, or being entertained in one way or another – they got a cab almost immediately.

'I never asked where you were going,' said Felicity. 'Is this remotely on your way?'

'Not an issue. I'm along for the ride.'

'Hmm. Just so long as it's understood I'll pay my share …' She stopped in response to his 'Halt' gesture, and laughed. 'What?'

'Please. Allow me to be a gentleman; it'll be a novel experience for me.'

'I'm sure that's not true, Will. But all right, I'll accept graciously.'

Will could not imagine her doing anything other than graciously. He had expected the pleasant, at-home sensation to end when he left the party, but in her company it was still there. He said:

'You know, I should so like us to meet up again.'

'Me too.' Her openness was delightful.

'Perhaps – God, this is so corny – I could take your phone number?'

'Not corny at all, sensible.' She opened her bag and – rather to his surprise, he didn't know why – took out a card. There was her name, address, phone numbers and email, and in a different font: *Sitting Pretty*.

'Is this a business?' he asked.

'*Is* it …?' She cocked her head as if considering her answer. 'Yes, it jolly well is.'

'Excellent. Tell me about it.'

'I'm a sort of contractor. I organise house-sitting for when people are away, someone who'll look after everything, including any pets. I've built up a database and I can help you navigate your way around to find the right people for you. I'm not unique, but I'm local and reliable, and I've been doing something like it for years, only free.'

'Do all the friends you've been helping out mind you turning into a hard-headed businesswoman?'

'No, no, it was their idea! One or two of them had been urging me to go pro for years, and after Tony died – you know, once I was able to raise my eyes from time to time – I thought I might as well give it a try.'

'And it's a success?' he asked.

'So far, but then it would be, wouldn't it? Everyone's rallying round. I'm prepared for something of a dip this time next year.'

'Ah, but by that time word will have got round and the requests will come flooding in.'

'You think?' She had the readiest laugh he'd ever heard. There was nothing strained or nervous there; it was a proper full-throated laugh. He was prepared to bet she cried easily too. A healthy person, he thought. A natural woman.

When they got to Victoria, he paid off the cab and accompanied her to the platform. He felt suddenly bleak.

'I lead this ridiculously uncertain life,' he said, 'but I promise to ring soon.'

'I'll look forward to it, whenever it happens.'

The train came in and she at once put her hands on his arms and kissed him lightly on either cheek. He realised this was just her way, but he was still thrilled.

'Good night, Will. Thank you so much for the taxi ride.'

'*Au revoir*, Fliss.'

She smiled. 'See you soon.'

As the train moved off, she pulled down the window on the door and leaned out to wave. How long since someone had done that? He remained there, waving back, long after she'd withdrawn, until the train had disappeared round the long curve of the southbound line.

Outside it was a beautiful evening, and with no particular destination in mind he began to walk. He felt buoyantly happy – and could only conclude that this was because he had spent the last hour with someone who honestly, and for no particular reason, liked him.

Chapter Thirty-Five
1999

There were times and places Kate chose not to dwell on, but with the passing of the years this mental editing became harder. Uninvited memories would burst, flashing, on to her mind's eye, like the unexpected darts of pain that afflicted her joints, a reminder of how violently alive those long-ago events were to her, and how much, still, they formed a part of her.

There was no special trigger that she was aware of and could avoid. Across half a century – more – those memories still had the power to render her faint. She would be walking, eating, in the company of family or friends, talking or watching television, and then suddenly, out of the blue of the past, there would be Bill's face – not at a polite, social distance but close, too close for comfort, so she could see the texture of his skin and smell its smell, feel the brush of his clothes against hers, and his encroaching sensual heat. The sensation of swooning pleasure and jagged anxiety would drive her heart rate up, making her breathing shallow and her face cold. She would have to force herself to move and speak, to regain control before something unimaginable happened.

The memory of her life with Lawrence, her real life, the one in which she'd borne children and been a good wife, loving and loved, her husband's comrade in war and peace time companion, lay sweet and calm as an English field; but not far beneath the surface there boiled this dangerous, unstable substance, and it scared her.

Stella had touched on it once. It was not long after Jack and Thea had died, within a year of one another, and Stella was taking a secretarial course in London. Kate had been blue. After a period in England, they'd been on their third posting in Germany, a huge BAOR HQ near Dusseldorf, and Stella had taken a few days' holiday to come and stay. Lawrence had gone on a shoot organised by a German landowner who lived in a handsome *Schloss* a few miles south of the camp; he'd accepted a lift from a brother officer, so Stella and Kate were making an expedition to the weekend food market just over the border in Holland. Stella hadn't yet passed her test and expressed her admiration for Kate's intrepidity.

'You didn't drive when you were in Germany before, did you, Ma?'

Kate shook her head. 'Even if I'd had a licence then, I doubt whether I would have done – we were in the middle of Berlin and the conditions that first winter were terrible.' She looked at Stella. 'How well do you remember being there?'

'Surprisingly well,' said Stella. 'Some things really vividly. The snow and ice, the crunching sound of walking on the pavements and the crackling and hissing of the car tyres ... all those ghastly clothes we had to put on!'

'Yes, awful, they took ages, and no nice well-insulated man-made fabrics. When they got wet they took forever to dry ... And no central heating, of course – we must have been tough! You used to sleep in your pram in the garden with icicles like dragon's teeth round the hood, but it doesn't seem to have done you any harm.'

'What else?' Stella mused. Kate felt a prickle of apprehension. 'The thin, pale children begging for chocolate.'

'Oh, the people, the Berliners.' Kate shook her head. 'That was terrible. None of us felt like victors.'

'And we had a maid – a housekeeper – Gisela?'

'That's right. Gisela was a darling, I think she honestly loved us. Especially Lawrence, she worshipped him.'

'Was that usual?' asked Kate. 'I mean, the old enemy?'

'Do you know, I really believe ordinary Germans were just glad the war was ended, and the awful time they had at the hands of the Russians was over, and in that sense we were liberators. I had a letter from Gisela only last year, in wonderful English. She got married at forty, and had a baby. She sounded so happy.'

'How sweet.'

Stella gazed at the road ahead, but Kate could tell it was her mind's eye she was scanning. They came to the border, produced their passports and were waved through – wives from the camp plied this route regularly. As always, she experienced a little rush of something like relief as they entered Holland.

'I remember a Christmas party,' went on Stella. 'In that school. I was terribly worried about it. In fact I didn't want to go at all, but you bought me some lovely new shoes.'

'Shameless bribery,' murmured Kate. Her head swam slightly and she slowed down.

'It worked ... Ma, what's up?'

'Do you mind if we stop for a moment? I need a breather.'

They were passing through an area of low-density woodland – larches and poplars quite well spread out, a wide, sandy path winding away between the silvery trunks through a carpet of bilberries and bracken.

'Stop right here,' commanded Stella.

Kate pulled over and switched off the engine. She opened the door, got out, and walked a little way, arms folded, breathing in the fresh air. Stella opened her door as well but didn't follow. When Kate turned round, her daughter was sitting sideways on the passenger seat, her face turned upwards to the sun, eyes closed.

'I'm sorry, darling,' said Kate. 'I felt a bit funny for a moment. Nothing serious.'

Stella opened her eyes and stood up. 'It's lovely here. Shall we walk a little way?'

'I wouldn't mind.'

They locked the car and set off slowly, side by side, along the path. There wasn't much traffic on the road, and soon all they could hear was birdsong and the soft whisper of their feet on the sandy soil. Stella tucked her hand through Kate's arm.

'I'm sorry. Was I going on too much about the past?'

'No, not at all.' Kate patted Stella's hand. 'Really. It's interesting the things that stick.'

'I remember Hildegarde took me to the party. Dad came to pick us up.'

'Did he?'

'You'd been called away – you had to go out somewhere, or meet somebody. We were rather lost without you.'

'Well I'm glad to know I was missed.' *Please, leave it there,* she thought. *Please!* 'I used to have to dash off sometimes if there was a crisis with one of the women in the wives' club; the Colonel's wife was very keen on everyone doing their bit.'

Stella didn't comment on this, but said, in the same reflective tone, 'You were very late back. I was already in bed, Dad was reading to me. You had snow on your coat. Anyway,' she turned her gaze on Kate, 'we were very glad to see you.'

Perhaps, thought Kate, Stella's suspicions about that night had been based on a young child's instinctive, animal understanding. She probably had read, uncomprehendingly, the unspoken signs; but Kate found it unsettling that she had been pondering those signs since in an attempt to interpret them. No direct questions had been asked, but they were still there in Stella's head. Over the intervening years she may even have got close to something like the truth, but it was in both their interests to remain at a safe distance.

Anyway, Kate told herself now, she had done nothing wrong. Not then, not on that occasion. Confronted with the starkest and most brutal choice imaginable, she had made hers, and it had been not just the right and honourable one, but the one she had thanked God for every day since. She had turned her back not just on him – on Bill – but on a whole part of herself, a part that most who knew her these days could never have imagined; and she had walked away, without once looking back.

She had walked all the way home through the frozen streets, with her tears turning to ice on her cheeks.

As for Lawrence, she had always been aware of his understanding. He had welcomed her back from wherever she'd been, and no questions asked. When, not very long after that, they'd been to see the film *Brief Encounter*, she'd been deeply moved by the reaction of Celia Johnson's husband in the film. Afterwards, she'd asked:

'Would a man really do that? Know everything and say nothing? Forgive in silence?'

'I reckon so,' said Lawrence, 'if he truly loved his wife, and trusted her. After all, what's the alternative? Rows? Recriminations? She came back, so better to leave things undisturbed and have each other. Anyway,' he smiled at her, 'it was bloody good but it was only a film.'

Neither the film nor the thoughts it provoked were ever mentioned between them again.

But recent events had been a painful reminder of those old, unhappy, far-off things and the part of her that had provoked them.

She was Dulcie's daughter. The wayward and dangerous strands of her nature, the strands that for a while had made her a liability to herself and others, had a source, of which she had been made fully aware. To be pragmatic, she had found an excuse for her behaviour. In fact, she reflected, if the relationship between her and Dulcie had been the conventional one of mother and daughter, they would in all probability have torn each other to shreds. Distance and discretion had enabled them to be friends.

It may have been as a sort of security, a shoring-up against unwelcome memories, that Kate began for the first time seriously to consider Ian Macky's offer of marriage. She was a realist; she had at most ten years of good life left. Ian was a kind, intelligent, amusing man who was smitten with her. She was not smitten with him, but the *coup de foudre* was not something she expected to experience again. What Ian had become over the past year was a true friend, unselfishly devoted and always ready to lend help and support without presuming on her time or privacy. As the survivor, like her, of a long and happy marriage, he implicitly understood the special status of that part of the past. They laughed together, ate together, took outings together, shared several interests and acquired a few new ones, and enjoyed a mutual respect and admiration with the occasional gentle flicker of romance. She could even imagine living with him, a couple of contented elderly flatmates. Roommates was harder, but he was an attractive man; it was not out of the question.

What concerned her more was her family and how they would react. Would they be astonished? Appalled? Delighted? Or would they simply take it in their stride? Those who had met Ian – Stella, Evie, Joe, even, on one long-ago occasion, Will – had liked him, and appreciated his being there as a good neighbour, a second port of call if they weren't around. Raff was at the age when the mere thought of a wrinkly marriage would make him gag, or pretend to, in that cartoon way of the young.

Then (the thought made her smile) there was always the possibility that Ian himself would have cooled off. It was getting on for a year since his courtly proposal, and though he had, in his own words, left the offer on the table, he was probably too much of a gent to withdraw it even if he'd changed his mind. She told herself that in the event of either of them raising the subject, she would know at once if there were any reservations on his part. That would be fine, she wouldn't be in the least affronted; the problem was that they ran the risk of losing their friendship by allowing something else to get in the way.

Through the autumn, this consideration of Ian's proposal was something to hang on to, a hostage to fortune. When she heard people (usually on the radio) speak of learning to 'let things go', she wondered how they squared that advice with the things that would not allow you to let them go – those past experiences against which you were powerless to protect yourself, which leapt unexpectedly out of the dark cave of memory and clung to you with claws and teeth.

And then, one wet and dreary afternoon in late October, she made a discovery.

Since her last visit to Ernest Mallory, there had been no more from that quarter. On good days she told herself that she had seen him off and put him in his place. (She also characterised him, to herself, in an unattractive and unpleasant way that she was not proud of and was very glad other people did not know about.) On not so good days she recognised that she hadn't really seen him off at all, because he had successfully initiated an unstoppable process of re-evaluation. She even attributed the disquieting mental intrusions of her old lover to this process. Until recently they had been very occasional and muffled by distance; now they seemed to be drawing nearer by the day. So though Ernest had gone quiet, his influence held sway.

On the weekday afternoon in question, with persistent rain smearing the windows, she embarked on a project. She went into her bedroom, turned on the overhead and bedside lights, and Radio 3, and moved the upright chair close to the ottoman chest at the end of the bed. Once she'd done that, she lugged an occasional table from the living room and placed it next to the chair.

One of the reasons she hadn't addressed this task before was because it was physically awkward and if she was going to have a bash now, she had to remedy that.

So she was already slightly puffed when she began, though some of that was due to nerves. It was a long time – years – since she'd dived into this lot. She regarded the chest as a kind of archive, not to be thrown away, but destined to be looked through with a certain amount of hilarity and a few tears by her family after she was gone. Now, however, she was in the mood to confront it.

She pushed up the lid and let it rest on the end of the bed. Beneath the surface layer of Scrabble, Monopoly and card games, the contents of the chest were a dismaying mess: worn envelopes, dog-eared manila folders, battered albums of all sizes and a host of frail paper wallets containing snapshots, many of them in black and white, with their attendant strips of negatives; the accumulated photographic records of over half a century of family life. Why, Kate asked herself, would she want to go through all this now, when she had never bothered before? God knew, her heart had sunk the first time, when the ottoman descended on her and Lawrence after Thea's death. She knew it was her duty to hang on to it, and its contents, that she had been appointed a kind of de facto archivist – a rotten one, as it turned out; she didn't have a filing-and-ordering mentality. They'd spent one Sunday rummaging around in the chest as thought it were a bran tub, pulling things out and exclaiming over them, how some people had changed and others scarcely at all; many were completely unknown to them, their identities unacknowledged and lost to memory, not even to be guessed at. They'd made plans to sort through and create a whole set of albums, in chronological order, but it had never happened. The present was far too pressing and important. About once every five years this process would happen again – someone or other, one of the children, or Joe, or his kids, would have a rummage – but the result was always the same: an hour's entertainment and then the lid would be closed on an even greater muddle than before.

Looking at it, she felt ashamed, but then thought, *What the hell?* She'd kept it all, given it house room, which was in precious short supply, and nothing had been damaged. Now she had a reason to look; she was searching for something, she wasn't sure what, but the scale of the task drained her resolve.

She remembered something Thea used to say to her when she was daunted by some unwelcome task:

'Don't sit staring at everything and sighing! Just look at what's nearest to you, and start there.'

Nearest to her was an assortment of plastic wallets of family holiday snaps. During a brief phase of organisation these had been labelled and dated. The photos most likely to yield answers would be pre-1945. Since what she had to do was narrow the field, she began by taking these out and tossing them on to the bed in front of her. Once she'd done that, she began to speed up, resisting the urge to look at anything after a certain date. Operating on this basis, she soon got on to a roll, and half an hour later the bed was covered with discarded photos, her hands were grey with dust and print and the level of the chest's contents had dropped by half.

Needing a break before the next phase, she got up stiffly and went to the kitchen, where she washed her hands and put the kettle on. Her mind was still so concentrated on her task that she jumped when the doorbell rang, and even muttered 'Damn!' to herself as she went to answer it.

It was Ian, in a Barbour jacket, rain dripping from the peak of his Donegal tweed cap. On seeing her, he removed the cap and slapped it against his thigh.

'Kate, I'm so sorry to turn up unannounced. I took a rather ill-advised constitutional and wondered how you were doing on this horrible afternoon.'

'I'm doing fine, but look at you, Ian, you're drowned – take that thing off! I was just making tea; would you like a cup?'

'Are you sure?'

'Come on, quick.' She held the door wide, ushering him in. She took his cap and hung it on a hook by the door. 'Put that coat over a chair in the kitchen, I'll train my fan heater on it.'

She was prattling because she felt a little grumpy, resenting the intrusion, though she knew that on any other wet afternoon she'd have been pleased to see him.

He followed her into the tiny kitchen, draped the Barbour as instructed and stood with his hands in his pockets as she made the tea. She handed him the tray with mugs, milk and sugar.

'Shall we go through?'

The phrase was a joke between them, a reference to the bijou accommodation at Rectory Court. She'd left the bedroom door open, and he could scarcely avoid seeing the open ottoman, its tumbled contents and the blizzard of photographs on the bed.

'I do hope I'm not disturbing you, Kate.'

'Not at all. I was sorting through old photos.'

'A major undertaking, in my experience.'

'It is rather.'

She added milk to the tea and let him help himself to sugar. When they'd sat down, he said, stirring, 'I'm rather ashamed to say that I kept a handful and dumped all the rest of mine on my son. It's up to him what he does with them. The past is the past, after all.'

'But is your son interested?'

'More than me, probably. And my daughter-in-law, an absolute gem, is keen to put together some sort of family history, so I'm only too happy to indulge her.'

'I'm not sure I entirely agree with you,' said Kate, 'about the past. It is history, as they say, but it's *our* history. Part of us that we carry with us whether we want to or not.'

'Only a small part, and one we have no control over. Whereas the present and future we can control.' He smiled ruefully. 'To some extent, anyway, allowing for changing circumstances, dodgy hips and so on.'

'Yes.' She wondered if he might have some special motive in saying this, but decided she was overcomplicating things. She said, 'I feel the past strongly at the moment, for some reason.'

'All those old photographs,' he suggested, 'and their attendant memories.'

'Before I started that.'

There followed a short silence, not awkward, a mutual provision of space, a politeness.

'How are the family?' he asked. 'All well?'

She thought he'd phrased that nicely, allowing two meanings.

'All well, yes. Stella may have found a mate at long last, and Evie, that's my granddaughter, is happy in the modern way.'

Ian smiled. 'What way is that?'

'All rather fraught and complicated, about personal fulfilment and self-esteem and so on.'

'I do know what you mean.'

'Of course she's a single parent, so anyone she falls for or who falls for her has that to contend with.'

'Or run the risk of being a wicked stepfather.'

'Absolutely. Her young man' – she caught his amused look – 'all right, her beau, her admirer, whatever you want to call him, is a policeman. A bit of a rough diamond, but you couldn't ask for a nicer man, good-hearted and devoted to Evie.'

'And the boy – Raphael, is it?'

'Raff, well remembered. I think there may have been some awkwardness in that quarter, but there's goodwill on both sides, so I'm sure they'll work something out.'

They drank their tea. Outside the wind got up and the rain lashed like a whip against the glass.

'Do you know,' he said, 'I'm going to make a run for it.'

'But it's pouring,' said Kate. 'A deluge.'

'I've only got to go a hundred yards or so. Do me good to break into a run. See if I can, anyway.'

He got up, put his mug down on the tray. She found herself regretting her inhospitable thoughts.

'Please, Ian, you don't have to.'

'I must.' He headed into the kitchen and took his coat off the chair. 'I have things to do and I want to leave you in peace to go through your photographs.'

'I can do that any time, it's not important.'

'Yes, it is,' he said firmly, shrugging on the still damp Barbour. 'And you need to get on with it while you're in the mood. I just hope I haven't fatally broken your concentration.'

'Of course you haven't.'

'Good.' He stepped into the tiny hallway and lifted his cap from the hook. 'Why don't you phone me when you've completed the task? Let me know what you've found, how you got on?'

'Very well, I will.'

He opened the door, nodded in the direction of the bedroom. 'Go on, go to it. Thank you for the tea.'

He didn't, on this occasion, offer even the most formal of kisses.

'Goodbye, Ian,' she said. 'It was so nice to see you.'

There was a fierce hiss of rain as he opened the outer front door, and he was gone. She closed her own door and looked at the slew of photos, the still open chest.

As she returned to her search, it struck her that this small exchange with Ian proved, as much as any carefully thought-out courting, that he was a man she could marry.

In fact it did take her a little while to get back into the task. Ian's arrival and his tactful departure had left her feeling a squeak self-conscious. She had not after all told him the whole truth about what she was doing; their friendship hadn't reached that level of confidence. Would he, she wondered, have been shocked? Perhaps not – she liked to think that in her own mind she allowed plenty of room for the secrets and transgressions of others and would never presume to pass judgement. She knew surprisingly little about Ian; there were probably any number of things he would keep from her, and she was entitled to do the same.

The rain stopped and the sky lightened. To welcome this change in the weather she got up and opened the bedroom window. All too soon it would start to get dark. The long winter was about to begin. She leaned her forehead on the glass for a moment and closed her eyes, thinking of Lawrence. The thoughts were in the nature of a prayer – for peace, for strength. For wisdom.

By six o'clock she had had enough. She was stiff from sitting, her eyes were tired and she felt slightly queasy from continually refocusing on different photographs. She was near the bottom of the chest and had found nothing to satisfy her curiosity, though she had set aside one or two that she might have framed. Heavily, she got to her feet. The bedroom looked a mess, but she wanted at all costs to avoid the trap of shovelling everything back into the ottoman and making the muddle even worse than before. Tomorrow she'd be fresh and would replace the contents in an orderly way; for now she had to clear the bed and pick up what had slipped to the floor so she didn't trip over it in the night. She closed the lid of the ottoman, then, congratulating herself on her lateral thinking, she pulled the corners of the bedspread together, knotted them loosely and slipped the resulting bag on to the floor by the dressing table. The photos on the side table at the end of the bed could stay there for the time being. The handful she'd earmarked for framing she tucked under her silver hairbrush, the one with Thea's maiden initials on the back.

She drew the bedroom curtains for now – she'd open them a chink when she went to bed – and switched off the light. But on leaving the bedroom she turned on all the others in the flat. Blow the expense – she wanted a blaze of light. In the kitchen, she hesitated briefly before pouring herself a gin and tonic. Was it altogether a good thing, she asked herself as she banged the ice tray, to mix oneself a stiff drink when on one's own? Might it be the thin end of the wedge, the start of a slippery slope? She decided not, and took the tonic to the top.

In the living room, still standing, she picked up the handset and dialled Stella's number.

'Hello, Ma.'

'One of these days it won't be me.'

'Yes, but I keep telling you, I'll know, because my little magic screen shows me.'

'I'm standing here with an enormous G and T in my hand.'

'Delighted to hear it. Have you got company?'

'No, that's why I'm telling you.'

Stella snorted with laughter. 'In case you turn into a secret drinker?'

'Well – I'm not sure it's a good idea.'

'Ma, you're entitled. What have you been doing?'

'Nothing very much. The rain's been rather depressing, but at least that's over now, and the garden smells lovely. How's your day been?'

'Classic curate's egg. Sometimes I think I'm not cut out to teach.'

'But you're so good at it!' Kate was pleased to be talking about someone other than herself, especially her daughter, towards whom she felt a surge of love that needed to be expressed. 'The difference you're making in those people's lives, darling, you must take tremendous satisfaction from that.'

'I regret it when I'm bad-tempered, like today.'

'Everyone has off days.'

'Yes …' Kate heard the clink of a glass the other end – Stella had joined her. 'But I'm dealing with highly motivated intelligent adults who deserve to be treated properly.'

'And I'm sure you do.'

'Ma, I was there, remember?'

The touch of sarcasm put Kate and her partisan support in their place. 'Point taken.'

'Sorry.'

'I understand.'

Kate sat down. There was a short silence, broken by Stella.

'I miss Alan.'

Here, then, was the point. 'Oh, Stella.'

'If only he wasn't so damned far away. We can talk and email, but we can't be together, or not easily. I'm beginning to think there's no future in it.'

'Don't say that, you don't know. '

'I mean, look ...' Kate could hear now that Stella was slightly tipsy, had been drinking for a lot longer than her. 'His life is over there, and mine's over here. We're two middle-aged, bordering on elderly people with jobs, and family, and commitments—'

'If,' Kate interrupted, 'by your life you mean me, I do hope you'll put that to one side. I'm in clover. I couldn't be more comfortable. I'm happy and I have plans. Your life should be about you.' She remembered her earlier conversation with Ian. 'The past is the past and you can't change it, but the future is in your hands.'

She was pleased to hear Stella laugh. 'What's this, Ma, a burst of philosophy?'

'If you like.'

'There's much in what you say, but don't forget I *like* my life here. It's mine and I made it and it suits me. And that applies to Alan, too.'

'I suppose the two of you do talk about all this sort of thing?'

'Not as much as we should. Too big.'

It seemed to be Kate's day for appropriating other people's wisdom. 'Start small,' she said, 'and go on from there.'

The next morning she woke to beautiful sunlight, shiny from yesterday's rain, streaming into the bedroom. As she bathed and dressed and had her breakfast of muesli and banana, she felt full of energy and purpose. Today she would get things done, throw away the dud photos and reorganise the others, so some good would have come of her gloomy rummaging the day before. No reason why that should take more than an hour or so. And then she'd ring Ian and remind him of the trip to St Petersburg they'd discussed a few weeks ago; she longed to see the Hermitage.

There was an old newspaper covering the bottom of the ottoman, and in her new, ruthless mood she grasped the edges and lifted it out like a sort of tray bearing the remaining photos, blowing off a cloud of dust and one or two dead flies as she did so. The newspaper itself – she twisted her neck to glance at the headlines – was nothing memorable, a copy of the *Daily Express* from August nineteen fifty-something. Beneath it, plastered flat to the wooden base, was a final stray Kodak wallet.

She picked it up, leaving some of the paper behind, held by a residual stickiness. For a moment she thought the wallet empty, but when she peeled it open, there was one black-and-white snapshot inside. She glanced at it, and was about to shy it in the direction of the counterpane-wrapped discard pile when something snagged her attention and she looked again.

The photo was of Dulcie, with a friend. It seemed to have been taken at the same time as the one she had on her dressing table, which she thought of as the carefree one – Dulcie wore the same clothes and was laughing, mouth wide, head tilted back, not at all the cool, controlled fashion plate of some other pictures. And the friend, a man, was laughing too; they had their arms round one another's waists but his head was turned to look at her, enjoying her amusement, egging her on. He was a little shorter than Dulcie in her high heels, but broad, strong ... Kate remembered that strength. He had been shorter than her, too, even in stockinged feet, but well built, with powerful shoulders. She remembered the grin, a touch vulpine, displaying strong teeth, a grin like a challenge. His hand was a shade higher than Dulcie's waist, the forefinger almost touching her breast, not quite accidentally. The touch was casual, proprietorial – oh, she knew it well! There was no mistaking the look, the attitude. They had been hers, too. She had ridden it out, this knowledge, years ago, but this evidence – so immediate, so full of casual sensuality – was too much.

Her lover, and her mother's.

On the back were three words, written in black ink now faded to brown: *You and me.*

She wasn't over it. The taste in her mouth turned liquid and she stumbled the few feet to the bathroom and lurched over the lavatory, one hand on the cistern to steady herself, the other flattening her skirt back against her legs. When she'd done, she rinsed her face and hands and sat down on the lavatory seat clutching her bath towel, her face buried in its cool, damp folds. It was years since she'd thrown up so suddenly and violently – the vomiting was a measure of her shock. When she finally stood up, the world swam for a moment and she had to hold on to the towel rail till the faintness passed.

Back in the bedroom, she abandoned all intentions of tidying up. She pushed the snapshot beneath the others under Thea's brush and then began shovelling the remainder back into the ottoman chest. The counterpane she simply undid, allowing the contents to cascade back where they'd come from. When all was back in, she closed the lid and replaced the bedspread, smacking and smoothing it into place. Then she restored the chair and the occasional table to their normal positions and went into the living room. Drawn by the sun, by brightness and normality, she opened the French window and stepped outside: air, warmth, the sounds of other lives. There was a plastic chair out here, tipped forward against the wall so that the seat had remained dry. She righted it and sat down. She was still trembling.

Once again she thought of Lawrence. She clasped her hands in her lap and pretended it was his hand holding hers. She sat there for a long time, in silence, and when the doorbell rang, and later the phone, she answered neither.

Chapter Thirty-Six
1964

It wasn't unusual for Thea to wake and find that Jack was no longer beside her in bed. Over their many years of establishing and running the farm in Gilgil, he often made an early start, before dawn. These days, when poor health meant he no longer slept well, he sometimes moved to the camp bed in his office, or even the sofa in the drawing room, for a change of scene during the night, and so as not to disturb her with his fidgeting. Thea never told him, but no matter how quietly he moved, her antennae would register his departure.

But not, for some reason, today. She awoke fully alert, clear-headed and refreshed, and was surprised when she reached out her hand and opened her eyes that his half of the bed was empty; in fact barely slept in, the bottom sheet smooth and the top edge of the upper one, though rolled back, still folded over the thin blanket. She must have slept particularly soundly; that would account for her not having heard Jack during the night. Through the soft focus of the mosquito net, it looked like a beautiful day. Many days were beautiful out here, but she wasn't always able to appreciate them. Today she had that pleasant sense of anticipation she used to have on fine mornings as a child at Chilverton House: of golden hours to fill, of happy speculation on how to do so, of all the thrilling possibilities that lay ahead.

There was no rational explanation for this mood; the day would be routine, full of the smaller tasks with which they now filled their time when the business of the farm was largely given over to the manager, Peter Durbridge. They were hanging on here because Jack was unable to let go and make the break. Thea understood without being told that for him, a return to England meant going back to die, an acknowledgement that the active, effective part of his life was over and the good night beginning to cast its shadow. She didn't see things in this way, but kept the difference to herself. Though she yearned to be near the family while there was still plenty of time, over the years she had come to see – to know – that her first loyalty would always be to Jack, the man she had chosen. Family was nature at work. Occasionally the natural order was disrupted by a rogue event, like the death of Maurice at a young age, or Dulcie before her time, but successive generations would still march forward into the future long after she was gone. It was more than forty years since Thea had made her promises to Jack. She could never have guessed what those promises would demand of her, but her resolve had never wavered. Her place was with him.

So here they still were, their horns drawn in a little, their horizons narrower, their belts looser, their pace slowing. The farm jogged along, with coffee and flowers now the primary crops, just about managing to 'wash its face', as Pete put it. Most of their old friends from round about had gone – confidence and product- ivity had been shaken by Mau Mau; some had died and others had returned to England or simply retreated to Nairobi, where one's neighbours were within hailing distance. The Kingsleys had been in the van of a pioneering enterprise, had made a go of it and enjoyed the prosperous, confident times when everything was secure. They'd stuck it out through the rebellion and accepted that things would never quite be the same afterwards. The wise and generous paternalism they – Thea especially – had believed in and practised was outdated. Kindness and civility were still the best way to manage, but must now be underpinned with a hard- headed realism. The country that had never been theirs had been reclaimed.

She pushed back the bedding, lifted the mosquito net and swung her feet out, shaking each slipper before putting it on. With small, stooped early-morning steps, she went to the window and drew the curtains. The bedroom was on the west side of the house; the sun was just coming round the corner of the roof and she gazed out from shadow into soft brightness, a haze in the middle dis- tance masking the mountains. She breathed deeply, pushing her shoulders back and lifting her arms.

Walking back across the room, she moved more easily. On the back of the door hung the cotton dressing gown that Kate had given her on their last visit, printed with a profusion of flowers in soft pinks and blues. She slipped it on and went out into the corridor, which, being windowless, retained a special smell of wood and polish and linoleum that reminded her of houses in England. There were some hunting prints of Jack's hung here, the only place she'd tolerate them – terrible old things with straight-legged primitive horses and hounds, and sharp-faced huntsmen waving their riding crops. Before Mau Mau there had been a hunt in Gilgil, which she had thought ludicrous at the time, even more so now that it had restarted, an embarrassing parody of Englishness. She was very glad that, prints notwithstanding, Jack had never taken part.

The kitchen was quiet, tidy, and empty, but she could hear a distant trickle of voices. Her present indoor dog, Buck, an elderly yellow Labrador, heaved himself from his basket by the back door and waddled to greet her. She stooped to give him a pat and a 'Hello, boy' before unbolting the door and letting him out. By the time she'd made her tea in its coronation mug, Buck had returned, and now he followed her back through the house, his paws clicking on tiles, linoleum and wood, falling silent as she went into the drawing room and crossed the faded Turkish carpet to the veranda door. He stood next to her, tail swinging, already panting gently, as she unlocked the door and went out, pushing the insect screen shut behind the two of them.

In the few minutes since Thea had woken, the equatorial sun had climbed above the roof and its growing warmth brought the smell of Africa – scorched dust, acacia and jacaranda, early cooking from the shambas.

Jack was lying on his side near the big flower border. He was in his pyjamas and leather slippers. The soles of the slippers were almost worn through – more were on order from Nairobi. He looked asleep. Buck trotted towards him, tail wagging, ears lowered in greeting. Thea quickly overtook and kneeled down on the grass.

'Jack? Darling?' She put her hand on his head, brought her face down to look into his.

He was not asleep. His narrowed eyes focused on her at once.

'Hello, my love.'

His voice was low, but clearer and younger-sounding than she'd heard it for years. One of his hands was curled into a loose fist against his chest, the other lay open in front of him, the fingers spread, and she took it in both of hers, chafing it between them as she would have done with a cold child. And like a child's, it felt relaxed and acquiescent.

'What are you doing?' she asked, beating his hand gently on her lap. 'Are you all right?'

'I came for a walk.'

'A walk? When? It must have been still dark.'

When he didn't answer, she said, 'You should come back to bed for a bit. Can you get up?'

'No.' Now his thin, dry fingers encircled hers and exerted a light pressure. 'Stay here.'

She was torn, briefly, between the impulse to practical action and doing as he asked. But there was really no decision to be made.

'For a little while then.'

Her legs were already quite numb from kneeling, and she had to get awkwardly on to all fours before dragging them round and sitting heavily, almost toppling over backwards. There were marks on the front of her dressing gown.

'The ground's still damp,' she said. 'Are you cold?'

Jack gave a small shake of the head. Their hands had come uncoupled when she moved, and he felt for hers again. Thea glanced down at him. His eyes were still open and his lips slightly parted. He seemed to be thinking, watching something in his mind's eye, and she took comfort from this.

'How long have you been here?' she asked. 'Did you sleep at all?'

'Not much. I sat in the office. Came out when it started to ... get light.'

'I'm surprised the dogs didn't bark.' She brushed at the shreds of grass on her lap, steeling herself for the next question she must ask.

'Did you fall over?'

'No.' He shook his head again. 'I just lay down.'

'Have you got any pains?'

'No.' He made a little sniffing sound and she realised he was laughing. 'Don't worry.'

'I can't help it. Look, Jack, darling ...' She withdrew her hand and laid it firmly on his shoulder. 'We really have to' – she was going to say 'get you back to the house', but stopped herself – 'go in for breakfast.'

'All right.'

'Can you sit up?'

'I'm not sure ...'

'Wait.' Laboriously, she got back on to all fours and then to her knees, shuffling sideways so that she was behind him and could hook her arms beneath his. Though so dreadfully thin, he was also weak, and a dead weight. She could feel him trying, putting his right hand flat on the ground and exerting what pressure he could, but they were getting nowhere.

'Sorry,' he said.

'We need help.'

'And tea,' he suggested.

She smiled. 'Good idea. I'm going to run back to the house and fetch Dorelia. I'll get her to make you a cuppa and bring it out. I'll come straight back. Don't go away.'

Getting up wasn't a pretty sight; she hoped no one was watching as her bottom rose in the air like a camel's and she moved her hands from the ground to her knees and then finally to her hips, where they rested as she caught her breath.

'Right. I'll be two ticks.'

She glanced over her shoulder as she limped at something between a walk and a run back to the house, Buck (after only a moment's indecision) at her heels. In spite of their combined attempts to sit him up, Jack lay exactly as she'd first seen him, as if he were made of sand and had simply settled back. But the sun was full on the garden now, and the temperature rising.

She flipped the screen door open and let it smack shut behind her; Buck only just made it through.

'Dorelia!' In the house, she was suddenly overtaken by panic, a sense of having deserted Jack. She wanted only to get back as soon as possible.

'Dorelia!'

Dorelia had only just arrived; she was sitting at the table drinking coffee.

'Sorry, *bibi*.'

'That's quite all right. Look, Mr Kingsley is outside, I think he's had a fall, I need some help. Can you please make a cup of tea, lots of sugar, and bring it out? When he's had some, we can help him back to the house.'

'Right away.' Dorelia stood, brushing crumbs from her dress. 'Is the *bwana* sick?'

'I don't know. Well, he is, of course – no, I don't know. Maybe I should call a doctor …'

Water rattled into the kettle. 'You go back to him.'

'Yes, yes, I will. Thank you, Dorelia.'

'I be there in a minute.'

'Thank you. Oh …' Thea ushered Buck into his basket. 'Keep the dog here, would you?'

'I will. You go.'

Thea flew back into the drawing room, and paused, hovering for a second by the telephone. Should she call the doctor? You weren't supposed to move people who'd fallen, were you? But Jack said he hadn't fallen, simply lain down; there was no sign of injury and he was perfectly lucid.

'No,' she said out loud.

She went out through the French window and stumbled across the lawn. Her dressing gown tie had come undone and the sides flapped open. When she reached him, she was out of breath.

'Jack? I'm here – I'm back.'

To her enormous relief she heard a small sound – an exhalation, a sigh that carried the merest shading of his voice.

Painfully she got back down on to one knee, then the other, then down via all fours to sitting, thinking drily that this was probably good exercise for her exhausted joints. Once established, she laid her hand on his head.

'Dorelia will be here in a moment. She's making your tea.'

This time there was no answer. She stroked his head, gently tilting it, and leaned forward. His eyes were still open, but she could tell at once that he had gone. There was a shocking, split-second intimacy to this realisation, as though by sheer force of will he had pulled her close to him, to say goodbye. *That little sound*, she thought. *That must have been it. He hung on until I got back, and then gave up the ghost.*

She shunted herself sideways and lifted his head so that it rested on her lap. With careful fingers, like a blind person, she felt for his eyelids and closed them. Now she could imagine for a little while that he was sleeping there. She no longer felt any discomfort sitting on the hard ground without support, her dressing gown rucked up, her legs sticking out in front of her. It seemed easy and natural, as if she were young again.

She heard the click of the screen door and Dorelia's footsteps crossing the veranda, and raised a hand, before looking round as far as she could – more than ninety degrees was impossible. Dorelia, carrying a mug of tea, had reached the foot of the steps and now moved cautiously to one side into her range of vision, free hand to her cheek in an attitude of anxiety. Thea shook her head and put a finger to her lips. She did not want to speak and she did not at that moment care how her message was interpreted as long as she and Jack were left together in peace.

It wouldn't be long. The story of Mr Kingsley's accident would already have flown round the shambas. It was only a matter of time before it reached Pete, who would be compelled by every decent instinct to take charge, and whom it would be harder – not even right – to deter.

She did not want to think anything, to do anything, but simply to sit here with the sun on her shoulders, cradling her husband's head in her protective shade, not looking at one another but gazing together at some shared objective.

The warmth was drawing out the scent of the garden. Directly in front of them were the English wild flowers, and the bush of wild thyme that had been one of Thea's earliest plantings – a survivor of decades of cutting, pruning and thinning, its stem thick and woody but its smell as sweetly pungent as ever. She had not very often used it in cooking; its role in her life had been to remind her of home. She would sometimes pick sprigs to have in the house, tucked into picture frames, propped among the photographs on the mantelpiece or laid in her clothes drawer. The plant was a faithful friend; where Jack had chosen to lie down.

She felt for his left hand, the one that was closed, and gently, firmly unfurled the fingers that seemed already to be stiffening.

Inside was a tiny, crumbling twig. She did not need to see what it was. When she rubbed it between her own fingertips, the smell of it rose from his palm to greet her, like a last warm breath.

Chapter Thirty-Seven

1999

Very occasionally, Evie attended a weekday Evensong in the chapel. She went straight from work and sat at the back in her business suit, without a prayer book. She was there not for any religious reason but for Raff. Privately, though, she did derive some peace and comfort from the service. She liked the idea of being defended against all the perils and dangers of the night, and the music was beyond beautiful. It humbled her that her own son was contributing to that spine-tingling, ethereal sound. The voices of the choir moved and calmed her.

And boy, did she need calming on this unfriendly November evening. Work had been a nightmare, and outside, the streets were scoured by a bitter wind all the way from Russia. She wasn't dressed for the conditions, either; there had been only a mild and gentle drizzle when she left home that morning. Her feet were frozen, her small umbrella was reduced to something like a dead bird and her hair was bedraggled. One side of her throat was sore and swollen, which boded ill – her tonsils had always been the barometer of Evie's general health. Her defences were low.

A well-meaning chapel official whom she had not encountered before and who therefore knew no better invited her to move forward, and when she declined made the mistake of encouraging her.

'You'll find it a good deal warmer up there.'

'No thank you, I'm fine.'

'Can I get you a prayer book?'

'No thank you.'

'As long as you're all right.'

'I will be.' The words had an edge of sarcasm.

'Ah ...' He stepped away, raising a hand. 'I do apologise.'

That, she knew, had been rude. The man meant well and didn't deserve a dusty answer. Evie didn't look at him as she took her place. She drew the line at kneeling, but she did close her eyes tightly for a moment in an exasperated prayer for patience. As so often, she felt beleaguered, and the sidesman, poor guy, had come within range.

It was now a month since she'd accepted Owen's proposal, but they had not yet told anyone else, let alone set a date. There was an element of bet-hedging – while the wedding was not in the public domain it remained mutable, something that was their business alone, hers and Owen's, and within their power to change. This was not to say that she had doubts, exactly. She could look her reflection in the eye and say without blinking: 'I love him.' They had been together for nearly two years, long enough to understand one another, to know when to give support and when to allow space. Sex, when they weren't too tired, was great. And she rated Owen – as a human being, as a man. He had strength and courage and the gentleness and modesty that should accompany them. They had a laugh. But oh God – she pressed her fingers to her closed eyes – what about Raff? He seemed to have come round, things were a whole lot easier, but she couldn't escape the feeling that perhaps she should have consulted him before making her decision. Then again, why should a grown woman have to consult a child? Well, because the child in question was her rapidly maturing son. And anyway, what if, when she had made a unilateral decision, he objected? What then? Was it a case of 'Trust me – it's my life and I know best'? Could she stand the responsibility? She remembered so vividly the night back in the spring when she had lain in bed and confronted her divided loyalties, and come down swiftly and unequivocally on the side of Raff.

The choir entered and she stood. Raff was towards the back; even at this distance she could pick out his exuberant dark hair, the upward tilt of his head. She watched the boys and the lay clerks take their place in the stalls. The weight of history held them all in place. Into the deep, disciplined silence the voice of the Dean rolled out, intoning the collect; she was by now just about familiar with the forms of the more regular services.

A hymn was announced; the organ played an introduction.

Lord of all faithfulness, sang the choir and the small congregation.

So what had changed? Raff's attitude, certainly – she hoped and believed that he would not now be against the idea. But she could not know for sure because she hadn't asked him. Not for the first time, she wondered what passed between him and his father when they were together. Did Mick ask whether she had a boyfriend, and if so, how did Raff characterise Owen? Louise, her friend from work, a woman with a healthy belief in the pleasure principle, had outlined over a bottle of rosé her analysis of the three post-divorce Rs: retreat, riot and resolution. Evie considered she had been through the first two, though 'riot' might not have been quite the word to describe her bout of bad choices and inter-net dating, all discreetly concealed from Raff. As far as resolution went, she felt less confident about that now than she had four weeks ago.

The hymn ended. The Dean's sidekick, the one she thought of as Robin to his Batman, did some more intoning, and then everyone kneeled. Evie remained seated, gazing out over the other bowed heads. She had her reservations about the conventional attitude for prayer. Was it humility, or in most cases a kind of vanity, a public declaration of institutionalised virtue? Owen had been along to one or two services and been blown away by the whole thing, far more eager than her to embrace the ritual. She'd found that touching, but also baffling. In response to her question after-wards, he'd been typically direct.

'No, never been a church-goer. My father was chapel, my mum never rated either side, load of tosh in her opinion. And mine till now, but that – showtime!'

She had to laugh. 'That's one way of putting it.'

'Loved it, darlin'. Really. At last I know what it takes to drag my mind on to a higher plane.'

'What about a lower one?'

His eyes narrowed, looking at her mouth. 'Now you're talking, girl …'

These were the moments when she knew that, given a world free of all other allegiances, they could be perfectly happy. Mick had found someone – Catherine, God help her – and according to Raff she seemed to be there most of the time. He quite liked her, enough to stop Evie worrying, not enough to make her jealous. Evie couldn't imagine that Mick would ever get married again; in retrospect, their union had been an aberration. The only surprise was that it had lasted as long as it did. He must have loved her; there could be no other reason for something she now saw was completely out of character. She could almost have felt sorry for him, getting all tangled up with a young wife and a baby when all he wanted was fun.

They stood for another hymn.

The day thou gavest, Lord, is ended,
The darkness falls at thy behest ...

'Behest' – there was a word, one of many, that one would never hear outside of church. Or Shakespeare. She thought of that *Midsummer Night's Dream* in the college garden. Owen's absence and the generosity behind it had been another of those ticks of the clock towards her decision.

During the last verse of the hymn she saw the sidekick heading towards the pulpit. So there was going to be a sermon, not always the case at Evensong. Evie made a quick calculation – Raff would be going straight back to school for a piano lesson, and didn't know she was there. She was at the back, and within easy reach of the south door. If she moved quickly and decisively, she could escape.

A moment later, she was in the porch, effectively trapped between the service she'd just left and the quadrangle across which the winter rain was blowing in shuddering curtains. There was no cover between here and the comfort of the road outside the college, with its cosy cafés and wine bars.

The chapel door opened behind her. It was the official again, the one who had caught the sharp edge of her tongue earlier.

'Saw you hurry out – is everything all right?'

'Yes thanks. I just realised I was going to be late for something.'

'I apologise if you already know this,' he said, 'but there are some spare umbrellas in the corner there.'

There were three, in a wooden stand. 'Don't they – I thought they belonged to people?'

'They did once, but they've never been collected so we keep them here for emergency use. Which might – excuse me – mean you.'

'I think it does.' She looked down at her own umbrella, its spindly limbs sticking out at sickening angles. 'May I borrow one?'

'Of course.' He spread a graceful, offering hand. 'You must. Just drop it off next time you're passing.'

'Thank you.'

'And why don't you give that other one to me? I'll dispose of it.'

'Are you sure? That's kind.'

She handed over her own and took a large one from the stand. Under the circumstances, she felt that some acknowledgement was due of her earlier rudeness.

'This is very Christian of you,' she said, and looked him squarely in the eye. 'And I'm afraid I don't deserve it.'

'You're most welcome. I hope the time you spent here did you good.'

There was a brief burst of Robin's sermon as the door opened and closed behind him. Evie put up the umbrella and strode out into the rain, protected by its overarching wingspan. Under cover by the porters' lodge, she got out her phone and rang Owen.

'I know you're busy,' she said.

'Not all that. The criminal fraternity are keeping out of the wet.'

'I just wanted to say, let's set a date.'

'Why don't we, it's about time.'

'And go public.'

'Whoa! You ready for that?'

'Yes,' she said. 'I am.'

Chapter Thirty-Eight

1999

Exactly how long was it, Will asked himself, since he had spent any time in someone's home? In Felicity's, he experienced a pleasant sensory overload from the gentle clutter of a shared life still hanging on: coats, hats and boots in the hall; a grate with a fire laid on yesterday's clinker; bookshelves so full that some of the contents were stacked sideways on top of others; postcards and invitations tucked into the mirror over the mantelpiece; a jug of winter greenery, copper beech and orange flowers standing on a side table, surrounded by a scattering of petals; family photographs all over the place; a border terrier, Bramble, who seemed to take to him. Most astonishing of all was to see the kitchen where his food was to be cooked, the fridge, larder and cupboards where the food itself was kept, the garden where some of it, she told him, actually grew! Once a family woman, always a family woman

'Do you have any help with all this?' he asked.

'Oh lord, yes. Since long before Tony died, the garden was his thing. During all our years in married quarters he never cared for it, a bit of dutiful lawn-mowing was about his lot, but once we came here, he took it on, like he did everything. A challenge, you know? Not one of nature's gardeners, but he liked getting the better of it.'

Will stared respectfully out of the window. 'He certainly did that.'

He was keeping her company while she made supper. She said she liked people there when she was cooking and he'd taken her at her word, though he wouldn't have felt comfortable sitting. He stood leaning against the work surface, moving from side to side when she needed something from the cupboard behind him.

It had been quite a while between their meeting at the reunion and his contacting her; months during which Crispin and Pauline had invited him down and he'd refused because he didn't want to run the risk of meeting her at their place and feeling beholden. He wanted this to be on his own initiative. But time had gone by – he'd been first in the States, then Spain, and back to the States – and it reached the point where he had been almost embarrassed to ring in case it appeared rude. When he had finally called her she had expressed neither surprise nor reproach, only delight that he'd got in touch.

'It's so nice to hear your voice. Are you coming down to see me?'

'Well – that rather depends on you ... Would that be all right?'

'I'll be terribly disappointed if you don't. This weekend?'

'If that isn't too short notice.'

'I prefer short notice,' she said. 'It means I don't have to go to too much trouble.'

She'd pressed him to stay the night, declaring that the spare bedroom was always ready to receive; that way he could have a drink and they could take a walk next day.

'It's the most lovely country round here,' she said on the Saturday while browning pieces of duck in a frying pan. 'Do you know the Weald?'

'No. I'm shamefully ignorant about England.'

'Not shameful at all; your job is to travel the world. But weather permitting, after breakfast we'll get in the car and go up to the top of the escarpment. It'll be a treat for you.'

Treated was how he felt. Spoilt, indulged – cherished, even. She was perhaps the most naturally hospitable person he'd ever met. There was something soothing in the knowledge that this hospitality was not an exercise of womanly wiles, but how she was, and would be, with everyone. There was no pressure; he was happy simply to be there. The ubiquitous pictures of her dead husband and her casual references to him were likewise not a problem – rather the reverse. Felicity was a woman used to loving and being loved. That, he perceived, was the source of her confidence and cheerful serenity. The only thing that bothered him was the inevitable questions, but she was discreet.

'How's your daughter?' she asked over the duck with red

cabbage, and the first of the two bottles of Saint-Émilion Will had brought with him. 'Emily?'

'Evie.'

'How is she? I remember she married very young and in next to no time you were the most youthful grandfather any of us knew.'

Emboldened by two large G and Ts and the wine, Will was disposed to be reckless. 'My relative youth will have to be my excuse, then.'

'Excuse?' She shot him a puzzled smile. 'What on earth for?'

'For being the worst father and grandfather in the world.'

She laid down her knife and fork. 'Now that can't possibly be true.'

'Believe me.'

'I doubt whether I will, but explain anyway.'

'Struth, where do I start? I allowed myself to be sidelined by Evie's mother, and didn't have the gumption to get back in. Or the inclination – I was lazy.' He shrugged unhappily. 'Still am. As we speak, I haven't seen my daughter for well over a year.'

He wasn't looking at her face because he was avoiding the politely stifled shock that he feared would be there. But all she said was:

'That's sad.'

'Oh, yes.' He was beginning to enjoy himself. 'And it doesn't end there. The rest of my family as well – my sister, my mother. I'm an exile.'

'Self-imposed, surely.'

'They're better off without me.'

'That, if I may say so, is an excuse.'

For the first time he detected a hint of censure in her voice. Though he hadn't meant to provoke her, he found himself rather glad to have done so. There was something comforting in being gently ticked off by felicity.

'And a pretty lame one to be honest,' she went on. 'You must know in your heart of hearts that it would be a lot better for everyone, including you, if you had contact with them all.'

He laughed shortly. 'They've managed pretty well up till now.'

'Now you're being sorry for yourself.'

'Someone has to be.'

'I'm sorry for you, Will,' she said, more gently. 'You're in a real bugger's muddle, aren't you?'

'I couldn't have put it better myself.'

'Which is a rotten place to be.' She got up, picked up their plates and put them on the side. 'There's pudding, but shall we hang on for a minute?'

'Good idea.'

'I'll have a top-up if I may,' she said as she sat down. 'And you might as well open the other one. This has the makings of a two-bottle conversation.'

'If you say so.' He filled both their glasses and uncorked the second bottle. 'I don't normally do this, you know.'

'Which? Burden people with your problems, or get sloshed?'

'The first.'

'You came to the right place, then. I like listening and hardly ever feel burdened. Not by friends. Children are different; you can't help shouldering their worries, can you?' She glanced quickly at him. 'Sorry.'

'Mine is a slightly different experience,' he said drily. 'How many do you have?'

'Two – James is married with three children, Victoria's unmarried with two.'

'Single or divorced?'

'Single. The girls have different fathers. She's what you'd call a free spirit.'

This slightly unexpected information, the small cloud in the otherwise blue sky of Felicity's domestic life, pricked his curiosity. 'Where do they all live?'

'James and co. live near Paris; he's CEO of the French arm of a pet food company. Mariette has a kitchenware business; she's quite terrifying.'

'You run a business,' he pointed out.

'Not the same thing at all!' She waved her hands to dispel any notion of a similarity. 'My daughter-in-law has six employees and is wooed by manufacturers.'

'All right, so that's them. What about your daughter?'

'Victoria and the girls are up in Cumbria, in a tied cottage that looks like something out of Beatrix Potter. Pretty but primitive.'

'I take it you mean the cottage.'

She laughed. 'I do, but come to think of it, that could just as easily describe Victoria.'

'What does she do?'

'She makes pots – some for gift shops and some more unusual ones on commission. She's very good, but it's not a living.'

'Idea. Could you get her and her *marmites* together with Mariette?'

This provoked a hoot. 'Oh my God! You have to be joking! Quite aside from the fact that Victoria's pots are *art*, I don't know who would kill who first!'

'Just a thought.' He was pleased to have amused her. 'So – how often do you get to see them all?'

'A few times a year. Mariette and James usually bring the children over in the summer – they came the day after the reunion this year – and leave them here for a week or so while they take off. And Tony and I used to go to Paris often. I've only been once on my own.'

'What about the others?'

'You'd wait a long time for an invitation from Vic, and she'd never come here. I just drive up there and call her when I'm half an hour from her front door.'

Will laughed. 'She's okay with that?'

'It's that or nothing. And believe me' – she reached her glass out to touch his – 'that's better.'

They never got round to the pudding – she said she could freeze it – but continued to sit at the table. After another glass of the red, Felicity made herself camomile tea, leaving Will to finish the bottle. He was nowhere near 'sloshed', as she so quaintly put it, but his tongue was sufficiently loosened, and she such a good listener, that he drifted back into confessional mode.

'Another thing,' he said. 'I'm afraid I don't know how to do it any more.'

'How to do what?'

'Be a parent. I was never really given the chance early on, so I decided to dip out altogether. Now I'm in a funk. I've not had the practice, and that would show.'

'Will. Being a father isn't a job.'

'Just as well, eh.'

'It's just a – a *thing*.' She shook her head. 'That awful word '"parenting" has a lot to answer for. Most people go into it with their eyes half closed and wake up when it's too late.'

She never ceased to surprise him. 'Not you, though, surely.'

'I'm a classic example. I always wanted to be a wife and mother, and I thought all I needed was a nice man who loved me for everything to work out.'

'Which it did,' he suggested. Hoped, almost.

'Nope,' she said. 'I forgot one thing. I had to love him as well.'

This was so unexpected that he took a moment to process what she'd said, and couldn't help sounding taken aback. 'Fliss.'

She coloured slightly. 'I did love him, of course I did. But not enough. Nothing like as much as he loved me. Now *that's* a burden. Much worse than unrequited love – knowing you've hijacked someone's life under false pretences.'

'But everyone said—' he began.

'I know what they said. We were the best team anyone knew. We *were*. Being a good sport is my speciality. That I can do.'

'It is a real gift,' he said.

'Anyway,' she was brisk, 'I just thought you should know that it's all smoke and mirrors.'

'But you were happy?'

She considered this. 'Yes – most of the time. I had what I wanted, after all.'

'And the children?'

'Do you know, Will, I believe they knew the score? I think one's children take in an awful lot through their pores, without analysing it. Maybe ...' She pressed her lips together for a second. 'Maybe that's why my two have taken off so determinedly.'

'That's good, surely,' he insisted. 'You've given them confidence and security and they've flown the nest. I mean, obviously I'm the last person whose views on child-rearing you should listen to, but isn't that what people say?'

'Yes, and to some extent it's true.' She turned her wedding ring. 'They were secure, they are confident, reasonably so anyway. But they're not daft. They've got my number.' She smiled suddenly, and rather too brightly, as though realising she might have overstepped the mark. 'But nothing's ever been said between us. We're loyal to Tony's memory.'

Will was more shocked than he cared to let on. His own

confession had been returned with interest. He picked up the wine bottle, but it was empty.

'We have Scotch,' she said.

'Is that permissible?'

'Stay there, I'll get it.'

He sat at the table, absorbing what he'd just been told. Nothing so dreadful, after all – simply that there had been an imbalance in her marriage, that the weight of affection had been greater on her husband's side. A man he remembered well: quiet, dignified, reserved, slow to smile and to anger; a good bloke, but not easy, one who required – and rewarded – some perseverance. Will was sure that he would have shown great fortitude in his illness. There was a photograph of the two of them on the wall in here, taken at some party, Tony in a suit and tie and Felicity a bit slimmer than she was now, in a pink shirtwaister and pearls. She was standing a little in front of her husband, his hand on her waist, beaming at the camera; his smile was more restrained, lips closed.

'Here we are.' She came back in with a half-full bottle and a tumbler. 'I don't do Scotch, so I'll leave you to help yourself. I forgot to make ice.'

'Never touch the stuff.' He poured. 'That's a nice picture over there.'

'Our silver wedding.'

'You look wonderful. And both of you,' he added pointedly, 'look so happy.'

'It was a happy occasion. Lots of old friends. You'd probably have been there if there'd been any way of getting hold of you.'

He doubted this, though it was a nice thing for her to say. 'Were Crispin and Pauline there?'

'Oh yes.'

'Do you see much of them?'

'I do, Pauline especially. She's an absolute gem; I don't know what I'd have done without her.'

He realised this was precisely what the Hamburys had said of her.

'You mean recently – during Tony's illness?'

'And before, all the time. In the regiment and since. She really is someone I could call at three in the morning and she'd pitch in without turning a hair.'

Will summoned up his mental picture of Pauline, somewhat blurred by time: a tall, sporty girl with a pleasantly no-nonsense manner, not to be trifled with. Later, a woman who had the mild and uxorious Crispin well under the thumb.

Felicity had obviously been reflecting along the same lines. 'Now there's a solid marriage,' she said. 'From the outside they seem an odd couple, but they are completely devoted. We used to play tennis with them – Crispin would leap about at the net getting all hot and bothered and minding terribly, while Pauline, who was much the better player, scooped everything up and got it back, usually in the right place and with the minimum of fuss.'

'Sounds a successful partnership.'

'It was.'

They sat in silence, reflecting on their exchange of confidences.

Felicity got up. 'I think it's bedtime. Let's take this lot as far as the dishwasher and deal with it in the morning.'

He followed, picking up his glass and plate. 'Chocolate mousse for breakfast, then?'

'Lemon tart.'

'Even better.'

They took the things to the kitchen, and she returned to turn the dining room light off. The Scotch bottle, their discarded napkins and unused spoons and forks were still on the table. Will sensed she wouldn't normally leave things this way. She seemed suddenly tired, her sparkle doused.

'Well,' she said. 'You know where you are. Sleep well, Will. No hurry in the morning.'

'Thank you for a delicious dinner.'

'Away with you. Night night.' She moved towards the back door. 'I'm just going to let Bramble out and lock up.'

He was sure this was a formula, a way of creating space between them at what might have been an awkward moment.

'Good night, Fliss.'

There was a washbasin in the spare room. When he'd cleaned his teeth, he drew the curtains back. The house was on the edge of a village; there were still one or two lights visible. He stood there for a couple of minutes, trying to put his impressions in order, but it was like catching feathers, and he gave up and got into bed, turning out the reading lamp at once.

What with the duck, the booze and the even richer food for thought, he half expected to lie awake for hours. But the bed was comfortable and the pillows had a fresh scent; in no time he'd drifted down, softly, into a deep sleep.

He offered to drive, but she was firm. 'I know where we're going.'

'That is an advantage.' He looked over his shoulder. Behind the grille, Bramble was sitting with his paws on the back seat. 'He's excited.'

She glanced at the dog in the rear-view mirror. 'The car means we're going somewhere interesting. He gets a bit sick of all our usual circuits.'

'How old is he?' asked Will. 'Have you had him long?'

'Not all that long. He's coming up to two. I got him as a puppy when Tony was ill. Everyone thought I was completely mad, but he gave us something else to think and talk about – not to mention a lot of pleasure at a time when fun was in pretty short supply.' The road was beginning to wind up the side of the escarpment. 'You want to keep looking to your left, the view's gorgeous.'

He did so, and she was right. As they climbed, a vista of picture-book English countryside unrolled below them – snug fields and woods, low hills and shallow river valleys, the occasional curl of smoke or church tower signalling a village. When Felicity pulled over at a vantage point, he could hear a peal of bells.

'Would you be going to church,' he asked, 'if I weren't here?'

She tilted her head from side to side, signalling uncertainty. 'Sometimes I do, sometimes I don't. I'm afraid it's a mood thing with me.'

'Me too,' he said. 'And I haven't been in the mood for years.'

'Not since church parade, I bet.'

''Fraid so.'

They continued driving to the top of the hill and parking on the edge of a wood, among the trunks of bare winter trees, their black branches embellished with clusters of rooks' nests. Bramble, released, leapt from the back of the car and wove around with his nose to the ground, tail waving, trembling with excitement.

'Come on,' she said, to both Will and the dog. 'This way.'

They fell in step along a track edged with drifts of dead leaves. They walked in silence, a silence intensified by the soft rustle of their footsteps, the patter and snuffle of the little dog, the creak of the branches in a hilltop wind they could not themselves feel. Will was accustomed to think of silences as threatening: the calm before the storm in combat; or in a domestic setting as due to some shortcoming on his part, or the withholding of unfavourable comment. But this one was tranquil, and a comfort.

'I can feel this doing me good,' said Felicity. 'I'm a bit hung-over, if truth be told.'

'Me too.'

'I do hope,' she said, her eyes following the dog, 'that there was nothing in last night's conversation that – you know – that bothered you.'

'Absolutely not,' he said, and, realising this wasn't quite true, added, 'Quite the reverse.'

'It was really good to talk. For me, anyway. I may have a slight headache but that's not because I regret anything I said.'

'Good.'

She glanced at him. 'What about you?'

'I regret the self-pity ...'

'I'm afraid I was a bit harsh.'

'No, you were quite right. The rest was true, and it was a relief to spit it out, frankly. They say you can't fool all of the people all of the time, but I do – including myself. The ones I can't fool are the ones I choose not to see.'

To his surprise – and pleasure – she tucked her gloved hand into the crook of his arm.

'What a pair we are!'

They emerged from the trees like that, linked together. Admiring the view, with the wind in their faces, he laid his hand over hers.

They had a late lunch in a pub that couldn't have been bettered, a seventeenth-century building that was scarcely altered, with historic real ale from the wood, and a dog-friendly landlord.

Afterwards, as they walked to the car, she asked, 'When do you have to go back?'

'Let's put it this way,' he said. 'There's no one waiting for me. On the other hand, I don't want to outstay my welcome. I was thinking about six?'

'Ideal.' She popped the lock and opened the driver's door. 'In that case, I can take you back via the scenic route.'

It was all quite lovely, but half an hour later, Will, on the outside of two pints of best, was in danger of getting drowsy. His eyelids were heavy, and he had the sensation of hauling them up when they stopped and the engine was switched off.

'A bit mean of me,' she said. 'I should have let you snooze, but I think you'll like this.'

'No, thank God you woke me up ...' He peered around. 'Where are we?'

'Just a house I love. Gone to rack and ruin, waiting for the developers, I'm afraid. It was a school, and then flats – Tony and I knew someone who lived in one of them. That's when we got to know it, and now that it's on death row, I bring selected individuals over so I'm not the only person who remembers.'

'Good thought. I'm glad I'm one of them.'

They left the dog to sleep. The afternoon air felt raw after the soporific warmth of the car. The house, with its tall chimneys and boarded-up windows, was like some grand old person, abandoned, blind and crippled but still, with its history gathered about it, a tremendous presence.

'Don't worry,' said Felicity, 'we can't go in. I thought perhaps we could just take a turn down the garden. There's a path as far as the church and back; it's only a few hundred yards.'

'Fine, lead on.' They began to walk. He could sense her odd pride in this house that she liked so much, and didn't want to injure it in any way.

'Do you know how old it is?' he asked.

'Not all that ancient. Nineteenth century, I should think. And although it's big, it's not pompous.' They reached the back of the house, and she stopped, and turned to look up at it. Will did the same.

'I think that's why I like it so much,' she said, and he could hear the real tenderness in her voice. 'Because it feels like a home, for a family, and their pets.'

'And their servants,' he pointed out.

'And their servants, of course; our friend had one of those old multiple bell-pulls in his living room. But anyway,' she was impatient with this nit-picking, 'it doesn't matter. Whoever lived here, I'm sure it was a happy place.'

Will took a few paces back. Though no expert, he could see that it was, certainly, a nice house, well proportioned and large, with high gables, many windows and two great clusters of chimneys like sentinels on the tiled roof. They had come through an arch at the side of the house, past a door, perhaps leading to the kitchen. Here he could see another single door and a large French window – blocked off with full-length wooden shutters as well as half a dozen crossed planks – opening on to a tangled terrace with a broken stone balustrade. In the middle of the house, midway between the two gables and between ground and roof, was a bay window, at the turning point, he guessed, of a large staircase.

He heard Felicity at his side give a little sigh as she turned to walk away.

'I hate to see it like this,' she said. 'There must be some million-aire out there with the funds and the imagination to restore it. A rock star or somebody.'

He fell in step beside her. 'Not the sort of thing people are after, I suppose.'

'Do you like it?' she asked, almost anxiously. 'Do you know what I mean?'

'I do,' he said. 'Both.'

They were walking down the ghost of a broad path, through a jungle of shrubbery, towards what must once have been a great lawn and was now a field of withered brown hay and the desic-cated spikes of dead weeds.

'Like Manderley,' she said.

'I'm sorry?'

'Never mind.'

He resolved to look it up. It had become important to him to understand her, to follow her train of thought – to be close to her. At the bottom of the lawn, about a hundred yards from the house, the path passed through a rusted black swing gate in a beech hedge. Beyond that there was another half-acre of ground, even less kempt, a paddock possibly, bounded by a brick wall and a broken five-bar gate sagging open on its hinges. By the swing gate they paused again. With the council's depredations softened by distance, the house reclaimed some of its grace.

'I bet they played games out here,' said Felicity. 'Don't you think? Badminton and croquet.'

'French cricket.'

'Yes! That was the only game I was ever any good at. Because I'm short' – she demonstrated, bending forward and flicking her arms – 'less leg to aim at.'

'And I reckon that was where they had their bonfires.' He pointed to a circular patch in the meadow, where the vegetation was slightly different. 'Over there, look.'

'Oh, yes!' She was delighted with this observation. 'Well spotted!'

She pushed open the gate. 'There's the little church. This must have been their short cut.'

'Fancy wanting one,' he remarked drily. 'Wouldn't be much of a selling point these days.'

'I like to think of the family trooping down here – not necessarily all willingly, but together.'

He smiled. He was having to walk quite fast to keep up with her now. 'You really feel you know these people, don't you?'

'Yes,' she said. 'Yes, I do.'

'If they existed.'

'Of course they did – well, somebody did.'

'Ever done any research into them?'

She shook her head. 'I wouldn't want the facts to spoil a good story.'

They reached the church gate. The graveyard on the other side was well kept, the province of a prosperous parish, if not a God-fearing one. The pattern of summer mowing was still visible even now; the grass over a radius of ten metres from the church itself was cut military-short. Beyond that – nearer to them as they came through the gate – it was trimmed only to create paths between the graves, with the graves themselves left stranded in islands of shaggy growth. To their right was a large holly tree covered in berries, to their left the lowering bulk of a giant yew, its ragged black arms reaching out towards the church like an arboreal grim reaper. The building was cute and compact, a village church from central casting, stone- and flint-built with a tiled oast-house tower.

'Isn't this pretty?' murmured Felicity, then cast over her shoulder, 'If it's open, shall we go in?'

'I'll pass if you don't mind,' said Will, who didn't care for church interiors, with their stern, spiritual tap on the shoulder. 'You go ahead, though, I'll be happy having a wander out here.'

'If you're sure.'

He followed her round to the south porch. The outer gate was open. The door was framed by a garland of dark greenery and white flowers that gave off a slightly oversweet scent.

'A wedding yesterday, I suppose,' he said.

'Last week, I think.' She touched a rose, and a shower of brown-edged petals fell to the stone flags. 'At least – these are dead as anything.' She lifted the latch and pushed the door, which swung heavily away from her. 'Open – good. I won't be long.'

'Be as long as you like.'

He continued his perambulation of the graveyard, thinking, with a sort of shy pride, that this was what regular couples did – separated according to whim, then rejoined one another to share what they'd seen. On this side of the church was a lychgate leading on to a lane, with a couple of attractive red-brick pantiled houses visible. The air was cold and still. A light came on in one of the houses opposite, reminder of the rapidly shortening days. He went round the east end of the church beneath the tower, brushed past the heavy, black-sleeved arms of the yew and looked back the way they'd come. From here he could see that the house, though below the hills of the Weald, was on gently rising ground; it was clearly, even commandingly, visible. The pale late-afternoon sun, smudged by cloud, caught the broken glass of the bay window, the one he'd supposed to be on the main staircase, and this flash of brightness brought the place to momentary life, as though it were sending out a last defiant signal before sentence was carried out.

He agreed with Felicity. What a damn shame.

Folding his arms against the chill, he began an inspection of the graves. Many of them were so weathered and overgrown by moss and lichen as to be illegible. He paused by one that was very simple, a plain white headstone with a rounded top, reminiscent of a regimental war grave, and with very few words:

A short life, then, and ended – how? He was still looking down at the stone when Felicity joined him, shoulders hunched, hands in pockets.

'Brr, it was even colder in there than out here! What have you found?'

'This.' He pointed. 'Rather striking.'

'You're right.' She peered at it. 'And rather mysterious.' She tucked her hand into his arm again and turned him towards the gate. 'Come on, we need to warm up with a cup of tea before you hit the road.'

The dusk was deepening as they walked back up the central path of the garden, and the house was a dark, lifeless hulk. Felicity turned on music in the car before pulling away, and put a couple of notches on the heating.

'I tell you what,' she said, as they turned out into the road. 'When I do my research, I'll try and find out who that person was.'

'Maurice,' he said. 'Yes, why not? Do – and let me know.'

Chapter Thirty-Nine
1999

'I'm sorry,' said Alan. 'I can't come.'

Stella lowered the phone to her lap. She could hear him saying her name. She lifted it again.

'Why not?' An automatic response, a sound she could make to buy herself time.

'Work. You'll understand – I hope. My partner's wife's seriously ill, he has to take time off to be with her while he can. The hospital's pushed, too, they really need every hand they can get. I can't just swan off.'

'Swanning? Alan – taking a fortnight's holiday you'd booked in advance, that you and they both knew was in the offing.'

There was a short silence. 'You know how things are, Stella. I've told you.'

He wasn't playing. She felt all the hot, toxic feelings boiling up inside her, the bad words spilling out.

'Not really, no.'

He sighed. 'Don't make me crawl. You know how sorry I am – how sorry it's turned out like this and how sad that I'm not coming. However wretched you feel, I can double it.'

'Who cares? You may feel sad and bad, but I'm fucking furious.'

'I can tell.'

'Really? Can you? I suppose you didn't get where you are today without being able to spot the problem.'

She knew she was being childish – or was she? No, she was entitled to be this angry. She'd been let down and he seemed, in truth, not that bothered, as if this were all run-of-the-mill stuff. And if she didn't get angry, she was going to cry. She wanted to make *him* cry.

'Anyway,' he said, 'there it is. You either believe me and

407

understand and we get over it, or …' his voice dropped, 'I don't know.'

'Or I toss a wobbler typical of my sex when mildly disappointed and you sit it out before breathing a sigh of relief and getting on with your busy life.'

He didn't reply, and his silence enraged her still more.

'You know what?' she snarled. 'Who cares? I'm tired, Alan. Sick and tired.'

Not long after she'd rung off, he called back; the screen proclaimed INTERNATIONAL but she didn't pick up. She couldn't have spoken to him even if she'd wanted to. She couldn't remember when she'd last wept like this, an uncontrolled vomiting-up of her misery.

The following morning there was an email, sent by him the previous night, just after they'd spoken.

Stella my darling – I love you, and can't bear that you are so hurt and angry. I did consider simply telling my colleagues I was going to be away, but they have a crisis of manpower and my practice patients need someone there that they know. Whereas you and I have no crisis (or so I thought) and plenty of time ahead of us.

Do, please, look after yourself and try to feel better about this. I'm not doing it lightly, and only felt able to do it at all because I've got every faith in us.

I hope you do too.

Alan

Bruised and resentful as she still was, she recognised that he could not have put it better, or said anything more likely to soothe her. But she was not ready, yet, to be soothed. Alan had not made her a priority. His talk of their having plenty of time smacked to Stella of taking her for granted.

She was going to look after Toyah while her mother went to London with some girlfriends to buy a wedding dress for one of their number. Shannon, attuned to the emotion upheavals of other women, noticed at once that all was not well.

'What's up, Stel?' she asked, as Stella scooped the charging Toyah into her arms. 'Hey, have you been crying?'

'Yes.' There was no point in denying it, when her face so obviously bore all the signs. They went into the living room and Stella put Toyah down.

'Coffee?'

'No, Shannon, really – you have things to do.' Toyah crawled on to her lap, carrying a book. 'Let's look at this.'

'I'm making us a quick cup,' said Shannon. When she returned, she put the mugs on the table, and switched on the cartoon channel. Toyah, her eyes fixed on the TV, slid off Stella's knee and plonked herself on the floor.

'You've got two sugars in there.'

Stella felt herself welling up. 'Thank you, lovely. I really don't want to hold you up ...'

'You won't. I'd rather talk. Or listen – I'm a good listener.'

'Oh dear.' Stella took a sip of the sweet coffee and wiped her eyes with the heel of her hand. 'I am sorry about this.'

'Don't be. Man trouble?'

The phrase made Stella laugh in spite of herself. How were the mighty fallen! That she, who had always been in charge, always the dumper, never the dumpee, should be accused of having 'man trouble'!

'I suppose so, in a way. I've had a disappointment.'

'He let you down?'

She thought about this. 'He had his reasons.'

'Huh!' Shannon's whole stock of world-weariness – large for one so young – was invested in this one syllable. 'Typical.'

'He has a very demanding job, and that has to come first.'

'I don't see why,' said Shannon. 'If he loves you.'

'He's a paediatrician, he can't just drop everything.' In the face of Shannon's knee-jerk girl-power disapproval, she found herself (uncharacteristically, she realised) defending not only Alan but their whole generation, weighed down with commitments and notions of duty and loyalty. Something occurred to her. 'Think how you'd have felt when you were going back for Toyah's tests if you'd always seen someone different.'

'We did till you got on the case and we started seeing Mr Pennington!'

'Okay, fair point.'

Unused to even the smallest disagreement – their professional friendship didn't allow for such things – they paused to regroup against the background chirrup of the cartoons. Shannon was the first to collect herself.

'I'm really really sorry, Stel. You must be devastated.'

'I was last night,' said Stella, 'after he rang. I'm starting to see I overreacted.'

'No you didn't!'

'All right, let's say it doesn't seem quite as bad. Talking to you has helped.'

'Not quite sure how, but that's good. Right, time I wasn't here.' Shannon took the mugs out to the kitchen, and came back wearing her bright turquoise coat with the black buttons. 'Her lunch is by the microwave. Help yourself to anything in the fridge; there's a pasta salad in the plastic box.'

'Wonderful.'

'See you later this arvo. Bye, babes.' She knelt down by Toyah and embraced her extravagantly. 'Give us a kiss – mmm! Be good, have a lovely time.'

It was a relief to Stella when the front door closed behind Shannon. The exchange had been invigorating in its way, but Shannon's spirited encouragement had left her debilitated, as if the real emotions engendered by Alan's call had been hijacked, pushed around and summarily rejected. She felt drained. For once, she allowed the screen to hold sway and went out to make a second, stronger coffee.

After an hour of guilty passivity, she turned off the TV and went through her usual repertoire of activities with Toyah: reading stories, colouring, an elaborate pantomime of childcare with various dolls and stuffed cartoon characters, and a failed attempt to put together a dismantled fairy grotto whose inventor should have been executed for crimes against supervising adults. Then came action songs – some she remembered from her own childhood and one or two she'd learned from Shannon. All this, and – she consulted her watch – it was still only ten thirty.

'Come on,' she announced. 'Let's go to the swings.'

'Swings, swings!'

One of many useful lessons learned over the past year was that 'going to the swings' was an exercise that could be stretched to fill almost any required time span. There was the initial suggestion (always greeted with wild enthusiasm); the 'couple of things' that had to be done first (these could range from rinsing coffee cups to a full load of ironing – the principle of deferred gratification held good); the discussion and selection of clothes (Toyah had quite a few) for the expedition; the putting on of the selected clothes, and her own outdoor things; and finally the assembling of paraphernalia to be taken with them – toys, a drink, wipes, purse, shopping bag – on the bottom shelf of the buggy. Following departure, the route to the park could be broken down into a series of intermediate objectives: admiring the fruit outside the Asian supermarket (and conversing with the indulgent proprietor); studying any passing dogs or cats; going 'up the snicket', where Toyah could safely get out of the buggy and walk; posting a letter, or pretending to; finally, the pressing of buttons at the crossing opposite the park gate.

On arrival, an energetic burst of swinging could be followed by quite elaborate sessions of 'timing' – how many seconds would it take Toyah to run from here to the roundabout? To climb on and off the bouncy elephant? To go round the wooden playhouse? This exercise was best in the summer, when Stella could sit on a bench in the sun while gazing at the second hand on her watch. Today, with a dark sky and seasonal temperatures, it was better to keep moving. Dutifully, on autopilot, she trudged from one piece of equipment to the next – pushing, hauling, lifting, making train noises, singing snatches of songs as required, and responding reflexively to Toyah's stream of questions and observations.

There were a handful of other people at the playground on this inclement weekday morning, mostly young women with preschool children and one older lady, a grandmother probably, with a toddler and a small baby in the lower part of a double buggy. A couple of the mothers seemed to know each other and were moving about as a pair, chatting; the rest of them emitted a kind of inaudible, bonding bleep, an assurance of mutual understanding. Remarks addressed to their charges – 'let the other little girl go first', 'don't push', 'good boy, that's right', 'careful on that now', 'say sorry' – were also for the benefit of the nearest adult, to show that everything was under control.

Toyah was an adventurous child these days; she didn't allow her slight limp to hold her back. At two and a half, she spurned the baby swings in favour of the 'big-girl' ones and the tall slide. The swings weren't really a problem, since she couldn't climb on to one unaided, but the steps to the slide were set into a bank and were fairly easily negotiated by even the littlest legs. When Stella had asked about this, Shannon had replied with a young woman's breezy confidence that she'd be fine, but to keep an eye out for other, bigger children who might become impatient and try to overtake on the way to the top. 'It's like driving,' she explained. 'It's the rest of them you got to be careful of.'

Stella, *in loco parentis,* was very careful. But her own confidence had grown with that of Toyah, who now went up the steps at a great rate, leading with her right foot, and hurtled down as light as a beanbag to shoot off the end and land with a *flump*, shrieking with excited laughter, on the carpet of wood chips at the bottom.

Today, though, it was the climbing frame that was the big attraction; or more specifically the four-year-old boy, older charge of the grandmother, who had risen intrepidly to the top rung. The frame was a large, igloo-shaped structure with a central pole. Bigger children could swarm up one side, over the top and down the other, or slide down the pole like firemen. Toyah reached the third rung before hesitating, and pedalling frantically with her small, bent foot for the rung below in order to come down again. Stella assisted, guiding one boot after the other against a background of frustrated wailing. A sisterly look passed between her and the grandmother. The boy came down and headed for the roundabout, with Toyah in hot pursuit.

'I think he's scored a hit,' said Stella, following.

'And he knows it,' agreed the grandmother.

They left it at that – there were protocols to be observed in these exchanges – and drifted, separately but driven by a common impulse, like cows at milking time, towards the roundabout.

'Stella!'

Not expecting to hear her name in this context, she assumed the shout was for someone else.

'Hey – Stella!'

She stopped and looked around. He was walking, half running, across the grass from the direction of the tarmac path that bisected the park, the familiar beanie pulled down over his ears, hands thrust into the pockets of his donkey jacket.

'Ted?'

'I thought it was you.' He reached her side. She noticed a little duck of the head as if he'd considered kissing her but changed his mind; his hands stayed firmly in his pockets. 'How's it going?'

'Very well, thanks. Nice to see you. You?'

'Good, yeah – really good.' He stared at her, beaming. 'This is the last place I'd expect to bump into you. What are you doing here?'

'There's a young mum I help out. That's her little girl' – she looked over her shoulder towards the roundabout; the granny gave her a reassuring wave, which she returned – 'there.'

'Good for you,' he said. 'You're always helping people out, aren't you?'

Coming from Ted, this was an unprecedented effusion. There was something different about him. She had hoped not to encounter him again after their sad and acrimonious parting. Even now, if she'd seen him first she'd probably have looked the other way, pretended she hadn't. But he'd spotted her and sought her out. That was the difference in him, she realised – confidence.

'I suppose you're tied up with the little 'un,' he said, 'or I'd ask you to come for a coffee.'

'Nice idea, Ted, but no, you're right, I can't.' She glanced over her shoulder. 'I've got responsibilities.'

'I hope you don't mind my saying, Stella – you changed my life.'

'Me?' She laughed. 'I don't think so. Any changes you made all by yourself.'

'Straight up. What I learnt with you, I carried on with. I'm okay now with the reading.' He grinned. 'I've got a Jeffrey Archer on the go.'

'That's great, Ted. I'm really glad to hear it.'

'And I'm looking to expand the gardening – do a bit of design. I did some for a lady a few weeks ago and she's chuffed. I'm going to give her a new garden, make it happen for her.'

'That's wonderful.'

'Like you made it happen for me.'

Stella felt the old wariness kick in. Where was this leading? In her emotionally weakened state, she could not face a second-wave onslaught from Ted, with who knew what consequences.

'Nonsense.'

'It's true.' He planted his feet apart. His attitude was resolute, but she could sense a deep breath being taken.

'I'm getting married.'

'Oh!' She couldn't help it, the little poison dart of jealousy. 'Ted, that's brilliant news, congratulations!'

She stepped forward and gave him a brief hug and a kiss on the cheek, to protect him – and herself – from her moment of chagrin. When she tried to step back, he held her firmly a moment longer, but leaned back to look into her face.

'It would never have happened if I hadn't come to you.'

'Don't be silly, of course—'

'Ah-ah!' He raised a finger close to her mouth, not quite touching it. 'Shut up, for once. I was a loser, and you turned me around. Take it on the chin, all right?'

'All right.' She smiled. 'I'm so pleased for you.'

For the past minute – no more than that – she'd been lost in the exchange, and so hadn't heard the shout from behind her. It was Ted who stepped back and said:

'Something's up – think you'd better go.'

He was already taking his mobile from his pocket, his eyes on something over her shoulder. Her stomach and face felt cold, and her vision swam slightly as she turned to see the grandmother waving, stumbling with an elderly person's stiff, knock-kneed gait over the grass, her mouth wide. The continued shouting reached her a split second later. All her senses seemed to be on a time lag.

Ted, the phone to his ear, gave her a push.

'Go on, Stella – go! I'm going to the gate.'

She went to meet the other woman. Beyond her, near the swings, a small knot of people had gathered. She knew, of course, what must have happened, could feel the panic ballooning inside her, rising, pushing, at the back of her throat.

'I'm so sorry – she fell, it was so quick. Has your friend …?'

She ran past the grandmother, without answering. Rudeness was not an issue – all she wanted now was to be there, where she was supposed to be, to see for herself and take back the responsibility that should have been hers. The group by the swings turned to meet her and stepped back to let her through. Was it her imagination, or was there a kind of grim self-righteousness in their faces, a *Schadenfreude* that it had been she, not they, who'd screwed up? The other children had been ushered away and were being supervised by a volunteer in the sandpit. The grandmother's smaller child was wailing fretfully in its buggy.

Toyah lay on the ground just in front of the swing. A young woman in a business suit, not one of the mothers, was kneeling next to her. She looked up as Stella arrived.

'Is she yours?'

'I'm looking after her, yes,' said Stella, gasping, and saw a look of contempt flit over the girl's face. She knelt down beside her. Toyah's eyes – thank God! – were open, slitted, but she was a terrifying yellowish white, and the hair just above her right ear, near where the now stained pink scrunchy held her bunch, was thickly clotted with blood.

'Toyah?' Stella took her hand, which felt cool and limp, and held it in both of hers.

'She can't hear you.'

'Jesus, oh Jesus …' For the first time in years, the words were not an oath, but a prayer. Her eyes still on Toyah, she asked, 'What happened?'

'You'll have to ask one of these ladies,' said the girl, getting to her feet and swiping at the knees of her black trousers. 'I was just taking a short cut, but I've got a first-aid certificate, so I came over.'

'Thank you …'

'Has someone called an ambulance?'

'Yes, I believe this lady's friend—'

'He has, he's gone to meet it.'

'It's the internal injuries you have to—'

'What *happened*?' Stella's voice was a screech. 'Will someone please tell me what happened?'

'She ran in front of the swing.' Stella recognised the friendly grandmother's voice; she was bending down next to her with her hand on her shoulder. 'They move so quickly, it happened in a flash. The corner of the swing caught her on the head.'

Sensing the woman's sympathy, Stella whispered, her voice breaking on a sob, 'I should have been here!'

'It was a pure accident. We were all keeping an eye out, but none of us was quick enough to prevent it.'

In the background, Stella heard a familiar urban sound, its shrill urgency now directed accusingly, terrifyingly, at her.

'Here's the ambulance,' said the first-aid girl. There was a general buzz of relief, but also a kind of excitement – what would the experts say?

'I'll stay for a moment in case I can tell them anything. Otherwise I think we should leave it to them, we'll only be in the way.'

The onlookers began to step away. No one wanted to be thought a mere gawper.

'I'll hang on for a bit too, if I may,' said the grandmother. 'I feel partly responsible.'

Stella shook her head. 'No.' She touched the hand on her shoulder briefly. 'No, you aren't. Not at all.'

The paramedics, a man and a girl, arrived accompanied by Ted.

'Do you want me to stay?' he asked. Stella shook her head. 'In that case, call me – I want to know.'

'Okay.' She was embarrassed, for herself and for him – what must these people think? 'Go!'

What followed was one of the unhappiest and most humiliating experiences of her life. In the centre of it all, Toyah, lay small, broken and helpless, like a doll, as the paramedics did their stuff. Their questions came quickly, calmly, in strict order. Who was in charge of the child at the time? Had she seen what happened? Then who had? Had anyone touched Toyah after the accident? What did you do? After the first question Stella was sidelined, of no more account, except: 'Has a parent been contacted?'

'No – not yet.'

'You'd better do that now, I think.'

'What's the matter, how is she?'

They didn't look up. 'We're still finding out, aren't we, Toyah? If you could contact a parent, please.'

Miserable and ashamed, Stella stood to one side, still a novice with her mobile, fumbling through the list of numbers in her diary, dialling Shannon's number with cold, clumsy fingers. The sounds of the park and her own blood thudding in her ears prevented her from hearing, and she turned her back on the scene by the swings and put a hand over her other ear before trying again. There was a short tone followed by a voice telling her that the person on this number was not responding.

What did that mean, for heaven's sake? That Shannon's phone was switched off? That was so unlikely as to seem impossible. She tried a third time and got the same response. Stella put her hands to her face to shut out everything except what she needed to focus on. What was the name of the bridal shop the girls had been going to? The restaurant afterwards? Both places had been mentioned, but she had never thought to make a note. She was helpless.

She returned, wretched, to the group by the swings. The paramedics were transferring Toyah to a stretcher, swathed in a red blanket. Her eyes were a little more open but she still had that white, floppy, doll-like look which turned Stella's heart over.

'May I speak to her, please?'

They didn't answer, but paused to let her lean over the stretcher.

'Toyah? Toyah, darling, it's me, Stella. Can you hear me?' There were tears running down her face now, she couldn't help it. She felt for Toyah's hand under the blanket and held it, rubbing the soft skin on the back of it with her thumb. 'Toyah, it's Stella – can you hear me?' She thought, believed, that there was a slight change in the child's face, a widening of the eyes, a twitch of the lips. 'You're going be all right,' she said, not caring how stupid she sounded. 'Mummy will be here soon.' She bent and kissed her. 'I love you.'

She clambered to her feet, wiping her cheeks. 'Okay.'

'Any joy with the phone call?'

'There was no reply, I can't understand—'

'Keep trying, please. We're taking her to the Galloway, you know where that is?'

'Yes.'

She was left with the business-suited Samaritan, reeking of disapproval, and the grandmother, whose children had been returned to her, the red-faced baby now asleep, the four-year-old, peevish with boredom, swinging on her hand. Toyah's laden buggy was drawn up alongside.

'Thank you both so much,' said Stella. 'I can't tell you how grateful I am.'

'I'd better get to work,' said the young woman, unsmiling, hitching her bag over her shoulder. 'Good luck.'

'Thanks again. Do you – have a card or something?'

'Don't worry about it.'

For a second time, Stella felt the sting of her disdain.

The grandmother placed her arm lightly across Stella's shoulders. 'Are you all right?'

'Worried sick. I must go.'

'Do you have a car here?'

'Shit!' Stella clapped a hand to her forehead.

'Nor me, unfortunately. Get a cab. I've got a number on this thing, my daughter put it there – you never know when it'll come in handy. I'll come with you to the main gate, if you could just grab him by the hand.'

The toddler – Jack – was loud in his objection to this arrangement, but Stella was in no mood to take prisoners. In the end she picked him up and held him tightly, still protesting, as her companion called the local minicab company.

'They'll be here in five minutes.'

It was nearer seven – Stella counted every second – but the grandmother remained at her post, refusing to leave until she'd seen Stella on board, with the buggy and its contents squeezed into the boot. She handed her a scrap of paper – a shopping list – with her number on it.

'I don't want to add to your problems, but I'd be so pleased if you'd call me and let me know how she is. Edith Chappell.'

'Stella Drake. I will, I promise.'

Edith and the now recovered Jack waved her off. She couldn't help it, she was glad to be relieved of the woman's kindness and her company; she needed to lick her wounds. Trembling with anxiety and fatigue, she leaned back. The driver looked at her in the mirror.

'A and E, that right?'

'Yes.'

'Oh dear, someone in trouble?'

Shut up, she thought. *Just shut up.* Her mobile rang and she snatched it to her ear, inadvertently cutting off the caller in the process. She hadn't recognised the number, but when, almost at once, it rang again, it was Shannon.

'Shannon!'

'Stel? You okay?'

'I've been trying to ring!'

'Yeah, sorry, I left my phone in the Ladies' and didn't realise. Just got it back. How are you guys?'

'I'm fine, but Toyah had an accident at the swings. We had to call an ambulance – I'm on my way to A and E at the Galloway now.'

'What? What happened?'

'One of the big swings hit her on the head.'

'On the head? What was going on? Is she – how serious is it?'

Stella concentrated on the last question – time enough for the recriminations when – if – Toyah was out of danger. 'I don't know, Shannon. The paramedics didn't seem too worried, but obviously they weren't saying, and I wasn't able to contact you …'

'Fucking hell!' It was rare for Shannon to be angry, let alone swear; the words came over the line like a blow, and Stella flinched. 'They must have said something!'

'No – no, they didn't. But her eyes were open, a little, and she responded, I think, when I—'

'You think!'

'She did – only slightly, but she definitely did.'

'I'm coming now, right now, but it's going to take me an hour, hour and a half. You stay with her till I get there, yeah?'

'I will, I promise. I wouldn't dream—'

But Shannon had gone. Stella, battered, wept. She could feel the cab driver's eyes flicking her way in the mirror, but she didn't give a damn and she couldn't help herself.

'Nearly there,' he said. 'I'm taking you the back way.'

At twelve on a weekday morning, A and E was mercifully quiet. There was a man in builder's overalls with a cloth wrapped round his hand, two women in tennis whites and an old man with an impatient-looking woman, probably his daughter. The receptionist told Stella that Toyah Atherton was being seen by the doctors and that she should wait with the others until summoned.

'Do you know if there's any news – about how she is?'

'I'm sorry, I don't, we don't deal with the medical side, but I'll let them know you've arrived.' She spotted the phone in Stella's hand. 'You do know you can't use that in here?'

'Right, yes, I do – of course.'

She sat down on the end of the front row of orange plastic chairs, the buggy parked alongside. On the wall opposite was a noticeboard covered in leaflets, advertisements and admonishments relating to health, safety, treatment and even, she noticed glumly, compensation for accidents. Beside the board was the regulation fish tank, its occupants drifting languidly around their underwater pagoda like Christmas tree decorations in a draught. Above these, a neon stream of information circulated on a loop. Waiting time was currently estimated at fifteen minutes, but whether or not that applied to her she had no idea. Two more people came in, a woman with a burned hand and her friend from work, and were processed by the triage nurse. Along the corridor the four curtained cubicles gave nothing away – was Toyah in one of them? Stella could hear a murmur of voices from that direction, but no child's voice, not one that might have been Toyah's. Panic, which had subsided a little with her arrival at the hospital – the place where things could be put right – rose in her again, and the shriek of an approaching ambulance brought her out in a sweat. The ambulance pulled up outside and suddenly all was focused urgency and purpose; she heard running footsteps in the corridor behind her, the slap of double doors being pinned open, the words 'major RTA', the rattle of trolley wheels. She couldn't, wouldn't look, and put her hands to her face.

'Stella Drake?'

A young Indian doctor – a houseman in a short white jacket, a stethoscope over his loud tie – was standing next to her. Now he bent towards her, politely solicitous.

'Excuse me – are you Stella Drake?'

She got unsteadily to her feet. 'Yes, I am.'

'You're with Toyah Atherton?'

'Yes – how is she?'

Behind them, the background hubbub ebbed away. 'Don't worry, she will be fine.'

'Really? She will? Oh!'

'Steady.' The doctor put a hand beneath her elbow. 'Sit down, sit down.'

'No, I'll be okay. Honestly. Can I see her?'

'You are not her mother, I understand?'

'No, I was ...' The awfulness of what she was about to say

420

washed over her. The personal injury ads glared at her from the wall. She slumped back on to the chair.

'You were looking after her for a while?'

'Yes, I was – I was supposed to be.'

Considerately, he let this go. 'Have you contacted a parent?'

'I've spoken to her mother; she was in London for the day. She's on her way, but she won't be here for at least another hour.'

'No problem, we want to keep Toyah in overnight anyway.'

'So can I see her now?'

'Yes, in fact we'd like you to stay with her till her mother arrives. She's a little woozy at the moment, but she may be upset when she starts to notice where she is.'

The hand under her elbow again. She stood, and drew a breath, noticed the buggy.

'Can I leave this here?'

'Bring it with you, that'll be fine.'

They left A and E and walked briskly along a wide corridor lined with framed children's pictures and bland corporate art, through swing doors that sighed shut behind them.

The doctor said, 'She'll be glad of some of those things from home in a little while.'

Stella was weak at the knees, grateful for the buggy to lean on. 'I can't believe this has happened. I feel so terrible, I was responsible.'

'Accidents happen.' He was a nice man but low in the food chain; he was in no position to assuage her guilt. They turned left, went through a second door, and he indicated that she clean her hands with the antiseptic gel on the wall before tapping in a code and entering a side ward. She saw Toyah at once, lying in the second bed along on the right, a nurse standing beside her, holding her hand. She was wearing a hospital nightie in pink, with red and white smiley faces on it (well, that would please her anyway, thought Stella); the shiny tip of a thermometer peeped out from the armhole. There was a large pad of dressing taped over the side of her head, and the rest of her hair – her beautiful, silky tendrils of baby hair – stuck out roughly around it. As they approached, the nurse removed the thermometer, read it, shook it and replaced it in its glass of pink fluid on the trolley at the end of the bed. She smiled at Stella.

'Normal. She's doing really well.'

'Is she?' Stella went to the side of the bed. For the first time in what seemed like aeons, Toyah was looking back at her, round-eyed and solemn – not exactly her old self, but at least fully present.

'Hello, sweetheart.' Stella was not given to terms of endearment, but this one, now, came to her quite naturally. She kissed her fingers and touched them lightly to Toyah's left cheek. The houseman moved a chair so that it was behind her, and she sat. 'You're such a brave girl.'

The round eyes filled with tears. 'I want Mummy.'

'She'll be here very soon.'

'Mummy ...' Toyah cried quietly, almost motionless, only her lips stretching and quivering, the tears trickling down into the wadding above her ear. Stella could hardly bear it. 'I want Mummy.'

'She's on her way, sweetie. She'll be here any minute.'

The nurse handed Stella the floppy, crazily quiffed donkey – star of a recent hit animation film – from the buggy.

'Maybe she'd like this.'

'Yes, good idea.' Stella took the zebra. 'Toyah, look who's here, it's Merv.'

Toyah whimpered again, but when Stella tucked the toy into the crook of her arm, she nuzzled her face into it and her eyelids drooped.

'She'll want to sleep,' said the nurse, who in this situation appeared to be the young doctor's superior. She touched a carton with an angled straw on top of the locker. 'And drink, as much as she will take.'

'Thank you.' The nurse moved quietly away, and the young doctor took her place on the far side of the bed. Stella asked, 'Has she had stitches?'

He shook his head. 'No, we've taped it. Small children have efficient healing mechanisms. It should be fine. We just want her in overnight to keep an eye on her.' His eyes moved beyond her, and he took a step to the side. 'Here's Mr Pennington. I believe he'd like a word with you.'

A tall, weary-looking man in a crumpled suit appeared next to her and held out his hand. 'I'm David Pennington, consultant paediatrician. How do you do.'

She half rose to shake his hand. 'Hello. I'm Stella Drake.'

'I know, I've heard all about you. Please do sit down.'

For the first time Stella felt acknowledged, and even accorded a little respect for her role in Toyah's life. Pennington addressed the houseman.

'How's she doing?'

He was softly spoken and had a gentle manner, but the younger doctor still displayed the air of a man standing to attention.

'Very well considering. The signs are all stable and the wound is clean.'

'But we're keeping her in, I hope?'

'Tonight, yes.'

'I'd like to see her in the morning.'

In some indefinable way the houseman had been dismissed, and left the bedside. Pennington perched casually on the far side of the bed, so that he was facing both Toyah and Stella.

'This must have been a horrendous business.'

'Awful,' she agreed. 'Awful, and I feel—'

'Of course,' he interrupted mildly, 'I know Toyah and her mother quite well. I've had one or two meetings with them about Toyah's juvenile arthritis.'

'Yes – how is that?'

'Let's say we're watching it. It's certainly no worse. But you'll probably have noticed she still has some slight distortion of the left foot. It may make her a little unsteady.' He looked pleasantly at Stella. 'It could easily have contributed to this accident, for instance.'

She could have kissed him. 'You think so?'

'It only takes a second off balance and something can happen. By far the most likely cause is simply a two-year-old's inattention, but it's worth bearing in mind.' He looked at his watch. 'Any idea when Miss Atherton's likely to be here? I was going off duty, but I particularly wanted to see Toyah as she's one of my patients.'

'She's coming from London. At least half an hour.'

He glanced over at the houseman, now hovering beyond the end of the bed. 'Dr Mandalia, please will you let me know when Toyah's mother arrives?' He stood up, and this time Stella did too. 'Bye for now.'

'Bye.'

He headed for the door, the houseman following. Before he

reached it, the nurse waylaid him, and after a brief discussion he came back down the ward to the bedside of another child. Stella was aware of the pale, calm light of his concentration being focused on someone else. She looked back at Toyah, who slept, the faintest hint of colour now in her cheeks, the toy's mad wide eyes staring out from beneath her arm.

Stella herself fell asleep several times, in the ward before Shannon's arrival and in the minicab on the way home. The moment she saw Shannon, she embarked on her litany of agonised apology, but Shannon wasn't interested; her one concern was for her daughter. Stella had never seen her like this before – tight-lipped, peremptory, commanding respect. There were no tears, this was a young woman with neither the time nor the taste for recriminations. Like the paramedics, she took things in order, questioning Stella, the nurse, the houseman and, when he arrived, Pennington with white-faced composure. During the exchange with Pennington, Stella left, with just an absent-minded 'Cheers, Stel' from Shannon and a cursory wave from the doctor. She had not, in the end, been blamed for anything, but she was now surplus to requirements.

She couldn't face making calls, but she did leave a message with Shannon, asking her to ring when she could, before collapsing on the sofa. Her last thought as she lay there full length, her head on a cushion, her feet up on the arm, was that today she had been vouchsafed some invaluable insights, and must act upon them.

It was six when she woke; her head was aching, but the thought was still there, shiny and clear. She swallowed two paracetamol and made a cup of tea, syrupy with sugar, before going straight to the computer.

No matter how tired she was, she needed to email Alan. Now.

Will was walking by the river on the outskirts of north Oxford. It was eight thirty on this midwinter morning, not an hour he was specially familiar with, but he was restless these days. In spite of sleeping only lightly, he was waking early and was often gripped by the impulse to get going, on what he wasn't quite sure. He had the strong sense of being at a dangerous corner, of decisions coming at him from all directions that before too long would need to be addressed. All of this was energising, but there were times when he needed to direct the energy into something undemanding, like exercise, before it began to turn in on itself and become unproductive fretting. In other words, he thought as he stamped along the towpath, before the lurking decisions came into focus.

He liked Oxford for a variety of reasons. In and of itself it was a beautiful, ancient and interesting town; and the colleges reminded him of Raff, and what he was up to; also, it was a good place for pottering. He could walk for hours around the streets, straying into college grounds, browsing in book and antique shops, idling in pubs and teashops, eavesdropping on other people's conversations, without a sense of time wasted. In Oxford, reading, thinking, drinking and observing one's fellow man constituted a perfectly proper use of time. Of course the students were no longer around, but the dons were, and those wonderfully characteristic denizens of the prosperous suburbs like Jericho, who, while they may not have been dons themselves, affected a donnish air, the women not unattractive but pleasantly unkempt, with dirndl skirts and long, uncoloured, loosely pinned-up hair, the men skinny and mopheaded in corduroy and tweed.

Will was staying in one of the college rooms that were available for hire during the vac. The room was in one of the newer colleges, but still central. A plain cooked breakfast and the use of the comfortable JCR was included in the very reasonable price. This morning he had confined himself to a cup of strong sweet tea (facilities were in the room) before leaving, and was planning to stop at a greasy spoon in the Cowley Road on the way back.

He loved it out here. He felt like a king. The morning wasn't cold for the time of year, but there was a scudding wind with rain on its breath. A pale sun lit the edges of the clouds above the distinctive uneven skyline of the town. Between him and the network of Victorian streets that was north Oxford lay half a mile of broad water meadow lit by ruffled pewter-coloured puddles. This was common land where a mixed herd of horses grazed between patches of low scrub. One of the horses, startled by something or simply on some strange equine whim, began to run, and a dozen others joined in, heads nodding, manes tossing, their hooves sending up fountains of spray as they thundered towards their distant, unrecognised objective.

On the opposite side of the river from Will, a row of ancient grey willows trembled and creaked like galleons at anchor. On his side, below the towpath bank, a mat of brown winter reeds and rushes lay on the surface of the river; at its edge, moorhens, coots and the odd duck sculled about on the rain-pocked water. The packed earth beneath his feet was fast becoming a mud slick, and he moved to the edge of the path to get a purchase on the flattened grass. It would have been sensible at this time of year to buy wellingtons or walking boots, but he was always deterred by the feeling that such a purchase implied a commitment to life in England. So he squelched on, prissily avoiding the worst of the mud.

He could see one other person, with a dog on a long lead, over a hundred yards away; otherwise he had the place to himself. But the moment he'd made this observation he felt the buzz of the mobile in his pocket. There was no need to bring it out at this time in the morning, but the habit of on-stream contact, with its promise of work, was hard to break. He debated whether to ignore it, but that too proved impossible. He dug the phone out.

'Will Drake.'

'Hello – you're not in the car, are you?'

'Fliss, I didn't cop the number.' He was warmed and delighted to hear her voice. 'No, I'm taking a walk by the river in Oxford.'

'Gosh. Outside my window it's dark and dreary and blowing a gale.'

'Same here. But it means I have the place to myself.'

'That's quite enough of that. What are you doing at the weekend?'

His mind raced. 'I'm not completely sure at the moment. I may have to go away.'

'You're so elusive,' she said cheerfully. 'I wondered if you'd like to come down here, but it sounds as if that won't be on ... will it?'

'Can I call you later today?' he asked, feeling foolish now for keeping her at bay and setting up this unnecessary complication. 'I really would like to come if I can.'

'That's fine. I'll keep my fingers crossed. If you do come, I might invite the Hamburys over for kitchen supper. Would you mind that?'

'Not at all.' He had the impression she'd seen through his evasiveness for the defence mechanism it was and had already discounted it. 'That would be fun. But I'll give you a ring in a couple of hours if that's okay.'

'I may be out by then, but leave a message.'

He locked the keypad and put the phone back in his pocket. He very much wanted to go. Since his last visit, he'd seen Felicity in London a couple of times, once when she'd been coming up to Christmas shop and they'd had lunch together, the second time for a show and dinner at his invitation. He'd stuck his neck out a bit with the choice of play, a smart modern revival of a sixties farce, but happily they'd both rocked with laughter and gone for a Lebanese feast afterwards. There had been the now familiar trip to the station, the brief hug and touching of cheeks on the platform, his return to the club with a light heart and a restless disinclination to read his book in bed. With their growing acquaintance he had started to notice things about her, things that stirred him. Not in the furious, helpless, overwhelming way in which he had been *bouleversé* by Jacqueline all those years ago – Felicity could not have been more different, and he was, what, more than thirty years older – but just as powerfully. He observed the round cushion of flesh beneath her chin ... the swift delicacy of her hands with their uptilted fingertips, that reminded him of birds ... a small brown spot on the grey-blue iris of her left eye ... the surprisingly lush and buoyant curve that swelled below her slim waist. She reminded him of a Flemish painting. He felt an intense curiosity, an insistent tender longing to know this woman, to peel off not just her clothes but her layers of accumulated experience, so different from his, to the point where the two of them shared a common soul. In other words, Will wanted to sleep with Felicity, but the rules of engagement, unlike the brutally simple ones of most of his encounters, were unclear. He wasn't sure how to proceed, and that was another reason for his craven prevarication now.

The moment he'd got back to the college, after a breakfast with an unparalleled cholesterol count, he sat in a chair in the corner of the JCR, looking out over the garden, and dialled her number. Her recorded voice answered, with a lively charm that brought her face before him: *I'm so sorry I missed you! Please do leave your name and number so I can call you the minute I'm back. Or you could try my mobile* (she repeated the number). *Many thanks.*

He couldn't quite match the natural warmth of her tone, so opted for simplicity:

'Fliss, I'd very much like to come down at the weekend if the offer's still open – I'll get there around five on Saturday unless there's any problem. Cheers.'

The minute he'd rung off, he wished he hadn't said 'cheers' – how much of a prat did that make him sound? And how inadequate when he was in the grip of this – this yearning. But it was too late now. And one thing she wasn't, he told himself, was judgemental.

At her insistence, he got there a little earlier, at four – there was something she was 'dying' to show him. There was already a warm, winey fragrance in the air from the beef stew simmering in the oven. The living room was untidy, a litter of papers scattered over the sofa and on the floor. A well-established fire glowed in the grate. She brought in mugs of tea and date loaf and sat him in an armchair with everything to hand. He couldn't take his eyes off her, with her round pink cheeks and shining eyes, her delectable figure swamped in a huge Aran jumper (Tony's, he surmised) over faded jeans and suede boots.

'This is all very mysterious,' he said. 'I can't wait.'

She chuckled. A sexy chuckle – he was beginning to find everything about her sexy. 'Are you sitting comfortably?'

'I'll say.'

'You remember when you came down the first time, and I took you for a walk through the gardens of that old house, down to the church?'

'Certainly. You were speculating about the people who used to live there.'

'I was! And in the churchyard there we saw a mysterious grave.'

'Maurice.'

'That's right – I'm so glad you do remember.'

He wanted to say that of course he did, because he went over and over their meetings in his mind. Instead he smiled and frowned, as if cudgelling his brains.

'And something about peace ...'

'Which is pretty common on gravestones, but which in his case had a special significance. He was a conscientious objector.'

'How do you know?'

'Because as a result of that day, I finally got round to doing my researches on the house, Chilverton House, and it turns out he was part of that family.'

Will felt his interest shrink back a little, guarding itself. 'Chilverton House?'

'That's right.' She stared at him intently, her face bright with enthusiasm. 'Why, does that ring a bell?'

'Sort of. The place where my grandmother grew up was called Chilverton House.'

'And is this where it was?'

'It was in Kent, certainly.'

'You've never seen it?'

'No, but I gather it was quite a pile.'

'Will!' Felicity brought her hands together, fingers laced. 'This might be your family!'

'I never heard of anyone called Maurice.'

'Maybe he was airbrushed out, if he was a conchie. And the poor chap died in nineteen eighteen, when he was still quite young. It's so, so sad.'

Will pulled a wry face. 'I should think the exercise of conscience at that time could wear a man down.'

'Or the Spanish flu – that's my theory.'

'Who knows.'

He was backing off fast now, propelled by the old habit of putting distance between him and the tentacles of family involvement. But if Felicity had noticed, she was too polite to show it.

'I think I missed my vocation, I should have been a journalist.' She paused, perhaps waiting for some encouragement or a question, which didn't come. 'I began with the parish records, which showed Maurice's funeral, and then I went to the office of the local newspaper armed with my one bit of information and they sat me down in front of a computer screen and away I went.'

He felt obliged to say something now, if only for form's sake. 'Electronics have revolutionised that sort of thing. No more grubby old cuttings libraries. Though I have to say, I had a fondness for them.'

'The family were called Tennant, but as far as I could tell, he was a cousin who lived with them, because he didn't have the same surname. Does that mean anything to you – Tennant?'

Will felt himself trapped. Netted.

'Yes.'

'It does? I knew it! Are they connected to you?'

'It seems likely. I believe Tennant was my grandmother's maiden name.'

'And she lived at Chilverton House – of course it's her; this was your family, Will! The house originally belonged to people called D'Acre, and when Lady D'Acre died, their daughter went to live there with her husband, who was called Ralph Tennant – your great-grandfather! They moved there from London with three young children. They must have walked along that path, the one we went along, just as I imagined. Oh, this is so exciting – look ...'

She began picking up pieces of paper from the floor, the sofa, and tried to give them to him, but he held up his hand.

'Actually – Fliss, do you mind? I don't feel – I'm not quite ready for all this.'

'No? Don't worry, Will, it's not a problem.' She was trying to cover it up now, to regroup, but he could tell she was crestfallen. 'I got carried away with the whole thing. I'm so ridiculously proud of myself for finding this out, but presumably it's all there in some corner of a family cupboard.'

'Presumably.'

'I tell you what.' She glanced at him. 'I'm going to put everything in a Jiffy Bag and you can take it away to look at in peace.'

'Maybe. I'll see.'

'I needed to do this anyway ...' She began tidying up, shuffling papers together and putting them in two piles on the coffee table. Her voice shook slightly. 'Some of this is my Sitting Pretty accounts. My nice financial adviser would blanch if he could see the way I carry on. And Tony was forensically organised, but I do manage in spite of appearances.' He half rose to help, and she flashed a smile without meeting his eyes. 'Don't bother. All done.'

'I'm so sorry,' he said. 'I just—'

'Will. Enough. I understand. I jumped on you.'

'I hope you do understand, Fliss. Things are all a bit tricky with regard to my family.'

She didn't reply to this, but picked up the papers and their tea mugs, and touched his shoulder lightly as she passed his chair. For the few minutes that she was out of the room he sat there shaken, drained by a mixture of shock and relief. He had worked so hard – and so far succeeded – to keep his association with Felicity separate, but now it was being encroached upon by these 'discoveries' of hers. He couldn't share her pleasure in them – it was not in him. All he wanted was to push them away, to turn the clock back to how things had been before.

She re-entered and kissed him lightly on the cheek. 'I'm going to do things in the kitchen. You make yourself at home – papers, telly ... Or you can keep me company, I always like that.'

He remained where he was, and found an old film, *Double Indemnity*, to fill the cell of silence that surrounded him.

It was inevitable that over supper with the Hamburys, the subject of plans for Christmas should arise. Crispin and Pauline were staying put, hosting the day for their offspring and grandchildren, deflecting all expressions of sympathy about the amount of work that would entail.

'To be honest,' said Pauline, 'we rather like it when it's our turn. No driving, our own beds, and everyone pitches in. What about you, Fliss? Coming to Boxing Day drinks, I hope?'

'I'm afraid I shall be on my travels. I'm going up to bring a little seasonal cheer to my daughter in Cumbria, and then to France for a big new year with the other lot. In some ways I'd be quite happy here on my own, seeing a few friends, but they'd all worry if I did that.'

Crispin turned to Will. 'What about you, somewhere exotic? Santa in the sun?'

'Actually not. It seems likely I shall be where they do Christmas best, in Germany – Heidelberg, as a matter of fact.'

There was a murmur of polite envy, then Pauline just had to say, 'Not on the day itself, surely?'

'Well, Christmas Eve, *Heiligabend*, is the big thing over there, and it's important I'm there for that – so yes, I imagine I'll still be there on the twenty-fifth.'

'Where will you stay?' asked Crispin. 'I bet these jaunts do you pretty well.'

'Not always the most expensive, but characteristic.'

'I'm sorry, but I'd hate it,' said Pauline. 'However nice it was, I'd still be horribly lonely.'

Without looking at Felicity, Will said, 'Not necessarily. Fliss just said it, she'd rather like to be home alone.'

Pauline was having none of it. 'But that's the operative word, "home" – by her own fireside, and with friends she can be in touch with whenever she wants to. Not stranded on her tod in some foreign city.'

He shrugged. The others had turned to Felicity for her endorsement, but she was putting plates in the dishwasher and was not to be drawn.

Talk became louder, looser and more general as the wine flowed, and Will gave good conversational value; not the lonely unmarried man but the unfettered singleton, the life and soul. Felicity was the quietest of the four, but she too listened and laughed like the good hostess she was, relaxing now that dinner was over, letting her guests make the social running.

The party broke up just before midnight. When the others had left, he helped with the last of the clearing up. Bramble was already asleep in his basket by the Aga. Will was mellow with drink but all his senses were alert too, like those of a teenager aching for sex. They stood together in the doorway as she turned out the kitchen light and he could no longer contain himself; it was the most natural thing in the world to put his arms round her. She stood quite still, neither responding nor withdrawing. She felt wonderful – soft, warm, tremendously alive, her body still humming with the conviviality she had generated.

'Fliss …' he whispered. He looked down, and she turned her head to one side, looking away from him, her cheek just touching his shoulder. 'Fliss?'

'No, Will.'

He wasn't sure whether he'd heard her; or, if he had, what she meant. 'What?'

'I don't …' She lifted her hands and pushed gently outwards at his arms. 'I don't want this.'

'Not now? You're not ready …'

'Not at all.'

'God, Fliss!'

He was mortified; sickened. She pushed at his chest, and he realised that in another second she'd be struggling, and released her.

'I apologise. I got it wrong.'

'That's all right. Let's go to bed.'

Will couldn't remember when he had last felt this crestfallen. He had been so sure, the circumstances so perfectly easy and natural, and yet he'd been rejected, and not conditionally, either.

She said, quietly, 'Good night, sleep well.'

'Good night.'

Will couldn't bring himself to follow her up the stairs, like a child banished to his own room. Instead he went back into the kitchen. The blind was up and there was a faint wash of light on the lawn from the moon and a couple of upstairs rooms as Felicity got ready for bed. He sat down at the table, now bare as an altar, and laid his clasped hands on the surface, praying to someone for something, he wasn't sure what. Bramble rolled an eye at him before losing interest and sinking back into gently wheezing sleep.

The optimistic, sociable phase of the alcohol was wearing off, its departure accelerated by humiliation. Glumly, he recalled the earlier awkwardness about her researches into the Tennant family. Why the hell had he been so prissy about that? He had only to pretend interest, to admire the work she'd done, to say he'd check it out elsewhere. To do so would have cost nothing and achieved, simply and gracefully, the desired outcome. He pressed his linked fingers bruisingly against his brow. *Listen to yourself*, he thought. *You wish you had behaved better, so you could be in bed with her now.* But in answer to his plaintive question she'd replied 'Not at all'; so perhaps nothing he'd done tonight would have made any difference. She simply didn't fancy him, didn't want him, was still mourning her husband.

Jesus H Christ ... He rubbed his knuckles in his eyes. *Grow up!*

The next morning, at first anyway, a brittle normality prevailed. He hated the sham, her making breakfast and talking about the Hamburys, and producing the neatly sealed Jiffy Bag containing her researches, pretending nothing had happened. After a couple of cups of strong coffee he nerved himself to say:

'I think perhaps I should get an earlier train. If there's one mid morning.'

She didn't demur. 'Eleven thirty. A slow one, but it'll get you back to town in time for lunch.'

'That sounds fine.'

They'd taken the cafetière into the living room, and she was lighting the fire. When, he wondered, had she cleared the old one? She was tireless, she got on with things.

'Will.' She had her back to him, striking a match.

He steeled himself for whatever was coming. 'Yes?'

'I'm sorry about last night. I mean, in the sense that it was unfortunate. Not that I have anything to apologise for.'

'I think the apology's my bit, isn't it?'

She didn't answer, but sat back on her heels, watching the fire catch and blaze, adding coals one by one with a pair of brass tongs. He didn't know what else to say to her; the fire gave them both something to look at, to cover the silence. A moment later she kneeled up and held out her hand.

'Could you?'

He leapt up and offered his hand to receive hers, to help her to her feet.

'Thank you.'

The gesture, and the feel of her that travelled the length of his arm, had rekindled his hopes, but as soon as she was standing, she let go and stepped away from him, a little awkwardly, with her arms folded. When she next spoke, it was in a tone that made his heart plummet.

'Did you mean it – about going to Heidelberg for Christmas?'

'I did, yes. Trip's not finally confirmed, but—'

'I can't believe it, Will. I simply can't.'

'Why? It is my job, after all.'

'But this is Christmas we're talking about.' She leaned slightly forward, arms still folded, even more tightly, as if restraining herself. 'People have time off.'

'What about nurses – people like that?'

'You're not "people like that", you're a journalist. And you have a family, Will!' Here it came. 'A family who would like to see you, and who you should be with.'

'Both of those propositions are debatable,' he said, pompously.

'Don't be pathetic!' Now she loosed her arms and threw her hands up in a gesture of furious exasperation. Her cheeks were pink and he was astonished – horrified – to see tears in her eyes. 'You are pathetic, do you know that, with your excuses and evasions? Do you honestly think that your mother and your daughter and your grandson would gasp in disapproval if you showed up, for once? Of course they wouldn't. I'm the last person to be holier-than-thou, but I'll be running around like a headless chicken in a couple of weeks' time in an attempt to see my lot, who live miles away and in opposite directions, and you can't even be bothered to take a short train ride to be with yours, after all this time.'

'Fliss, please …' He sat down, utterly deflated.

'It's a disgrace, Will! Didn't you say your grandson was a chorister? He's probably doing something amazing at Christmas, singing his heart out, and you won't be there to see and hear him! And I hate to be cruel, but how many Christmases does your mother have left?'

'She's in excellent health as far as—'

'As far as you know, quite! And your daughter, what's going on

435

in her life? You said she was divorced, she's on her own; don't you think she might like you to show just a little fatherly interest?'

Feeling at a serious disadvantage, Will stood up. At once she turned away from him and stomped – there was no other word for it – to the window, where she remained with her back to him. He'd never seen her like this; it was both impressive and a little frightening. The thought of his advance the previous night made his flesh crawl with shame all over again. He cleared his throat.

'It isn't what I wanted, Fliss.' Silence. She swiped her hand back over her hair; he thought she might be crying. 'They were angry with me for letting Jacqueline take charge of Evie, for being a lousy father – and I suppose it became a self-fulfilling—'

'Shut up!' Now she turned on him. She had been crying; her face was hot and fierce. 'Go!' She picked up the package of research papers and threw it at him, hard. 'Take these, in which it's obvious you have no bloody interest whatsoever, and clear out! You're a sad, cowardly man, Will, and I just wish that was all you were, because then I wouldn't have invited you into my life!'

The package had struck his shoulder and fallen to the floor. She rushed forward and picked it up again before he could; he actually flinched a split second before she smacked it across his face and then again in the direction of his heart, so that his arms instinctively went around it, protecting himself. One of the corners had caught him in the eye, which now began to stream. He heard but could not see her leave the room and run up the stairs.

He was shaking when eventually he went up to collect his bag. There was no sound; her bedroom door was shut. He briefly considered knocking, or even going straight in, but did neither. Downstairs he found the telephone pad and a pencil and began to write a note of apology, but all the phrases he came up with appeared so abject – 'pathetic' – that he didn't do that, either. His reflection in the hall mirror showed his left eye suffused with red.

It was a half-hour walk to the station. His arm ached; the MO had said he might get arthritis later on. Along the way a car drew up and the window rolled down to reveal Crispin Hambury.

'Need a lift?'

'I'm fine,' he said. 'Walk'll do me good.'

'Everything okay? Where's Fliss?'

'Having a lie-in.'

'Good idea.' Crispin plainly didn't believe him but was too nice a man to probe. 'Right, well, if you're sure … Happy Christmas, if we don't see you before. And we're having a bit of a bash for the millennium, if you're not doing anything else – you don't have to let us know, just turn up. Pauline's ordered fireworks.'

'Thanks, Cris.'

'Enjoy Heidelberg.'

'Cheers,' he said. 'I will.'

Chapter Forty-One

1999

'Of course you should go!' said Kate. 'You mustn't give it a second thought.'

'Are you quite sure, Ma?'

Stella wanted to be certain, and for that she had to go through the motions of unselfish filial reluctance, even though she was almost positive both she and her mother were of one mind. 'I do so hate to rat on you at this time of year.'

The small room was bright and gently seasonal – Kate would have no truck with an artificial tree and had no room for a real one, but she had her usual creamy poinsettia, and Stella had brought her a big spray of Scotch fir, which stood in the tall African pot, strewn with small white lights and a scattering of sparkly decorations. The decorations were among Stella's earliest memories – they were German, bought in Berlin just after the war, tiny angels of gold wire, clad in white cotton embroidered with stars.

The two of them were having their traditional large G and Ts; on a table between them sat a plate of M&S sushi canapés, brought by Stella, to which they were doing full justice. Each privately considered that the other was looking particularly attractive tonight. Kate beamed indulgently.

'You know me better than that, surely. For one thing, I would *never* think you were ratting on me, and for another, this is exactly the time of year for doing these things. I shall have plenty of people around me; in fact the way things are going, I shall be spoilt for choice. Evie has asked me, and I've also been invited out by Ian for Christmas lunch at the Watermill. Who knows, I may well do both.'

'You are so popular, Ma. In that case, I shall stop worrying.'

'Please. Tell me, how's the little girl …?'

In the hall, Kate placed her hands on Stella's shoulders. Stella had forgotten how commanding her mother could be, even in old age. She felt a flicker of apprehension.

'What?'

'Don't look so nervous! I only want to tell you something.'

'And that is … ?'

Kate removed her hands and touched Stella's cheeks lightly. 'That I am very like Dulcie. And so, in some ways, are you. Ah –' she stopped Stella from speaking – 'you'd be surprised. A very, very long time ago I nearly threw everything over and ran away. But I made a decision not to, and I've been glad for it every since. What I'm trying to say is, we may own the past, but we don't belong to it.' There was a pause; they looked into each other's eyes, almost too close for comfort. Kate tilted her head.

'Hm?'

'I hear you, Ma. I do.'

They exchanged a simple, everyday kiss. Kate opened the door.

'Now off you go. Safe journey.'

When Stella had gone, Kate took the sushi plate and her daughter's glass into the kitchen, and poured herself another drink. Her appetite was healthy but her capacity small these days; she wouldn't need any supper.

She felt wonderfully light-hearted, and knew it wasn't just the gin. At last, she had said her piece. For too long her daughter had been becalmed, treading water, doing worthy work that neither stretched her nor made her much money, and associating with a succession of men who weren't nearly good enough for her. This may have been a stereotypical maternal response, but it was also plainly true. Stella's line was that she had her life, in the modern parlance, sorted; that she was a free agent. But to Kate it had always looked more as if she had arranged boundaries and remained within them. There had not been enough impulsiveness. Recent reminders of her own past should perhaps have acted as a dreadful warning against acting on impulse but there was, surely, a middle way? Kate did not wish her daughter married, but she did wish her happy, exhilarated by love. When the Canadian boyfriend was over, there had been a light in Stella's eye that Kate had never seen before; her whole person and manner had acquired a shine, a glow designed to gladden a mother's heart.

Kate had half expected that Stella might not return from Montreal that first time, or that the return would be brief, a mere interval in which to put things in order before taking off for a new life. But no, Stella had come back, and the weeks, now months had gone by, and he'd had to cancel his next visit. Kate had needed to remind herself that at their age she had been married for twenty-five years and had two grown-up children; perhaps the course of true love ran more slowly in the second half of life. But all the more reason why the moment, when it came, must be seized.

She took her drink back into the living room and switched off the table lamps. Then she drew back the curtains and sat down in her chair, in darkness but for the lights on her Christmas bough. Rectory Court was on the edge of the village, and the windows of her flat faced across the quadrangle, with only the low roofs opposite between her and the East Anglian fields; there was little light pollution, and the broad rectangle of the midwinter night sky was pricked with stars. Kate's mind seemed to break free, and float. For the first time in, oh, years, she felt entirely herself, unshackled by the complexities of family life, present and past. The blessed clarity was like a drink of cool water after a long, hot walk.

Some good had come of Mallory's interference. Acknowledgement, resolution … closure, as it was now called. Stella was going to take her advice. Now, as her mother's daughter, she must take it herself.

The local amateur operatic society were putting on *Oklahoma!* as their pre-Christmas production – she had bought two tickets back in August, with an open mind as to who might come with her, but now she rang Ian and invited him.

'Remember this time last year, at dinner – Dolly played some of the tunes.'

'And such wonderful tunes. How much do I owe you?'

'Nothing, my treat. You be i/c transport for the evening.'

'And dinner afterwards, perhaps, at l'Artista?'

'Even better.'

When, at six forty-five on the Friday before Christmas, he

turned up to collect her, she saw a white-lit 'Taxi' sign in the road behind him.

'Such extravagance!'

'I want to be able to enjoy a glass of l'Artista's rather decent Chianti.' He held the door open for her. 'And it is the festive season.'

'I think it's an excellent idea.'

In the back of the cab, he gazed at her with undisguised admiration. 'You look smashing, Kate.'

'Thank you.' She looked down at herself, touched Lawrence's brooch. 'Not too overdressed?'

'I shall be the proudest man at the show.'

Both agreed they couldn't have liked it more. On the short walk from theatre to restaurant they laughed at themselves for singing choruses and snatches of the wonderful lyrics. L'Artista was buzzing with seasonal cheer: a full house, decorations hanging from the ceiling, tinsel garlands draped from lamp to lamp along the walls, greenery around the candlesticks and Dean Martin warbling in the background (so much nicer, they agreed, than the ubiquitous canned Christmas carols and seasonal pop).

It was ten o'clock – late, by their standards – and they were hungry; they decided to work their way through the card in the Italian manner, but sharing the antipasti and pasta courses. Kate had a veal cutlet with spinach, and Ian steak and chips. With that they were almost ready to call a halt, but a fifteen-minute break and another glass of wine persuaded them to take a leaf from the book of the couple next door and order three scoops of ice cream in one dish, with two spoons.

'I don't know about you,' said Ian, shaving off a mouthful, 'but my parents would have had a fit.'

'No,' she shook her head, 'mine wouldn't. Not my mother, anyway.' She realised that she was talking about Thea, and hesitated. She had two mothers now. 'No, she definitely wouldn't.'

'Anyway,' he said, 'it's one of the more sensible modern habits. And neighbourly.'

'Neighbourly!' She laughed at him.

'Friendly, then.'

They had coffee – who cared if they were wakeful; uninterrupted sleep was a thing of the past anyway – and Ian accompanied his with a glass of Italian brandy. He raised it to her.

'This has been the most wonderful evening. Thank you, Kate, for inviting me.'

'I can't think of anyone I'd rather have spent it with,' she replied. 'And it's not over yet.'

'Not quite – taxi's here.'

The white light waited patiently at the kerb as Ian finished his brandy, moved Kate's chair and took her coat from the attentive waiter.

In a typically chivalrous gesture, Ian had settled up with the driver at the beginning of the evening, so there was no rustling of notes and clinking of change on the pavement, simply thank you and good night. He accompanied her to the door, and she opened it – she had left the Christmas lights on, and the radio tuned to music while she was out.

'How nice everything looks,' he said.

'Why don't you come in for a nightcap?'

'I don't know …' He turned his left wrist in a small, involuntary gesture. 'Isn't it a little …?'

'Does that matter?' She smiled, eyebrows raised. 'What are you doing tomorrow?'

'Point taken.' He stepped over the threshold. 'If anyone can afford to be night owls, we can – thank you.'

They hung up their coats and went into the living room. This time Kate had closed the curtains, and the little apartment was beautifully warm and full of the scent of pine and the sound of mellow jazz. She didn't switch on the lamps, but turned to face him.

'What can I get you, Ian?'

'I don't know … I think I've had enough to drink.'

'So – what would you like?'

They stood close together in the twinkling half darkness. Surely there could be no mistaking her meaning, but she sensed his hesitancy, and stepped towards him, laying her palms flat on his lapels. 'Ian?'

'Kate …'

'I know what I would like,' she said, in a voice barely above a whisper, just audible through the gentle music. Eye to eye with him in her high heels, she leaned forward and touched her lips to his. At once she sensed that lovely, familiar response, heard a small sound in his throat and felt his lips part and his body first tense, then release, moving into that other, unpredictable place where who knew what could happen ... Oh, how she had missed this!

'Come.' She took his hand and was astonished, thrilled, to find he was trembling. Her mother's daughter.

'Come – come with me.'

Chapter Forty-Two

1999

Will liked Germany, always had. He was of the view that the Germans weren't just like us, they *were* us – or we were them. Given any mixed group of tourists in any city in the world, he prided himself on his ability, born of his many years' professional travelling, to identify different nationalities at a glance, but Germans were the trickiest, the people you were most likely to mistake for Brits, and vice versa. He liked their towns, their buildings, their homes, their language, their comforting cuisine – and their motorways.

On the autobahn between Frankfurt-Hahn and Heidelberg, he let rip. The hired VW estate took off like a bird and for about an hour his speed scarcely dropped below a hundred and thirty, which even in translation was going some, and all guilt-free – he was legal. His flight had landed at midday, so there was plenty of light, and for added value his storming drive took him between vast rolling vineyards, winter-brown just now but a reminder of some of the many pleasures that awaited him.

He could scarcely forbear to cheer as he overtook a white Mercedes E-Class as if it were standing still. He had escaped. He had not allowed himself to be pussy-whipped; he'd got his head back up and bloody well got on with the job he was paid to do. This was who he was: a free spirit, a loner, an independent operator. If Felicity, or any other woman, wanted something different, they must look elsewhere.

He was not entirely without conscience or a sense of family duty; he had bought and posted presents for Kate, Stella, Evie and Raff, and sent Raff a special card wishing him well for the Christmas Eve service and expressing regret that yet again he couldn't be there. Oh, and Jacqueline; he'd seen her a couple of days ago and bought her dinner, but they had not slept together. He had been ready for it to happen, but somehow the mood hadn't been right. She'd asked whether he was going to Raff's service.

'No, unfortunately. I've got a job over Christmas.'

'That's ridiculous. Anyone would think you were in some sort of essential occupation.'

'The money's good.'

'Oh well.' She'd offered up her glass for more wine. 'That's all right then.'

She always seemed to think she had the right to needle him. 'I take it you're not?' he asked. 'Going to the service?'

'Certainly not. Parenting was quite enough for me; I don't do grandparenting and I certainly don't do church, as you well know.'

He was amazed at her ability to state, without a hint of self-consciousness, what her own rules were. The full weight of his family's disapproval descended on him, while Jacqueline did exactly as she pleased and got off scot free.

'I saw Evie a couple of weeks ago,' she went on. 'You know she's going to marry this policeman?'

He didn't, but neither was he going to let on. 'I did get that impression.'

'In the spring.'

'I'm pleased for her. She's been alone too long. Is Raff happy about it?'

'I imagine so. I'm sure they've discussed it. Maybe' – she slid him a mocking look – 'you'll be asked to give her away.'

He thought about this now, as the steep wooded slopes of the Neckar valley appeared to the south-west. The remark had been intended as a joke, of course, albeit a cruel one and in poor taste, because hadn't he given Evie away a long time ago?

He'd tried to turn her comment back at her. 'What about you – the mother of the bride? Floral hat and tears?'

She laughed her hoarse, sexy laugh. 'Can you imagine?'

'That's not an answer.'

'It won't be that sort of wedding. They're going for a small civil ceremony in the garden of a riverside pub. Mostly friends and a few close family.'

She'd used the phrase as if that excluded (and perhaps exonerated) the two of them. But then she'd added, airily, 'She did ask me if I'd go, and I very well might ...' She left the comment hanging for him to make of it what he would. Remembering, he shook his head, admiring and resentful in equal measure; she was a piece of work.

He slowed to come off the autobahn, and joined the briskly moving stream of traffic on the Heidelberg-bound dual carriageway. Spring was a long way off; anything could happen between now and then, a lot more water under the bridge. But if there was any chance Jacqueline was going to be at the wedding, he couldn't see himself being there. Anyway, Evie hadn't mentioned it to him, let alone extended an invitation. It was safe to assume she'd written him off. Time went by and situations hardened and set, like scar tissue.

He was glad he was here. Free. And safe.

The hotel exceeded his expectations. Bang on the cobbled central *Platz*, timbered and gabled, the windows glowing with hospitable warmth, the sign a gilded flourish of Germanic script, smoke curling up from a chimney on the lower slopes of the tiled roof. The great church on the other side of the square was surrounded by brightly lit stalls buzzing with music and people, like an animated Christmas wreath. Taverns heaved with revellers, food shops were all piled high with more abundant, beautiful and enticing fare than Selfridge's food hall, and the pedestrianised streets swarmed with cheerful people of all ages, dressed colourfully for the cold like characters on a Christmas card. On the forested slopes on either side of the river house lights twinkled in the trees. The forbidding castle overlooking the town had become a floodlit fairy palace. This place, he would tell his readers, was a dream of Christmas.

He handed over the VW to be valet-parked in the car park beneath the square, and checked in, his modest German put smoothly in its place by the barely accented English of the receptionist in his maroon and gold uniform. The green spire of the tree in the centre of the lobby reached up as high as the first-floor gallery; hard to imagine how they'd got it in there, let alone decorated it with strings of white candle lights, flights of silver doves and constellations of gold stars. A log fire burned in the enormous fireplace, and guests were helping themselves to tea, coffee and cakes from a white-clothed table.

The room where he left his bag was about as picturesque as it could be, with ash-coloured beams, exactly the right amount of comfortable repro furniture, a magnificent four-poster and a diamond-paned dormer window overlooking the square. A square slab of plain dark chocolate, four squares by four wrapped in brown paper and red string, lay on a white plate by the bed. Perfect. The room was warm, deliciously so after the glittering late-afternoon cold outside, but he still tried the window, which opened easily and had a sturdy latch. So far, ten out of ten.

But the nuts and bolts of what the magazine termed the 'hotel experience' were not what Will's columns were all about. He needed to get out there to test the water, soak up the atmosphere, observe locals and visitors at play – particularly today, with the afternoon drawing in. He needed to be one of the crowd. He unpacked his few things, then shrugged on a fleece gilet, replaced his coat, stuffed gloves and a cap in the pockets and left his key at reception.

Will had never suffered from that special urban loneliness of which one read and heard. To be on his own in the throng of a city – especially a foreign one – was for him the quickest way to peace of mind and body. Alone among strangers he felt most himself; or, more truthfully, he could turn on a sixpence and become whoever he wanted to be. As he stepped out into the brilliant, tuneful bustle of the square, in this city enfolded by dark forest, he felt his heartbeat grow steady and his breathing slow to a more gentle rhythm; the blood in his arteries seemed to flow strong and clear as the river beneath its ancient bridge. Calm and content, he walked first to the bridge and stood at the halfway point. In front of him, downstream, he could just make out the paler dark where the valley opened out. When he turned to look back, the darkness was deeper and more mysterious, pricked by the small lights of houses among the trees. Across the sliding black surface of the river wriggled the pale shimmer of the weir beneath which the devil – visitors were told – lay in wait for the unwary.

Back in town, he walked the streets, going in and out of shops, browsing the stalls around the church and winding up in a tavern where there was music, wheat beer and mountainous comfort food. When he'd finished there, he went to another, and then a third. By the time he strolled into the church, he was pleasantly pissed and disposed to be friends with everyone he met. He shouldn't get ratted on the job, he knew that, but he had three more clear days in which to write his piece, and he reckoned he deserved a break; God knows, everyone else was enjoying themselves.

There were people in the church, and the organ was twiddling away merrily; the window sconces were full of greenery with fat white lighted candles like blossoms growing out of the branches, and further up, near the chancel steps, was a thatched crib, as big as a small cottage with – how the dickens had they done that? – a lighted star hanging over it. Everything was nice, welcoming. A man in a black clerical gown greeted him with a smile and asked him something in German, which he didn't quite catch. The man repeated the question in English.

'We are going to have a short service, some Christmas music – would you like to join us?'

'Why not?'

'Please.' The man pressed a book and a sheet of paper into his hand. 'Sit where you like.'

'Thanks. Okay.'

Will meandered up the south aisle and slid into a pew about halfway back. There were a couple of smart middle-aged women in fur-trimmed coats at the far end of the pew, with whom, from habit, he exchanged a warm smile as he sat down halfway, and unzipped his jacket. He looked at his watch – eight o'clock local time, only seven for him. The night was young; he could afford this religious interlude in the interests of research. He must be early, because the place continued to fill up round him; this must be the equivalent of ... His mind drifted, halted, backed off; of he didn't know what.

A family came into the pew on the other side of him – a handsome, well-turned-out couple in their early forties – she might have been a squeak younger – with two children, a boy and a girl of thirteen or fourteen. The girl was tall, already a young lady, in tight jeans, black boots and a faux-fur jacket; the boy handsome but still growing and gauche, looking out from beneath a dark curly fringe and beetling brows. The woman nodded hello to Will, and leaned forward to wave at the closer of the two older women. It was clear they knew each other, had been intending to sit together. Filled with goodwill, he rose to his feet and made ushering gestures.

'Please ... I'll go on the end.'

After a certain amount of polite whispering, the family allowed him to slither to the end of the pew and they all changed places. When they were seated once more, the man, his face dark and a little haggard above his sheepskin collar, offered a '*Vielen Dank, mein Herr.*'

'My pleasure.'

'English?'

'Yes.'

'Welcome to Heidelberg.'

They consulted their service sheets – it might have been Sanskrit as far as Will was concerned – and the people continued to come in. A fat elderly gentleman with troublesome adenoids demanded to squeeze in on the end of Will's pew. Two boys in red cassocks used tapers to light the candles – as tall as they were – that stood on the altar. The organ played something pensive.

Covertly, Will observed the family on his left. The woman with her friend on the far end was clearly the grandmother of the two children, though whose mother she was he couldn't say, since whether daughter or daughter-in-law the younger woman – red-haired, chic in a suede trench coat – was the sociable one. The teenage girl was abstracted and cool, sitting tall in her seat, her programme held loosely on her lap, her perfectly made-up eyes gazing at some point above the altar, probably at a rather less spiritual image in her mind's eye. The boy was – well, the boy reminded him of Raff. Physically he was the same type – the luxuriant dark hair, the pale skin and grey eyes, the long, fidgety hands – but a year or so on. This lad provided a pretty good picture of what Raff would be like when puberty really kicked in and before confidence caught up with it.

The organ boomed; the service began. A red-robed choir trooped in, a brace of clergy in festive kit bringing up the rear; the congregation rose to its feet.

The whole thing took a lot longer than Will had expected. Longer, more formal and full-on, and incomprehensible – his restaurant German did not stretch to a full-blown Catholic liturgy. He realised he had been expecting something like a traditional Nine Lessons and Carols, but this service was heavy-duty worship. There were no familiar tunes, and about forty minutes in, the older of the two clerics delivered himself of an interminable sermon, which was closely followed by an equally lengthy giving of communion. His earlier warm benevolence began to wear thin. He was tired, his feet were cold and he was developing a headache. He considered slipping away during the mass, but neither the children's father nor the stertorously breathing old man went up to the altar, and he didn't quite feel up to rudely edging past them. When the clergy and choir finally began to process out and the last chords of the recessional sounded, any idea of partying the night away had gone. He wanted only to get back to the hotel and lie down.

The old man on the end had the most terrible difficulty getting to his feet and Will assisted as best he could, praying that he wouldn't have to help him the whole way to the door, or worse. Fortunately the German father was on the case, taking the old man's other arm, making reassuring remarks and steering him on his way. It was now Will's turn to say '*Vielen Dank*.'

The man smiled – comforting to see that he looked a great deal more cheery and approachable now the service was over. 'No problem. I think he has been toasting the season.'

'You could be right.' Will wondered if his own breath smelt of beer and aquavit. 'Well. *Fröhliche Weihnachten*.'

Any plans he'd had for a quick escape were thwarted by the crush of people moving slowly down the aisle towards the west door; he found himself once more ranged alongside the family, who were all beaming at him. Even the boy had got his head up. The mother leant across and offered her leather-gloved hand.

'Happy Christmas to you.'

'And you.'

'You enjoyed the service?'

'It was most impressive.'

The man asked, 'You're here on your own?'

'I am, yes. I'm working,' he explained. 'I'm a writer.'

The grandmother chipped in with something in German; they were an insanely sociable lot. The woman laughed. 'My mother-in-law asks why working? Over Christmas?'

Will smiled weakly. He'd come all this way to escape this kind of stuff, and here it was happening to him anyway. They emerged into the church porch. Outside, snow was falling, enormous Disneyesque flakes drifting down into the medieval square. He was conscious of some sort of brief murmured exchange between the woman and her husband, and then the man said:

'We are Gerhart and Marianne Karol. This is my mother, Liselotte, and our children Frieda and George.'

'How do you do.' Will shook more hands. 'Pleased to meet you. Will Drake.'

'If you would like to have dinner with us tomorrow – *Heiligabend* – we would be delighted.' The man produced a card from his breast pocket and handed it to Will. 'Where are you staying?'

'At the Berghof.'

'Beautiful,' said the woman approvingly. 'But we should like it very much if you would come to us. We have fish, you know.'

The grandmother leaned across and tapped his wrist; she spoke slowly and loudly, as if she'd been building up to this: 'Zere – house – is – byudderful.'

They all laughed; she'd done well, apparently. People were surging past into the snow. Will told himself he would not – need not – ever see these nice, decent, generous people again. What did it mater if he offended them?

'I'm sorry,' he said. 'It's extraordinarily kind of you, but I can't. I have to work, Christmas or not. Thank you so much. I'm sorry.'

He didn't wait for their reaction, but pushed his way roughly through the crowd and headed off in the direction of the bridge, away from the cobbled streets and the shops, the car parks and taverns, to where he could most easily disappear.

Shaken, he stood on the bridge, his chest heaving, spewing out great clouds of steam into the ever-heavier snow. They probably thought him slightly mad.

His defences had been breached. He was no longer safe, sound nor sure. The devil lay at his back, beneath the weir.

If you didn't count the polite surprise on the face of the receptionist, there was no problem checking out – the account was taken care of.

'You are leaving us already, sir?'

'Something's come up – a family crisis.' He reassured himself that this was the simple truth. 'I need to get back to England.'

The man shook his head. 'That is going to be extremely difficult.'

'I know.' Did he think Will was stupid? 'But I hope not impossible. Anyway, I intend to try.'

'Would you like me to call the airport for you, sir?' He lifted the receiver. 'Which one will you go to?'

'I don't know … I flew in to Frankfurt-Hahn.'

'It's snowing hard. Shall I ring both?'

The question was rhetorical. The hotel had all the numbers stored; the man clicked a button and adopted a waiting face, while Will paced fretfully. He longed, needed, to be gone, while the adrenalin was still pumping and he still felt sufficiently single-minded not to care about anything else.

The man tilted the receiver under his chin to speak to him. 'Don't worry about the car; you can leave it with the company at either airport.'

The two calls seemed to take forever. Will saw the VW pull up outside; the driver came in and plopped the keys down on the counter. He dragged a five-euro note out of his pocket and handed it over. What the hell.

'So …' At last. The receptionist put the handset down. 'You have a better chance at Frankfurt. There is nothing at the moment, but if you go right away and present yourself at the desk …'

'Thanks.' Will picked up his bag, swiped the keys off the desk and headed for the door. 'Sorry about this, can't be helped. You have a great hotel here, by the way. *Auf Wiedersehen.*'

'Goodbye, sir. Good luck.'

By the time he got to the airport it was ten thirty and his head was cracking open. He knew that for most of the drive he'd been dangerously exhausted as well as way over the limit, and in shocking driving conditions too. But to stop, to pull over for even a moment, would have been to think twice; and he didn't want to think twice.

The airline staff had seen it all before, presenting a flat-faced patience, only just the right side of politeness. It was Christmas; everyone had somewhere they needed to be. He wasn't the only one under pressure, either – he was third in line for any seat that came free. He found himself scanning the hundreds of faces of the milling crowd in the check-in area, wondering which of the cunts had a prior claim to escape. Will didn't usually dislike his fellow man but tonight he found himself weaving between them, avoiding contact, muttering 'excuse me's through gritted teeth. He got back in the ticket-sales queue and after forty minutes told the young woman – a different one – that he didn't mind which airport he flew into, his only priority was to be back on English soil. She said she'd make a note of that, but her expression and tone declared unequivocally that it was out of her hands and special pleading would do nothing to improve his chances. After this encounter he made his way to the nearest bar, waited a further noisy, nerve-jangling fifteen minutes to order, and got in two large whisky macs, which he poured into one plastic beer beaker. There was nowhere to sit; he found a space near the window and stood with his bag between his legs, chugging down half the drink right away, knowing it would do him no good.

At midnight he was paged. There was a seat on a flight to Birmingham at six a.m. The price was a joke, but he paid up instantly, without comment. He mustn't think, mustn't start making calculations, examining what he was doing. Now that she was putting him out of his misery, the girl on the desk was nice.

'Happy Christmas, sir.'

'Thank you. And you.'

With only a handful of flights in the small hours, the crowds were thinning out; there'd probably be another surge in the morning. He checked in, shuffled through security and headed straight to the departure gate. Here, as he'd hoped, there were enough empty seats to enable him to lie full-length with his head on his flight bag. He was on his way; for a while at least there was nothing more he could do. What with the excess alcohol swilling around his system, and nerves pinging with nervous exhaustion, he didn't sleep properly, but managed to doze, lurching in and out of consciousness, aware of people arriving around him. By four a.m. his fellow passengers had reached critical mass; a young woman shook his shoulder and asked if he'd mind sitting up so that she and her friend could use the seats. The look on her face told him that he probably looked terrible. His eyes felt gritty, his breath certainly smelt of booze and his clothes were crumpled; he needed a pee, but if he went to freshen up he'd lose his seat. When his bladder began to complain in earnest, he gave in and went to the Gents'. Looking in the mirror in his relieved state, he saw that his reflection wasn't quite as bad as he'd feared. He washed his hands, slooshed water over his face, raked his hair with his fingers and swallowed three paracetamol out of the packet in his wash bag. As he returned to the gate, he found himself thinking with keen anticipation of the in-flight breakfast.

Arrival in Birmingham at six forty-five local time presented another series of challenges, but energised by the airline's ham omelette and croissant (flaccid and cool), and plentiful coffee (weak but hot), he was ready for them. With no checked bags he shouldered his way through the seasonal mob to the hire-car zone and didn't quibble over having to cough up for the Nissan Altima which the young man claimed was the only model available, all the runarounds having been snapped up in a seasonal frenzy. He caught the courtesy bus to the car park, signed forms, arranged to deliver the car back the day after Boxing Day at the Stansted office.

Once the young man had left him to it, he sat in the insulated privacy of the driver's seat and left a brisk, not too apologetic voicemail with his editor, and one with Felicity, saying simply: 'I wanted to tell you I came back. I'm on my way to the carol service. Happy Christmas.' She'd be on her travels; that was the best he could do. At a more civilised hour he'd call her mobile.

He didn't contact Evie, because he was by no means sure how she'd react, and he didn't relish the dilemma consequent on her telling him not to come. He had at all costs to keep moving.

As he turned on to the southbound carriageway of the M6, the dashboard digital clock read 8.15. Conditions were atrocious; not cold, but lashing rain, and it was barely light. He twiddled with the knobs and found Radio 2 – Chris Rea's 'Driving Home for Christmas'.

That's me, he thought, his heart in his mouth. Me!

Chapter Forty-Three

1999

Spontaneity needed organising, Stella found. She had sent cards and delivered presents, made arrangements with her neighbour about post and plants, and adjusted the timer and thermostat on the boiler to keep it ticking over – this wasn't the time of year to leave the system cold for two weeks. Then, with a light heart, she had packed.

Most importantly, she had everyone's blessing, including – thank heavens – Shannon's. She had been dreading the aftermath of Toyah's accident and had delayed her departure until 23 December in order to see the little girl back on her feet and to establish a rapprochement with her mother. In the end, that had not been necessary. In the days immediately following the accident Shannon was conscientious with bulletins, and when Stella had asked if she could come and visit Toyah at home, she'd been welcomed, literally, with open arms. She was almost too weak with relief to return Shannon's hug. Toyah clutched her round the knees and she covered her emotion by bending down and picking her up. Shannon led the way into the living room and turned off the TV, sure sign of an important moment.

'I think she's pleased to see you, Stel.'

'Not half as pleased as I am to see her.' Stella plumped down on the sofa and Toyah at once skidded off and transferred her attention to a large, complicated-looking model house full of cutely dressed plastic squirrels. Stella couldn't help wondering what the place would be like once Santa had been. Shannon perched elegantly on the edge of a chair, her long legs in immaculate black trousers (how *did* she do that?) crossed at the ankle. Behind her, a small silver tree with integral lights shimmered and sparkled.

Above the mantelpiece cards, graded according to size, hung on a length of red string.

'I've got cake – do you fancy a slice?'

'I'm fine, thanks. Shannon …'

'Glass of wine? There's some Pinot in the fridge.'

'No, really …'

'Mind if I do?' Shannon was already on the move. She came back with two glasses, and placed the smaller one in front of Stella. 'Just in case.'

'Thanks. Shannon, I can't tell you how sorry I am – about everything.'

'It wasn't your fault, Stel.'

'Not directly, perhaps, but it was on my watch.'

'Yeah, but …' Shannon took a sip. Stella had rarely seen her so self-possessed, and there was no rancour in her voice when she added: 'You weren't there when she fell.'

'I know. I was talking to someone else. That's what I'm apologising for.'

'It doesn't matter. You're allowed to have friends. I trust you, Stel. I don't know what we'd do without you. And she's always falling over – Mr Pennington said her foot's still not right, but it's not serious – not rheumatoid. We've got an appointment to see him again next week. If this hadn't happened, I might not have noticed – you see what you want to see, don't you?' She bent a fond look on Toyah. 'And she's fine, look at her.'

'Yes. Thank God.' Stella snatched up the glass and took a swig. 'That was one of the worst days of my life.'

'You need a break, Stel,' said Shannon. 'You really really do.'

'Well … As a matter of fact, I'm going to get one. I'm going away for Christmas.'

'No!' Shannon's astonishment was unfeigned. 'Where?'

'To stay with my friend in Canada.'

'Your bloke?'

'Actually yes.' Stella couldn't help it; a smile bloomed and spread all over her face. 'As it happens.'

'That is so great, Stel!' Shannon put down her glass, came over and enveloped Stella in her second fragrant hug of the afternoon. 'Oh wow, I am so pleased for you!'

'I'll be away for at least two weeks,' said Stella. 'I hope that's—'

'Two weeks?' Shannon exclaimed. 'I think you should never come back!'

Then it had turned into a celebration, and Shannon fetched the bottle from the kitchen. They'd clinked and laughed like a couple of girls. Stella's laugh had been one of pure happiness.

Now, as the rumble of the plane's undercarriage signalled their descent into Montreal, the idea didn't seem quite so strange. This was her second visit; she knew what she was going to – the city, the locations and the cast of characters. The freezing air round them was spectacularly clear and blue. She gazed out of the window at the gleaming silver swathe of the St Lawrence, and the skyscrapers rising out of the snow, glittering in the low afternoon sun. The city was all down there waiting for her. Alan too. She was already a part of it; she had presents in her suitcase for Alan and his mother, and for Pierre and Ben, who were going to be there. It would be a family gathering, but to her surprise she felt not the least trepidation. The others would see that this was what she and Alan wanted, that they were sure, and confident; and that would make it all right.

She knew Alan wouldn't be there to meet her; things were crazy at the hospital at this time of year.

The cold outside the airport building was like walking into sheet glass; for a moment it stopped her in her tracks. The sun had dropped below the higher buildings, and the dazzle of the city skyline was in sharp contrast to the freezing shade of the taxi queue. By the time she reached the front, she was chilled to the bone.

The cabbie, a French Canadian, glanced at her in the mirror as they pulled away.

'*Premier fois?* First time in Montreal?'

'Second – I was here earlier in the year.'

'Work, huh?'

'No. Visiting a friend.'

'A friend? That's nice.' He looked over his shoulder as they hit the main airport exit road, inviting her to expand on that, and when she didn't, he added, 'Staying over for Christmas?'

'Yes.' Stella, who was suddenly weary, could have done without the cabbie's amiable interrogation, but he'd read the handbook on tourist-schmoozing.

'Great, you'll have a good time here. This is a superb city, but you know that.'

'Yes.'

'Where you from?'

'England.'

'I'd never have guessed!' He chortled, peered at her again. 'Long day, huh?'

'It has been, rather. Travelling, it's always, you know …' She tapped her watch. 'It's nearly midnight for me.'

'I get it, I get it!' He shook his head. 'You sit quietly and enjoy the ride.'

Easier said than done, because from here on in he diverted his energies into showing his mastery of the city-bound freeway and everything on it – slaloming from lane to lane with one hand on the wheel and the other raised in faux exasperation, and hurling French curses at other road-users.

Within half an hour they were coming into the suburbs; all the lights were on, and the blue sky beyond had faded to gunmetal, darkening by the minute. The traffic, as her driver pointed out, was something else. She realised she had no idea where they were, and for all she knew he could be driving her in ever-decreasing circles. When her phone began to play a high-pitched 'Alouette', she snatched it up; she had never been more eager to hear Alan's voice.

'Hello? Hello?'

'Stella, sweetheart – you're there.'

'We were on time.'

'Where are you at this moment?'

'Sitting in a taxi, in traffic.'

'In that case – look, I'm still at the hospital. Why don't you come straight here? I should be done in half an hour; we could stash your stuff and go for dinner.'

'Alan, I don't mind what I do, I want to see you. Where shall we meet?'

'Tell the cabbie the main entrance on Holroyd Avenue. There's a coffee shop on your right as you go in. I'll be right with you, that's if I'm not there already.'

458

'Okay. See you at the hospital.'

'Cab's on me.'

'Don't worry about it, I can't wait.'

'Me neither.'

This change of plan created another conversational opening for the cabbie.

'Hospital? Everything all right?'

'My friend's a doctor. He's had to work late.'

'Doctor? Is that right?' A knowing, indulgent smile appeared in the driver's mirror. Stella realised, too late, that she had let slip a vital piece of information. Before this line of enquiry could be pursued any further, she said, 'Excuse me', picked up her phone again and pretended to study it, with a great show of frowning concentration.

The hospital was *en fête*. A group of nurses and doctors, muffled up against the biting cold, were singing carols in the covered area outside the main entrance. Stella dropped a dollar bill in their tinsel-wrapped charity bucket. The lobby was bright with hanging decorations, a Christmas tree and a grotto with model reindeer (one red-nosed) and elves. The girls behind the counter in the coffee shop wore Santa hats with white pom-poms. Tense, tired-looking visitors sat at tables in the centre of the concourse or patrolled its perimeter, some of them accompanied by patients in wheelchairs or on crutches. The effect of this among the seasonal glitz was surreal.

Stella bought a hot chocolate and found a free stool at the counter overlooking the concourse. She didn't want the drink but she needed the seat. Her eyes felt gritty and her mouth was dry – she'd have been better off with a bottle of water.

A young woman came to stand next to her at the counter. She was crying as she broke up a muffin on the plate in front of her. In the minimart opposite, a distressingly thin young man on a saline drip waited at the checkout, his friend alongside carrying a basket containing shrink-wrapped apples, bottled smoothies and a magazine. At a nearby table a family of four, parents and two young teenagers, tucked into polystyrene platters of yellow fast food with furious concentration. Too many stories. Stella's tiredness overwhelmed her again and she pushed away the

459

remains of the hot chocolate and put her face in her hands.

'Hi there.'

She felt his hand on her shoulder at the same time as she heard his voice. Her eyes were wet as she slid from the stool and sank into his embrace.

'Hey ...' he said, kissing her hair, her damp cheek. And then: 'Thank you, thank you, thank you, for coming.'

She shook her head against his shoulder, felt in her bag for a tissue, smiling now, overcome with relief and happiness.

'Okay.' He took the handle of her case. 'You ready?'

'Yup.' She kissed him on the lips. 'Composure restored.'

'Let's get out of here.'

As they left, he exchanged a greeting and a pumped fist with the fast-food family; there were smiles all round.

'You know them?'

'Their youngest is my patient.'

She glanced at him, noticing now how tired he looked, thinner than last time, his hair a little greyer; but his face was bright and animated, the face of a man who did good work. The man she loved, and who loved her.

'Will they have a happy Christmas?' she asked, as they emerged into the snow, the carol-singers declaring that it was the season to be jolly. An ambulance howled past on the slip road, heading for ER.

He smiled. 'Yes,' he said. 'I guess they will. And so will we.'

Will had forgotten about queuing. Somewhere in the back of his mind had been the unexamined notion that as the grandfather of a chorister he would simply walk in. It was only because of the need to stretch his legs that he discovered, on turning into the street flanking the college, that there was already an orderly line of about forty people waiting outside the porters' lodge, kitted out for the long haul with day bags, Thermoses and folding chairs.

His immediate, split-second reaction was one of defeat, followed by rebellion – *I'm not doing that!* – before he pulled himself together. He had come thus far at considerable cost to his wallet, energies and professional reputation, because for once he wanted, really wanted, to do the right thing. All these people, he reminded himself sternly, were standing here in the cold to hear his grandson – *his grandson* – sing, something he'd had plenty of opportunities to do over recent years, all wasted.

It was ten thirty, and the queue was growing steadily. He made a quick calculation. The corner offie, sadly, was largely a thing of the past, but he was pretty certain he'd passed an Oddbins en route from the car park. He sprinted back the way he'd come and bought a quarter bottle of Jameson's. There was an M&S next door, and he dived in there too and picked up a chicken tikka wrap and a Mars bar. As he rejoined the lengthening queue, he found himself reflecting quite cheerfully that all this – hanging about in freezing conditions with hard rations in your pocket – was a bit like the army.

At two thirty he saw them arrive, his daughter and his mother, marching at a smart pace towards the college gate from the direction of the town centre. He stared, transfixed by longing and fear. Evie was wearing a black leather jacket with a fur scarf, tight jeans and biker boots, bright red lipstick (that was different); she looked great. Kate was in boots too, knee-length suede edged with sheepskin, and a camel trench coat, collar turned up; gloves, of course, and a brown velvet pillbox hat – he betted it would be the only hat in the place. They were two smart, good-looking women; he was choked with pride. But not brave enough to greet them. Not yet. People saw what they expected to see, and he was the last thing they'd expect. He was sitting on a low wall and ducked his head as they approached. When they'd gone past, a sweat of shame and embarrassment had puddled in the small of his back.

Getting here, he realised, had been the easy bit.

Raff wasn't nervous. This was his fourth Lessons and Carols, and the service was a doddle compared with some of what they did; the music was mostly straightforward and the audience really easy to please. Also, this was the best of the three – they'd already done the schools' service three weeks ago, the chapel full of fidgeting kids and tired teachers; and the BBC television recording, which was boring, boring, with endless reruns and no atmosphere. This one went out live, so at least you could crack on without interruptions. They were doing one interesting new piece, but the rest was all the usual stuff. He was on the shortlist for the solo, but it would probably be Sean who got the nod, because he would be off next year.

They were changed except for their surplices, which hung in a row like headless angels in the corridor. Matron, a businesslike New Zealander in a dark blue uniform, was carrying out her inspection – which was okay; her eagle eye was protection against Dowd's far less comfortable scrutiny. Alfie was playing with his Game Boy, and she removed it and put it in one of the cubbyholes beneath the surplices.

'Save that for later. Hands?' They showed her front and back. 'Fine.'

Alfie turned to Raff. 'Who you got coming?'

'Mum and my great-gran.'

'What about your auntie, the one who came on tour? She's cool.'

Raff shook his head. 'She's gone to Canada to see her boyfriend.'

'Count yourself lucky. My sister's bringing hers,' said Alfie.

'What's he like?'

'Not bad, actually.'

'Mum's getting married,' said Raff. It was the first time he'd said it, and now he'd spat it out it didn't sound too bad. 'In the summer.'

'Wow.' Alfie was impressed. 'He's a policeman, right?'

'Yes.'

'Not here today, though?'

'No,' said Raff. There was something else he half wanted to say, but thought better of it. 'No.'

Matron clapped her hands. 'All right, let's get these surplices on. Mr Dowd is on his way.'

Will was in the quad, only about ten metres from the chapel entrance, when his phone buzzed.

'Hello?'

'Will – it's me. Fliss.'

'I thought you were in France.'

'No, that's new year, for their millennium party. I'm at Vic's in Cumbria for Christmas. I got your message just before I left.'

'Oh.' He still felt sheepish and ashamed at the sound of her voice. 'Drive okay?'

'It's a stinker, but I'm here now … Will?'

'Yes?'

'What you're doing – I am so, so pleased. I was being a complete prig the other night, but you should be proud of yourself.'

'Too early to say,' he said, but he was beginning to glow.

'Have you seen everyone?'

'Not yet – Fliss, I'm nearly at the chapel, I'll have to go.'

'Will you come and see me in two thousand?' she said.

'I'd love to.'

'Soon?'

'Very soon.'

Felicity's 'Happy Christmas, Will' was ringing in his ears as, for the second time in twenty-four hours, he entered a full church. Her approval and pride warmed him as he passed from the grey of the winter's afternoon to the lofty, luminous beauty of the nave.

On their outing in the summer, Raff had told him he might be in the running for the solo, so Will knew where he wanted to sit – as close to the back as he could without running the risk of putting Raff off his stroke if he got lucky. He positioned himself in the centre of a pew three from the back on the south side, flanked by tourists, American and Japanese. Remembering Heidelberg, he kept his mouth shut and studied the order of service. Somewhere way in front, among the shining ones, the entitled and those with a ticket, were Evie and Kate. He closed his eyes for a moment and pictured them. Fliss, too – and Jacqueline, wherever she was. And Raff, drawing closer. Even himself, God help him. His hands, with the service sheet between them, pressed together.

God help me.

The choir left the school building and processed down the path, through the gate and across the quadrangle towards the chapel. As they drew nearer, they could hear the strains of the organ.

The playing of the merry organ …

Raff, a veteran of three previous carol services, failed to suppress a shiver of excitement. They all felt it. The whole world was waiting for them.

Will stopped praying. He was here. Even if (which he doubted) a higher authority had helped him get this far, it was down to him now. The chapel door opened, and he turned towards it.

The choir paused for a moment in the porch while their arrival was signalled to the front. The organ ceased, and they filed in, past the standing rows of people, and took up their positions in three ranks in front of the west door. Mr Dowd stood in front of them, in his eyes the iron gleam that demanded their full and complete attention. It worked. That face was all Raff could see. He was in the second row, but he knew that down by Dowd's feet was the box that would give them the green light. The people near the back of the chapel had turned to watch; they wanted to be in at the beginning, to see the famous, spine-tingling moment. Raff was aware of them, of being the focus of their massed and fascinated stares, but his whole vision was filled by Dowd's imperious glare. Then the glare changed, moved, considered. The green light was on.

Dowd lifted his hand, and pointed.

The British Council employee who ran the White Gates centre outside Gilgil turned on the digital radio, tuned in earlier to the BBC World Service. She liked listening to this little bit of home while they geared the place up for the party tomorrow. She suspected the rest of the staff merely tolerated it, but what the hell? It was an oasis of tradition, and culture, much-needed peace, in amongst all the hectic activity. She loved her work with a passion, and loved too the people she worked with. They were a great team, and they were doing a good job. The school, the sports facilities, the various community activities, the mother-and-baby clinic; all met real needs in the surrounding area.

She went out on to the veranda to sit down, just for a moment. Behind her, the screensavers floated in their separate universes, messages hurtled silently on to invisible lists, the ceaseless, unsleeping network of cyberspace hummed with activity. There were times when she wished she could unplug the whole thing and cut herself off. She was shattered, but then she was part of a long tradition; everyone who'd ever sat out here had probably been tired. Whatever else you thought about the old days, they must have been tough.

Thomas Ojukwu, the office manager, joined her.

'I'm going now, but I'll be back tomorrow morning.'

'Thomas, you're a star.'

'I've updated the accounts, but I don't want to ruin your day.'

'I appreciate that.'

It's him.

Evie touched her grandmother's gloved hand. 'It's him.'

He's a soldier, thought Will. Still, straight, disciplined. *A soldier, and I'd walk through fire for him.*

Thomas paused at the screen door. A thin, pure sound trickled through from the office beyond. 'Your programme's started.'

'I'm going to take five and listen.' She turned her head slightly to catch the sound. 'Turn it up a squeak, would you, on the way out?'

'Sure.'

'And leave the door.'

The massed voices swelled. She let herself relax, go with it. Give in.

Christian children all must be
Mild, obedient, good as he.

Insufferable, but there was something sweet, too, about that sort of certainty. Mildness and obedience were considered a bit suspect these days, but she hoped they were doing good here.

Steps in the office, voices, at first strident above the carol, then lowered. They'd seen her sitting here and decided to leave her in peace.

And our eyes at last shall see him ...

Well, maybe.

The garden was still lovely, even though all they had time for was to keep it mowed and cut back. The farmers – the couple who were buried side by side in the Anglican churchyard in Gilgil – had done a good job. One of them (the woman, she liked to think) had created a patch of England here: roses, hydrangeas, peonies, even the occasional sturdy buttercup and foxglove, and some herbs that had long since grown into shrubs. That reminded her of an idea she'd had; she rose and went down the steps.

She crossed the grass to where a great shock of mint leaned over the grass, its dry flowers shedding a dust of small blue petals. She picked a few spears, and then moved to the thyme, her favourite. This was almost a small tree now, its central stem and main branches bleached and gnarled, not much in the way of foliage, but enough for her purposes. With difficulty, she succeeded in twisting some twigs until they snapped off and she had a small bunch. The strong, pungent fragrance rushed up at her like a cry, making her eyes smart.

She was going to put these sprigs in amongst the decorations. But for now, she sat down again on the veranda, with her nostalgic bouquet in her lap, and listened to the English carols.

It was dark when they left the chapel. The sky had cleared, though – there would be a frost, people said, as they hurried, shiny-eyed, along the path that led around the quad to the porters' lodge and the town, whose furious commercial heatbeat was at last beginning to slow down.

Will stood on the path beyond the porch. The choir had gone, and Raff with them. He could scarcely believe it. He had naively imagined embraces and laughter, a reward for his efforts. But his inital disappointment was tempered by a slow tide of peacefulness, a recognition of the right order of things. There was to be no quick fix; he didn't deserve it. He had merely made a good beginning, started something that now must be seen through. When Evie was born, he remembered how quickly she'd been taken away – for weighing, for checking – before being returned to them. And this, after all, was a rebirth.

Now Evie was upon him, silently, her arms around his neck. He thought he heard the one word, 'Daddy …' His girl, his sweet. She'd give him hell later, but for now, they stood locked together, united.

Over his daughter's head he saw his mother, tall and composed, a pillar of strength, smiling a quizzical smile that told him it was all right – that he was recognised, acknowledged and forgiven. After a moment, she stepped forward and kissed him, removing her glove and wiping his cheek dry with her hand.

'My darling,' she said, with clear, brave good cheer. 'Welcome! Welcome home. And now, shall we find somewhere warm?'

They set off, the three of them, with arms linked, towards the gate, and Christmas, and the last days of the old year.

The End

Acknowledgements

My heartfelt thanks to Rob and Jane Greening, Malcolm Simpson and Benedict Williams for background information; to Liz Green, Ros Holbrow and my husband Patrick for moral support, and Martin Pickett for the technical variety, without which this book would have been lost in cyberspace.